Mr. Naughty List

(Mr. Christmas #2)

By Leta Blake

An Original Publication from Leta Blake Books

Mr. Naughty List
Written and published by Leta Blake
Cover by Dar Albert
Formatted by BB eBooks

First Print Edition, 2019
ISBN: 978-1-626226-5-31

Other Books by Leta Blake

Any Given Lifetime
The River Leith
Smoky Mountain Dreams
Angel Undone
The Difference Between
Omega Mine: Search for a Soulmate
Raise Up Heart
Heat for Sale
Bring on Forever

The Mr. Christmas Series
Mr. Frosty Pants
Mr. Naughty List
Mr. Jingle Bells

The Training Season Series
Training Season
Training Complex

Heat of Love Series
Slow Heat
Alpha Heat
Slow Birth
Bitter Heat

Stay Lucky Series
Stay Lucky
Stay Sexy

'90s Coming of Age Series
Pictures of You
You Are Not Me

Co-Authored with Indra Vaughn
Vespertine
Cowboy Seeks Husband

Co-Authored with Alice Griffiths
The Wake Up Married serial
Will & Patrick's Endless Honeymoon

Gay Fairy Tales
Co-Authored with Keira Andrews
Flight
Levity
Rise

Audiobooks
Leta Blake at Audible

Free Read
Stalking Dreams

Discover more about the author online
Leta Blake
letablake.com

Gay Romance Newsletter

Leta's newsletter will keep you up to date on her latest releases and news from the world of M/M romance. Join the mailing list today.
letablake.com

Leta Blake on Patreon

Become part of Leta Blake's Patreon community in order to access exclusive content, deleted scenes, extras, bonus stories, rewards, prizes, interviews, and more.
www.patreon.com/letablake

Acknowledgements

Thank you to the following:

Mom and Dad, without whom I couldn't be following this dream of being a writer. Brian and Cecily, my lights to travel home to. All the wonderful members of my Patreon who inspire, support, and advise me. Keira Andrews for editing. DJ Jamison for proofing. Kate Hawthorne for beta reading, and Annabeth Albert for helping me untangle a few knots. Jennifer Stanford and Crystal Lacey for beta reading. Rough-DraftHero for writing the book *Rorschach Blots* which partially inspired this book. Jennifer Niceley for her music and memories of her farm. Emmy the Great and Tim Wheeler for the song that inspired the series, and Knoxville, TN for the setting inspiration.

Most of all, thank you to my readers for making all the blood, sweat, and tears worthwhile.

For my patrons with my love

Can this teacher's former student spank some holiday spirit into him?

Is Aaron allowed to want a hot holiday fling with his young former student? Even more forbidden, is he allowed to want this student to *spank* him?

It's another Christmas, and Aaron is still in the closet as a gay man and a natural submissive. With one youthful indiscretion blacking his ethics record, he can't afford to indulge his desires no matter how pent up and needy that leaves him.

Until his former student comes home for the holidays.

Dominant and charming, RJ knows what Aaron needs—intense, steamy encounters and a firm hand. As Christmas nears, RJ helps Aaron unlock his true self. But family and fallout await, and all good things must end.

Or can their hot holiday affair turn them into lasting lovers?

Mr. Naughty List is a steamy MM romance set in the *Mr. Christmas* series that began with Mr. Frosty Pants, but **can be read as a standalone**. Featuring light D/s, spanking, an older sub with a younger Dom, former student/teacher dynamics, and all the warm, sweet holiday feels complete with a strong happy ending.

Chapter One

FRESHLY SCRUBBED AND eager, Aaron fairly skipped by the glittering storefronts in Market Square. Knoxville was all done up for Christmas with lights and ribbons and wreaths, and he hummed along to "Jingle Bell Rock" as he passed the outdoor ice rink on his way to the cozy, familiar pub where he usually met his hookups.

He paid Scruffy City Hall's leather-clad bouncer the $10 cover charge for the night's band and headed inside to find the dim, wood-lined interior already packed with people. Needing a drink sooner rather than later, Aaron forced his way through the crowd and up to the bar to put in his order with the hipster, bearded bartender and was gratified by a glorious whisky sour within mere moments.

An unfamiliar and yet very Christmas-y song rang around him, emanating from the next room. Visible through an arched doorway, the small, crowded stage flashed with spangled lights from a disco ball.

The holiday spirit was evidently rampant amongst the patrons, a mix of college students and single thirty-somethings, dancing and singing along to the catchy, Christmas-themed chorus. Silver, gold, and red decorations hung from the pub's ceiling, adding a sparkle and shine that lifted the room out of mediocrity and into joy. Aaron's spirits rose even higher.

Gazing around, hoping not to see any familiar faces and pleased to find nary a one, Aaron moved into the room where the band responsible for the jangling array of Christmas tunes amped up the excitement of the drunk and adoring crowd.

Dodging elbows and squeezing between dancers, Aaron sought out a place where he could watch, listen, and drink. The rock-n-roll carols vibrated his bones, a cheering, holiday-infused hum that made his eardrums ache, but Aaron didn't plan to be here long enough to worry about his hearing. Fingers crossed, anyway.

He'd already been blown off once that evening by a potential hookup. In his desperation to secure an end to his current spell of celibacy, he'd been less choosy than usual in arranging this one. Aside from a photo of a handsome, if rather cruel-looking face, to identify the guy by, Aaron only knew his screenname—CaptainKY—and wasn't even sure if that referred to the state or the lube.

Aaron had resisted the lure of hookup apps for almost six months. He'd been proud of himself for making good use of the Internet and his right hand to satisfy his needs instead of requiring the sexual services of a stranger. Not that he *wanted* to be celibate. It was just that it was so damn hard to find no-strings-attached fucks in a town the size of Knoxville. Not as a teacher trying to keep his sexuality quiet.

The last thing Aaron needed was to find himself face-to-face with a student's closeted dad on parent-teacher night, or discover he'd screwed the older brother of one of his current students, or to trip and fall into some other horrible situation that could cost him his already tattered reputation and maybe his job.

Thus, his usual preference was to pick up men passing through town: business travelers for the most part, though truckers would do just fine if he was looking for a certain *expérience spécifique*. That'd been the plan tonight, actually. A tough-looking man who'd been trucking through town had offered to meet him for drinks and a long, slow blow job, followed by a nice, hard spanking. But the trucker had backed out at the last minute for an unspecified reason.

Which, okay. Fine. Whatever.

Aaron sometimes backed out of hookups too. It happened—second thoughts, or some protective instinct warned him against a particular rendezvous, so he flaked. But he'd *needed* it tonight. He'd been aching for it for weeks now. So, no sooner than the trucker had ditched him, Aaron had been back on the apps, scrolling for a new catch.

And he'd found one.

Cruel face. Baseball cap. In town for a monster truck show.

Aaron could totally *not* relate to that interest, but all the better. It was so much less likely they'd have to spend a lot of time talking. Instead, he'd test CaptainKY out here at the club, make sure he felt safe with him, and then go back to the hotel where the guy was staying. Probably not the Hotel Oliver, since that was a bit posh for the stereotypical monster truck fan, but maybe the new business-class Marriott, which was right around the corner from his apartment. Aaron wouldn't even be tempted to spend the night.

Sipping his cocktail, he meandered closer to the stage, attracted by the glow of the fake stained-glass windows on the balcony above the room and the optical illusion of the castle-like hall behind the stage itself. The sound was tight, and the performers were dressed up in Christmas glitz—reindeer antlers, wristbands made of tinsel, and the girls wore shimmery hair and makeup. Entertainment, Knoxville style.

Aaron was meeting CaptainKY between nine and nine-thirty, but he'd been too anxious and horny to wait at home, so he'd come out a little early. He figured a drink in advance would soothe his jitters and make him looser all over. For whatever happened in the hotel. God, he hoped the guy was hung. He needed a cock in his ass more than he needed air.

Aaron drowned that desperate thought with another mouthful of whiskey. Fixing his attention on the band, he noted that it was made up of two girls and two guys: a glittering, probably Korean woman on drums, a pixie-looking lady with blue hair seated at a decorated, stand-up piano, and two fine, wiry pieces of man-flesh on bass and guitar. Both of the guys weren't too precious to play up the Christmas theme either. One wore jingle-bells on reindeer antlers, and the other had tinsel bracelets and necklaces shimmering with every move.

Aaron's gaze hung on the lead-singer-slash-guitarist. Beneath the reindeer antlers, the man wore his light brown hair shorn close to his scalp, and he possessed an easy sexuality that made Aaron's nipples tingle and his overeager cock rush hot with blood.

Aaron rolled his eyes at his own horniness, annoyed to be like a raw nerve, needy and twinging with every semi-arousing stimulus in sight. Like this tall, handsome singer with his beautiful, angular body. *Damn.* Nothing *semi*-arousing about him. More like a total hard-on.

Finally finding an empty corner to lurk in while he waited for CaptainKY to arrive, Aaron stared at the stage, chewing his bottom lip and nearly drooling over the lead's muscled arms and attractive hands. It was like a poem, the way the tendons of his forearms moved with each chord change. Aaron's skin felt alive just watching.

As minutes passed and Aaron slowly sipped his whiskey sour, letting the alcohol relax his high-strung nerves, he admired the singer's strong jawline and the wiry ligaments of his neck as he sang Christmas songs both strange and familiar. His voice was a scratchy baritone that sent shivers down Aaron's spine.

Aaron licked his lips again, spinning out a fantasy where he got this man on a bed somewhere, straddled his long legs, and unwrapped the nice package showcased by the tight fit of worn jeans.

Flushing with want, Aaron fanned himself. He shouldn't have worn a sports coat. Christ. Given that he'd been horny as hell before he even arrived at the pub, it wasn't surprising that he was steaming hot in here now, or that his imagination had taken such a dirty turn when faced with a man exactly his rough-looking type. This was the kind of man who clearly knew what to do with his hands—based on the work those fingers were doing on the fretboard, anyway.

Standing there, sporting wood beneath his sports coat, Aaron was unprepared for the effect a certain toss of the lead's chin would have. That quick move, followed by his piercing gaze raking over the crowd, triggered Aaron's memory.

In a flash, he knew him.

RJ Blitz, former high school senior, sat in back row of Aaron's very first English Composition class as a teacher. He'd glared at Aaron like he'd wanted to turn him inside out, or beat him up, or do something else that had left Aaron feeling eternally anxious for that whole school year.

Fuck.

Even now Aaron battled the fear that a student would guess his sexuality and use it to hurt him—either professionally or physically. He only needed one more strike and he'd be out. Even five years ago, before the mistake and the humiliation, RJ Blitz had been a student Aaron had avoided interacting with.

RJ had been just as tall and lanky as he was now, but he'd also radiated an intensity that had shaken Aaron to the core. Violence. Attraction. Aaron didn't know, but he didn't risk reaching out, even when RJ's grades had been subpar despite his clear intelligence.

Once RJ had graduated, not only had Aaron been glad, but he hadn't ever anticipated seeing him again. Well, maybe on the local news, arrested for God only knew what. Drugs probably. Though, to be fair, that had been a mostly subconscious opinion he'd formed of RJ's possible future based on the anxiety RJ had always made him feel, the lack of effort he put into his work, and classist biases that Aaron was ashamed even now to admit to.

He blinked at RJ on the stage, all coiled sexuality and shimmery Christmas-coated lust. How was his former student the total hottie he was hungering for as he owned the small stage at Scruffy City Hall? A student. *His* student. And here Aaron had been ogling him for nearly thirty minutes. *Hard* for him even.

Fuck.

Based on the friendly smiles shot out to the giddy audience, as well as the affectionate, happy glances sent toward his bandmates, RJ was no longer the furious young man he'd once been. But there was still some underlying *something* in him that sent a shiver through Aaron's body, riled him up, and, at least tonight, engaged his lust.

Maybe it was because on stage, all of RJ's formerly pent-up, hostile energy was transformed into pure sex. No matter what song he pulled out—a rock version of an old Christmas standard, or a cheesy rendition of "Frosty the Snowman"—sexuality simply rose from him like a glowing aura of hotness.

Yes, his former student was quite possibly the most delicious thing Aaron had laid eyes on in ages. At least since the last Cocky Boys porn clip he'd jerked off to several days before.

RJ tossed his head again, and Aaron groaned. Definitely even yummier than porn.

Aaron stayed in his corner, sipping his drink. Watching. In the dark privacy of his mind, he allowed himself to imagine all sorts of dirty things: RJ shoving him against the alley wall behind Scruffy City Hall, RJ's hand against his neck as he jerked Aaron off, huffing small growls in his ear like the ones he'd just let loose in the middle of an artsy rendition of "Rudolph the Red-Nosed Reindeer." RJ plowing him as Aaron cried with joy.

He squirmed against the wall and took slow breaths. He wished CaptainKY would arrive already so he could get fucking laid. And he also hoped CaptainKY took his time, so he could watch RJ's whole set. He didn't want to miss a single, sexy minute.

Jiminy Christmas. What was wrong with him? He seriously needed to get fucked tonight. That was the only explanation for the appealing wrongness of wanting a former student—one wearing tinsel on his wrists, jingly reindeer antlers on his head, and a sexy smirk on his face—to fuck him silly. As messed up as it was, there wasn't much Aaron wouldn't do to get a chance at RJ Blitz. *Just look at him, for God's sake...*

But Aaron had never been quite that good, or quite that bad. Santa didn't give out presents like that. At least, not in his experience.

CaptainKY would just have to do. Now where the fuck was he?

HOPPING DOWN FROM the stage with adrenaline still rushing all wild and jangly, RJ tugged off the reindeer antlers and tinsel bracelets. Tossing them into the small crowd to the sound of a half-dozen girlish squeals, he made his way to the bar. Strange hands clapped his back, guys offering up congratulations, and young women trying to catch his eye to offer up *more* than congratulations. Unfortunately, girls in general weren't his type, and he had eyes for only one thing at the moment: a cold beer.

RJ motioned for the bartender and was rewarded with a frosty, fresh-ly poured mug. He took a deep gulp, closed his eyes, and moaned as the bitter barley taste filled his mouth and slipped down his dry throat. Perfect.

"Did you hear them?" Madison, the band's pianist said, appearing at his elbow with the rest of the band just behind her. She grinned up at him with shining blue-green eyes they same color as her hair. "They love us."

RJ shrugged. "Hard not to love Christmas music if you're a fan of the season."

Still, he knew just what Madison meant. The crowd had *really* loved them tonight. They could have played another hour if they'd had the material ready. His entire body thrummed with the kind of giddiness that only performing well in front of a receptive crowd could arouse. It was almost as gratifying as playing stadium tours as a professional guitarist with big-name bands. The roar of the crowds, the lights from the cellphones held up in the air, the screams... It all got his heart pumping like nothing else.

"Well, what now?" Madison asked, leaning against the bar and peer-ing up at him. "Are we all going to party or...?" She shrugged.

"No partying for me," Joel, the bassist and RJ's old friend from high school, cut in. "I have a store to open in the morning." Joel owned a local home and garden store, and t'was the season for fir trees and poinsettias. He squeezed RJ's shoulder. "Casey and I are gonna pack up and head home. Want us to grab your stuff too?"

RJ glanced toward Joel's boyfriend standing nearby, smiling, blond, and oozing with pride. Casey was RJ's friend too, and he'd been closer to him over the years than he'd been to Joel, but now that they were a couple, RJ hardly ever saw Casey alone. "That'd be great. Thanks. Let me finish this beer and I'll come help load out."

"You stay here and enjoy your drink," Joel countered. "Casey and I can take care of loading out. It's just your guitar and amp. Becca always deals with her drums. How she fits them into the back of that Forester, I'll never fucking know. It's magic or something. But, yeah, man. Relax. Have a beer."

Casey approached, gripped RJ's arm, and squeezed warmly. "You don't have to get up early tomorrow. Unlike us." He winked. "Have fun tonight. You deserve it."

RJ wasn't sure why, exactly, Casey thought he deserved to get off scot-free from the pain-in-the-ass job of breaking down their equipment and loading it out, but he didn't argue. He'd gotten used to roadies handling that stuff when he toured with big groups, and it was nice to pretend that he was a big enough act all on his own to not need to bother with it now either.

"Practice on Friday again?" their friend and drummer, Becca, asked, sidling up closer behind Madison and wrapping her arms around her middle. Becca's long black hair was shimmery with glitter product, and she hadn't removed her tinsel halo.

"Yeah. Seven o'clock at Joel's place." RJ nodded.

"Good. 'Cause we need it."

Casey scoffed. "From where I sat, you guys already sounded great."

Becca laughed and tweaked his chin. "Like you'd know. You always think anything Joel does is amazing."

Casey kissed Joel's cheek and shrugged his agreement. A vague jealousy settled under RJ's skin. What would it be like to have someone to greet him like that as soon as his feet were off the stage? What would it be like to have someone who looked at him that way? Even Pan, his last boyfriend, had never shone with love like that.

Then he let it go. Casey and Joel were cute, but they didn't live the kind of life RJ wanted for himself. Too settled. Too domestic. Too...*sweet*. If he ever committed to a relationship, he'd want something with more of a bite to it. A sharp, hot spark.

After final goodbyes and reassurances that Joel and Casey really didn't mind loading out without him, RJ grabbed another beer and headed out the front door. Scruffy City Hall's patio faced Market Square proper. Though a few people lingered, chatting with the bouncer, it was mostly empty, folks preferring to be inside on this chilly December night in Tennessee.

RJ wore only jeans, combat boots, and a black T-shirt, and he dropped into a chair at a wrought-iron table, shuddering as the sweat on his skin prickled in the cool breeze. Normally, he'd want a jacket at the very least. But after the heat of the packed interior and the bitter cold of the winter he'd spent in Finland last year, the chilly night air felt good on his sweaty skin.

Stars popped between folds of darkness, obscured by the lights of the square, and the scent of buttered popcorn drifted over from the outdoor ice rink the city slapped up every year at Christmastime. Squeals and gurgles of laughter spilled out from the walled oval of ice, providing a bittersweet sense of innocence offset by the thrum of dance music coming from inside the pub behind him.

RJ scrubbed his hand over his closely cropped hair and sighed with pleasure. Kicking his feet up into the chair next to him, he slung back another gulp of beer, then pulled out his phone to open his latest hookup app. There had to be a hard-up hottie in the holiday crowd somewhere, either in the pub itself or in another establishment in Market Square. It was Knoxville, for God's sake. Home of tons of closeted, horny men.

As he swiped mindlessly, holiday shoppers went in and out of the Market Square stores. All of the windows were beautifully decorated with greenery, lights, colorful ribbons, bows, and shining stars. RJ had just decided to give up on the app and on getting laid when Scruffy City Hall's door flung wide and a slender man in his late twenties stalked out with a cell phone pressed against his ear. His shoulders curved against the punch of cold wind, and he shivered hard despite his tweed sports coat.

"Sorry, I couldn't hear you," the man said breathlessly. "Are you running late?"

RJ's heart stumbled. The man might have his back to RJ, but RJ would recognize *that* voice and *that* hot ass anywhere. Any. Fucking. Where.

An electric thrill shot up RJ's spine.

Sitting up straighter, he dropped his feet to the ground and ran a hand over his hair to smooth it again, before quickly sniffing his pits. Not too ripe. Not too fresh either. Sweaty, like a man should be.

Yes, a *man*.

No longer a boy. It'd been five and a half long years since he'd last seen Mr. Aaron Danvers in person, and RJ most certainly hadn't been a man back then.

"Oh." Mr. Danvers's head and shoulders dropped. Puffs of condensed breath lifted around him, and he shifted from one foot to the other. Suddenly, he raised a hand and flipped off the sky. Then, totally casually, like he hadn't just expressed rage to the heavens, he said, "Of course. No problem. I completely understand. Have a good night." Mr. Danvers ended the call and cursed softly before dropping his phone into his jacket pocket.

With his back still to RJ, he leaned his weight against another empty patio table, gazing toward the skating rink. Several slow seconds ticked by with music from the rink drifting over to them, Mariah's "All I Want for Christmas Is You" along with the giddy yells and bubbling laughter of people too young to know how crap the world could be. Or what it was like to be let down.

Mr. Danvers loosed a long, frustrated sigh. "Fuck," he whispered finally.

"Get stood up, Mr. Danvers?" RJ asked. His insides trembled with fizzy-popping excitement, like someone had slipped Pop Rocks into his beer. But he leaned back in his chair, crossing his boots at the ankle, and tried like hell to look calmer than he felt.

Mr. Danvers's shoulders tensed again, and he whipped around.

RJ caught his breath. *God, he's still perfect.*

Mr. Danvers's golden-brown hair, highlighted by the white twinkle lights all around Market Square, shifted in the breeze and looked soft to the touch. He'd maintained the compact, twinky build that had made even teenaged RJ feel like a hulking giant next to him. Everything about Mr. Danvers's lithe body had always been arousing—his long neck, his delicately tapered fingers, and especially his juicy ass, which was currently encased in sexy, fitted trousers that hung perfectly to show off its shape.

Fuck.

RJ had often fantasized about biting into that bouncy flesh. Of course, he'd never had the pleasure. After all, Mr. Danvers had been his teacher. Off-limits and out of bounds. Not to mention completely oblivious to the desperate crush suffered by the gangly, acne-faced, long-haired, queer kid in the back of the sixth-period Senior English Composition classroom.

A surge of confidence lifted RJ's chin. His face had cleared up since then, and he'd cut his long, greasy hair years ago. He was an attractive, *grown ass* man now. He'd traveled the world, for fuck's sake, and screwed *a lot* of dudes. He wasn't the awkward kid he used to be. As Mr.

Danvers stared at him in surprise, and with a hint of confusion in his furrowed brow, RJ tried to put all that hard-earned adult experience into his expression.

Because, while there had never been any confirmation, or even any real rumors around school about Mr. Danvers, RJ had killer gaydar. And Mr. Danvers was as gay as a rainbow flag busting out its best colors over the Pride Parade.

He just knew it.

Mr. Danvers stared at him for a long, awful moment, and RJ's bravado wore terrifyingly thin—*had Mr. Danvers forgotten him?*—before a smile of recognition broke across Mr. Danvers's fine-featured face. "RJ Blitz? Is that you?" His adorable dimples grew deeper. "I didn't recognize you up on the stage."

RJ cocked a brow.

Weird. RJ wasn't sure why Mr. Danvers had lied, but he knew bullshit when he heard it. Maybe Mr. Danvers hadn't recognized RJ for a moment in the dark of the patio outside the bar when he'd first turned around, but he'd damn well known who he was on stage. Small inflections of Mr. Danvers' voice and a sudden strain in his eyes had given that much away.

Curiosity about Mr. Danvers's lie bit into him, like the way he wanted to bite into Mr. Danvers' butt. What had prompted such a denial? Surely it couldn't be…

There was no way…

Right?

And yet, in an instant, he knew. Mr. Danvers had found him attractive. Mr. Danvers thought he was hot. Mr. Danvers…*yes*.

A plan formed.

First, he'd get Mr. Danvers to chat with him right here and now. *Then* he'd convince him to get a drink and talk longer. And *then*, the coupe de grace, he'd seduce the man. Though he'd start with just the drink. Thinking too much about anything more would cause him to explode like a cheap amp plugged into an overcharged circuit. But, with any luck, he'd find out just how tender Mr. Danvers's ass truly was tonight.

"Did you enjoy the show?" RJ asked, taking another slow pull of beer, pleased his hand didn't shake.

"Of course!" Mr. Danvers's dimples blessed RJ again. "You guys were great. You *are* RJ, right? I didn't misremember, did I?" Mr. Danvers shoved his hands into his pockets and rocked back on his heels. It was that familiar, smug, teacher-stance that used to make RJ want to bend Mr. Danvers over his wide, messy desk, and spank the man until he didn't act so distant and *adult*.

After all, Mr. Danvers was only four or five years older than RJ. That small age gap had been a thorn in RJ's side back then, keeping him from even hoping he could have what he wanted, and he wasn't going to let Mr. Danvers act like he was that much older than him now, either.

Offering what he hoped was a winning grin, RJ lifted his beer in a salute. "Yeah, that's me. RJ Blitz."

"Sixth period. Senior English Comp. My first year teaching," Mr. Danvers said with a smile. He rocked back on his heels again. His hair ruffled in the breeze, and the music from the ice-skating rink swelled with a new song: Dolly Parton's "Here You Come Again." Weird that it wasn't a Christmas tune. "Sorry if I wasn't that great of a teacher back then," Mr. Danvers said with a shrug. "I was still getting my feet beneath me. That year feels like forever ago."

Perfect.

They were agreed then that there was no need for any student-teacher deference. Maybe this seduction would be easier than RJ had anticipated.

"For me too." RJ kicked the chair beside him out from the table. The heavy wrought iron slid across the patio concrete with a screech that momentarily blocked out Dolly's sweet voice from the rink and the bouncing dance music from within the pub. "Have a seat."

Mr. Danvers stared at the chair for a long minute, a small furrow digging in between his delicate eyebrows—did he tweeze them to be so perfect?—until his expression broke into a smile again. "Sure, what the hell? Why not?"

"I mean, unless you have something else going on tonight," RJ said, with a knowing wink.

Mr. Danvers rolled his eyes and gestured toward the phone in his pocket. "Apparently, I don't. And I'm not ready to go home just yet. I'd love to catch up with a former student." He gave RJ an almost flirty glance. Or was that wishful thinking on RJ's part? "Let me just grab a drink to keep warm." Mr. Danvers nodded toward the bar inside. "Want another beer while I'm at it? On me?"

"Sure."

Mr. Danvers's smile grew deeper, again revealing the dimples RJ had mooned over from his desk in the back row. "Your ID?"

"Seriously?"

Mr. Danvers shrugged.

"C'mon. You know I'm old enough."

Mr. Danvers swallowed and flushed. "You look plenty young."

"Like you're one to talk." RJ pitched his voice back, making it flirty as fuck, testing the waters. "I mean, get real, baby-face. Do you even shave?"

Mr. Danvers laughed but didn't relent. RJ narrowed his eyes at him and thought back to the torture of having to watch Mr. Danvers teach every day, fighting off increasingly ferocious hard-ons. Back then, Mr. Danvers had looked like an uptight, arrogant, baby-faced dream, and the intervening years hadn't aged or changed him much at all. Soft-looking cheeks, supple lips…

God, RJ still wanted to fuck him blind.

"It's been five and a half years," RJ said, lifting his chin and gazing at Mr. Danvers with determination. "I was nineteen when I graduated. Do the math."

Mr. Danvers put out his hand with his beautiful, pale fingers out-stretched toward RJ. "ID."

This time he used his teacher voice, and RJ wanted to just grab him and kiss the smug look off his stupid, gorgeous face. Instead he grumbled in annoyance as he dug his wallet out of his back pocket to produce his driver's license.

Mr. Danvers plucked it from his hand to examine it with a raised brow.

"See? Twenty-four years old. I'm really damn legal."

Mr. Danvers darted a quick, startled glance at RJ. The potential double-entendre of his words gripped RJ like a hand around his balls, as Mr. Danvers's eyes darted down to RJ's mouth and back up again. RJ's heart thudded with terrifying pride.

Yes, Mr. Danvers, I saw that.

He'd made his prissy, hot teacher think about kissing him. Probably fucking him, too.

RJ smirked to cover his glee, and when he took the ID back from Mr. Danvers, he was glad his hands weren't sweaty because their fingers brushed.

"I'll be right back," Mr. Danvers said, his voice a little husky. "You want anything stronger than another beer?"

"Nah, good old YeeHaw will do."

"Great." He nodded at RJ's sleeveless arms currently free of tats. Hashtag goals for the upcoming years. "Need your coat from inside? I can grab it."

RJ had left his coat in the band's van and, from a quick glance over his shoulder back inside the pub, it looked like Casey and Joel were long gone. Becca and Madison were still dancing, though. He could see Madison's blue hair bouncing in the crowd.

"I'm good. Thanks." He put his chin up again, determined to stay cool. "This so-called 'winter' has nothing on Finland mid-January. Now *that's* cold as tits."

Mr. Danvers snorted. "Surely I taught you how to use descriptive language well enough that you don't *need* to resort to crudeness."

RJ laughed. "Fuck yeah, you did."

Mr. Danvers rolled his eyes. "I don't remember you being such a brat."

RJ shrugged. "I'm surprised you remember me at all. I was quiet back then."

"Sure. If you call that whole angry, goth-punk vibe you had going 'quiet.'" Mr. Danvers grinned again, dimples digging into his cheeks. "I'll be right back with drinks. I want to hear about what you were doing in cold-as-tits Finland in the middle of January."

The familiar sounds of "Do They Know It's Christmas?" rang out from the sound system in the bar as Mr. Danvers swung the door open to go back inside. The crowd was still in a jovial mood. Gazing in through the wide, front windows, RJ saw Becca had joined in with the folks who were singing along, dancing, and swaying with raised glasses or beer bottles.

The buzz off the crowd was hot enough to intensify RJ's already strong headrush. Patience was never his strong suit, and he tapped his foot to the beat, eager for Mr. Danvers to be back even as the door closed against him and the music. RJ hummed the cheesy melody under his breath while fingering the chords on his beer bottle. He couldn't believe he was talking, *flirting* even, with Mr. Danvers.

What kind of holiday fever dream was he in? The best kind.

He grinned, remembering the last time he'd dropped acid. He'd been in Rome, and he'd promised himself he'd never do that shit again. Not after the entire world had breathed in and out like a big lung, expanding and contracting around him. Not after flowers had told him secrets that, even now, he was afraid to repeat. And definitely not after he'd nearly fallen into a chasm made by his own mind. Real or not, it was all too terrifying.

But here he was, mostly sober, sitting in downtown Knoxville positively *tripping balls* because he was talking to his high school crush. RJ didn't know if he was scared or excited. Mostly both. He rubbed a hand over his short hair again. A cold wind blew across the square. RJ shivered hard.

Even letting his mind toy with the idea of touching the man he'd obsessed over, ached for, and lusted after was nearly too much for him. He'd wanted Mr. Danvers since he was a teen. He couldn't stand to blow it.

Blow it. Ha.

He was going to seduce the pants off Mr. Danvers's intoxicating ass tonight, and finally get the kind of Christmas homecoming he'd always wanted but never thought he deserved.

Chapter Two

ARON ORDERED HIS second whiskey sour of the evening and a YeeHaw for RJ. Standing by the bar with a cocked hip waiting to pay, he blew a bit of hair off his sweaty forehead and let his gaze wander back to the big windows that looked out at the patio and Market Square.

His gaze hung on RJ Blitz sprawled at the iron patio table, looking far too grown up for his own good. Forcing himself to look away, Aaron watched as the bouncer, standing a few feet away from the patio table, checked some college girls' IDs. But his attention quickly drifted back to RJ. He licked his lips as he noticed again the casual stretch of RJ's long legs in the beaten-up jeans, and the sexy way RJ's T-shirt stretched over broad shoulders. The epitome of careless and cool.

Another rousing chorus of "Do They Know It's Christmas?" lifted up around Aaron, and, determined to get a grip on his thrumming lust, he closed his eyes and swallowed hard. What was he doing? He couldn't afford any trouble. Not after what had happened with Coach McAllister.

He took a steadying swallow from his whiskey sour and wiped the sweat from his forehead. Everything was fine. This was a completely different situation from that mortifying experience. RJ was a former student, not a fellow teacher. A *married* fellow teacher Aaron had been foolish enough to dally with in the man's office.

He'd told himself it was late at night and no one would know, and he honestly hadn't realized the asshole was married. He'd barely ever seen the coach in the staff room, and they'd hooked up unwittingly on an app before meeting face-to-face. That should have been the end of it, but they'd been stupid and horny.

Did he mention stupid?

Aaron had learned the hard way upon breaking the school board's code of ethics that winning football coaches were far, far more valuable than young English teachers. He was lucky to still be teaching at all, and probably wouldn't be if not for...

He pushed away the twist of guilt and gratitude. He gulped his drink and mentally scanned the rules for ethics. RJ was in no way connected to Aaron's current school, Pineview Middle. There was no reason Aaron couldn't share a drink with the man. And he *was* a man—Aaron had checked his ID and everything. See? He was playing by the rules.

Besides, it wasn't like he was going to sleep with him. They were just going to chat. Catch up. There was no reason at all for him to be thinking about the situation with Coach McAllister. None at all.

Never mind that RJ was sexy as hell and that Aaron's entire body had twitched alive with shocking arousal as soon as he'd kicked that chair out from the patio table like he was the boss and Aaron his obedient servant. Never mind that Aaron's nipples were still singing in anticipation of a good tweaking, and his balls hummed in hope, as if they sensed an imminent orgasm on the horizon.

He wiped at his forehead again and tried to get a grip on himself.

The best thing he could do was to talk with RJ. Get to know him a little for the undoubtedly boring, stupid, or flat-out weird guy he probably was, and this unreasonable attraction would drop away effortlessly. RJ was a young musician. He'd barely gotten a C in Aaron's class. He probably had nothing of interest to say.

There was no reason to expect he'd be any different from any other man Aaron had ever made the mistake of talking with. A conversation was always the best way to kill his lust. Which was one reason he preferred hookups with guys he had nothing in common with. No expectations aside from sex meant he was rarely let down.

Aaron grabbed the beer from the bar and headed out to the patio, letting the chilled drinks against his palms do the job of cooling him down. He and RJ were just going to talk. Nothing more. Nothing less.

"Keep it all superficial. He'll ruin it. No problem. Everything will be just fine," Aaron whispered to himself as he pushed the door to the patio open and plastered on a smile. His stomach dropped as he stepped out the door.

Fuck.

RJ was just as hot as he'd been when he'd left him.

THE DOOR SWUNG open and Mr. Danvers stepped back out, a beer in one hand and some sort of whiskey drink in the other. His cheeks were flushed and fresh sweat glistened on his forehead and narrow nose.

RJ's heart raced, and his palms went damp.

He took a deep breath and let it out slowly. Right. So, getting into Mr. Danvers's pants was going to be no different than learning a hard song on the guitar: cut it into achievable sections, take it piece by piece, and then let it flow.

RJ smiled as he took the replacement beer from Mr. Danvers's hand. Cool relief rode him like the night's breeze as Mr. Danvers sat down across from him. Dimples broke out again and, to RJ's amazement, they were somehow prettier than the last time Mr. Danvers had flashed them.

"Cheers," RJ said, and put his beer out for Mr. Danvers to tap his whiskey glass against.

After they'd both taken a drink, RJ kicked his feet out. "So," he said with a smirk. "You didn't like my emo, goth-kid look, huh?" Cold wind stung RJ's eyes, and Mr. Danvers pulled his sports coat tighter around his body.

"No, I can't say that I did. But kids." Mr. Danvers shrugged and smiled fondly. "They're still trying to figure themselves out. It's not easy work, is it? Sometimes they take a few ill-advised detours along the way to their real selves." He shrugged again and took another swallow of whiskey, his cheeks and chin pinking up even more from either the cold, or the alcohol, or both.

"Yeah, well, I gotta admit, eyeliner and greasy hair weren't my best looks," RJ conceded. He indicated his current casual punk style and ran a hand over his tightly shorn head again. "I prefer what I've got going on now."

When he was younger, he'd thought guys who dressed like him were scary, neo-Nazi skinheads, but now he just knew it was easier to keep his hair short than to deal with the risk of lice from all the dubious lodgings he stayed in while traveling the world with the less-than-famous bands.

"I have to agree," Mr. Danvers said, sounding a bit breathless. Then he swallowed a healthy gulp of his drink. Out of nowhere, he started chuckling. It was a sweet, effervescent sound that made RJ tingle all over. And Mr. Danvers didn't stop. It went on long enough that Mr. Danvers had to wipe at his eyes with his fingertips.

That made RJ bristle a bit, despite the tingle. "What?"

"Nothing."

"Rude, Mr. Danvers." He put on his dominant voice. The one his kinky German friend, Pieter, had taught him how to use during their D/s training sessions in Berlin. Leaning forward and making eye contact, he demanded, "Tell me."

Mr. Danvers caved like a sweet baby sub, and RJ swallowed hard, making note of that. *Damn, Mr. Danvers. Damn.*

"All right." Mr. Danvers leaned forward, stage whispering. "Truth is, I was afraid of you back then. When you were in my class, I mean. You were always so *intense.* Stared at me like you wanted to hit me or something, and, well, I..." He trailed off, chuckling again. "How ridiculous is that? So ridiculous."

"Why would I want to hit you?" RJ didn't understand how Mr. Danvers could have interpreted his lustful gaze, inspired by watching that fantastic ass shake every time Mr. Danvers wrote on the smart board, as violent.

"It doesn't matter. Never mind." Mr. Danvers bit his lower lip, and his eyes dropped to RJ's mouth again. "You're more approachable now. I like it."

Yes. That was a response he'd take with no complaint.

After another sip of beer, RJ untangled his tongue and offered, "I had a lot of shit going on back then."

"Yeah. I think that's called high school." Mr. Danvers closed his eyes and shook his head. "Who didn't have a lot of shit going on at that age? I wouldn't go back to it for the world."

"What do you mean? You go back there every day."

Mr. Danvers arched one fine brow. He *had* to shape them. They were just too perfect. RJ kind of wanted to lick them. "Believe me. Going to school as a teacher is a very different thing."

"I don't know. Seems like it's pretty similar. You've still got home-work, even if it's called grading, and you get summers and holidays off. Plus, you have to hang around with teenagers all day. So, where's the difference?"

"When you put it like that..." Mr. Danvers winked. "Though I teach middle school now. So, I guess I went back to seventh grade. Which was, if memory serves, even worse for me. Maybe I'm a maso-chist."

RJ's fingers clenched his beer bottle reflexively. Had Mr. Danvers meant to use that particular flirty tone on the word masochist, or was he imagining things?

And RJ hadn't known about the switch in schools. How had he not gathered that from stalking Mr. Danvers's social media? Probably because he'd been more obsessed with pictures than anything else. Deciding to leave innuendo aside for now, RJ asked, "Oh, yeah? Why the change?"

"I prefer the age group. They're fun."

"What's fun about a stinky, emotional preteen?" His mom had one living in her home right now, and RJ didn't think his moody, snarling stepbrother was all that amusing.

"When they aren't yours, a lot of things." Mr. Danvers smiled again, and RJ's heart did a funny little flip. "They're all so damn sincere and trying so hard." His eyes went fond and pitying. Then he brought his gaze back to RJ, who found it impossible to think that there could be a gay man alive who wouldn't think that Mr. Danvers was the stuff dreams were made of.

"But enough about me." Mr. Danvers waved his hand, batting away the topic of his career. "Tell me what you do now, RJ. Play music, obviously. But is this just a hobby or is it a career for you? And what's this about Finland in January?"

RJ relaxed back in his chair again. *This* he could do. Talking about his work and adventures as a touring guitarist for various bands was easy and usually entertaining. He didn't start at the beginning. He didn't bother telling Mr. Danvers how, on graduation day, he'd gone back to his mom's trailer and packed up his things while she cried.

He didn't start in the middle either, with his disappointing first year in Nashville.

No, RJ started his tale for Mr. Danvers with his first big tour as guitarist for a little-known band, Society Demons, opening for The Cure. The band's regular guitarist had injured his hand in a fireworks accident and Society Demons had required a last-minute replacement. RJ'd been thrilled to snag that opportunity.

Afterward, he'd toured with band after band. Any genre—country, rock, funk, soul. The tours lasted months or weeks, it didn't matter. All that mattered was being out there on the stage, feeling the music rise in him, and being part of it all. He didn't *love* living on the road. It was tiring and strange. But, after that first stint with Society Demons, he'd never been anywhere in the world long enough to call a place home. Nothing held him down. No apartment, or car, or student loan. None of the things that so many of the kids he'd graduated with claimed as their own.

What he did have were a ton of stories, a lingering, now-never-indulged desire to snort coke and smoke pot, a history of a few shitty relationships, and memories of being on stages of all shapes and sizes, and in so many different countries that he'd once started a list to keep track of where he'd been.

And he wouldn't trade any of it. Not really. Even if the traveling life ate at him as time went on, wearing him down, killing him little by little with the lack of stability. God, his head was kind of a muddle. He both loved and hated his career right now.

But RJ knew how to paint over the whole messy business with the rosy brush of humor, fun, and scandal, keeping the dark side of the industry out of it. Plus, he wasn't an idiot. Mr. Danvers wouldn't be seduced by stories of feeling burned out and too old for his years, or how much he wished he'd put some serious cash aside earlier in his career so that he could buy a little house to call his own.

Maybe here in Knoxville, maybe not. He didn't care. He just wanted to crash for a few weeks now and again to catch his breath in a comfortable place he could recall from the chaos of Singapore and know it was there waiting for him.

Burnout stories *did* work to seduce certain kinds of men. The ones who wanted to take care of RJ, soothe his pain. That sort of thing. But that wasn't really RJ's jam. He didn't like to play that role. He preferred to be the one doing the soothing. After he'd inflicted pain of the fun variety, that is.

And RJ could tell… Mr. Danvers would be seduced by the awesome stuff: the wild fans, the huge crowds, the beautiful theaters, and the long, spangled nights when RJ was too keyed up after a show to get to sleep. He'd seen some of the most glorious sunrises because of that post-show high. Including one from Montmartre in Paris, on the steps of Sacre-Coeur. That sunrise had changed his life.

"It made me want to be a better person," RJ explained. "That's why

I came home for Christmas this year. I wanted to get to know my little half-siblings and make peace with my past. Well, that sunrise and the religieuse I was eating at the time. Have you had one? Better than an éclair." RJ smiled. "They don't taste the same outside of France. Different butter, you know. So, you'll have to go there to experience the real, life-changing deal. But it's worth it."

Mr. Danvers had listened with bright-eyed enthusiasm, and now sat with his nearly entirely empty whiskey glass clutched in his beautiful fingers, and with a fond, pleased expression on his face. "I haven't been to Paris," he murmured. "I haven't been many places, to be honest."

RJ shrugged. "You're young. You've got time."

Mr. Danvers laughed, his eyes scrunching up adorably. "I'm *young*. So says my former student."

"Well, I've heard that the student becomes the teacher."

"So true. They often do." Mr. Danvers rubbed his fingertips around the side of the whiskey glass. "And now what? You're here in town, playing some gigs with some local friends, or…?"

"Yeah. Joel, Becca, and Casey have been pals of mine since high school. We were in a band back then. Don't know if you remember it? It was pretty bad. We called ourselves the Old Skool Millennials."

Mr. Danvers snorted softly. "I think I remember seeing a flyer or two around the school, yeah. Any bigger plans?"

"You could say so." *Seducing you.* He gave Mr. Danvers a coy smile.

"I'm impressed, RJ. What a life you've been leading." Mr. Danvers's gaze lingered on RJ's mouth, before he brought it back up to RJ's eyes again. He hesitated but asked, sounding a bit breathless, "What else is the holiday bringing you? Anything good?"

"I doubt it. I'm pretty sure I'm on Santa's naughty list." RJ grinned.

"Come on, Mr. Naughty List," Mr. Danvers teased. "There must be something you're especially looking forward to?"

In that moment, Mr. Danvers sounded exactly like the middle school teacher he was. RJ could just imagine him asking that same question to a thirteen-year-old like his stepbrother, Carter. He chuckled under his breath and Mr. Danvers laughed too.

"I haven't gotten any truly great presents in years." RJ supposed his little siblings weren't bad gifts in of themselves, but they'd both been summer babies. "Maybe ever. Christmas was always a disappointment growing up—no money meant no presents."

Mr. Danvers winced, and RJ reconsidered his revelation. Exposing his vulnerabilities wasn't the way to seduce this man, so he went back to the happy stuff. "But as an adult I've found it the merriest time of the year. That's why I wanted to do Christmas gigs, specifically. Seeing all the people having a good time, with all the Christmas packaging to go with it? Always fun."

And he'd hoped playing to small, enthusiastic crowds like this one might act as a kind of holiday medicine to ease his travel-weary heart. So far, with one show in the bag, he could say it was helping to mend his worn-down soul.

Mr. Danvers smiled. "You were fantastic up there. Have you ever thought about doing your own album? Instead of just playing for other people?"

RJ raised his brow and smiled prettily, sucking on his teeth and thinking of the best way to answer. "I have." He pondered his small group. Madison had mad talent, but he wasn't about to go down the path of putting together a band with her. Too much hassle. "But I really love touring. I'm just in town to get my bearings and visit my family."

And, yes, okay, also to record a little demo record for his agent to pass around. But he didn't need a band for that. After a few weeks here, he'd hopefully be rested and ready to get back out on the road. He wasn't in Knoxville to make commitments, just amends.

"Is that all you want out of music? To tour for other people?"

"Maybe," RJ said, kicking back in his chair again. "I'm young yet. Who knows what I really want out of music, or life?"

Besides, RJ didn't know the last time when he wasn't on a stage that he'd gotten what he truly wanted out of anything. Maybe that morning on Montmartre. Maybe that's why he'd brought it up.

"It's all good, though. Don't worry about me, Mr. Danvers. This Christmas is bound to be a decent one."

Sitting in the cold on the Scruffy City Hall patio with Mr. Danvers was already his favorite night since that Montmartre sunrise. He'd enjoyed watching Mr. Danvers's reactions to all his crazy stories. The crinkle of his eyes, the guffaw of disbelief followed by wide-eyed amazement, and the way he'd thrown his head back when he laughed.

It was adorable to watch the man give in to the humor so thoroughly that laughter shook his body. And getting that kind of reaction out of the teacher he'd crushed on so desperately in school—and remembered obsessively ever since—was a pretty damn awesome high.

It definitely beat cocaine and was way more exhilarating than pot.

RJ ached to know more of Mr. Danvers's non-teacherly reactions. Sexy ones especially. As soon as possible. But he wasn't entirely sure how to pivot from telling stories about touring to getting Mr. Danvers to consider him as a viable hookup option. He knew that'd been his plan, but somehow the execution was harder than the fantasy.

"Some life you're living, RJ," Mr. Danvers said again. He tucked his hands between his legs and shivered despite his coat.

RJ shivered too. He rubbed his hands up and down his arms over the goosebumps. Breaking eye contact with Mr. Danvers, he checked the weather app on his phone. The temperature was dropping, nearing forty-three degrees now. Cold enough that when the breeze came through it really bit into him. Maybe he should suggest they take this somewhere inside? That could be the pivot?

"Here," Mr. Danvers said, shrugging out of his tweed sports jacket. "Put this on to warm up a little. I'm wearing long sleeves. You're in nothing but a T-shirt."

"Or we could go inside," RJ suggested, hoping he sounded seductive.

Mr. Danvers pondered the offer and then scooted closer. "It'd be harder to talk in there, and, well, I'm enjoying this conversation." Mr. Danvers bit into his lower lip, a coy gleam in his eye. "You get me?"

RJ's cock twitched. He licked his lips and his voice almost cracked as he said, "Yeah. Me too. And I get you."

"Good." Mr. Danvers held the coat out again. "Put it on."

RJ's cock rushed hot as he pulled the tight jacket on.

Maybe he'd managed the pivot after all. Maybe he was on exactly the right track.

Chapter Three

WELL, THIS WASN'T going to plan.

RJ, as it turned out, was an intelligent, funny, thoughtful man who had seen more of the world than Aaron had at this point. So much for him being dull or stupid. RJ, with his stories about Paris, Finland, and Singapore, made Aaron feel like the student. A very naughty one who kept thinking about his young teacher's lips, and hands, and package. God help him.

And now, shivering in the cold wind, he couldn't stop imagining a scenario where he breached the space between them and curled up on RJ's spacious lap to share the warmth of the too-small tweed coat that barely covered RJ's arms and tugged at his broad, angular shoulders.

Truly, RJ looked ridiculous in it, but sexy too. Like a big, sexy man in a doll's jacket.

Christ. Aaron rubbed his forehead. He was absurd.

"Everything okay?"

"Tonight didn't turn out like I'd planned, that's all."

"Typical of a Tinder date, I guess." RJ shrugged.

"Grindr, more like," Aaron said, taking a gamble. A flush chased through him as he reached for his glass and downed the last drops of his whiskey.

Silence held for a few beats, save for the pop music from the ice-skating ring and the beat of the dance music in the pub behind them.

"Yeah. I'm more of a Grindr man, myself," RJ finally said, meeting Aaron's gaze with a challenge.

Aaron had known. Of course he had. He'd known deep down as soon as he'd seen RJ sitting at the table, he'd known by the way RJ had kicked out the chair and looked up at him with heated eyes. RJ was gay and wanted him.

Still, his heart raced, and his palms went damp despite the cold.

Was this happening? Was he really going to do this?

Oh God, those questions always preceded his hottest, most reckless fucks. His dick thickened in his pants. His nipples ached.

RJ said, "Don't get me wrong, I've met some nice guys on Tinder." He huffed a laugh. "The truly nice kind, I mean. Men who are always looking for more than I'm prepared to give."

It was Aaron's turn to chuckle. "Oh? Is that how you are? You like to hook up and then...what? Hit the road again?" He smirked. "Go to Finland mid-January with some band?"

"Something like that."

Aaron licked his lips and tilted his head.

That's good. That could be...perfect.

Gathering bravery to him like sticks to burn, he leaned forward. "Your ID said you're twenty-four now." He swallowed thickly. "I'm twenty-eight. Just another two years and I'm thirty. Ancient in gay years."

"You're still hot." RJ met his gaze head on, warm and knowing. He was no child. He clearly understood exactly what Aaron was getting at now, and he wasn't running from it.

Aaron stared at him a moment longer. "I hadn't thought about you in years until I saw you on the stage earlier tonight. Something about you up there..." He groaned softly.

"I know."

Another laugh punched through Aaron.

"I have stage presence." RJ shrugged. "It's a problem sometimes with the front men I tour with. They think I pull too much attention." He rolled his eyes.

"Yeah?"

"Yeah." RJ smirked. "For what it's worth, I've thought about *you* a lot over the years. Found your Facebook, your Instagram." He appraised Aaron again with a long, slow, up and down that made Aaron's insides turn to goo. "Your cat's pretty cute. So are you."

Aaron stared at him, his palms sweating, filled with desire and hesitation. What was he doing? He knew better. This man was a former student. He couldn't afford another Coach McAllister situation.

But…fuck, his cock was hard, and his asshole was hungry. He had a strange feeling that RJ Blitz really knew how to fuck. Rough, and strong, and right. With a creamy ending, like that French pastry he'd mentioned, the one he'd eaten during a beautiful sunrise in Paris. If RJ ate ass with half as much enjoyment…

Aaron shivered and licked his lips. "So, what you're saying is it'd be a dream come true for you, then?" His heart shot off wildly. He didn't remember the last time he'd been this nervous picking someone up. Had he ever?

RJ's eyes widened, and he sucked in a sharp breath. "Yeah. You could say that. You've been a long-time fantasy of mine."

"My place is just up the street." Aaron rashly threw his gathered-up courage onto the fire of lust. "Why don't you walk me home?" He took a deep breath. *In for a penny…* "You can tell me everything you've ever imagined doing to me."

RJ almost knocked over his chair standing up, all coltish, raw eagerness. He lost it again immediately, though. Suave smoothness replaced the lapse. His eyes went dark as he stripped off Aaron's small sports coat and handed it back to him. "Let's go."

Aaron stood more slowly, sliding the jacket back on, shuddering at the delicious body heat RJ had left behind. Then RJ put his hand out for Aaron's, and when he put his fingers against RJ's palm, excitement shot up his spine. RJ's hand was bigger and more calloused than Aaron had expected. Guitar strings left their mark.

"Oh God," Aaron whispered.

"Lead on, Mr. Danvers." RJ's gritty baritone seemed to wrap around his balls and tug.

"Yeah, okay." Aaron's knees felt weak. "It's this way."

Leaving their empties on the patio table, Aaron pulled RJ away. A tremble started deep in his muscles: anticipation or cold, he didn't know or care.

Holy shit. He was taking a former student home. Some part of him knew it couldn't possibly be a good idea. But when RJ's big hand released his, only to settle against his lower back, silently urging him toward his apartment and all the things they were going to do there, Aaron no longer gave a shit about prudence or good judgment.

He just wanted more.

The jingling Christmas songs of the busker on the corner followed them as they left the holiday cheer of Market Square and started toward the lights of Gay Street, which was more fitting than ever.

Without warning, RJ rumbled low and soft in Aaron's ear, "I imagined bending you over that desk and spanking your sweet ass. With a ruler."

Aaron's nipples tingled. "You thought about that…in…in class?"

"So many times. Nearly came in my pants most days." RJ's hand drifted lower, gripped Aaron's left ass cheek possessively, and then quickly released it.

Aaron almost choked on his own spit. How had this happened? How had he gotten lucky enough to run into RJ, who admitted to wanting exactly what Aaron needed tonight? What he'd tried and failed to get before?

"*That* was my obsession," RJ added. "You'd write on that fucking smart board, so serious and earnest as hell, going on about grammar and symbolism or whatever. But all I could imagine was you on your stomach, ass shiny red from my hand, begging for my cock, pleading for me to fuck you. I'm amazed I passed, actually."

"Me too. Holy shit."

"Have I left you speechless, Mr. Danvers?"

"No."

"Are you into that fantasy?"

"Fuck yes."

He should probably tell RJ to call him Aaron, but there was something so dirty about him calling him by his teaching name.

RJ shifted his hand from Aaron's lower back to his own crotch as he groaned. "How far is this place of yours?"

"Just around the corner. Not far."

"Thank fuck."

The twinkle lights in the shop windows along the street, the blue lights of the massive Christmas tree erected just ahead, and the shining bulbs of the Tennessee Theater sign couldn't distract Aaron from one bright, pulsing thought: praise the baby Jesus, he was about to get his ass beaten and then get *laid*.

"It's just up here."

RJ squeezed Aaron's ass cheek again, and Aaron shuddered. "I'm going to fuck you, Mr. Danvers, until you can't see straight."

Hallelujah!

Chapter Four

T HEY STUMBLED INSIDE Aaron's loft, and RJ had him pressed up
against the door forcefully as soon as it was shut. Aaron gasped. Oh
yes, *hallelujah*. Praise Santa for delivering the early present he needed *so
badly*.

Still fully dressed, they rubbed against each other, breath mingling as
RJ said, "I'm going to get you on your knees. On your back. On your
stomach. I'm going to have you every way there is, and you're going to
fucking love it, Mr. Danvers. I'm—" RJ sniffed, his nose wrinkling up.

Aaron sniffed too and groaned.

Shit.

Literally.

Dammit, Constance, I love you but...really? Tonight?

He considered hustling RJ back to his bedroom and starting the fun
and games, but the air usually pulled back that way if he turned the
overhead fan on. And he hoped to get hot and sweaty enough to need
the fan. Aaron cleared his throat, wondering how to maintain their
boner-making banter and a sexy ambiance while cleaning up putrid-
smelling cat shit.

Damn Constance for being so cute and fluffy and for choosing *right
now* to lay a massive turd.

Rubbing his palms against his pants, Aaron cleared his throat. He
gestured toward Constance's litter box, placed on a towel near the door
out to the side entry by the kitchen. "Cat box. Let me just deal with
that? I think we'll both enjoy ourselves more without the..." He

wrinkled his nose and waved his hand in front of it.

"Yeah, good idea," RJ said with a warm smile. He took off his boots, crossed the loft's living room, and dropped down onto Aaron's green mid-century sofa, long legs spread wide. His still swollen crotch was on display. "I'll wait." He placed his hand over the bulge in his jeans, and Aaron flushed hot all over.

On either side of the couch, drawn close enough to use the table easily, was a set of matching green chairs. Constance rested in one of them, her golden eyes glowing, shining bright against her black fur. Aaron glared at her.

"That's Constance," he said, motioning toward her. She hopped down from the chair and sauntered from the room like she was putting on a show just for RJ. Aaron chuckled. "She's a stinky brat, but I love her."

"I know. I've seen your Instagram account. Or should I say Constance's Instagram account?" RJ laughed easily as Aaron knelt to lift the lid off the litter box, the scent of Constance's gift rising even more strongly through the loft. The bedroom and bathroom were down a brick-lined hallway, and the windows in Aaron's room looked out on First Presbyterian Church. Which felt decadently transgressive, given the porn Aaron watched in that room whenever he had a chance.

"It's all yours? Or do you rent?" RJ asked.

"It's all mine. Thanks to an inheritance."

RJ stood and made a slow turn around the open space, taking in the kitchen table by the long counter. The stove, the microwave, and the refrigerator were all in a neat row, and the dishwasher and sink were installed in the counter facing the living room—the better to wash dishes while watching TV, Aaron guessed. He'd never actually done it himself.

"No Christmas tree?"

Aaron shook his head. "I have those, though." He nodded to the small string of colored Christmas lights he'd hung over the loft's big front window.

RJ sauntered over to the window and switched on the light. "I have to admit, Mr. Danvers, I expected more holiday spirit out of the man who turned his classroom into a blizzard of hand-cut snowflakes, à la the movie *Elf*. Or do you just save all the merry for the students?"

"Pretty much." Aaron never decorated his loft for the holidays beyond a string of lights and whatever trinkets he got as teacher gifts from the kids.

On Christmas Eve, he always headed out to his father's farm in Strawberry Plains, where he, his dad, aunts, uncles, and cousins spent the evening together. Then they exchanged small gifts beneath his father's tree. And Aaron always spent Christmas Day itself with his mom in her condo, where he enjoyed her tree.

"Are you a secret grinch?"

Aaron laughed. "No. I love Christmas. It's my favorite time of the year."

RJ's brow quirked, interest gleaming in his eye, but then he gestured around at the apartment. "Could have fooled me, Mr. Danvers."

"It's a long story, but I split my holiday between my parents, always have. I help them decorate their places. It just seems like overkill to decorate here too when I'm the only one who'll see it."

"Right. *You'd* see it." RJ shoved his hands in his pockets, rocked back on his heels, and appraised Aaron. Flushing, Aaron really wished he was on his knees naked instead of holding a poop scoop. "That's important too," RJ said. "To do things just for yourself."

"I know. It's just I'm barely here." Were they going to discuss his decorations, or lack thereof, or were they going to fuck? *Damn you, Constance!* He grabbed a plastic baggy from the stash he kept near the litter box and dipped the scoop into the litter, covering the giant turd so that it would clump easily.

"I decorated my hotel rooms when I was on tour," RJ said. "Trees, lights, the works."

Aaron laughed awkwardly. "Did you come here to fuck me or would you rather we went down to the corner and bought a Christmas tree?"

RJ smirked. "We could do both. So your folks are divorced?"

"Yeah." Aaron slipped the giant poop in the bag. He might as well clear out all the clumped pee while he was at it since now they were making small instead of dirty talk. Then he'd spray some air freshener and try to move things back toward sexy times.

"Mine too. Kinda. They were never married, but they aren't together."

"Do you see them both?"

"Nah. My father wasn't part of my life. Except when he was. And that's not worth talking about. It was best when he was gone." He shrugged. "I liked being the man of the house."

"I bet you were good at it."

RJ ignored that as he sat on the couch again, legs spread. Tone casual. "You said you still split the holidays. How's that work?"

This hookup was rapidly devolving. Aaron hoped he could find a way to get it back to *evolving*. Hopefully into a red-hot, role-playing spank-fest, but at this point even a quick fuck would do. He scooped faster and waved off the question. "Doesn't matter."

"This is a pricey place for a teacher's salary," RJ said. "Family money, you said?"

A glance RJ's way showed he held one hand over his crotch and was absently rubbing the soft fabric of the sofa with the other. "Nosy much?"

RJ smirked but didn't deny it.

Aaron finished shoveling the litter. "Not family money, no. Well, not anymore. I used what my papaw left to me when he died to buy this place. I figured it was a good investment. Downtown was growing again, and this place was a bargain. It's tripled in value already." He couldn't help but brag a little.

RJ whistled low. "Hot damn. That sounds lucky."

"It was."

Papaw's legacy had covered the entire mortgage and left enough for him to furnish the place. He'd been free and clear of any family financial obligations and able to live on his measly public-school teacher salary. It was one less way he had to answer to anyone else for his life choices. Papaw probably wouldn't have appreciated Aaron's life choices, though. He'd died without knowing Aaron was gay—and for good reason. Aaron shrugged off those thoughts and finished up with the litter.

"Nice piece," RJ observed, nodding toward the antique chest of drawers Aaron used to store his less attractive books. No sense in putting ugly books out on shelves where people could see them.

"It was Papaw's. Took it from his old place out on the farm. My cousins didn't want it."

"I like your apartment," RJ said with a nod. "Spic and span, just the way I knew it would be. And books. Lots of books." He eyed the bookshelves lining the opposite wall.

Aaron had cleaned the loft earlier in the day, but Constance had ruined the perfect presentation with her shit. Tying off the baggy, he grimaced. He supposed he had nothing to hide now since his cover of being a fantasy fuck had been blown by his cat.

RJ didn't seem to notice his frustration, though. He lounged on the sofa with his hand on his crotch, looking around the room with a piercing, judging gaze. Aaron's stomach flipped over, imagining RJ looking at his naked body like that: judging him, appraising him, and hopefully finding him satisfactory.

But what if he didn't find him pleasing? What would RJ do then?

Aaron's gut curled with lust. He had a feeling RJ would have a very good idea of exactly how to handle any situation where Aaron didn't please him. And Aaron was dying to know what that would feel like. Maybe he should be just a little bit of a tease, a bit of a brat. See if RJ pushed back. If he *handled* him the way Aaron needed to be handled. Or was he just expecting too much now?

Constance meowed and returned to the room without any evidence of shame. She proceeded to sniff the cuffs of RJ's jeans, checking him out. Aaron grumbled, trash bag in hand.

"She's pretty," RJ offered, putting his fingers down to let Constance butt up against them. "Black cats are my favorite."

Aaron smirked, taking the collected litter out the side door to a small balcony area, putting it in the lidded can where it wouldn't stink. He'd take the whole thing down to the big dumpster by the church later. When he returned inside, he said, "A punk rocker with a preference for black cats. Try not to be such a big cliché, RJ." He sprayed air freshener around liberally.

"Mr. Danvers," RJ smirked. "C'mere, and I'll show you how big my cliché is."

Yes. Let's get back on track. Aaron bit down on his bottom lip and chuckled, shoving the air freshener back into the cleaning closet.

Aaron's gut fluttered, and he stared at RJ, who raised a challenging brow at him. He was tempted to get down on the floor and crawl right up into RJ's lap, but... "Let me wash my hands first."

"Always so prissy," RJ said, squeezing himself. "Luckily, I've always liked that about you."

Running his hands under hot water in the kitchen sink and lathering up, Aaron's mind tripped on itself. "Prissy?" He'd never considered himself especially feminine. He didn't think he read as overtly "gay" even, but that was because his mother had strictly forbidden any behaviors that could be seen that way.

As a teen, he'd worked hard to reduce his so-called lisp, and to prevent his swiveling hips and fluttering hands from outing him before he was ready. Some days, when he really thought about it, the amount of effort he'd put into training himself out of his natural behaviors pissed him off. He could have done something so much more interesting with all that energy and stress. What would it be like to be free and loved for who you were born to be?

But, on other days, like at parent-teacher meetings, when he was seated across from a big, burly football dad, he was glad of his mother's training. Most of the time. Hell, he wasn't sure how he felt. He just knew that when he'd started working as a teacher the last thing he'd wanted was to be read as queer, so he'd worked extra hard to stifle it. Now, acting masc just came naturally. Or so he'd thought.

"You always…" Aaron cleared his throat again, trying to keep the squeak out of his voice. "You found me prissy?"

"Yeah. Uptight, fussy," RJ clarified with a hot grin. "You kept your things on your desk *just so*." He groaned like that was incredibly sexy. "And you always dressed like a magazine had decided to feature you in a best-dressed teacher spread." He smiled again. "You know the type, Mr. Danvers. You *are* the type."

"I'm not—" He wanted to deny it, but even as the words left his mouth, he found himself carefully folding the kitchen towel he'd wiped his hands on and placing it on the counter top like RJ had said—"just so." Aaron stifled the rest of the denial and instead said, "You like that type?"

"Like it? I lust after it. After you. For years." RJ grinned again. "C'mere, Mr. Danvers. Get on my lap. I want to see if you taste as good as you always look."

Aaron's heart skittered and his cock thumped with blood. He stepped carefully toward RJ like he might be dangerous, his mind trying to gauge just how much trouble he was getting himself into by letting this boy, this *former student,* boss him around.

He didn't care. He wanted it.

"You should call me Aaron."

"I'll call you whatever I damn well please."

Aaron's blood rushed. He peeled off the tweed jacket he was still wearing, sweat dampening his armpits now, and dumped it on a chair, trying not to be fussy or hang it "just so." Touching the top button of his shirt, he swallowed hard. "Should I…?"

RJ shook his head. "I'll do it. Just get on my lap. Now."

Aaron didn't know what came over him, an undeniable longing to obey perhaps. It didn't escape his notice that he'd yearned for this exact thing as they'd chatted outside the pub: to sit on RJ's lap, to be held by him.

Aaron straddled RJ's long legs, his own pants rubbing against his now fiercely hard dick. They both groaned.

RJ's head went back on the sofa, exposing his long neck and prominent Adam's apple. He gripped Aaron's ass and held him down while shoving his hips up, pushing his hard cock against Aaron's butt. "Mr. Danvers, you have no idea...fuck."

Aaron got the idea very quickly when RJ gripped a handful of his hair and tugged him down into the hottest, wildest kiss he'd ever experienced. Tongues and teeth, lips and spit, and both of them breathing like racehorses. His chin burned with the scrape of RJ's stubble as they made out hot and heavy like teens hopped up on fresh testosterone and the newness of their bodies.

"Damn," RJ whispered when they broke apart to breathe. "I knew you'd be hot for it. Knew you'd be just like this." And then Aaron was on his back on the sofa, his legs spread, and his body undulating under RJ. Their clothes scraped and rubbed as he escalated toward what promised to be an earthshaking orgasm, bearing down on him hard and fast.

Before he could get there, though, RJ pulled back and knelt between Aaron's spread knees. "Look at me."

Aaron met his blue eyes and shivered.

RJ peered down at him, gaze hungry and intense. Then he reached to unbutton Aaron's shirt. His big fingers fumbled with the first two at the top. He cursed under his breath. "This a favorite of yours?"

Aaron shook his head.

"Would you miss it?" RJ gripped both sides of the collar and gently tugged in imitation of ripping it open. "This okay?"

Aaron gulped. He did like the shirt, but he liked this more. He whispered, "It's okay."

RJ grinned and tore the shirt open, buttons bursting, fabric tearing, and cool air rushing over Aaron's chest, raising his nipples. Aaron's torso jerked up with the force of the rip and he cried out before collapsing back against the sofa, shirt destroyed.

Aaron's breath heaved and sweat popped on his bare skin, making him shiver.

"Mr. Danvers, I think you'd let me do anything to you," RJ murmured, running his finger down Aaron's chest, circling each sensitive nipple, and then down toward his belly button. "Is that right? You gonna let me do anything?" He poked his finger into Aaron's belly button and then trailed it back up again.

Aaron nodded.

His words had flown somewhere far away, and he hoped RJ wasn't one of those guys who made him say yes to everything they did before they did it, because that just wasn't happening. He could barely think through the white noise of lust in his head and the throb of his cock, and the wonder of this man kneeling over him, holding him to the sofa with just one finger and the heat from his eyes.

Who'd have ever thought?

RJ Blitz. Christ.

Making Aaron weak with need.

"Good. Because I like it when I can do anything." RJ bent and sucked Aaron's nipple into his mouth. Aaron arched and gripped RJ's head, his hands slipping through the soft, short hair.

"Fuck!"

"Mmm, yeah. For sure," RJ hissed. "But first we're going to play. I think I'm going to like playing with you, Mr. Danvers. I think you're going to like it too."

Constance darted from the room in a surge of movement, and RJ laughed. "I think I scared her. Or maybe you did, with all that noise you're making."

RJ's single finger reached Aaron's belt buckle, and he started to undo it. As he worked it off, and Aaron lifted his hips to help him pull it through the loops, RJ grinned. "Good God, Mr. Danvers, I think this is going to be the best night of my life."

Aaron still couldn't talk, but he was starting to feel exactly the same way. Cat shit and all.

Chapter Five

MR. DANVERS'S LOFT apartment was tidy and neat, and so was his body. He was shorn and shaven, tight and firm. His chest hair was light, and his nipples peeked out pink and perfect. His stomach wasn't a ripped six-pack—it was just a bit soft. But in the best way, displaying a tender vulnerability that made RJ feel protective and hot all over.

He wiped the sweat off his upper lip and stared down at the man beneath him, still struggling out of his pants and looking shy about his boxer briefs, hung up as they were on his hard cock. Mr. Danvers was like a miraculous present wrapped up just for RJ by the baby Jesus himself.

Holy shit. Merry Christmas to me. Fuck.

RJ ran his hands down the length of Mr. Danvers's body, fitting his palms into the grooves at his hips, and then rapidly freed him from the boxer briefs, shoving them down and leaning back to tug them off. "Yes," he hissed. "That's better. Fuck, look at you."

Mr. Danvers shivered lightly, and RJ couldn't resist touching again, smoothing his hands down and up again, rubbing his torso, plucking his nipples, and then skimming past his gorgeous cock to stroke his thighs and spread them apart. RJ popped open his own jeans, shoving them down to mid-thigh.

"Condoms?" he breathed.

"Bedroom."

"Mmm." RJ bent low and kissed Mr. Danvers again, his red lips still swollen from the ferocious kisses they'd shared before. "Gonna make you come so hard." He trailed kisses down Mr. Danvers's scratchy cheek to suck his earlobe, gratified when Mr. Danvers arched and whimpered. "Gonna make you come so many times."

"Fuck," Mr. Danvers said, gripping RJ hard and tugging at his T-shirt. "Get it off."

"You want me naked?"

"*Fuck*," Mr. Danvers said again. "Want you."

"Yeah? How much?"

Mr. Danvers groaned and kissed RJ hard, tugging him down so that their dicks lined up as they rutted together. RJ tugged Mr. Danvers's head back and licked up his neck, loving how Mr. Danvers's breathing hitched and wobbled, how he gripped RJ's ass harder and pulled him in tight.

"Like that?"

Mr. Danvers moaned. His eyes were closed, and he was working himself into a frenzy, his cock jamming against RJ's hard stomach and rubbing against RJ's aching cock. They were both going to come if they kept on much longer.

RJ wanted that, but he also wanted Mr. Danvers to beg. He lifted off Mr. Danvers's body and resisted his urgent grunts and reaching hands long enough to stand up, tug his jeans back up over his aching dick, and reach a hand down to the teacher he'd wanted to fuck for six years.

This was happening. Holy fuck.

He was about to bury himself in that hot ass. He'd never believed in miracles, but this sure as hell had the hand of God written all over it, as far as he was concerned.

"Bedroom," he ordered. "Now."

Dazed, Mr. Danvers seemed to have a hard time getting to his feet. His eyes were far away in the haze of lust, but he let RJ pull him up, unsteady and naked, a vulnerable sweetness in his whole body, so on display and so aroused. His ass jiggled as he moved ahead of RJ down the hallway that must lead to his room.

Constance streaked past them again, scampering around before bouncing off the sofa and then under the chair she'd been sitting on when they first came in. Mr. Danvers ignored her, so RJ did too, following him with his eyes trained on that ass which had given him so much trouble in high school.

It was every bit as luscious naked as he'd imagined. His balls tightened, and he was glad he'd pulled his jeans back up. If he touched himself right now, he'd shoot all over that sexiness. When he really wanted to shoot inside it.

The bedroom was sparsely decorated with a comfortable looking bed and a chest of drawers. Nothing more. The bedroom window curtains opened to let in the glow of a neighbor's outdoor colored Christmas lights. Mr. Danvers hastily flipped on the standing light next to the bed and drew the curtains closed with a fast twitch.

And then he was digging in the top drawer of the chest against the wall, rattling the few framed photographs atop it, as he finally yanked out a tube of lube and a half-used strip of condoms.

It made RJ's stomach flip to imagine that Mr. Danvers might bring other men—other hookups—here. Sweat gathered at the base of his back, a feeling of nausea washing over and through him. Like Mr. Danvers was his, and the men he brought up here to fuck were betraying something that'd never existed between them.

Mr. Danvers turned to him with the supplies in hand and stared up at RJ wide-eyed. RJ gazed down at him, wonder, lust, and sweet, crazy disbelief rattling in him. He realized he was shaking only when he reached out to take the lube and condoms to toss them on the neatly made bed.

"I'm about to come in my pants just looking at you."

Two bright spots appeared on Mr. Danvers's dimpled cheeks just like when RJ had stared overlong at him back in English class. He drew close enough to feel Mr. Danvers's breath gusting gently, and then chucked his chin up. He rubbed his lips against Mr. Danvers's, refusing to turn it into a kiss, even as Mr. Danvers swayed up, trying to lock onto him.

"Beg," RJ whispered, brushing his lips over the soft plumpness of Mr. Danvers's mouth. "Beg me to bend you over this bed and smack your ass. Beg me to fuck you."

"Ah, damn," Mr. Danvers whispered, his eyes squeezing closed. RJ could feel him trembling, his hard cock brushing against the front of RJ's jeans. He opened his eyes and stared at RJ's collarbones exposed by his V-neck tee. "Please," he gasped. "Just please. Anything."

"Mm-hmm," RJ murmured, ducking his head to nuzzle the side of Mr. Danvers's face, breathing in the scent of his peppery cologne. "Be. More. Specific."

"Spank me."

"I can do that for you, baby. You want me to do that?"

Mr. Danvers shivered and grabbed hold of RJ's biceps like his knees had gone weak. "RJ…"

"Let me just…" He breathed him in again and then trailed his lips over the rough, golden shadow growing in on Mr. Danvers's cheek.

Mr. Danvers breathed harshly through his mouth, his fingers gripping RJ's biceps hard. When RJ kissed him, his mouth opened like a soft, wet, bloom, and he claimed it, driving his tongue in until Mr. Danvers moaned and collapsed against RJ's chest, kissing him back greedily.

Breaking the intensity, RJ kissed Mr. Danvers's ear, then spun him around, tugging that sweet ass back against his thighs, wishing his pants were off and he could feel Mr. Danvers's soft skin against his cock. Instead, he gripped his hips and pushed him forward. "Bend over. Hands on the bed."

Mr. Danvers whimpered, nearly collapsing, but holding himself up so that RJ had a great view of his ass. The soft, light dusting of hair over his ass cheeks, the thicker hair on his thighs, and the tremble in his haunches that reminded RJ so vividly of when he'd written on the whiteboard at school, his butt shaking with the effort.

"Mr. Danvers," RJ said, but then no more words came. He put his hands on that ass, cupping it, sensing the heat from his skin and the tremble in his muscle. He wanted to spread the cheeks, get a look at his asshole, but he held off. He savored the heaving breaths Mr. Danvers took, his ribs expanding and falling enticingly, his hands knotting into the comforter.

"Mr. Danvers, I'm going to spank you now. You want that?"

Mr. Danvers froze slightly and then said, "Anything. You can do anything you want."

"Beg me to do it."

"Please."

"Please what?"

"*Please* spank me." Mr. Danvers's voice cracked, like he was shocked by his own words. But RJ took it for the permission it was, and he let his hand fall hard on Mr. Danvers's right butt cheek, grunting as the flesh wobbled and Mr. Danvers let out a bitten-off cry.

"Let it out. I want to hear." Mr. Danvers cried out again when RJ slapped his left cheek. "Used to imagine you over your desk just like this. Your grade book shoved off on the floor, and me spanking you while you shouted the school down. Spanking you until your ass was bright red and you were begging to be fucked."

"Oh *fuck*," Mr. Danvers whispered. He buried his face in the sheets and lifted his ass up higher, inviting RJ with his body.

RJ pulled back and smacked his left butt cheek again, watching his handprint flare on the pale flesh, and hissing in pleasure when Mr. Danvers humped air with his hard cock, driving forward and back, seeking something more.

"Yes," Mr. Danvers groaned.

RJ hesitated. Part of him wanted to go easy on Mr. Danvers, he didn't seem like the kind of man to get spanked very often, but another part of him wondered if he'd ever have this shot again. He was pretty certain they'd agreed on a one-night thing. No strings. No repeats. He didn't want to waste it.

But, fuck, he already wanted a repeat. Ten repeats even. Just to hear Mr. Danvers make that sound when RJ's hand connected with his flesh, just to know he was going to get to put his cock inside that beautiful body, and that he was going to make that beautiful man come. He stood back, still dressed and desperately hard, staring at Mr. Danvers, and he already wanted so much more than ten repeats.

He was screwed.

He was also in too deep to even consider stopping. He squeezed his cock, unzipped his jeans, and tugged himself out to stroke while ogling Mr. Danvers's hot ass.

"Please," Mr. Danvers whimpered, looking back over his shoulder. "Do it. Spank me like you—" He licked his lips, eyes glazed. "Like you always wanted."

RJ released his shaft before letting fly with his hand, smacking Mr. Danvers left and then right, and then left and right again. Mr. Danvers jumped around the bed, biting off his cries still, but shoving his ass back for more every time RJ paused to shake out his hand. He stared in awe as Mr. Danvers arched his back, taking every smack like a greedy whore.

Mr. Danvers groaned and cried out, "Please! I...I need! Just fuck me!"

The words shot to RJ's balls. He had to grip himself hard, breathing through his nose in slow, even inhales and exhales before he could trust himself to shove his pants down to his knees, rip off one of the condoms from the strip, and roll it on.

Lube was messy, and one squirt was enough to cover his sheathed cock with plenty to spare for Mr. Danvers's asshole. He slicked the tight muscle up good, tempted to push his fingers in to prepare Mr. Danvers a little, but also too desperate to get his dick inside that sweet hole before he shot and ruined the night entirely.

Breathing heavily, he stepped up to the side of the bed, gripped Mr. Danvers by the hips, and grunted, "Ready?"

"God, yes." Mr. Danvers shoved back, drawing RJ's gaze from the side of his flushed face down to his narrow waist and then to his red, handprinted ass. RJ's handprints, like claims of ownership on that sweet butt he'd wanted for so fucking long. And it was about to happen. Right now.

Right fucking now.

RJ bit his lower lip hard, holding back with all he had as he pressed his cockhead against the small entrance to Mr. Danvers's body. He pushed and gasped as Mr. Danvers shoved back and bore down.

He was finally taken in—so tight, and so *practiced.* Heat enveloped him as Mr. Danvers's ass opened for him, his lower body swiveling in a gorgeous, wanton dance. A grunting moan fell from RJ's mouth and he sank in to his balls.

"Fuck," RJ whispered, gripping Mr. Danvers's hips hard enough to leave bruises, trying not to blow immediately. "Mr. Danvers, *fuck.*"

Mr. Danvers chuckled softly, convulsing around RJ with each burst of breath. "You're one to talk," he finally got out around his moans and soft laughter. "You're huge."

"Surely you can use more a descriptive word, Mr. Danvers," RJ gritted out. "You're a composition teacher. 'Huge'? C'mon. Dazzle me." He rubbed Mr. Danvers's hot haunches; his handprints were edged in white around the red. "Or I'll have to spank you while I fuck your ass."

"Enormous. Colossal. Mammoth. Gargantuan."

RJ laughed now. "You make me sound like an animal."

"You make me feel like one," Mr. Danvers said, squeezing his asshole around RJ and then releasing. He rocked back, fucking himself slowly on RJ's dick, and then he broke, his hips speeding up, moving recklessly. Tossing his head back, he reached down to jack himself.

"Fuck. Always knew you'd take my cock like a champ," RJ gritted out. "Used to watch you in class and imagine this. Knew you'd be hot.

Knew you'd *want it*."

All of that was true, and RJ was about to go off at any second because of it. But he hadn't known about Mr. Danvers's sounds. The delicious, urgent noises that puffed out of him with each aroused breath. He groaned, wanting to see Mr. Danvers's face when he came.

He pulled out, and Mr. Danvers cried out in surprise, reaching back with a greedy hand to grip his thigh and try to pull him forward.

"Turn over."

Mr. Danvers didn't hesitate, flipping onto his back, his stomach exposed like a sweet thing to be protected and his hard cock leaking pre-come against it. "Yes. Take me like this," he said, pulling his legs up to expose his hole for RJ's dick. "Fuck me now. Hard. Like you mean it."

RJ didn't hesitate. He thrust in fast and pounded Mr. Danvers, nearly bending him in half with his urgency.

Mr. Danvers's eyes went wide and vulnerable with lust as RJ continued to fuck him with long, regular strokes. His noises escalated, loud and reckless, like RJ was ripping pleasure from him in strips and giving it to him in punches.

Mr. Danvers scrambled at RJ's shoulders, his fingernails scraping skin as he fell apart. His eyes rolled back, his body convulsed, and his heels kicked against RJ's ass in seizure-like spasms.

"That's it, Mr. Danvers," RJ crooned, sensing the coming explosion. "Come on my dick."

Mr. Danvers groaned and shivered all over, his stomach jumping as he twitched and strained. RJ didn't stop pumping, his hips slamming against Mr. Danvers's hot ass cheeks again and again.

"Yes," he whispered when Mr. Danvers's legs hitched even farther up, and his asshole clenched rhythmically around RJ's dick again. "Give me everything. I want to see you, baby."

Mr. Danvers quivered and shook, his body wracked in the throes of some delicious bottom boy ecstasy that RJ could only imagine. He yelled, tendons standing out on his throat, and his face going as red as his ass as he gripped RJ's shoulders with sharp nails and orgasmed. Come shot from his cock, spattering over his stomach, his neck, and hitting RJ's arm and chin.

"Oh God!" Mr. Danvers cried, his body shaking and jerking as he took RJ's still slamming cock. He jerked and came more, what seemed like a full-body orgasm wracking him. He shot another small load as RJ gripped his hips and shoved into him as hard and fast as he could.

When he reached it, RJ's climax was New Year's Eve fireworks bright and Christmas morning perfect. He thrust deep into Mr. Danvers's sweet, flailing body and yelled his pleasure. He kept his eyes open, staring into Mr. Danvers's hot gaze, grunting with each long, nearly painful burst of pleasure.

Collapsing onto Mr. Danvers, breathing in his sweat and the scent of jizz and whatever laundry detergent he used on his sheets, RJ's head spun. No gift in the history of man had ever been as good as what Mr. Danvers had given him tonight. Forget frankincense and myrrh. Forget Santa Claus. A truly perfect Christmas gift was Mr. Aaron Danvers offering up his jiggly, red-hot ass for mutual screaming orgasms.

"Thank you," he breathed in Mr. Danvers's ear as they crash landed from their pleasure high.

Mr. Danvers laughed, but he sounded shocked too. "No, thank you. That was…" He stopped. "That…"

RJ kissed his cheek. "I fucked all descriptors out of you. Wow."

"You and that ginormous, titanic, immense dick of yours."

"Oh no, I left some behind." RJ rose up, pulled his dick free, and took off the used condom. He spotted the trashcan by the chest of drawers and tossed it in, making the goal. "I guess I'll have to try again. If that's all right by you."

"That's fine with me." Though Mr. Danvers's voice shook with the words.

"You sure?"

"Yes." Mr. Danvers stroked a hand over RJ's cheek, drew his fingers down to the slight dimple in RJ's chin, and said, "You fuck like a dream. Merry Christmas to me, right?"

"No, Mr. Danvers. Merry Christmas to *me*."

Chapter Six

"WHAT THE FUCK?"

Aaron reached out to slam his hand down on the alarm clock, shutting off the horrific bleating noise. He scrambled out of bed. If the bedside alarm was going off already, then he'd left his phone in the other room, and now he was late, late, *late*.

Fuck.

A yawn from the bed next to him, plus long arms and legs stretching widely, jolted him even more thoroughly from his deep sleep. Fuck, he'd let RJ stay over. After such incredibly intense sex, he'd been unable to resist the lure of curling up next to RJ's long, strong body, and resting together. He hadn't meant for them to fall asleep.

He scrubbed at his face and eyed RJ's prone form. RJ was awake, though just barely, peering up at Aaron through slitted eyes that were so clearly eager to close again, obviously on the very edge of going back to sleep.

Aaron's stomach tumbled anxiously. Letting a hookup stay wasn't his usual MO. Especially on a school night, but RJ had fucked him senseless. Not once. Not twice. Not four times. Not even five.

Six times.

Fuck.

Aaron had nearly cried in sheer, wrung-out pleasure the last time. He'd keened out weird, hitching, begging sobs he didn't understand. But RJ had held him through it, kissed his cheeks, and told him that he'd never fucked a sexier man. The final orgasm had actually hurt. But when it was over, Aaron had still whimpered for more.

Jesus.

He'd never had a night like that. Ever. He ached all over. His balls, his cock, his hips, his butt—which might even be bruised from the spanking—and his asshole all felt tender and well-used. A temptation to call out sick from work came over him. He almost never did that. It wasn't fair to his students to stick them with a substitute who couldn't advance their learning just because he'd gotten his freak on the prior night.

Still, he was exhausted, raw, and so very tired. He'd just decided to do it, to hell with the kids, when he remembered he'd promised Carter Ward some one-on-one time today. The kid had been a wreck lately, and he'd asked Aaron with a tremble in his voice to please talk with him. There was no way Aaron could let him down on that. Not when a middle-school boy had been brave enough to ask.

He glanced toward RJ again. His eyes were open now, regarding Aaron with curiosity, obviously waiting to see what would happen next.

Oh God. What had he done?

A groan tore from him as he climbed from bed. Fuck, he really was sore.

"You okay?" RJ asked, sitting up fully, his cropped hair somehow messy-looking despite being so short. "Did I hurt you last night?"

"I'm fine." Aaron said, glancing at the clock. "I'm just really fucking late for work."

"But the alarm just went off?"

"That's my final warning alarm. It goes off when I'm supposed to be leaving. I have two more on my phone, but I guess it's still in the living room."

"Shit."

Aaron opened the bedroom door, and sure enough the tinkling chimes of his alarm on his phone came from the living room. He hustled in to grab the damn phone, turned the alarms off, and checked Constance's water and food bowls before walking down the hall to the bathroom. Every step was a reminder of what had happened last night. Of how much he'd needed it. And how fucking good it had been.

RJ stood by the bed, naked as a jaybird and gorgeous as an Adonis. Every sinew and muscle was visible in his body. His shoulders, his arms, his thighs, the six pack at his stomach. Damn. He was hot. A sort of wild fear gripped Aaron. It filled his whole body, making him want to either throw himself onto the bed and submit to RJ's cock again, or kick him out right fucking now. No in-between.

Aaron shook his head, trying to clear it of the lustful thoughts that were creeping in already. It wasn't right, fucking a former student like that, or rather being fucked by one. Still, there was no denying it had been the best sex of his life. Hands down. No comparison. He couldn't regret it. Not even a little.

But it was time for it to be over now.

RJ strolled down the hall toward him, obviously planning to follow him into the bathroom.

"I think you should go," Aaron said, trying to keep his voice calm, to not let the morning-after, how's-this-gonna-end-now? panic leak through. But his voice still trembled, and he hoped RJ thought it was just usual morning frogginess, and not indicative of the weird, unnerved feeling in his stomach that he couldn't put a name on.

He didn't wait to see RJ's expression, ducking into the bathroom quickly.

Constance was curled up in the sink, sound asleep and adorable. She opened one annoyed eye when he began to relieve himself in the toilet. As he pissed, RJ appeared in the doorway. Aaron didn't meet his gaze, but he found the annoyance he needed to harden his voice. "I mean now. You need to go now."

"Sure. I'll piss on the sidewalk I guess," RJ said, a flint in his tone that made Aaron wince.

"Fuck. Sorry. Just..." He shook the last drops from his cock and motioned at the toilet. "Go right ahead. I have to hop in the shower."

Embarrassment heated his skin at what a rude dick he was being. He didn't *do* this morning-after thing. Any of it. Ever. He got fucked and got out. That's the way he always did it. He hated this jittery, confused feeling.

"I'd let you take a shower too," he lied. "But I really have to get out of here and—"

"And I need to go now. Got it."

RJ sounded hurt, but he obviously wasn't going to push it, and Aaron didn't have time to be sweet. Especially when this, whatever this was, could never happen again. It'd been hot. Wild. Perfect.

But no.

Aaron wasn't able to be in a relationship. Not with his current job situation—issues with his principal, that pesky black mark on his record… And, besides, RJ had made it clear that commitment wasn't his style. It was best to call it quits straight away. Put the entire thing in the past. RJ would remain forever a fond memory of the hottest night of his life. And he'd hopefully be the same to RJ—a long-time fantasy come true.

Aaron started the shower over the sound of RJ's piss hitting his own in the toilet. When the water was the right temperature, he ducked under the stream, soaping up quickly. "Listen, I'm not trying to be an asshole. Really."

"I know. You're late." RJ flushed the toilet and must have dislodged Constance because she meowed in irritation. The sink water ran, and Aaron peeked out to see that RJ was washing his hands.

Aaron ducked back behind the curtain before their eyes could meet, his heart lurching. RJ was still naked, and he looked so vulnerable in the cold light of the bathroom. Not too young, necessarily, but too human. Shockingly so.

Aaron soaped up more, a new kind of regret he didn't understand filling him.

The shower curtain jerked back, exposing RJ in his entire naked beauty. He didn't get in, though. He just stared at Aaron like he was memorizing him, and then he smiled. "I just wanted to thank you again, Mr. Danvers." He gave Aaron another long up and down and added, "That was the best night of my life. The hottest for sure."

Aaron swallowed, his cock rising treacherously at RJ's heated gaze and sly smile. "Well, like we said last night, merry Christmas, right?"

"Yeah. Merry Christmas, Mr. Danvers." He reached out and ran his index finger up the underside of Aaron's cock, causing it to fully harden in one sweet swipe. Then he brought the same index finger to Aaron's chin and lifted it until Aaron reluctantly met RJ's gaze. "I'm in town until after the New Year. Does your phone have a password?"

"Yeah."

RJ released his chin and grabbed the phone from the counter. He held it out. Aaron stepped out of the shower stream and took it. "What?"

"Put your password in."

"Why?"

"I'm putting my number in your phone. You'll text or call me when you're ready to do this again."

Aaron's throat clicked. "I don't—"

"Don't make a liar out of yourself."

Aaron put in the password, not really sure why he was obeying.

RJ plucked the phone from his hand, thumbed at the screen, and then put it on the counter. He leaned into the shower to kiss Aaron. His breath was sour, but Aaron didn't care. He wanted to dive into RJ's arms and let him draw all of those hot noises and even hotter feelings from his body again.

RJ broke away first. "Bye, Mr. Danvers," he whispered.

Aaron's knees trembled.

"Call me." RJ's voice went a shade deeper. "Got it, *Aaron*?"

Then he stalked out of the bathroom, his bare ass all muscled and gorgeous.

Aaron closed his eyes and took some gulping breaths. Finally calming down enough to finish washing off, he shampooed and rinsed. His cock remained erect and aching, and his balls were sore as fuck. He didn't have time to think about his life choices right now. He had to get to school before Principal Shock realized he was late. Otherwise, he'd never hear the end of it.

Besides, he needed to have his head together by the time he met with Carter Ward after lunch. The kid deserved him at his best.

Shaving as quickly as possible, and thus cutting himself twice, he decided to shove RJ Blitz into the back of his mind for now. He could think about him later.

Maybe tonight after a glass of wine, alone here in his apartment. He could maybe text him or call, and, well, figure out a nicer way to turn him down.

A one-night stand he could manage. But anything more, even a holiday fling? That might be taking things too far. Especially when RJ fucked like that. Like he'd reached right into Aaron's soul with his stupidly tremendous cock and then shattered it with pleasure. Yes, anymore of *that* would be more than he could possibly endure.

As Aaron left his apartment, hustling down the street to the garage where he paid a monthly fee to park his car, he resolutely ignored the twinge in his ass, the tug of his sore muscles, and the Christmas decorations going up all around. He ignored his own treacherous brain whispering that there were trees for sale on the corner. If he wanted, he could invite RJ over and...

No.

He didn't have room for romantic emotional entanglements, not in the past, not in the future, and not even at Christmas. He didn't have it in him to deal with that kind of pain. He'd seen enough of the fallout of love with his parents. He wasn't going to volunteer to endure it himself.

As he climbed into his car and started the engine, he groaned. He'd be at least fifteen minutes late. Principal Shock would probably notice. With any luck the only thing on the homeroom agenda would be a roll call and a run through of the daily announcements. He flipped on the car stereo. Spotify merrily picked up in the middle of "Tender Tennessee Christmas" right where it'd left off the day before, and he sang it under his breath as he left the parking garage.

A bing from his phone grabbed his attention. He glanced at it, even though he was driving, and what he saw made his forehead crease. He groaned. It was a reminder that he'd promised to play an elf to the Coach Ramirez's Santa Claus during the school-wide holiday pep rally for the basketball team the following afternoon, and he hadn't even picked up the costume from the rental place yet.

Crap! Why'd he ever agree to do that? Coach Ramirez was hot, but not that hot. And he definitely wasn't gay. So, wearing green-striped tights and a jingle hat wasn't going to get Aaron anywhere with the man. Ugh. What was it with him and coach-types?

And, speaking of getting anywhere with any man...

Why the *hell* hadn't he just thrown caution to the wind and spread his legs for RJ Blitz one more time this morning? Who knew if he'd ever get screwed like that again? One last fuck for the road would have taken the edge off his thrumming anxiety, especially since he was going to be late anyway. He glanced at his clock. It would have been worth it.

He put his foot on the gas, hoping he didn't get pulled over on his way to school. It was the last week before Christmas break and he was already on the principal's shit list. Christ. He just wanted to have a calm holiday season this year. No drama.

Was that too much to ask?

A nice, fun Christmas Eve with his dad's family and a nice, tolerable Christmas Day with his mom for once. No fights. No problems. And no tempting, handsome, former students with miraculous dicks that could plow him for hours. He shivered at the memory.

Yeah. Absolutely none of that.

Just regular wholesome, drama-free, family fun. He deserved that right? Because God knew he needed it. Almost as much as he'd needed RJ Blitz last night.

RJ CLIMBED OUT of the Uber he'd taken from Aaron's apartment and stalked up the sidewalk of his mom and Doug's place in the new West Knoxville neighborhood where they'd purchased a typical suburban house. He took in the various Christmas decorations that had been added since even yesterday.

Before RJ had left for his gig, Doug had already set out the blow-up Santa and reindeer on the roof. Now they had a Frosty the Snowman in the front yard, along with a glowing star hung in a tree and a full-sized glowing nativity scene that he recognized as having been on sale last week at Joel's store, Vreeland's Home and Garden.

"Doug goes all in for Christmas," his mom had told RJ yesterday afternoon over an early dinner while gazing adoringly at her husband of the last four and a half years. The kids had been shoving mac and cheese into their faces and being quiet for a change. His stepbrother had been at his mom's house for the night.

"Betsy loves it," Doug had said, gazing back at her with a lovesick expression that'd made RJ's homemade noodle soup suddenly taste gross. Though, truthfully, that adoring expression was the main reason RJ couldn't dislike the guy, even if some petty, idiot part of him really wanted to. Doug was devoted to RJ's mom, and RJ couldn't ask for much more than that. Especially since he wasn't around to take care of her. He just wondered how long it would last. Four years already seemed to be pressing their luck.

But what did RJ know about love? He hadn't even been able to pull off a decent morning-after with Aaron. How it'd turned into such a failure after such a successful night, he had no idea. When he'd held

Aaron, hot with orgasm and sobbing with pleasure in his arms, he'd never imagined the man would be so cold the next morning.

"RJ!" a voice cried from an open window above. He glanced up to see his little sister Perri hanging worryingly out the window, her round face broken into a grin. As she leaned out even farther, her dark brown hair flew in the cool December morning breeze. "You're home! Mommy's been so scared about you!"

Shit. He should have texted that he wouldn't be coming home. Frankly, he wasn't used to her caring. And not just because he didn't normally live here, but, before he'd taken off touring, living on his own, she'd been working doubles most of his life. She hadn't known, or had the time or energy to care, where he was, how late he came home, or if he came home at all.

She was a stay-at-home mom now, but she'd barely been a mom to him at all.

He'd lost his virginity as a teenager in a pretty disturbing situation with an older guy, but he'd never even thought to call his mom for help. She'd never have been able to get off work to come pick him up, anyway. So, he'd gone through with the sex despite his better judgment, and it still made him a little sick to think about that night.

But there were a lot of things from his childhood and adolescence that he preferred not to think about. And, frankly, Mom would be devastated to learn about them or remember them herself. She wasn't a bad woman. She'd just been in a bad position. Thank God he was old enough to understand that now.

"It's RJ?" another voice piped up from inside the house. "Perri? Is it RJ? Move over!" His tiny brother Beau's high-pitched voice was just a bit deeper than his twin sister's. It was the only way RJ could tell them apart on the phone, and one reason he preferred to FaceTime with them when he was away.

"Both of you get away from that window!" Mom scolded, coming over to shut it, her blond hair held back in a red scarf. "You know better than to—oh!" She raised a thin brow and scolded him with his full name, "Randall James Blitz! Where the fu…um, where on earth have you been, young man?"

"Mom, I'm sorry. I should have called. I didn't—"

"Get in the house!" She frowned and pointed toward the door beneath the window. "Now!"

RJ raised his hands in surrender as she tugged both kids from the open window and shut it firmly behind them. He'd just put his hand on the front doorknob when the door was jerked open from the inside by a pink-cheeked Perri, Beau stumbling down the stairs behind her.

A golden retriever called Brady came barreling from the kitchen, barking at RJ as he always did. Like RJ didn't belong in the house. Like he didn't *belong*.

"Brady, stop!" Beau yelled, wrapping his arms around his dog. "It's just RJ. He's come home. He's our brother, *your* brother, remember?" He spoke to the dog, as calmly and sweetly as his little four-year-old voice could, and it melted RJ's heart even though he wanted to find a way to be hard right now.

Hell, he'd been kicked out of Mr. Danvers's apartment. His siblings barely knew him. The dog didn't even believe he belonged here. Why should he feel any different?

But he kept those petty thoughts to himself. His mom wanted him here; his little brother and sister did too. Who knew what his stepbrother thought, but Doug claimed to be thrilled he was home. Never mind that RJ could see the lie in Doug's eyes. He wished he wasn't so good at spotting liars.

"RJ," his mother said, starting down the stairs with her hands out like she was going to either smack him or grab him in a hug.

He dodged her when she reached the bottom, remembering that he hadn't showered and that he was covered in the scent of sex and Mr. Danvers. No, the scent of *Aaron*.

God, what a sweet name.

He'd known Mr. Danvers's first name already of course. But a night of holding the man in his arms and breaking him open with pleasure again and again had somehow changed the ring of it.

"RJ!" his mother said more sharply, as he started up the stairs without acknowledging or hugging her.

"Sorry, Mom," he said, stopping on the second rung up. "I should have called or texted. I was...yeah." He grinned sheepishly.

Her brows shot up.

"Anyway, uh, I need to shower."

She blinked, shock falling over her face for a moment. But then she rolled her eyes and didn't try to stop him. "Say it won't happen again."

"It won't." Although it would because he was a grown man.

"And if it does, you'll text me."

"I will."

She rubbed her forehead before changing gears. She was good at that. "Come on, kids. We need to get some yummy breakfast in you and then we're going to Target."

"Yes! Target!" Perri fist pumped the air.

"No! Not Target!" Beau cried, his little shoulders slumping and a whine starting in the back of his throat. "I hate Target!"

RJ was grateful to disappear up to the second floor and down the hall to the guest suite before his little brother really got going. He knew he'd screwed up by not calling or texting his mom and might warrant a punishment. But listening to the whine of a discontented four-year-old had to be one of the most severe penances in hell. And RJ didn't think he really deserved that.

He flicked open the curtains and looked outside. It wasn't a cold day, not really. Especially not for winter anywhere else in the world, and it was barely cold by Tennessee standards either. But *he* was cold all the same. Being kicked out so unceremoniously from Mr. Danvers's apartment that morning had stung.

He'd tried to salvage it and left his number in Mr. Danvers's phone like he'd said he would. Plus, he'd left Mr. Dan—no, *Aaron*—he'd left Aaron hard as a rock and panting for more. But still…

After such a hot night, the morning had been like ice.

The steamy shower in the en suite attached to the guest bedroom was a blessing on his skin. He ducked under the stream and reluctantly scrubbed away all the lingering scents. His mother had put out fancy soaps in the guest shower, and he applied them liberally. He felt better afterward, more clearheaded, but also like he'd lost something important that he might never have again.

He flashed back to Aaron in the shower, remembering his rigid cock, open mouth, and dilated eyes. Surely RJ would get to see all that one more time, right? And maybe more than once? It'd been so good between them. Like Aaron was designed just for him—every sound. Every movement. The way he'd begged.

RJ's dick flexed, and he closed his eyes, willing it down. He was sore enough without wanking now.

Once he'd dried off after the shower, he checked his phone, hoping for a text from Aaron, but there was nothing.

There was a message from Joel though:

The van's at my place. I'm at Vreeland's. Casey's back home until eleven if you wanna get your jacket.

Right, his jacket. He checked the weather app on his phone. The temperature was supposed to drop that evening. Nothing wild, not like Finland in January, but he didn't really want to hang out here at Mom and Doug's house by himself either. Not with all this restlessness in his veins.

He threw on some clothes and headed downstairs to see if he could catch a ride with his mom on her way to Target. Casey and Joel's place was a little out of the way, but it would save him some Uber fees. He really needed to suck it up and rent a car, or maybe buy one soon, along with a little house. He didn't know. This in-between way of life was confusing. Was it worth the expense of a vehicle or a place if he was never around to drive or live in it?

But having nothing to call his own left him feeling like a kid. Everyone else he knew, from Joel and Casey to Becca and Madison, were advancing into adulthood: building houses, buying cars, getting hitched. Okay, so maybe not Becca and Madison, but even they had apartments they actually lived in and owned their own vehicles, like real adults.

RJ just traveled the world and made music with nothing but cool experiences to show for it. The eternal child. He didn't want to think of himself as Peter Pan, but if the Tinkerbell fit…

"RJ," his mother said as he walked into the kitchen, reaching for him with both hands. "Did you shave?"

He shook his head. He'd shave tomorrow. For now, he'd keep the stubble and leave the subtle beard burn from kissing Mr. Danv—*Aaron*—alone. He wondered how long it would take for him to think of Mr. Danvers by his first name. There'd been something hot, though, about calling him Mr. Danvers while they'd fucked. RJ licked his lips and ducked behind the wide kitchen counter when his dick threatened to react to that memory.

"Got any good cereal?" he asked, peering into a cupboard and seeing nothing that looked immediately edible in there. Just ingredients for meals.

"Cereal's bad for you," Perri informed him.

"Spikes your 'sulin," Beau added.

"What?"

"Oh, it's just something Doug's been telling them. We don't eat carbs for breakfast anymore." Mom blushed a little and shoved her hair off her brow, the large diamond Doug had graced her with glittering in the morning sun through the kitchen window. "We try to keep to proteins and veggies."

"Veggies," Beau repeated and then made a gagging noise.

Mom snapped her fingers at him.

RJ asked, "Because of something called Suhlin?"

She chuckled, but her cheeks were still pink. "Insulin. Doug says carbs in the morning spike your insulin and can lead to the development of Type 2 diabetes." She waved the words away like they were silly, but he noticed both the kids were eating eggs and bacon with a side helping of something green.

Mom shoved some coffee his way along with a heaping portion of eggs. "Here. I made this for you."

He cleared his throat and pushed the plate back to her. "I'm allergic, remember?"

Her eyes flew wide and for a moment he thought she might cry, but then she blinked rapidly, got it together and said, "Bacon then?'

"No. Just coffee. I'm fine."

She reached out and took hold of his hand. "Of course, I remembered. About your allergy. I mean, usually, I'd remember. I'm just too tired from worrying about you all night. That's all."

He squeezed her fingers in return. A childish part of him wanted to say that no matter how tired she was, it'd be nice if she'd remember that her eldest would swell up and die if he swallowed even a tiny bite of those eggs. But he didn't want to hurt her any more than he could help it, and he'd already hurt her enough just by existing.

But it wasn't her fault. She'd been the best mom she knew how to be for him. Things had been different when he was a kid. Being married to Doug allowed her to actually focus on being a mom this time around. And the fact that Perri and Beau, and maybe even Doug's older son, Carter, got a better version of her than RJ ever had well…that wasn't anything to resent.

And it meant he was a *really* shitty person that he *did* resent it, right?

Right.

She put together a plate of bacon and handed it to him with a tremulous smile. "I didn't use the same spatula as with the eggs. I did remember." He took it and ate the first piece like it was the most delicious strip of pork he'd ever had. Maybe he even over did it, because she looked hurt again.

Sighing, RJ wondered if Aaron would have taken him home the night before if he knew that RJ was a butthurt bastard who resented his little siblings for the house, the dog, the mom, and the life that he'd never had? Would Aaron have wanted a petty-hearted man like that in his apartment, much less in his body? Probably not. He was a teacher after all. He probably put all children first. A motherfucking hero.

With the hottest ass and sexiest whine and...*shh. Shut up, RJ. Mom's staring at you.*

"So, I guess you aren't going to tell me where you were last night?" She raised a fair brow at him.

"There's nothing to tell. Unlikely I'll be there again." Though, God, he hoped he was wrong about that.

Her lips twisted and she shot a glance at the kids like they might understand that their older brother was a slut. She drew close and whispered in his ear, "I wish you'd be more careful. HIV might be manageable these days, but it's still out there, and there are other STDs. I hear that they're all on the rise because of the success of PrEP, and—"

"I wore a condom," RJ said in a normal tone.

"Shh!" she slammed her hand down on the counter.

"What's a condom?" Beau asked.

"It's nothing," Mom said. "It's something for grown-ups."

"What's an STD then?"

So, the whispering hadn't worked either. RJ felt a little vindicated by that.

"A kind of disease," RJ said, reluctant to lie or obfuscate.

"Do you have a disease?" Perri asked, chewing her eggs slowly.

"No. Do you?" RJ tweaked her hair.

Perri giggled. "No."

"I'm 'llergic too," Beau said, shoving his plate with the eggs away and giving RJ worshipful eyes. "Like RJ."

Mom rolled her eyes but didn't argue with him. "C'mon. Get your shoes from the closet. We've got to get to Target and be home in time to fetch Carter off the bus."

The kids went off to get their shoes, one cheerfully, the other with as much woe as he could muster.

Mom rounded on RJ. "Listen, I know you grew up differently, and that's my fault. But in this house—"

"I know. Watch my language."

"And call your mother if you're going to be late...or not home at all."

"I promise. I'm sorry."

She rubbed her brow again and then offered him another smile. "Apology accepted."

"Can I catch a ride with you guys to Joel's place?"

His mother sighed and checked the clock on her phone. "Yes. But watch what you say in front of the kids."

"Don't worry. I won't tell them details about my wild night."

Mom shuddered. "Better not. Not unless you want me to tell you about mine."

He winced. "Ew."

Mom laughed and flipped him off before hustling out to the front hall to help Beau with his sneakers. RJ grinned to see a glimpse of the woman who'd raised him—the one who'd cursed and given people the middle finger. He missed her sometimes. Then he headed upstairs to grab his boots, wallet, and phone.

He checked his messages again.

Still nothing.

Oh well, one night with Mr. Danvers was a better Christmas gift than he'd ever expected to get. He'd have to be satisfied with it.

Hope was as stubborn as partridge in a pear tree, though, and RJ headed down the stairs with it chirping madly in his heart.

Chapter Seven

ARON WAS LATE to work but none of the kids seemed to care, which was perfect as far as he was concerned. When he walked into his paper snowflake-strewn room, they were all discussing the upcoming Winter Dance on Friday, negotiating meeting times, describing dresses, and bragging about the relative popularity of their "dates." They were so absorbed they didn't bother snapping to attention the way they usually did whenever a teacher entered the classroom.

The obedience granted to him by the kids wasn't earned, though, and it always grated on his nerves more than gratified him. The current disrespectful chatter and downright ignoring of his presence was infinitely preferable. He wasn't a taskmaster or a disciplinarian, and he didn't like that the school in general had been run in such a way that the kids expected that attitude from him.

Aaron put his bag down on the desk, cleared his throat, and spoke into the rustle of final whispers and the creaks of students turning around in their seats to peer curiously at him. "Sorry I'm late."

"S'okay, Mr. D," William Sandburg said, winking. "You probably needed the extra rest." He waggled his eyebrows.

Aaron's insides knotted up, confusion warring with the urge to stride back out of the classroom and down the hall to the teacher's lounge where there was a full-length mirror to investigate his appearance. Did he look like he'd just gotten banged all night or something? William's leering expression and the sniggering of the boys next to him certainly seemed to say so.

He smoothed his bowtie and lifted his chin. "Excuse me?"

"Don't mind him, Mr. Danvers," Chastity Lovell called out, flipping her blond hair over her shoulder. "He's just trying to get under your skin."

"Or *maybe* my mom's boyfriend works at Scruffy City Hall, and *maybe* she was there last night visiting him, and maybe *she* saw you flirting with another guy, and *maybe* you left with that guy, and—"

"William!" Aaron snapped. "Enough."

There was a low *oooooh* through the room from William's friends and a few wide-eyed stares from the other kids. Aaron forged ahead. "We have to get through roll call and announcements." He glanced toward the clock, sweat prickling his brow. "We're behind already. Michael Adams? Here. Okay, Shira Bernstein?"

He studiously didn't look up as he ticked people off as present or absent on his computer screen. No matter what William's nosy mother saw at the pub the prior night, it was meaningless. Aaron had ogled RJ on the stage over a glass of whiskey, taken a phone call, then sat and chatted with RJ outside before leaving with him. That proved nothing. RJ could have been a friend. None of the kids in this room had any reason to think he'd spent the night lost in paroxysms of pure pleasure with another man.

He was still safely closeted here where it mattered. He hadn't made another error in the magnitude of Coach McAllister. A titter of laughter rose from near William's seat along with speculative whispers. Aaron steeled himself against it. He *was* still closeted, dammit.

But, after he chose Lee Belle Rhodes to read aloud from the announcements sheet, Aaron's racing pulse and rising nausea bucked off the grip of reason and ran wild, hand-in-hand, with irrational fear. Vomit rose slowly up his throat. He rolled his shoulders, trying to shake free.

What was the worst thing that could happen if he got outed at school anyway? The kids would know their teacher was gay. So what? It wasn't as if he were sucking cock at the front of the classroom or getting pounded while explaining the finer points of grammar. He was a man like any other, who had sex like any other, just with other men instead of women, and there really wasn't any reason anyone should have a problem with that.

So why was he sweating like a pig?

Because people *would* have a problem with it: parents, other teachers, some of the kids, and definitely the principal. Aaron couldn't afford exposure. He'd made one stupid mistake his third year teaching and it'd been more than enough. The humiliation had gone so deep. He'd been lucky to get another job. Even though he wouldn't technically be breaking any rules to be out and openly dating men, it was safer to keep hidden.

Relieved when the bell rang and everyone in the class gathered their things for first period, Aaron leaned back in his chair and studied the hand-cut snowflakes he'd strung up around the room the week before. He'd made them every year since he started teaching. The kids liked them. He did too. Even RJ had remembered…

Oh, God, *RJ.*

He'd been so good at fucking. Thank Christ those other men had canceled, because RJ's hands on his body had been transcendent, and his cock up his ass had been—

"Mr. Danvers?"

Startled out of his memories of the night before, Aaron sat up straighter at his desk. He plastered on a professional smile and hoped he didn't look like he'd been thinking about strong hands, a cocky grin, and a giant dick. What on earth was wrong with him anyway? He was at school!

Red-headed, lisping Elsie Peters was a tiny little thing. She was almost thirteen and in seventh grade but looked closer in age to a fourth grader. That had to suck for her. Aaron could relate, having been a very late bloomer himself. He hadn't needed to shave until well into college.

Truth be told, some days he didn't really need to shave even now. He had a baby face, just like RJ had said.

"How can I help you, Elsie?"

"It's okay if what William says is true, you know."

"Excuse me?"

"If you're gay, I mean. My dads are gay and they're awesome. You're awesome too."

Aaron swallowed thickly. "Uh, thank you."

"I know that there's still prejudice out there. I deal with it every day. But I think a lot of people are starting to understand that gay people aren't bad, or whatever. For what it's worth, I don't think William thinks gay people are bad, either." Elsie pushed a long strand of orange-red hair from her face and shrugged. "His dad's just a jerk, that's all. My dads say they feel sorry for William because his father is a raging bigot. They say William hardly stood a chance, you know? But, with people like you and me in his life, my dads say William could still turn out all right. He's just got a lot of learning to do."

Aaron swallowed, compassion for Elsie and for himself coming to do battle with his anxiety. "Thanks for sharing all that with me, Elsie."

"So you *are* gay?"

"I prefer not to talk about my private life at school."

She shrugged. "It's up to you. But I have your back, Mr. Danvers. So do a lot of other kids. Most people won't care. And the ones who do don't matter. You should just come out and get it over with." She smiled, a light in her eyes switching on. "Maybe as a Christmas gift to yourself. I mean, if you celebrate Christmas. If not, Hanukkah?" Her expression grew a bit panicked. "Or Kwanzaa or whatever?"

"I do celebrate Christmas." Aaron chuckled. "Thanks, Elsie. You're a smart young lady."

The bell rang, and Elsie gasped. "I'm gonna be late." She darted from the room, her hair trailing out like a flame behind her.

As soon as she was gone, Aaron checked the small mirror he kept in his desk to make sure that he didn't have a giant hickey he'd somehow missed, or some super obvious beard burn on his chin. But, no, he looked all right. A little tired. Maybe his eyes shone a bit brighter than they normally did—lingering delirium—but there was no reason for William or anyone else to assume that he'd slept with a former student the night before.

God, it'd been so good. He squeezed his butt cheeks and closed his eyes, enjoying his asshole's remaining tenderness. RJ had been really big, the way tall, stringy men like him often were, thick and long, like the fucking eggplant emoji hookups used when sexting.

Shit. He shouldn't be thinking about this again. He shook the memories free as kids piled into his classroom with expectant eyes and freshly scrubbed morning faces.

Time to get his head out of his ass and into the classroom. It was showtime.

Chapter Eight

AARON'S FIRST PERIOD class went by in a flash. Advanced Composition for seventh-graders was his favorite. They were all intelligent, funny kids, and they never tried to half-ass their work. He'd given them all a creative writing assignment the weekend before to take their favorite winter holiday story from whatever country or tradition they preferred and update it.

They'd finished the draft over the weekend and now it was time for them to edit one another's work. He looked forward to seeing the end results. He walked around the room making sure everyone used Mr. Danvers's Three Rules of Criticism: Number one: praise. Number two: critique with the intent to improve, not insult. And number three: praise again.

Most were doing well, but he had to put a hand on Barrett Rogers's shoulder and lean down to whisper, "I'm fairly sure that, 'This entire thing is dumb,' doesn't follow rule number two, Barrett. Come up with something more specific that your partner can improve on."

After the bell rang announcing second period—his free period of the day—he'd eased himself back into his desk chair, pleased that his ass cheeks were still smarting a little from the spanking RJ had given him the night before. The speaker above his desk blared, and the principal's voice came through loud and clear.

"Mr. Danvers. Come to my office. Now. Thank you."

At school, Principal Shock never sounded anything but irritated and commanding, so the tone was meaningless. Still, Aaron's gut tangled with worry. Had William or some other kid actually gone to tattle on him for being at a pub last night? Drinking on a school night? And was he going to actually get in trouble for it like some little kid?

He rose from his desk and headed down the quiet hallway, avoiding the wayward backpacks that somehow hadn't made it into their owners' lockers and passing by the occasional child camped on the floor outside a classroom working on something alone. Christmas tree lights had been strung up on the ceiling by the janitorial staff three weeks prior, and they glowed like a runway leading him toward the main office.

As he walked, he grew more annoyed than worried. But that didn't mean he could just ignore the summons. He owed Principal Shock his job after all. She'd been the only one willing to take him on after the Coach McAllister debacle. And she liked to remind him of that fact.

The Christmas tree in the school office was decked out in ornaments made by the kids in art class, but the charm of that didn't take the edge off the sharp, antiseptic nature of the women who worked the front desks. They glared at him through their glasses—twin sets of disdain. They'd looked at him in that exact same way since he was twelve years old.

"Aaron," Jolene said, eyebrow twitching up. "She wants you."

"I know." He gave her a grim smile. If Jolene hadn't been wearing a gingerbread man shirt and jingly red Christmas bells for earrings, he'd think she was pure evil instead of a middle school office employee.

"Now," Rita added, pointing with her index finger, a long, red-and-green striped nail proving that she'd spent yet another Saturday at her salon getting her hair washed and set, and her fingers and toes done up in something gaudy. Was it a prerequisite for the front secretaries of schools to have no taste?

"Aaron!" Principal Shock called from her doorway. "Stop dawdling."

He held back a scoff. Dawdling with Rita and Jolene would never be something he'd ever do willingly. They'd been a torment to him in his childhood, and nothing about that had changed.

Principal Shock looked pissed as he stepped into her office. The jingle of carols from the radio next to her desk didn't help ease the palpable sense of danger in the air. Kids often peed themselves when brought in to sit in Principal Shock's office to await her judgment. She had that way about her.

Aaron cleared his throat and studied the chairs in front of her desk, trying to determine if one was less stained than the other. The last time he'd chosen the chair closest to the window, but that one now looked to have a new dark patch.

"Aaron!" Principal Shock said again, voice demanding his attention. "You and I need to talk."

He dropped into the chair closest to her desk without another glance at the upholstery and smiled. He hoped it was a winning one, but given how the morning was going, he had his doubts. "Yes, Mom?"

THE NEW LOG cabin that Casey and Joel were building on Joel's property by the lake had taken slow but sure shape over the last year. RJ had been privy to update photos by text all during his last tour.

When RJ hopped out of his mom's car and waved his family off, he barely turned in time to intercept the greetings of Bruno, Joel and Casey's pitbull rescue dog, before he could be knocked down by all that enthusiastic muscle.

The trailer Casey and Joel lived in while they built their dream home was decorated for Christmas. Lights were strung along the edges and gutters, a multicolored Christmas tree blinked by the front stoop, poinsettias rested on the stairs to the door, and a giant Blow Glow nativity set was arranged near the road so everyone passing by could see it. Like at Mom and Doug's, it was full-on Christmas at the Vreeland/Stevens's household. Unsurprising since Joel owned a home and garden store. It made sense that he'd indulge in his own wares.

The dodgy van Joel had scored to use as an equipment vehicle for the band, an older SUV, and a new Nissan LEAF all sat in the driveway area. RJ hoped Casey's parents weren't visiting. He'd never been the Stevens's biggest fan. And the feeling had been more than reciprocated. Though they seemed to loathe him a little less now that they thought he had connections to famous people and big money. Casey's folks had always loved connections and cash.

"Hey! How's it going?" RJ called out when Casey opened the door to his and Joel's trailer to check out who or what had Bruno so riled up in the yard.

Casey grinned. "It's going okay. Bruno, down!"

The dog ignored him entirely. "You got visitors?" RJ asked, nodding toward the extra car as he contended with Bruno's slobbery love.

"No." Casey whistled for Bruno, who continued to jump and lick at RJ. "Long story."

"Cool. How goes the wedding planning?"

Shaking his blond head, Casey smirked. "How'd you know that's what I was doing?"

"Just a guess." RJ finally freed himself from Bruno's affections and stepped toward the trailer. "You and Joel were arguing about the venue in the van on the way to the show yesterday."

Casey snorted, holding the door wider as RJ started up the steps. "That wasn't arguing. You know Joel. He has to act like he hates every idea at first so he can give in later."

RJ laughed, taking Casey's hand and squeezing it. "Sounds about right.

"I guess you're here for your jacket." Casey looked out over RJ's shoulder. "You caught a ride over here?"

"My mom. I'll get an Uber back home. Don't worry about it."

"You don't have to do that." Casey closed the door behind them, trying and failing to leave Bruno and his slobbery love out front. "I could lend you the SUV while you're in town."

"Why would you do that?"

Casey blushed and turned toward the living room, which featured a fully decorated Christmas tree with a tin star on top and electric candles in the window. "Because my folks got me that LEAF for Christmas? And Joel won't give up his old truck? So, I'm not quite sure what I'm going to do with the SUV until I sell it." He frowned. "*If* I sell it."

"Dude, it's a Lexus."

"I know."

RJ leaned against the back of the sofa, admiring the colorful tree. "I can't drive a Lexus."

"That's what Joel said when I tried to give it to him." Casey laughed.

"Thanks for the offer, but—"

"But you'll take it while you're here," Casey said.

"I can't."

"You can. You will."

"Stubborn."

"That's my middle name. Don't wear it out."

RJ rolled his eyes.

"Sit down," Casey said, motioning at the wrapping-paper-strewn couch. "Let me just..." He moved the colorful rolls down to the floor, and Bruno promptly sat on them, crunching them up. Casey patted the sofa. "Have a seat."

RJ did as he was told. He was tired, the night before was starting to catch up with him now, and in the cozy warmth of Joel and Casey's living room, he yawned.

"Long night?" Casey asked with a gleam in his eye.

"Maybe."

"Fun night?"

"Definitely."

"Ah." Casey cocked his head. "Was it with Mr. Danvers?"

RJ's drowsiness fled and he sat up straight. "How did you...? I never said that."

Casey laughed, his head flinging back as he shook with it. "Oh my God, you slept with Mr. Danvers!"

"Hey, now," RJ said, before groaning and covering his face, understanding dawning. "Shit. You saw me talking with him after you finished loading out."

"Yeah. We were gonna come make sure you didn't want a ride home, but when I saw who you were talking to, I knew better than to interrupt." Casey flashed an incredulous grin. "Wow. You did it? You really slept with him? Your high school wet dream?"

RJ rolled his eyes, but a sheepish smile drew over his face. "You could say that."

"Was it everything you wanted it to be?"

RJ flopped back on the sofa, eyes on the ceiling, and let out a long, wretched groan.

"Oh, wow," Casey said, chuckling. "That good, huh?"

"Unreal."

"So, what are you going to do about it?"

RJ pressed his hands to eyes and sat up again. "Something. I don't know what yet, but I've gotta do *something*."

"Isn't he kind of old?"

"Just twenty-eight. Not that old." Hell, RJ had been in a semi-long-term relationship with a guy way older than Aaron. Like in the second half of his thirties kind of old. Of course, he and Pan had seriously crashed and burned in the end, but who didn't? He just hoped Mom and Doug didn't napalm the kids' lives when they inevitably went down in flames.

Nothing was permanent.

Not bands, not tours, not homes, or relationships. It was best to try not to overthink anything or get too invested. Just take the rides as they came. And fucking Mr. Danvers had been one hell of a ride. He supposed this attitude was why he was so behind on the whole "being a grown up" thing.

"So you'll see him again?"

RJ hissed out his confusion. "I don't know. I want to. But...he wanted to keep it to just one night."

"Did he give you his number?"

RJ reached down to rub Bruno's head. "I gave him mine."

"But did you get his?"

RJ shrugged. He wasn't a fool. Of course, he'd sent a text from Aaron's phone to his own, so that he'd recognize Aaron if he called. But would it be a good idea to use it? He didn't want to be creepy about it.

Casey guffawed. "Why are you even hesitating?"

"Because...I don't know. It's probably best to just leave it at the one night. I mean, he's a teacher here in town and, from what I can tell, probably a closeted one. I'm a homeless musician on tour most of the year. What could really happen?"

Casey started to count on his fingers, "First, you could sleep with him again."

RJ groaned softly. That'd be reason enough.

"Second, you could make a real human connection outside of old high school friends and the messed-up assholes in the rock 'n' roll world. You know, the drug-addicted dicks you normally travel with. Third..." He smirked. "True love."

"Ha! True love." RJ rolled his eyes. "Just because *your* holiday fling with Joel turned into wuv-and-marriage-and-a-baby-carriage, it doesn't mean that mine would."

Bruno edged closer to RJ, flopping down on top of his feet and staring up at him hopefully. RJ relented, scratching behind his silky ears.

"Hey, hey, no one here's considering a baby yet. Or ever. Don't get ahead of yourself." Casey rolled his eyes. "You were onboard last year when it was me pursuing Joel. You were all about us falling in love. But now that it could be you going after a real happy-ever-after, you're resisting."

"Happy-ever-after?" RJ scoffed. "I banged the guy." A lot. So good.

Damn.

"You're a lot like Joel, you know that? Gotta fight the thing you want before you take it. Why not just take it?"

RJ rolled his eyes. "Mr. Danvers might not want to be taken."

"Seems like something you should find out for sure though. With your phone. Using that number he gave you."

"Well, the thing is…he didn't give it to me. I kind of took it. So ha!" RJ pointed at Casey. "I *do* just take what I want sometimes!" Bruno huffed at RJ's feet and shifted heavily against his ankles. RJ stroked his ears some more.

"Give the man a prize!" Casey chuckled, and punched RJ's shoulder. "Listen, here's the deal. He didn't tell you not to contact him, right?"

RJ shrugged. He guessed not explicitly, no.

"So try. If you text him and he says not to contact him again, then fine. Don't. Boundary drawn. Consent not given. But if you text him, and he doesn't reject you? Then you could have your high school wet dream in your bed for the holidays." Casey waggled his brows. "Freak your stepdad out."

RJ had never known for sure if the awkwardness between him and Doug was because Doug disapproved of RJ's traveling rock 'n' roll lifestyle or his queerness. A holiday boyfriend would definitely help clear that up. But wasn't it better for everyone if RJ just made nice with his mother, made time with the kids, and then disappeared again as soon as possible?

"When is Chip giving you that recording studio time?" Casey asked, thankfully changing the subject.

"As soon as I ask for it."

"Joel said he'd play for you on the demo if you want, but he needs time to learn the songs."

"Yeah." RJ rubbed at the back of his neck, pulling a face. "That's just it. I don't have any songs."

Casey blinked at him. "Seriously?"

"I know, I know. I thought I'd have time to put a few together on this last tour, but then I got back together with Pan for a while—"

Casey groaned. "Why dude?"

"I'm an idiot. What can I say? And that turned into mucho maximum drama-rama plus a drug overdose."

Casey's eyes went wide.

"His, not mine. Obviously." RJ sighed, thinking back to the mess of finding Pan like that. RJ had never been so scared in his life. "And he's fine, by the way. I mean, I think he's still using, but fuck if seeing him on the floor in that shitty motel bathroom with foam coming out of his mouth didn't scare me straight..." RJ scrubbed at his shorn head and shuddered. "I don't even smoke pot anymore."

"Damn, RJ."

"Yeah. But, hey, I can't pretend I didn't see that shitshow was coming. The music business is a lot of things, but healthy isn't one of them." RJ bit into his lower lip. "Truth is, I haven't even taken my acoustic out since I got home. That's the guitar I usually write on."

"Why?"

"It's so loud at Mom and Doug's. Always a kid crying, or yelling, or stomping. Sometimes they have friends over. That's like...whoa." He shook his head. "I'm glad my mom's happy, and I love the kids like crazy, I do. But being around them is not conducive to getting shit done." RJ shrugged. "Maybe I'll just let go of the studio time. Get back on the road after the holidays. Forget about making another demo. Where'd the first one get me anyway?"

Casey blew out a frustrated breath. "You were straight out of high school back then. Just a kid. You've got more to offer the world now."

"Save your pep talks for Joel," RJ said, winking at Casey. "I'm a lost cause for them."

Casey smirked. "If Mr. Danvers gave you a pep talk, I bet you'd listen."

RJ snorted. "If Mr. Danvers gave me a blowjob, I'd do anything he asked of me."

"Call him." Casey's phone buzzed and he glanced at it. "I'm sorry, man. I have to take this call. It's a client."

"No problem. I'll just head out."

Casey nodded and picked up. "Stevens Branding and Marketing, Casey speaking."

While Casey began to lead a local business owner toward the concept of rebranding to appeal to a younger crowd, RJ found his jacket on the coat rack by the door, gave Casey a wave goodbye, and patted Bruno on the head in parting.

RJ stepped out front and took his phone out of his pocket to summon an Uber, startling when Casey opened the door behind him. Cell phone still pressed to his ear, Casey shoved a car key fob RJ's way. "Take it. Don't argue. You'd be helping me out if you just took it off my hands for the next few weeks until I can convince Joel he's allowed to drive a Lexus. Or until I find a buyer. Probably the latter."

"Stubborn Casey Stevens," RJ said.

Casey smirked. "I've heard there's no arguing with him."

Chapter Nine

"You have to chaperone? Like, she didn't even give you a choice?"

Aaron groaned. "My mother never gives me a choice. As far as she's concerned, she's the parent, I'm still the child, and I have to do what she tells me to do."

The teacher's lounge featured a small fiber-optic Christmas tree by the coffee maker, but otherwise was devoid of the charm of holiday décor. Aaron sat across from Lauren White, his colleague and best friend from graduate school. She'd followed him from grad school to teach at Taylor High, and then afterward she'd come with him to teach at Pineview Middle, and today she'd followed him to the circular wood laminate table in the faculty lounge. Talk about loyalty.

Both of them ate their lunches. Aaron's was a bag he'd grabbed from the takeaway portion of the cafeteria before it closed, and Lauren's was a preciously prepared lunch from home.

"She'd never treat another teacher the way she treats you." Lauren patted Aaron's shoulder sympathetically and heaved a sigh. Her shoulder-length brown hair was up in a bun, and she wore a candy-cane-striped, button-up shirt over a black skirt. Very strict-teacher in her look today. Aaron knew she was a softy with the kids, though.

"Tell me about it."

"Plus, she's making you dress up as an elf for Jack's pep rally tomorrow, isn't she?" Her golden-hazel eyes flashed.

Aaron shrugged. He wasn't about to admit he'd volunteered for that humiliation himself. It was just that Coach Ramirez had been sweaty from running with the boys' football team when he'd approached Aaron in the hallway to ask for his help. And the optimistic, horny slut in Aaron hadn't been able to resist even the most hopeless of cases.

He wasn't going to tell Lauren about that. No way. Let her think the humiliating elf costume tomorrow was all his mother's fault too.

The teacher's lounge was empty aside from them, but Aaron still spoke softly. No need for word to get back to the principal that he was bitching about her treatment of him. Sometimes he thought he really should have considered looking for a job outside of Knoxville after the scandal with Coach McAllister. At least he would have stayed out from under his mother's thumb. But he'd just bought his apartment in the city, and he'd loved it dearly.

"Bring a date," Lauren said with a smirk. "To the dance."

"You know I can't."

"You realize they can't really fire you for being gay, Aaron. The situation with McAllister was because he was married. The 'affair' is what violated the code of ethics." She rolled her eyes. "Although why he got away with it and you didn't...well, let's just say I have thoughts about that. Still. To this damn day."

"I know you do, and I know you're right. They can't fire me for being gay, but they can make my life harder." He shoved aside his lunch, not feeling hungry now. "Besides, if I brought a date, Principal Shock would be so pissed she'd never ask me to chaperone again."

Lauren lifted her mug. "Score."

"You know I'd pay for it. She'd probably find a way to invoke the morality clauses in my contract."

"Pfft. Aaron, no. No one would let that happen. And your mom might be pissed, but she wouldn't take it that far."

"I know, I know. But she'd find a way to make me sorry. I do have to spend Christmas with her, Lauren. She'd spend the whole day letting me know how disappointed she was in me, how I'd humiliated her, and after all she'd done for me, blah blah blah…"

"You actually don't."

"What?"

"Have to spend Christmas with her."

Aaron swallowed hard, imagining what would happen if he told his mother he wasn't coming over for Christmas Day. "I know. But despite everything, all our differences, she's my mother. I love her. And I really want to enjoy my time with her this year."

Lauren put her own leftovers back into the square, sectioned lunchbox she used. "Why do you give her a pass all the time?"

Aaron didn't know that he gave his mother a pass, so much as he just hated to hurt her. He knew this wasn't the life she'd imagined as a young woman. He wasn't the son she'd wanted. His dad hadn't been the husband or father she'd hoped for. And Christmas was an especially vulnerable time for her, had been ever since the divorce.

"She's overly sensitive during the holidays because she thinks I have more fun with my dad."

Lauren shrugged. "It's the truth. You do. Rutty's the best."

Aaron rolled his eyes. "Don't call him that."

"Why? All your cousins do. When I was out on the farm with you for that Easter shindig last year, they were all going on about Uncle Rutty this and Uncle Rutty that."

"His name's Rutgers and it's much more dignified."

"Rutty's more fun, though. Like Christmas at his place." Lauren winked at him. "So, moving on, because I already know where every conversation about your mother ends up: you making excuses for her, nothing changing. Rinse, repeat. It's exhausting and fruitless."

Aaron jerked, the words a slap.

Lauren didn't stop talking, though, or acknowledge that what she'd said hurt. "Why are you so…" She waved a hand at him up and down, and around and around. "Like that."

"Like what?" What was so different about him today? Could getting laid really change his appearance so much?

"Rumpled? Haggard? I don't know. You just look like you didn't sleep at all last night. That Grindr date rough you up or what?"

Aaron flushed. "Nah. The Grindr dates *stood* me up. Both of them."

"Ah. Then why do you look...?" She grimaced and waved at him again.

Damn, he really must look a mess. "I picked up a guy at Scruffy City Hall. The, uh, lead singer in the band that was playing. Pretty hot guy."

"Oh, yeah?" Lauren's eyebrow shot up.

"Um. *Yeah.*"

Her eyes lit up with delight. "*Yes*, Aaron." She put out a hand for a high five. Aaron slapped her palm. "Get it, baby. What's his name?"

"RJ." Aaron tugged his lunch back over, his appetite not really returning, but he hoped a bite of his sandwich might obscure the last name. "RJ Blitz."

Lauren's grin fell off her face. She sat back and gaped at him. "Excuse me? Did you say RJ Blitz? As in our tall, gangly, *ex-student* from our days teaching at Taylor High RJ Blitz? Of the long hair and acne and scary glower that could explode a human brain from ten paces?"

Aaron swallowed and wiped his mouth with a napkin from his lunchbox. "He's twenty-four now, his hair is short, and that was ages ago."

"Holy shit, Aaron." Lauren glanced around the room like there might be spies listening in the corners. "That's...you know that's not okay."

"There's nothing illegal about it."

"No, but..." She blinked wildly, stunned. "How long ago was he a student exactly? We were still at Taylor High. That was, what, three years ago, right?"

"Yeah, but RJ was farther back than that. He was a student during my first year teaching. Your third."

Lauren winced, dropped her fork into her thermos of mac and

cheese, and stared at him. "I just...how can...? He was a *student,* Aaron."

"Yes, I know! But for God's sake, he's not now!"

"No, but..." She chewed her lower lip, conflicted. "What's...what's he like now?"

Aaron snarked, "Entirely adult."

"I mean, I'd hope so. But what's his job?"

"A guitarist. Tours the world. Home for the holidays." Aaron didn't know why he was being so stingy with information, but his defenses were up now. He'd known she'd react like this—any teacher would—but he wasn't doing anything wrong.

Doing? No, done. Past tense. He hadn't *done* anything wrong.

It was over and finished.

"I don't know about this, Aaron."

He put his hand on Lauren's forearm reassuringly. "Look, it was a one-night stand. It's no big deal. Nothing's going to come of it."

"I really hope not. I know I said that they can't fire you for being gay, and no one is actively looking to invoke the code of ethics against you. But hooking up with a former student *could* piss some people off. It could cause a ton of problems for you, fair or not. You know, parents would take it the wrong way. Or one of our asshole colleagues. And if your mom found out..." Lauren grimaced. "She really wouldn't like it."

Don't embarrass me, Aaron.

He could still hear the words his mother had hissed on his first day at Pineview Middle before she'd plastered on a smile for everyone else's sake, and then "proudly" introduced him to the rest of the staff and faculty as her son. Most of them had known him for years, of course. He'd grown up at Pineview, both as a student and as the principal's son, but his new position was clear to everyone: fellow teacher, to be treated as such. Don't go easy on him. Don't treat him as anyone special.

And his mother surely didn't.

"I'm not seeing him again," Aaron reassured Lauren.

"Really?"

"Yes."

"Good. I mean, if it's just a fling, it's not worth the drama." Lauren closed her lunch box with finality that signaled their hour was almost up. "I'm glad you got it out of your system. I know how you get when you've waited too long to take care of business. You make rash choices." She cleared her throat and winked. "Now you can spend the rest of the holidays the right way: relaxing at home with cocoa and Hallmark Christmas movies. Like me."

Aaron laughed, his skin prickling with embarrassment over her assessment. She was right of course. He did make poor choices when he was horny. As for the rest, well, Lauren was the happiest single person he knew. She loved her alone time in her apartment, and had never dated, and never wanted to date anyone. "I do love the whole 'stranded in a small town during the holidays' trope. It's got to be the basis for half those movies."

"Half? Try three-fourths."

Aaron grinned, grateful that Lauren had decided to stop scolding him and get back to their usual friendly, fun conversations.

"Oh, wow. Time has flown. Aren't you meeting up with Carter Ward?" Lauren asked, glancing at the clock on the wall above the vending machines.

"Shit," Aaron whispered, shoving the last bite of his sandwich into his mouth. "I am."

Chapter Ten

CARTER SAT SULLENLY at his usual place in Aaron's classroom. He kicked at the carpet and flicked a folded-up paper "football" back and forth on the desk in front of him.

"Sorry," Aaron said, breezing in and tucking his unfinished lunch into his satchel beneath his desk in case he got hungry later. He turned back to Carter. The young man's light brown hair looked freshly trimmed, and he had cut himself quite badly shaving that morning by the looks of his chin. No late blooming for him. "Time got away from me."

"S'okay," Carter said with a shrug.

Aaron sat down next to him in a student desk, folding himself up to fit into it, and smiled. "I do apologize, though. Students are important to me, and I know your time is just as valuable as mine. What's going on? How can I help you?"

"I dunno." Carter flicked the paper football with his right hand and caught it in his left palm. "I guess it's not a big deal."

"You're here. It was a big enough deal that you wanted to talk to me about it."

"Yeah."

"So talk to me."

"It's nothing."

Aaron smiled patiently. "Okay, it's nothing. But why don't we talk about it anyway?"

"Sure. I guess."

Aaron waited. Carter remained silent.

This was already way too much like his experience working with high schoolers. The sullen distance, the need for help, but the inability to actually ask for it. Those were all things that had made teaching high school less than ideal for him. But some middle schoolers faced a more rapid maturation rate, so they hit this stage young. And while it was frustrating to deal with, Aaron wasn't about to give up now. "Is it a problem at school? Or at home?"

"It's a problem with me."

"With you? How's that?"

"I don't think I'm like all these other guys." He frowned and flicked the paper football hard. It soared into the air and landed on the floor about eight feet away. Neither of them moved to retrieve it.

"In what way?"

"In every way."

Aaron waited for him to elaborate.

Finally, Carter offered, "I'm no good at sports."

"Lots of guys have other interests besides sports. Music, art, chorus."

"Meh."

"Robotics or—"

"I don't like any of those things."

"Okay. What do you like, Carter?" Aaron stretched his legs out in front of him, the shift making his butt ache a little. He cleared his throat and stayed focused on Carter.

Carter was edgy and silent for a long moment. "My stepbrother is home for Christmas. I don't like him."

Aaron tried not to visibly tense up. He'd asked what Carter *liked*, not what he didn't, but this was the first insight he'd had into what was bothering the kid. Was this stepbrother hurting Carter in some way? He waited a few beats until he was sure his voice wouldn't betray him. "Why's that?"

"Because he makes me feel weird."

"How so?"

Carter squirmed in his seat. "I don't know. I just don't like him okay?"

"Does he hurt you?"

Carter rolled his eyes. "No. He barely pays me any attention at all."

"Ah." Aaron tried to parse what he was being told. "And you don't want him to pay you any attention? Or you do?"

"I don't know. He's..." Carter shrugged. "He's my stepmom's son. He was already grown up when my dad married her. So..." He wrinkled his nose.

"So you don't like him?"

"I don't like him being in our house. He doesn't belong there."

"I see." Aaron sat back in his chair and let Carter's posture and attitude sink in. There was something more to all of this, but he couldn't quite put his finger on it. "Do you need my help talking to your parents about your stepbrother?"

"What? No!"

"All right. Do you need me to help you talk to your stepbrother himself?"

"No. I just...I guess I..." He grunted and then stood up. "Never mind. You don't get it."

"I'd like to get it."

"Well, you don't." He huffed again, hitched his backpack on his shoulder and said, "Besides, you're a fag."

Aaron jerked, but he quickly pulled himself together. Where had *that* come from? It didn't matter. He'd practiced for this moment ever since he'd started teaching. The fact that he hadn't been called the F-word since college was amazing really, especially since he worked with teens and tweens. He was well past due for some verbal harassment from someone. The fact that it was coming from Carter wasn't even a surprise. The kid was clearly dealing with something.

"We both know I could send you to Principal Shock for using that language."

Carter's shoulders drew up.

"But I won't. Because I don't think you'll learn anything from that." Carter's shoulders relaxed slightly, but he still looked scared, like maybe he couldn't believe he'd really said that word to his teacher. Aaron almost appreciated that Carter was invested in seeing this moment through. Like a dare to himself. A test of some sort.

Aaron stood up slowly, peering down at Carter, who was already beefier than him, more muscular for sure, but still shorter. "My private life is no one's business but my own. However, if you need me to help you at home, with your parents, or your stepbrother, I'm willing to do that. You don't have to leave it this way with me, Carter. I'm on your side."

Carter pondered him for a long minute, snorted derisively, and then stalked from the room.

Aaron sighed and rubbed a hand over his face. His day had already been a doozy between waking up to morning-after regrets, facing his dragon of a mother in her guise as principal, enduring Lauren's scolding, and then running late to meet a student. The actual meeting with Carter hadn't made things any better.

He just hoped the day wouldn't get any worse.

Chapter Eleven

A FTER LEAVING CASEY and Joel's place in Casey's Lexus, RJ went to the mall and did some Christmas shopping just to waste time. It felt weird to park a car that big and nice in the mall lot, but Casey had loaned it to him without any hesitation or limits, so if someone dinged it, then he reckoned that was at least partially Casey's own fault.

It hadn't taken RJ long to spend more than he'd intended to on some pretty, long-sleeved dresses for his mom from an upscale boutique and superhero toys for Beau and Perri from the only toy store left in the building. But then his spending spree came to an abrupt end. What should he get Doug or his stepbrother? He had no idea what thirteen-year-old boys liked these days. Or forty-six-year-old straight men for that matter.

Grabbing a Starbucks coffee from the kiosk, he pulled his phone from his pocket for the hundredth time. His messages remained stubbornly free of content from Mr. Aaron Danvers. He couldn't make up his mind about how to handle that. He bought some wrapping paper, and then decided to continue his shopping another day. There was still plenty of time to procrastinate on the hard-to-find gifts.

Back at Mom and Doug's, RJ parked Casey's SUV on the car pad usually reserved for guests. He went inside and was instantly greeted by the scent of baking cookies. He grinned, eager for them, but first he hustled up the stairs to his room to hide the presents in a high place where snooping four-year-olds wouldn't find them. Once that was done, he trotted down to the kitchen to snag a cookie or two.

Pausing in the doorway, he smiled at the sweet image of his two siblings decorating Christmas cookies. Even Carter sat at the table dutifully adding buttons to the snowman-shaped cookies' middles.

"Hey, what's up?"

"Making cookies!" Perri said, her cheeks smeared with green sugar sprinkles.

"C'mon, you too, RJ," Beau said, pointing an icing-covered finger toward the empty chair at the kitchen table. "Mom used the eggless egg-stuff just for you."

Carter shot a strange wide-eyed look at RJ, the meaning of which was indecipherable. Maybe it was fear? Or panic? RJ wasn't sure. It didn't make him feel very welcome, though. He grabbed two unfrosted cookies from the cooling rack and backed away with a regretful smile.

"Sorry, kiddos, but I have some things to deal with upstairs."

Like angsting over whether or not to text Aaron, or whether or not he should make a demo, or whether or not he should bother calling that real estate lady Madison had given him the number for so he could start searching for a little place to call his own. Really, maybe he'd be better off making cookies with the kids. But Carter gave him another weird look…

So, nah.

"Where's Mom?" RJ asked, surprised that she wasn't hovering with so much potential for mess on the table, what with the frosting *and* the sprinkles.

"Bathroom," Carter said, darting another anxious look RJ's way.

"Okay. You in charge while she's away?"

Carter shrugged but said nothing.

"We're big enough," Perri said, tossing her long, blond hair. "Don't need Carter to watch us."

"We're big like you, RJ," Beau said, sending him one of his sweet, wide-eyed, worshipful looks.

"Right." RJ watched them work a few more moments while he ate his cookies, noting Carter's extreme reluctance to look his way, and then finally said, "Okay, well, I'm upstairs if you need anything. Save a few more for me, all right?"

Carter nodded, and the other two moaned about him leaving, but he just turned and left. Brady, the dog, at least was out back in the fenced yard and hadn't barked at him. Carter's nervousness was enough to make RJ feel out of place yet again—as always—in the family.

As he trudged up the stairs, dusting cookie crumbs from his T-shirt, he remembered a conversation he'd had the week before with the little ones. They'd been eating a snack at the kitchen table, and Perri had told him all about the lights Doug was going to put up around the house for the holidays.

RJ had winked at Perri before saying, "Mom and I never put up lights when I was a kid—you guys are lucky."

"Why?" Beau had asked, one small finger shoved up his nose.

Laughing, RJ had pulled it free and then wiped it off with a napkin. "Mom had to work a lot back then. There wasn't much time for things like decorating. And she was tired all the time. Christmas was pretty low key when I was your age."

"But you got presents, right?" Perri had asked, her big blue eyes round and worried.

"I didn't need presents."

"Even from Santa?"

"Santa?" RJ had cleared his throat. "Santa was always good to me." That wasn't true, but he wasn't going to break her heart. Then he'd kissed Perri on the forehead and they'd dropped the subject.

RJ knew his mom wished things had been different for him growing up, but neither of them could turn back time. And even if they could, nothing would change. She'd still be broke. He'd still be white trash. They'd still be barely making ends meet. It had been their life, and that was that.

The phone in his hand buzzed and he glanced down at it eagerly.

Was it Aaron?

Rehearsal Friday at 3 instead? Ok by you?

Just Joel.

Sure.

Casey said you picked up your coat.

Yeah.

Good.

And, shit, why couldn't he have left something at Mr. Danvers's this morning instead? Then he'd have a reason to text, wouldn't he? Why was he just thinking of that now?

Locking his bedroom door so that the little ones wouldn't come barging in, RJ flung himself down on the mattress and curled onto his side to look out the big window. It opened out onto the street below. Christmas lights blinked and sparkled from the neighbor's houses across the way as the evening descended earlier every night.

Hell. He had to try. Casey was right.

He got comfortable on his bed, adjusted his pillow behind his head, and then spent twenty minutes getting the text just right before he sent it.

Hey. How'd your day go?

He'd considered sending something flirty, and he'd erased half a dozen texts full of innuendo before finally settling on this message. It was relaxed, easy, something any new acquaintance might ask after a misspent night together.

Bubbles appeared. Disappeared. Appeared. Disappeared.

He started to sweat. Fuck. Was Mr. Danvers not going to reply?

Bubbles appeared again. He breathed a sigh of relief.

I'm assuming this is RJ?

Aaron was pretending not to know who he was? Cold. RJ had texted himself from Aaron's phone with his own name and a smiley face. It would be there at the top of the text thread. He decided not to call Aaron out on the lie. If this was how he wanted to play it, then so be it. RJ braced himself for outright rejection, even as he typed his casual response.

Yeah. This is RJ.

Bubbles came and went again, until RJ had to get up and pace the room. Finally, his phone dinged with a new message.

Last night was incredible, but it probably shouldn't happen again.

Shouldn't wasn't the same as wouldn't, and RJ's heart tumbled. He'd been lucky enough to have Mr. Danvers once. He should be satisfied with that. But he really wasn't.

I'm grateful for last night. Thank you for letting me have it—and you.

He scrubbed a hand in his hair and waited for a long time, but finally a short and sweet reply came through.

It was a pleasure.

RJ didn't respond. He didn't know what to say that wouldn't be pushy after Aaron had made his position on another hookup clear. He stared at the screen until he finally gave up and stared at the ceiling instead. After a few minutes, he got out his acoustic guitar for the first time since arriving in town. It took him about half an hour to pick out a melody that pleased him, and another twenty to start making progress on some lyrics, but he was pleased to finally be writing a new song.

His phone dinged.

RJ paused. It was probably Joel again. But he snatched it off the bed anyway, heart thumping with expectation.

So how was your day?

RJ bit into his lower lip and put his guitar aside.

Yes. Fuck, yes. Aaron had given in and texted him. There was hope.

Chapter Twelve

24 hours later

S EXTING WITH A former student was probably just as bad as actually fucking one, but what Lauren didn't know wouldn't hurt her. And Aaron really needed the distraction tonight.

After dressing as an elf for the holiday pep rally, enduring the laughter of the entire middle school, and realizing that, after all he'd done to help out, Coach Ramirez now looked at him like…like maybe Aaron really *was* a raging queer—and worse, like that knowledge made Jack uncomfortable? Well, Aaron desperately needed something to take the edge off.

The fact that his preferred "something" was a little hit off his former student, RJ Blitz, was…not worth examining too closely.

The night before, they'd simply texted about life. They'd chatted about their day, the books they'd read recently, and had somehow ended up comparing memories of their favorite holiday movies from childhood. But when they'd signed off for the night, it'd felt good. Nice, like they'd agreed to be friends and nothing more. Maybe they'd shared an intimate, hot night together, but now they could be comfortable, casual buddies.

Tonight, though, right from the start, things had felt different for Aaron. When the first text from RJ came through around seven, right after Aaron had finished up his lonely Chinese takeout dinner and he'd settled down with Constance on the sofa to contemplate whether reaching out to RJ first was allowed, he'd nearly crowed with joy.

He'd flushed hot to see RJ's message on the screen. Never mind that it was another completely innocent *Hey, how was your day?* It still sent him up in flames. Aaron had never felt a full-body blush that hot and hard before. RJ might as well have asked him if he'd like to get rimmed.

Staring at the innocuous message, his dick chubbed up against his thigh. Aaron struggled with his conscience for about six seconds. And then he started it.

Later, if Lauren ever found out and chose to hang him out to dry, he'd have no excuse worth giving. He'd just wanted to feel wanted, special, and sexy for a few minutes. And his former student was really fucking good at making Aaron feel all of those things.

"If you were here with me tonight, what would you do to me?" Aaron's thumbs shook as he typed, and he had to correct several typos before he could send his question through. Then he waited, dizzy with the urgent need to know what RJ would say in response. His heart thumped and his dick surged, an anxious glee filling him as he watched the message bubbles appear. He waited for an interminably long time before gasping at RJ's response.

I'd bend you over your kitchen table, spank your ass again just to see it jiggle, and then I'd fuck you until you begged to come. Why?

Oh shit. That was real. That was exactly the response Aaron had hoped for. The spanking included. He'd been disappointed on that morning, only two nights after his encounter with RJ, to find the lingering swat marks on his ass had vanished while he was sleeping.

Aaron settled himself on his sofa, getting comfortable. He closed his eyes, remembering the way RJ had looked at him the night they'd been together. Like Aaron was a movie star, or the physical incarnation of all of RJ's hottest fantasies. Like Aaron's body was a Christmas gift that RJ was amazed to find beneath the tree, all his to unwrap and claim. Aaron had never felt so admired and wanted. Like he was RJ's dream come true.

Fuck, how often did he ever feel special anymore? Try never. Aaron slipped one hand beneath his silky robe and pinched a pebbled nipple. His hips twitched and he flipped his robe open to expose his hard dick.

Constance began to knead the fabric of the sofa where she sat perched next to him. Ignoring her and trying not to think about what she might witness, Aaron cupped his balls, fingered his taint, and considered his response. Finally, he managed to type in:

How would you fuck me?

The answer came without much delay. *Every way I know how.* There was a long, bubble-filled pause, and then, *I'd make you come until you can't handle it anymore. I'd make you sob and beg from how good it feels to have my dick in your ass. You wouldn't even know what you were begging me to do after a while. You'd say nothing but please.*

Aaron's dick ached. He fondled it, remembering the way RJ had reduced him to just that—a sobbing, begging mess—over the night they'd spent together. When he moaned, Constance shot him an aggrieved glare and hopped down, strolling away to hide beneath a chair. Aaron stroked himself more rapidly. He almost lost his grip on his phone, but he managed to respond with:

Why would you spank me?
Because you've been naughty. Very, very naughty.
How would you spank me?

He'd meant for RJ to give him more description (*hard, until your ass burns red, until you're crying out for me to stop*), but RJ's reply took his breath away and his cock jerked, releasing a pulse of pre-come.

With a ruler, Mr. Danvers. With a ruler from your desk drawer.

Oh, God, RJ was going down that teacher/student path again. It was so wrong, so, so damn wrong, but Aaron's dick didn't care, and neither did his left hand. It kept squeezing and pumping until leaking pre-come slipped down to coat his hand's glide. He swiped at the drips and swirled the slick moisture around his cockhead while he caught his breath and tried to type with his shaking right thumb.

Yes. I've been very naughty. I've fucked a former student.
It was a dream come true. A+ would do again.

Aaron groaned. His nipples tightened and tingled; his balls felt hot and full of come. *Tell me more about what you'd do to me.*

Say please.

Fuck you.

Naughty, Mr. Danvers. I'm waiting.

Please tell me what you'd do to me.

That's a good boy. I'd finger-fuck you. Rim your ass. Suck your dick.

Aaron's breath caught, and he nearly came imagining RJ's mouth sliding down over his cock. RJ's talented tongue teasing him and RJ's greedy throat wrapping around him. Fuck, it'd be so good. Another text came through: *Hang tight. I'll come over.*

No. Stay there.

Why?

I just want to know what you'd do if you were here, not actually do it.

Why?

We can't.

If you say so.

Aaron panted as he jerked himself, putting his phone aside for a minute to roll his balls in his other hand. Truth was, he wanted RJ to come over more than he wanted most anything else in the world right now, but he couldn't hold off on his orgasm for much longer, and he knew once he came, he'd find clarity again.

First, on the inappropriateness of fucking a former student, and second, on the emotional irresponsibility of starting a relationship—even just a holiday fling—with a guy like RJ, or with any guy at all.

Luckily, RJ didn't push the issue of coming over. He started up with the sexting again. Aaron's nipples stung they were so tight, and his balls rushed with jizz, orgasm holding steady just a few strokes away.

I'd put you on your knees, Mr. Danvers.

Yeah?

I'd grab your hair, force you down, make you kiss my balls.

Oh God.

I'd make you suck me until I decided I've had enough. Then I'd fuck your throat and shoot my load. You'd swallow it.

Aaron cried out. RJ wasn't exceptionally dreamy at sexting, lacking the descriptive powers of some men he'd done this with. But RJ *was* straight forward and certain, and Aaron knew he meant every word of it. If RJ were here in his apartment right now, he'd do those things to Aaron. He'd take control and make Aaron pleasure him, and, somehow, through it all, Aaron would feel cherished. He'd ache with joy while RJ wrung gratification from his body. God, he wanted that again.

Aaron gripped his phone hard as the crescendo consumed him, forcing him to achingly hot heights. His come arced from his dick in a long spurt so pleasurable that his eyes rolled back. It splashed over his chest and his throat. Shorter, sharp jolts of pleasure rocked him as jizz slopped over his still-pumping hand. *Fuck.*

Aaron's phone dinged with a new message from RJ: *I just came.*

Me too.

Wish I'd seen that.

Aaron swallowed and squeezed his eyes shut, laying the phone down on the sofa arm, riding out several aftershocks of pleasure. He wished RJ had seen him come tonight, too. He'd loved the way RJ had so ardently watched him fall apart when they'd fucked before. But…no. He couldn't do that. Lauren was right. This was a mistake.

He'd been an idiot. Christ, why was this all so hot?

Going to clean up, he typed to RJ with trembling thumbs.

There was no reply. RJ was probably doing the same.

After a fast shower, Aaron tugged on his favorite soft sweatpants and an even softer T-shirt. He slid his hand over Constance on the bed, and then lay down next to her, burying his face in her fur. She began to purr.

His mind was calm now, but his blood still seemed to fizz and pop inside him, a weird unsettled anticipation that even an orgasm hadn't extinguished. His phone dinged in the living room, and he rose to check it.

When can I see you?

Aaron stared at the message and then, somehow, almost like an out of body experience, he typed in: *Want to go to a middle school dance with me tomorrow night?*

Fuck, what was he doing? Why had he texted that? His mother would lose her mind if he showed up with a guy on his arm. She'd made it clear that his homosexuality had no place in a school setting and should always be kept separate from his work as a teacher. The situation with McAllister was proof of that, she'd said.

Aaron bit his lower lip and waited, not sure what he wanted RJ to do, accept his offer or reject it. When the text came through, his heart dropped.

I'd love to, babe, but I have band practice. Meet up after?

The strange disappointment warred with a flare of renewed lust. He should say no. Nip this in the bud. He shouldn't have texted RJ to begin with tonight, and the "babe" was a bit too much when they weren't naked together. But...

Yes.

Your place?

Yeah. Aaron's head spun. Oh, God, what was he doing? He was being a slutty fool. Since when had he ever let his dick be in charge? Not since McAllister. And look where that had gotten him...

Should I bring a ruler? ;)

Aaron quivered and swallowed hard. *Yes.*

What time?

Ten. The dance isn't over until nine, and I'll need to get home. Prepare things.

I'll be there. And don't worry, Aaron, I won't let you down.

Aaron shoved the phone away, staring up at where his string of Christmas lights glowed against the ceiling. He got up slowly, his insides humming with eagerness and dread.

When he crawled into bed and Constance curled up along the side of his leg to sleep, all he could think about were RJ's hands, his voice, and the surety he exuded whenever he stated what he planned to do to Aaron's body.

When Aaron finally fell asleep, he dreamed of being back in that damned elf costume—striped tights and green jingle-bell hat. But instead of being in front of all of his students, being mocked and laughed at, he was happily bent over RJ's lap, getting spanked.

The next morning, Aaron woke with soggy sheets for the first time in ten years.

While choosing the perfect bowtie for the day, he decided he'd wear the elf outfit for RJ that night. See where that took them. RJ seemed the type to be game for anything. And the outfit wasn't due back at the costumers for a week. Plenty of time to have it cleaned.

Aaron made his lunch, grabbed his school satchel, and plucked his keys from the counter before heading out. Yes, if he was going to risk double-dipping with RJ, he planned to milk it for all the kinky pleasure he could. Wearing the elf costume, putting that fantasy out there... It was a risk, but it felt like he already had nothing to lose. He might as well go for it. It was the right thing to do.

Or wrong thing, rather.

Former student, risky choice, potential damage to his professional reputation and all that.

But, hell. He was going to do it anyway. Might as well earn that lump of coal in his stocking.

RJ MESSED WITH his favorite, showy pedal, making his guitar ring out in the cavernous space of Joel and Casey's unfinished log cabin where they'd set up to practice. The downstairs was mostly complete, though they'd had to pull in wires from the temporary electrical panel set up for the construction company to plug in their amps, a few space heaters, and lamps.

Even with the space heaters, the room was chilly, but they all wore sweaters and were protected from the wind off the lake by the walls, even if the glass windows weren't in yet. Darkness closed around them in the winter gloom. RJ assumed the sound of their music must bounce off the lake and the cliffs around the property, especially without any leafy foliage to absorb it. He hoped the rich folks across the lake, including Casey's parents, enjoyed it. Bruno, for his part, didn't like the loud drums and always scampered off into the dark, bare woods to chase wild turkeys and squirrels.

Becca and Madison had already left, the rehearsal cut short by their need to attend Becca's holiday party at the hair salon where she worked. Becca had dismantled her drums and used her packing mojo to make it all fit in the back of her bizarrely roomy hatchback, but Madison was storing her keyboard at Joel and Casey's for now. She used the Scruffy City Hall's piano during the actual shows.

Luckily, they'd sounded pretty tight during practice, so RJ didn't mind that they hadn't gone the full two hours. The girls leaving early also gave him time alone with Casey and Joel for some guy talk.

"Wait, I don't get it," Joel said, frowning and scratching at his ear. "Mr. Danvers, the man you've wanted since high school, invited you on a date tonight?"

RJ nodded and strummed his guitar again before bowing his head and closing his eyes to noodle a little, enjoying the ring of the pedal. It was just so spangly. It matched his jittery excitement over the evening ahead.

"And you said no?" Casey asked, propped up on a pile of blankets in the corner with his iPad, making posts on Facebook and Twitter on behalf of his marketing clients. Always Old Skool Millennials' biggest fan, Casey hadn't wanted to miss their practice, so he'd worked through it like the good multitasker he was.

"Band practice is sacred," RJ said with a shrug. "That's always been my rule."

"Sure, back when we were dumb kids trying to be a real band. But now we're just fucking around playing some Christmas gigs for the hell of it," Joel said, furrowing his brow.

"It was a rule when we were kids, yeah," RJ agreed. "But it's a rule with every band I tour with. I can't just not show up."

"Well, of course," Joel conceded. "But you know this is different."

"It's really not."

Joel checked his phone and clucked his tongue at RJ. "You've still got some time. Text Mr. Danvers and say you can make it after all. Show up at the dance looking like a million bucks." He nodded toward Casey. "That's what I did. Showed up at his folks' holiday party in my best jacket. And look at us."

Casey gazed at Joel like a lovesick cow, and RJ rolled his eyes. "You guys are gross." He refrained from mentioning that Joel's surprise appearance at Casey's family's Christmas party had initially backfired on both of them. They were so in love and happy now, it was pointless to bring up the messy past. They were even on good terms with Casey's parents at this point. Everything had come up Christmas miracles for them. That's not how RJ's life worked.

"Really, you should crash the dance like Joel said," Casey offered. "He'd be impressed by that."

RJ scoffed. "Would he? A random dude shows up at a middle school dance. That wouldn't be, I don't know, fucking weird?"

"You'd be his date! It'd be romantic."

RJ didn't think it would be actually. "I don't have any clothes appropriate for a dance. I'm a touring guitarist. I don't own a suit or sports coat. I can't show up in ripped jeans, a T-shirt, and a studded leather jacket."

"Well, you *could*," Joel said. "It'd make things interesting."

"Nah." RJ didn't think Aaron would want that kind of attention.

Besides, he was pretty sure that saying no to the dance invite had hooked Aaron in even more. Aaron wouldn't have agreed to whatever was going to happen at his apartment tonight if RJ had accepted the invite to the dance. In fact, RJ was willing to bet that Aaron would have withdrawn the invitation entirely if RJ had actually said he wanted to go.

Some part of Mr. Danvers wanted to feel in control—wanted to be the one to invite, and offer, and sext. But what Aaron really *needed*, deep down, was to feel like someone else was in control. And that the other person truly *wanted* to be in control, and knew to be, and when.

By refusing the invitation, RJ had taken back the reins, and Aaron had given them over easily. It seemed clear: Yes, Aaron wanted to be wanted, but more than that, Aaron *needed* someone who could hold appropriate boundaries while Aaron lost his. That, more than being in control, made Aaron feel safe enough to do this again.

RJ had sensed that truth in Aaron all the way back in high school. He'd always dreamed of being the one Mr. Danvers surrendered to, and when they'd had sex the other night? Mr. Danvers *had* surrendered fully. Like a sweet bitch in heat—needful and desperate. And everything about it had been just as good as RJ had known it could be.

But none of this understanding was anything he could share with his friends. That would be a violation of the trust Aaron didn't even know he'd given RJ. But he knew he'd made the right choice in declining the invitation to the dance. The choice that would lead to Aaron willingly spreading his ass tonight to take RJ deep and hard.

Or maybe he'd ride Aaron's cock instead. RJ wasn't picky.

"I think you're missing an opportunity," Joel reiterated. "This school dance is the perfect way to show him you're serious."

"I want to fuck him, not marry him," RJ said, putting his guitar aside. "I'm *not* serious, and frankly, I think that's the last thing he'd want me to be."

"He just wants a holiday fling?" Casey said with an arched brow and a flash of crinkle-eyed amusement aimed at Joel.

"*He* wanted a one-night hookup. The fact that he's back for more at all is down to my ability to play it cool. I promise, I'm not blowing anything. Except him."

"So, deep down, you really think Mr. Danvers likes that you rejected him? Even though he asked you out?"

"Pretty much." RJ shrugged.

Down deep, Aaron liked a lot of contradictory things. But RJ didn't mind. He liked that about Aaron. Wanted to be the one to get to see that prissy, filthy man embrace all the naughty, sexy sides to himself.

"I'm not buying it. A guy that uptight wants a hell of a lot more than no-strings-attached fucks," Joel said, shaking his head. "He screams 'in need of commitment.'"

Given how tightly Joel had held himself back from what he truly wanted before Casey busted through his defenses, RJ figured he was probably speaking from personal experience. But that didn't mean the same techniques that had worked on Joel would also work on Aaron, or that RJ even wanted them to.

"Well, sure, Aaron probably wants more than he's asking for, just like anyone. But he's skittish." RJ left out the part where Aaron clearly needed someone to force him to come undone, to break him down into a puddle of goo just to relax enough to be held. "Coming on too strong will drive him away. Besides, neither of us is looking for more than sex right now."

"It's like petting a deer," Casey said, thoughtfully, poking away at the iPad again and not looking at either of them. "You set the feed out and let the deer come to investigate it. First, she'll come up, sniff the food and run off. Then she'll come back, sniff the food again, run off. And then, if you're very relaxed, and also lucky, she'll come back and eat right out of your hand."

RJ pictured Aaron as a deer and had to admit that Casey was on to something. And, just like the deer, even after Aaron had eaten out of RJ's hand, he'd scamper off to his forest again. Because that was the natural order of things between men like them. Aaron was far too edgy, and RJ traveled too often to ever train Aaron to be the kind of "deer" to come when called, or the kind of man to stay open and trusting between far-apart fucks.

"Is that what you do with your time while I'm slaving away at Vreeland's? You lounge around in the yard luring deers?" Joel asked Casey, laughing.

Casey shrugged. "Before I got enough clients to stay busy, let's just say I had some free time. And I only did it once."

Joel snorted.

"What? I got to pet her. She was beautiful."

Joel put his guitar aside and crawled on the floor to Casey. RJ rolled his eyes and started to put his things away. The murmurs and kissing sounds were more than he needed to witness. He was glad for their sake that they'd finally accepted what they were to each other, but they didn't need to turn everyone else's stomach with their sweetness.

At least Aaron was more into spankings and keeping things kinky. RJ knew what to do with a man who wanted that. But in his experience, attempting to build something based on true affection and tenderness always backfired. Not that he was building anything with Aaron, other than a possible connection for future hookups whenever he came to town. Not that he wouldn't be tender with Aaron, especially as a reward for taking cock so well.

He grinned and zipped his guitar into the soft case, rising and slinging it over his back. He'd definitely reward Aaron for that.

"I'm out."

Joel started to heave himself up and away from Casey's arms, but RJ waved him off. "I can see myself out. You keep on being disgusting. It's nice."

Joel and Casey laughed, and RJ left them to it.

After buckling up, he checked the time on his phone again. It was only six-thirty, but he had some errands to run. He needed to pick up a wooden ruler, and if he could find what he wanted at Wal-Mart or Target, he'd up the ante on their naughty list joke too.

A message popped up on his phone.

When will you be home? Doug's out with Carter tonight. The kids and I are going to watch Star Wars. Remember how often you watched it as a kid? Wore out the VHS tape. Want to join us?

RJ smiled at the vision of his brother and sister on the sofa with his mom. It was sweet to be invited, and he should probably take her up on it, given that spending time with his family was his number one reason for being in town at all. But there was no way he was missing out on a second night with Mr. Danvers.

Sorry. Have plans. Don't wait up. See you tomorrow sometime.

His mom didn't reply until he was in the Wal-Mart parking lot.

Be sure to cover your light saber.

RJ sent an eyeroll emoji back and was rewarded with a kiss emoji in return. Maybe he and his mom would figure out how to be in each other's lives again, and maybe they wouldn't. But he supposed this was a good start.

He swung by the condom aisle after getting what he needed from the school supplies, electronics, and holiday sections, and picked up a fresh box, along with his favorite lube. He had just one more stop to make, this time at a local sex shop.

RJ hoped Mr. Danvers was ready for a night of Christmas kink. Because he sure as jingle-hell was.

Chapter Thirteen

MIDDLE SCHOOL DANCES were pretty easy to chaperone. No girls or boys really wanted to be anywhere near each other, so it really was all about making sure the guys didn't come up with a dumb idea that would endanger them physically. Like, say, doing a back flip off the top of the gym's bleachers or something.

Aaron stood off to the side of the basketball-court-come-dance-floor sipping red, fizzy punch and trying not to think about RJ and what sexual pleasure might be waiting for him after the dance was over. Despite ruthless attempts to corral his thoughts, jittery excitement still climbed around inside him like a five-year-old on a jungle gym.

He couldn't wait for the dance to wrap up, and he hoped to duck out before he could get roped into any kind of cleanup. With his mother present, though, he was worried that he wouldn't be able to escape her clutches.

Carter Ward danced—if that's what all that flailing could be called—with his pals near the middle of the court to the latest dreadful song-sensation. There always seemed to be a new one, ever since the long-lost "Macarena" hit the charts when Aaron was just a baby. At least this one didn't have a required dance to go along with it or ask questions about what red-furred animals might say, though the repetition of a high fashion brand turned slang-word was a bit boring. It was only the fourth time the song had been played tonight. Aaron figured he'd have to endure at least two more.

The saving grace was that he knew old-school Whitney Houston had been cued up. He'd made sure of that himself, placing the request with the DJ during his last pass that direction.

"Nice tie," an adult male voice said from his left. Aaron turned to find Doug Ward wearing a green polo shirt and khaki pants. Tall and fit, he was handsome for a harried father. And if Aaron remembered correctly, he was a doctor, too. He wondered when Doug found time to work out.

Doug lifted his cup of punch at Aaron and asked, "Get it around here?"

"Picked it up in Atlanta, actually," Aaron said, glancing down at the subtle weave of color through the silk. Greens, reds, and whites. A Christmas tie for sure, but not an overt candy cane of stripes. "Can't recall the store. Sorry." He'd been there with a hookup, actually. A long weekend trip to Atlanta over his last Christmas break had satisfied his needs for nearly six whole months.

During the trip, he'd indulged in a series of Grindr fucks with a few different guys, but the real reason he'd gone down to the big city had been for a paid session with a Dom with a very good online reputation. And well-deserved, as it turned out. The man had spanked Aaron until he'd cried, made him come, and then took him shopping at a very fancy mall for silk ties as his reward for taking the pain so well.

Aaron hadn't even gotten fucked by the guy, and yet he still counted that experience as one of the most satisfying encounters of his life. Topped only by his night with RJ Blitz. Man, he was a kinky bastard, wasn't he? And he shouldn't be thinking about that now with Carter Ward's dad standing next to him watching the kids with a small smile on his face. This was a night for innocence. Aaron should have worn a different tie.

"So, how's Carter doing?" Doug asked. "He's been sullen around the house lately. I can't make heads or tails of it. Wondering if I should brace myself for his report card."

"His grades have held steady in my class. I can't speak for any of the other teachers, but I get the impression that it's not school that's bothering Carter," Aaron said carefully. He couldn't violate Carter's trust by revealing the content of their conversation to his father, but he might be able to hint around at it.

Doug nodded. "Me too. He's been squirrely lately. Do you think the other guys are bullying him? For being…" Doug trailed off and frowned. "He's never said the words to me. I don't know. Maybe he's not."

"Not what?"

"Gay. Or bi, like me. I don't know. I've just always thought…" Doug glanced around, confirming they were still mostly alone and that no kids were lingering nearby listening. "When he was a kid, he had a pretty big crush on his mother's male tennis instructor. I just assumed…"

"You're bi?"

Doug nodded. "Prefer women for the most part, but I've dabbled."

Aaron also confirmed their relative privacy before asking, "And Carter knows about that? The, uh, dabbling?"

"No! No, why would I worry him with that? If I'd started seriously dating a man after his mom and I split up, I'd have told him, of course. But I met my current wife and fell for her pretty fast. She's a great woman." His eyes went distant and happy, and Aaron felt they were in danger of losing the thread, so he directed Doug's thoughts back toward his son.

"If Carter is…how should I put it…not-straight—and I'm not saying that's his truth, because the thought never crossed my mind, frankly—but, let's say he isn't entirely straight, then it might help him to know that a man he admires and looks up to isn't either."

"He does look up to you," Doug agreed, nodding thoughtfully. "I think you're a good role model for him. I mean, from what I can tell. He speaks so highly of you at home. It's always Mr. Danvers this, and Mr. Danvers that. You're his favorite teacher."

How could the man be so oblivious? And given such an obtuse man had guessed his sexuality, it was clear that as Aaron had aged he'd become more obvious in his preferences despite his best attempts to keep it covered up. Was it his voice? His mannerisms? Or, fuck, the tie?

"I mean, I'm sorry." Doug flushed. "I assumed...you *are*..." He cocked his head, observing Aaron's discomfiture. "I'm not usually wrong."

"You're not wrong," Aaron said quickly. "But what I meant was that Carter could use a role model closer to home."

"His mother's brother is gay," Doug said thoughtfully. "Maybe I could ask him to talk to Carter."

"Maybe *you* should talk to Carter," Aaron suggested. "You don't have to confront him about his feelings but telling him about your own might help him feel safe to volunteer information about his, if he has any."

"I don't know," Doug said, shifting awkwardly. "Does he really want to know anything about what his father likes in the sack? Does *any* kid want to know that?"

Aaron blushed. "Well, no, but—"

"Mr. Danvers!" his mother's voice was sharp and demanding and coming from directly behind his back. It was like a knife plunging in, and his heart dropped into his stomach. How did she have such an instantaneous effect on him?

"Principal Shock," he said, turning around to smile at her. He motioned toward Doug. "This is Carter Ward's father, Doug. We were just talking about Carter."

She lifted a narrow, overplucked brow at Aaron, and then turned a less icy expression on Doug, offering her well-manicured hand. "It's nice to meet you, Mr. Ward. Carter is a great asset to our school community."

Doug laughed. "That might be laying it on thick, Principal Shock, but I'm glad you don't have anything bad to say about him." He glanced between Aaron and his mother and then said, "Pardon me. I'll get some more punch. Thanks for the chat, Mr. Danvers. Carter likes your class a lot." He headed away, eager, no doubt, to get away from the crackling tension between his son's teacher and the principal.

"What do you think you're doing?" his mother hissed, tugging Aaron farther away from the dance floor into a dark shadow behind the bleachers. "Flirting with a student's father like that?"

"I…what?" Aaron stared at her.

"That is utterly inappropriate."

"We were literally discussing his son, Mom. My student. I was not flirting with him." Aaron's temper rose hot and frustrated. "You're the one being inappropriate."

She loomed over him, using her height to dominate. "I know what I saw, and what every other adult with eyes saw. I've warned you not to embarrass me in this school. Not to embarrass me ever again."

"He's not even my type." Aaron could have bitten off his own tongue for saying that. He didn't need to defend himself. He'd done nothing wrong.

"God forbid this school ever knows what your type might be. We agreed when you came aboard here that you'd keep all of this—" she motioned at him, like whatever she disdained it encompassed the whole of him "—to yourself."

Ears burning, the words spilled out before Aaron could stop them. "You're treading perilously close to harassment, Mom."

"Excuse me?"

"If I were a straight teacher, talking with a student's father, this would never have come up. You're harassing me because I'm gay. Which, fine, it's something I've learned to live with at home, because God knows you're unable to accept me for some reason—"

"I accept you. How dare you say I don't accept you, Aaron? I simply don't condone your behavior. Especially not on school grounds. After what happened before, you should know better. You and I have made agreements."

Aaron's chin came up, righteous rage giving him courage. "For the sake of our relationship, yes. I've agreed never to bring a man into your home. I've agreed not to come out at school. I've agreed to hide who I am to make you more comfortable, but it's not working anymore."

"In what way?"

"You see homosexual intent where there is none, and you'd deny me the natural expression of my feelings with men that might actually matter—"

His mother shushed him, her nostrils flaring. "Keep your voice down."

"Fine." There were a few wallflowers who *had* scooted in their direction, seemingly to eavesdrop. A reckless part of himself wanted to let them hear. Maybe one of them could learn something about being true to themselves and standing up to their parents, even if it was years and years too late. But a more cowardly part of himself wanted to scrunch down and be small, unobserved, unnoticed, and safe.

He lowered his voice. "You already ask a lot of me, Mom, but it's never enough. I do my best not to embarrass you, to keep my love life to myself—"

His mother dragged him deeper beneath the bleachers. She hissed, "A 'love life'? Is that what you call these illicit and, quite frankly, dangerous assignations you engage in?"

Aaron had no idea how his mother knew anything at all about his sex life, but he wasn't going to ask. It was a small city. No matter what lengths he went to for privacy when getting a sexual fix, gossip would get around. It was why he so rarely indulged. His heart hammered, and he went sweaty and flushed.

"How long until other people find out about these disgusting depravities, Aaron? All it takes is one more complaint filed against you. I can't help you after that."

"It's not depraved to want—"

"To sleep with strangers? I certainly think it is! And the school board would agree with me. Imagine if my other teachers were doing that. Picking up random men. Imagine if a parent found out. You see where this ends up, Aaron. With you fired and me humiliated."

"Picking up random men?" Aaron gaped at her. "Don't you see? That's all you've allowed me, Mom. Your rules, your refusal to let me be myself, all that leaves me with is what you just described. I don't have the luxury of real intimacy, or love, or feelings, or even just having someone who cares for me—"

"Stop! This isn't the time or place!" She looked around to ensure they were still alone. Kids were scooting closer, whispering amongst themselves. A few other teachers had taken notice and were watching with raised brows. "You need to go home. People are staring."

"You started this." His statement encompassed so much more than the moment at hand. It covered all the way back to his teen years when his mother had made it entirely clear: if he wanted her in his life, then he couldn't have boyfriends, couldn't let anyone know the truth of him. In exchange for her love, he had to hide his feelings, his yearnings, and his needs.

Aaron was a grown man now, yes, but his mother had set him up. First as a mother, and then as his superior, and now he was stuck in a place where the very concept of getting his needs met made him feel selfish, and slutty, and bad. Even when following her rules, he was met with suspicion and disdain from the woman who should have loved him unconditionally, supported him whole-heartedly, and...

He straightened his shoulders. "You're right."

"Of course I am."

"I should go home. I'm not wanted here."

"Aaron—"

"Monday is our last day of classes before the break. I'll let you know by the end of winter break whether or not I plan to tender my resignation by year's end, Principal Shock. Because God knows I can't keep living like this. Something has got to give."

She gasped, her eyes growing round. Then she folded her arms over her relatively flat chest, sharp elbows sticking out at angles, and she hissed, "We will discuss this later."

Aaron shrugged. "Maybe. I've got a lot going on this weekend."

His mother flinched.

Aaron bit back the urge to taunt, *"Yes, Mother, I'll be too busy with illicit and dangerous hookups and fucking a former student to discuss this bullshit any further with you."*

Before he let the bile slip out, he whirled away from her scornful gaze. Without looking back, he stalked from the gym out to his car, slipped inside, and locked the door. Sweat damped his armpits and palms. He wiped his hands on his suit's pants legs, and then adjusted his rearview mirror to a view of the gym. The blue and white lights from the winter decorations glowed in the high windows, and he waited to see if anyone would follow him to his car.

Lauren wasn't chaperoning. No other teacher would want to intercede on his behalf in a fight with his mother.

If Doug Ward followed him out, his mother would feel proven right.

Aaron licked his lips nervously. He didn't know what had possessed him in there. He *never* talked to his mother *or* the principal like that. Not even as a teenager. Her love had always felt far too easy to lose.

When no one came, Aaron started his car with shaking hands and drove off school property. Heart racing, he pulled into the shadowy parking lot of a nearby church, choosing a spot well away from the building and out of sight from the main road. The church was dark, but the Christmas décor—big, fat green wreaths with gold and white bows—were still visible in the shadows. Aaron stared up at the cross stabbing into the night sky from atop the church's spire. There was a lot to unpack in that symbol and he didn't have the time or energy for it tonight.

He glanced toward the clock on his car dashboard. As bad an idea as it had been to invite RJ over at all, Aaron was grateful for the distraction now. Without RJ and the night of sex ahead, there was no doubt he'd have gone straight to the grocery store, picked up ice cream, chips, and Double Stuf Oreos before holing up in his apartment to gorge on junk while reliving every single moment of his conversation with his mother again and again.

She wouldn't call him. Not tonight. And maybe not tomorrow. Heck, it was possible she wouldn't call at all. She liked to let him stew and let him be the one to beg for forgiveness whenever they'd butted heads in the past. Not that they'd ever had words like they'd had tonight. Not even after the divorce. Not even when she accused him of loving his dad best. Aaron had always tried to placate and soothe her. What had come over him at the dance?

Thank God RJ would be over tonight. He'd be the best distraction. Aaron doubted he'd be able to give his mother's bullshit a second thought once RJ put his big hands on his body. Pulling himself together, Aaron left the church parking lot and directed the car toward his apartment.

Ruthlessly, he pushed pause on the automatic replays of his argument with his mom to make a mental list of all the things he needed to do to prepare. He wanted to shower and douche. Aaron wasn't a believer in douching before *every* anal encounter, since he ate a good diet of fiber-rich foods and everything down there was usually in good shape for spontaneous fun. But tonight, he wanted to be extra cleaned out, because he wanted to go long and hard.

Then he'd change his sheets and put some easy-to-wash blankets on the sofa in case they got into any play out there. He planned to quickly vacuum, as well as make sure everything in the bedroom looked tidy and neat. And he wanted to make sure Constance's litter was scrupulously clean after the disaster of last time.

He needed plenty of time to don the elf costume. He wasn't sure if he was in the mood now for such a playful game, but he didn't like the idea of his mother winning either. If he let her strip away all the joy and fun from his "illicit and dangerous" fling with RJ, then what was even the point of having it? Still, he wanted enough time to put the costume on and get back out of it again if he decided it wasn't the direction he wanted to go after all.

He'd opened a giant can of worms with his mom, but he wasn't going to let that destroy his chance to get thoroughly and completely banged by a super-hot former student. The one with a killer smile, big hands, and a sweet disposition. As he made his way home, he concentrated on his memories of RJ's body—his weight on top of Aaron, the width of his ridiculous cock, and the way he'd taken Aaron apart with pleasure the last time they'd hooked up. The images almost banished the gut-churning nausea left over from his encounter with his mom. They definitely left him straining with anticipation for the worry-obliterating events awaiting him.

Even if he couldn't expect love from RJ—or anyone, really—he already knew he'd get pleasure and respect from the man. That was more than he could say about most people in his life right now. The winter break would give him the space he needed to figure out if he'd meant what he said about resigning. And who knew what his mother would be like come Christmas Day if they hadn't made up by then?

At least tonight, he'd be fucked until he was nothing more than a quivering, warm pile of relaxed muscles. Blissed out on his self-procured Christmas gifts: RJ Blitz and his wondrous cock. And it would be worth it.

Of that Aaron had no doubt.

Chapter Fourteen

"OH DAMN, BABY. How did you know?"

Aaron held open the door to his apartment a little longer than usual, staring at RJ in shock. His nipples rose in the cold air, barely hidden beneath the elf costume's vest. He'd decided against wearing the entire thing and settled for just a few of the pieces.

"How did *you* know?" he whispered, confused laughter bursting from his chest. He tugged RJ inside, blocking Constance's dash for freedom with his stockinged foot, and quickly shut the door.

RJ reached out to stroke a hand down the elf costume's green, velvet vest decorated with gold buttons, and worn over nothing but the green-and-white striped elf tights. "Did you wear this to the dance?" RJ growled, possessive disbelief lining his words.

"Of course not."

"So it's all for me?"

Aaron raised a challenging brow and stroked over the red cloak with white fuzzy trim wrapped around RJ's shoulders. He tweaked RJ's red hat with the white fluff ball at the end. "Yes. And this is all for me? Santa?"

RJ grinned. "You're on my naughty list, Elf." He reached into the leather backpack he held loosely in one hand and pulled out a ruler decorated with a messily tied red bow. "This is all you're getting in your stocking this year." Then he shoved it back in his bag. "But that's for later."

Aaron hissed and swooned into RJ, lifting his mouth up for a hungry kiss.

When they broke apart, Aaron asked, "How did you know I was going to dress up for you?" He tugged RJ deeper into the apartment and led him over to the sofa to shove him down.

RJ complied easily, his long arms draping sexily along the top of couch and his lanky legs spreading wide, revealing the bulge in his blue jeans. "I didn't. We're just in sync." His dilated eyes roamed over Aaron, and then his hands did too. "C'mere."

Aaron straddled RJ's legs and let RJ slide his fingers over his exposed arms, into the vest to tweak his nipples, and then down to cup and squeeze his cock. "Mr. Danvers, I have bad news."

"What?"

"You've been a very bad elf."

"If you expect anything more to come of this," Aaron said breathlessly, "you have to stop calling me Mr. Danvers. Call me Aaron."

"Okay, Aaron." RJ gave a wide grin. "Except during sex. Then you're Mr. Danvers."

Aaron frowned but shivered involuntarily at the same time. "Okay."

"Ha! I knew you liked it." RJ tweaked Aaron's nipples again.

Aaron sighed. "You're a pill, did you know that?"

"A pill with a big dick and good aim."

Aaron shivered and tucked up close to him. "You're too cocky by half."

"All part of the show."

"I wish it was," Aaron whispered, kissing RJ's neck and squeezing tightly.

"What's that supposed to mean?"

Aaron groaned. "I don't know. I'm so turned on, I'm not sure what half the things I'm saying and thinking mean right now."

RJ stroked down Aaron's side. "You fuck like a wild thing, Mr. Danvers."

"Aaron," he corrected gently, a desperate thread in his voice that even he could hear. "And so do you."

"When you're in my arms, I'll call you whatever I damn well please."

Aaron moaned softly, his dick twitching in his tights. "Okay."

"Okay, what?"

"Okay, Santa."

RJ's lips quirked. "I'd meant for you to call me sir, just for kicks, but Santa works."

Aaron huffed a laugh. "You talk a big game, Santa, about how bad I am, and what you're going to do about it, but so far I'm not seeing any truth in your threats."

RJ blinked at him slowly. "Push all you want, Mr. Danvers, but I'm in charge tonight. So settle in. Santa's got plans for his prissy elf."

"I hope they include bending me over something and—"

"Shh. Hand me my backpack."

Aaron lifted the bag onto the sofa beside them. RJ whistled under his breath and smoothed his fingers over Aaron's soft abdomen, rubbing them over the treasure trail that led down beneath his straining tights. "Look at all this sexy elf on show for me."

Aaron felt his cheeks prickle with heat, a blush of pleasure. He wasn't used to praise from anyone, and he warmed everywhere with every bit of evidence that RJ was pleased by him.

Fantasy was well and good, meaningless hookups got his itch scratched, but sitting on RJ's lap and being touched like this, gazed at like he was someone of real importance was a rush that was definitely turning out to be addictive.

He shoved that thought aside and concentrated on what RJ was pulling out of his bag. The ruler. Condoms. Lube. An old portable DVD player and an even older DVD that looked like it'd been handled a lot over the years. Lastly, RJ removed a separate bag and unzipped it, revealing a very naughty toy.

Aaron squirmed on his lap. "What's all this?"

"Punishments for being on my naughty list, Mr. Danvers." He fondled the set of purple anal beads. The smallest looked easy enough, but the last one was more than intimidating. He quirked an eyebrow. "Elf, you're going to want to get comfortable for this."

He moved Aaron off his lap and set up the portable DVD player on the coffee table. "You mentioned this was your favorite Christmas movie the other day. Turns out I had a copy in a box of my old stuff in Mom's garage."

"RJ...." Aaron groaned. He was so aroused, and this wasn't what he'd bargained for. When RJ had showed up in a Santa outfit, he'd thought they'd get right to business. Spanking. Fucking. Orgasms. "Let's just have sex."

"We're going to have sex. Lots of sex. Everything I told you about and more." He moved the DVD player so that small screen faced the sofa. "Where's Constance?"

"I don't know."

"There she is," RJ said, nodding toward the top of the bookshelf where Constance was hiding to lick her paws. "Will it scare her if I make you scream?"

Aaron shuddered. "Stop making promises and then not keeping them."

"Take that vest off. Leave the tights."

RJ untied his Santa cape and draped it over the sofa, the faux-velvet side up. He pressed play on the DVD and sat back down on the cape with a cocky grin. All calm and confident with silly Santa hat on his head, he gripped Aaron's neck and dragged him face first into his lap. Aaron's elf hat fell off and joined RJ's Santa hat in a tumble to the floor.

Breathing in the scent of RJ's jean-clad crotch and sneaking his fingers to the soft strip of hair underneath RJ's soft, white T-shirt, Aaron shivered as the opening theme song of his old favorite Christmas movie began.

"You know what this place needs," RJ whispered, his fingers moving through Aaron's hair and down his neck, stroking and encouraging

Aaron's nuzzling.

"What?"

"A tree."

"So you said before."

"Open my pants. Get my dick out."

"Yesssss." Aaron had thought RJ was never going to get started, that they'd be trapped in this wrestle of almost-sex forever, maybe until one of them broke and the spell of attraction between them broke too. But, no, now he was hurriedly working RJ's zipper down and helping him tug his jeans halfway down his thighs.

RJ's cock was a shock again, even though Aaron had had it in his body just a few days ago. But it was just so wide, smaller at the head and flaring out into a thickness that made his heart thump. He opened his mouth and started to lower down the beautiful shaft, but RJ gripped his hair and pulled him off.

"Your mouth is beautiful, Mr. Danvers, but only good elves get to suck my cock. Bad elves have to watch a movie while I do whatever I want to their bodies."

Aaron shivered. As much as he wanted RJ's dick in his mouth, letting RJ do whatever he wanted sounded just as good, maybe even better. "Yes, Santa."

RJ grabbed a throw pillow and handed it to Aaron. "Across my lap. Ass up. Get comfortable. I plan to take my time."

Aaron did as he was told, using the pillow to prop up his head, left cheek pressed into the material and head turned so that he could see the screen. A cartoon mouse was ruining Christmas for his whole town by not believing in Santa. RJ massaged Aaron's ass through his tights as the mouse sang about his lack of faith.

"Relax."

Aaron tried, but he could feel RJ's bare cock digging into his hip, and his own cock throbbed where it was caught against the tights. RJ skimmed his warm hands up and down Aaron's back until he melted down against the pillow and RJ's legs.

"Lift up," RJ whispered. "Let me just…"

He tugged Aaron's tights down to the middle of his thighs and groaned before pushing Aaron back down again, spreading his own legs enough to wedge Aaron's aching cock in the tight place between his jean-clad thighs. Aaron hissed as the tip of his dick dragged against the fabric of the Santa cape.

"What a sweet ass," RJ whispered, caressing the swell and dip of Aaron's butt, and then running his fingers lightly in the crack to slide over Aaron's eager asshole. "A little pale for such a bad elf. Let's fix that."

Then his hand came down in a swat that jolted Aaron and sent his adrenaline rushing. "Thank you," he whispered, turning his face to the pillow and pushing his ass up.

"Eyes on the movie, Mr. Danvers."

With effort, he turned to look at the screen again. RJ set up a rhythm of slaps, almost like Aaron's ass was a drum and RJ was making music with it. "Love this jiggle. Look at that," RJ said with awe, as the rain of swats started to really sting and build heat. "You're taking your punishment so well. It's almost time for more."

Aaron rutted his cock between RJ's jean-clad thighs, the fabric of the seams rough and almost painful on his sensitive dick, but he caught a hard slap across his ass for that.

"Hold still, Mr. Danvers. Bad elves who come before Santa says they can, don't get fucked."

"What? Are you serious?" Would RJ really come here, key him up, get him off, and then walk away without plowing his ass?

"Don't test me."

Aaron held still again, keeping his eyes on the screen and the mouse who was now frantically trying to save Christmas instead of ruining it.

"Here. Unwrap your present." RJ held the ruler out in front of Aaron's face.

A shudder wracked him as Aaron lifted onto his elbows and reached out one arm to tug the ribbon free.

"Are you ready, Mr. Danvers?" RJ asked, rubbing his hand over Aaron's ass, then up his spine, pressing him back down to the pillow and holding a steady hand against the nape of his neck. "I've dreamed of this since I was in your class. Spanking you with a ruler. Seeing white and red stripes rise up. Because of me. And you. Letting me." His voice sounded wrecked. "Do you want that too?"

"Yes."

"Why?"

"Because I'm a bad elf, and I need to be punished."

RJ laughed. "You do. Look at this sexy ass, so round and perfect. Let's mark it up, Mr. Danvers."

Aaron gripped the edges of the sofa, turned his head from the screen, and bit into the pillow as a stinging stripe of pain broke over his ass. Aaron shivered and his cock throbbed as RJ squeezed his thighs around it. As the slaps from the ruler rained down, the stinging grew hotter, and stronger. RJ concentrated his strikes on the same spot, so that the pain escalated. "Like that?" he whispered.

Aaron moaned.

"Let's take you higher." RJ put the ruler aside and switched to hitting with his hand. Aaron pulled in a harsh breath, and within a few strikes, his mind was on fire and his ass muscles clenched tight. "Ready for more of the ruler?"

Aaron nodded, but the ruler hurt more this time. His flesh was burning from RJ's palm, and he grunted and twisted. The light, smarting stripes felt like firecracker-heat on his skin. It built and built. Stinging, and shallow, but fiery and growing.

When RJ switched back to his hand, the first strike made Aaron gasp and choke on his own spit. "So good, Mr. Danvers," RJ murmured, and then began to spank him with an intensity that made Aaron howl into the pillow. But RJ was strong and held him firmly. The elf costume tights strained against Aaron's thighs as he struggled, and the sense that he was trapped in them, trapped on RJ's lap was heady and hot.

His cock pulsed between RJ's thighs, and when RJ grabbed hold of his throbbing ass cheeks and squeezed, Aaron lifted his head, a mess of agony and bliss, to shout, "I'm going to come!"

"Come for me," RJ ordered. "Do it."

RJ's firm grasp on his ass, shoving his hips down into the tunnel between the hurtful seams of RJ's jeans, was all Aaron needed. He arched his head back, fresh sweat breaking over his skin, and came.

Rocket explosions of pleasure shook him, and he collapsed on RJ's lap, legs shaking and a shivery whimper sliding out of his mouth.

"That's right, Mr. Danvers," RJ said, fingers soothing in his hair and stroking down his neck and back. "You're gorgeous. So fucking sexy. Look at you. Never thought I'd have the chance. Thank you."

Aaron shuddered, white noise and shimmering glimpses of shame rushing into his mind. He started to stand, but his legs were too weak, and he slipped to the floor, tights still digging into his legs. RJ tore off his T-shirt to mop up the come that hadn't made it onto the Santa cape, pushed his jeans down to his knees, and nodded at his feet.

"Take my boots off. Then my pants. I think you earned a taste of my come."

Aaron shivered and nodded, the shame that had been trying to overtake the white noise losing its fight as renewed lust took up the available space in Aaron's brain.

As he worked the laces free and tugged the big combat boots from RJ's feet, he leaned into RJ's hand working through his hair over and over, soothing and commanding.

"That's it, Elf. Now, c'mere and open up."

RJ MEANT IT when he said he'd never thought he'd get this chance and he wasn't going to waste it. He might have already shot one load down

Aaron's greedy throat, but he was far from finished with his naughty elf. Not for the night. Hopefully, not for the weekend either.

RJ removed Aaron's tights and moved him to kneel on the sofa with his hands on the back of it. He dragged Aaron's vest off and tossed it to the ground with the Santa hat. RJ chose to keep his T-shirt and jeans on for now.

The red stripes on Aaron's ass were intoxicating, and he couldn't keep his hands off them. Aaron squirmed and moaned with every pass and squeeze, but he pushed back for more and bowed his head to his forearms on the back of the sofa, surrendering his body.

"What do you think comes next?" RJ said, trailing a finger up and down Aaron's crack, dragging through soft, fine hair to the hairless whorl of knotted muscle.

"Whatever you want," Aaron said, his breath hitching.

"That's right. Good answer, naughty elf." He lightly massaged Aaron's hole until it flexed and tightened, and then he spread his cheeks wide and bent down.

"Oh!" Aaron cried as RJ's tongue found its target. His head lifted and dropped again, another sobbing sound on his lips as RJ intensified his tongue's teasing strokes and pressed against the sensitive flesh.

Aaron's thighs trembled and shook, his weight shifting from knee to knee, his asshole flexing and releasing wildly. "Oh, fuck, RJ," he groaned. "It's been...shit. It's been a long time."

Hookups didn't always extend beyond a blowjob or a hurried fuck, RJ knew all too well. The pleasure of a good, long rimming was in short supply in most single, gay men's lives. He set about giving Aaron all the rimming his body could take.

It wasn't long before Aaron was arching back, reaching behind him to tug at RJ's short hair, barely able to grip it, and alternately tucking his ass like he was trying to get away before shoving it back for more.

The noises he let out stopped being groans or even whimpers and became full on hiccupping pleasure-sobs, high-pitched and desperate, lost and a little scared. RJ didn't stop. He pressed his fingers to Aaron's taint, rubbing and amping up the sensation. RJ grinned when Aaron suddenly froze in place, his asshole convulsing and a torn cry on his lips.

More come spattered the Santa cape. Aaron slid to the side and collapsed in a heap on the sofa, legs twitching, eyes rolled up, and hips jerking. RJ covered him with his body, rubbing his cock against Aaron's trembling stomach and pubic hair, finally clambering up enough to get his cock to Aaron's mouth so that when his red lips opened weakly, letting RJ push inside, RJ threw back his head and came for the second time that night.

And it didn't end there.

RJ hadn't gone by the Adult Superstore to buy anal beads for nothing.

Aaron lay draped over his lap again, red ass up and legs spread a bit, shocked little breaths coming and going as they started the Christmas mouse movie over. RJ took his time, starting with the small bead and working his way up with patience and lube until Aaron was sweating and shoving back to try for the last one—a bead nearly as big as a small fist.

"That's good," RJ said, holding Aaron's torso tight with one arm and working the fat bead in as Aaron strained. "Such a beautiful man. I can't believe how lucky I am to get to see you like this. Thank you, Mr. Danvers—*Aaron*. Thank you, baby."

He wasn't sure Aaron heard him, straining and full as he was, but he spoke the words anyway, sincere and from the depth of his soul. This was more than he'd ever deserved from a man, but damn if he wasn't going to take it. And he'd give as good as he got. He'd give Mr. Danvers anything.

"Oh!" Mr. Danvers—*Aaron*—cried, shock popping his eyes open wide just as his asshole finally surrendered and the final bead pushed in. "Ah!" he cried, shifting wildly, his hole swallowing the bead fast like it'd never been there, leaving just the sturdy cord dangling out of him to pull them free again.

"Oh, Mr. Danvers, look at that," RJ said, cooing with praise. "That's my man. That's my beautiful elf."

Aaron collapsed again, the movie soundtrack singing a cheesy song about Christmastime, and he swiveled his hips against RJ's thighs. His body shook all over, and he convulsed in short pulses. "Oh, fuck," he groaned, eyes rolling up. "It's so much. Oh, fuck." He convulsed again, his hips hitching.

RJ soothed his haunches, but the pleasure kept wracking Aaron, taking him farther and farther away on a journey of shaking bliss. He moaned and groaned, his body and cock flexing and releasing, jets of pre-come pulsing as he gripped RJ's thighs, struggled up to his knees, and straddled RJ's legs, holding onto his shoulders for dear life.

"Please," he whispered. "Spank me again. The table. Please."

RJ didn't have to be asked twice. He scooped Aaron into his arms, finding him a bit heavier than expected due to his sturdy muscles, but still easy enough to carry the few steps to the small table by the kitchen area. He laid Aaron out over it, hands gripping the opposite edge, and his cock just barely free of the hard surface, pointing down to the floor.

"That ass," RJ said softly, rubbing it again as Aaron twitched. "Mmm. Ruler or hand?" Aaron didn't answer, and RJ leaned closer, "Ruler or hand, baby?"

"Ruler."

"Hand it is," RJ said, examining the dark stripes he'd already left and deciding it would be too much for one night. Aaron was in no place to decide for himself.

"But—" Aaron tried to protest, but RJ smacked Aaron's ass hard.

"You're on my naughty list, Aaron."

He moaned and RJ swatted him until Aaron was crying and shaking on the table, rattling it against the hardwood floor. His cock was a furious red and the small puddle of pre-come was growing by the second. The scent of desperation filled the air, and RJ knew it was time.

"Ready, baby? You're going to come now. Take hold of your cock.

Make yourself come."

Aaron was delirious, but he could follow orders enough to do that. He wormed his hand down and started to squeeze and slide his cock through his fist.

RJ gripped the string holding the anal beads inside and pulled.

Aaron went still and a shout fell from his lips. Come exploded on the floor as the biggest bead shot free and the others came out in quick succession, his asshole grabbing and releasing each one as he came and came.

RJ wished he'd sheathed his cock earlier so he could shove in and come in Aaron's ass, but he hadn't. So he simply unloaded on Aaron's back, the white streaks getting into Aaron's hair, and slipping down to the table on either side of his shivering haunches.

"Mr. Danvers, you're so gorgeous," RJ moaned, working the last drops out onto Aaron's hip. "Thank you. For giving me all this."

Aaron shook hard, a combination of tears and exhaustion. RJ tugged him up, held him close, and then helped him to the shower, praising him the whole way.

Later, in bed, with his dick finally, *finally* buried into Aaron's trembling ass, he kissed Aaron's collarbones and whispered to him about the sweetness of his scent, the smooth pleasure of his skin, and the grip of his body around his cock.

Aaron didn't come again, wrung out for the night, but when RJ came in the condom, pulsing in Aaron's ass, Aaron whispered, "Thank you. I need this. More than you know." He swallowed hard and added, like a deflection, "Santa, I mean. Thank you, Santa."

"RJ. Thank me with my name."

Aaron closed his eyes, thighs trembling around RJ's torso. "Thank you, RJ."

"Merry Christmas, Aaron," RJ said, kissing his mouth. "You deserve it."

AARON WHIMPERED IN his sleep, but his arm was still heavy over RJ's chest and his leg hooked up over RJ's hip as he snuggled in closer. It figured that Mr. Danvers—fussy, sweet, adorable Mr. Danvers—was a *cuddler*.

And it figured even more that RJ loved everything about having him in his arms—his warmth, his heartbeat, his breath.

Safer than any hotel room or rented house or tour bus. More like home than anything had been since he was twelve and his father came back from wherever the fuck he'd been and tore their lives open again. But hell if he was going to tell Aaron that. The man was a jackrabbit, and he'd run.

No, he'd keep this moment for himself and store it up against the probability that in the morning Mr. Danvers—Aaron—would send him packing again with a stern lecture about not coming back.

RJ wondered what it would take for Aaron to admit he felt safe cuddled up together too. Probably more than RJ could take the time to give. He wasn't staying around for long after all. Just until the new year.

This thing with Aaron couldn't be a real relationship. Not like what Mom and Doug had with the house, kids, and golden retriever. Even that wouldn't last forever.

But this thing with Aaron could be a *thing*, couldn't it? The kind of thing worth coming home to after months on the road. The kind of thing where he got to sometimes see Aaron's eyes take on that urgent, almost-scared gleam right before he came. The kind of thing that kept him tethered to the earth.

But, in all likelihood, a *thing* wasn't what Aaron would want with him. Not that he had a clue what Aaron wanted other than a hard spanking and deep dicking. Though he'd like to find out.

Regardless, tomorrow he was supposed to meet up with Chip at the studio out in Strawberry Plains to play him a song or two and discuss making a demo together.

As of one day ago, and thanks to Aaron, RJ had a new, completed song to play for him. He stared out the windows of the bedroom at the church behind them, and farther across the rooftops in the city. Triangular-shaped Christmas trees glimmered in green, white, and red on the higher buildings and reflected in windows of the buildings all around. White flakes of snow started to fall, flecking the windowpanes and floating by on a breeze.

Aaron drooled on RJ's chest and snuffled in his sleep. Heart trembling with unexpected affection, RJ dropped a kiss on Aaron's soft hair. Tomorrow would take care of itself. Right now, he had Mr. Danvers in his arms, where he'd always wanted him. He'd cherish it.

A sweet feeling of comfort descended on him like a gift, and he closed his eyes, drifting off just as Mr. Danvers—his sweet Aaron—began to lightly snore.

Chapter Fifteen

N O ALARM WOKE him this time.

It was Constance who brought Aaron round from the deepest, most restful sleep he could remember. He cracked one eye open to find her sitting on his chest, face outrageously close to his, and a rattle in her body that would compete with an extra-strength vibrator in loudness. She kneaded the quilt he'd thrown on the bed last night after he and RJ had left the duvet cover stained with come. It was shoved into a corner, so he'd remember to wash it in the basement tonight.

"She's pretty into you," RJ said, his voice a gravelly whisper. "Should I be worried?"

Constance stared at him between slitted eyes with either adoration or loathing, Aaron could never be quite sure which.

"She wants her breakfast."

As soon as the word was out of his mouth, Constance chirruped like a furry bird, leapt from the bed, and began to stalk between the door and the bedside impatiently.

Aaron sat up and yelped. His asshole was definitely tender today, way beyond the sensitivity of even their first night together.

RJ roused more fully, sitting up too. "You okay?"

Aaron nodded and started to climb from the bed, but his legs ached. He moaned. Fuck, he felt like he'd done power yoga for five days straight and been plowed by the biggest dick in the world while in downward dog. Shit.

"Let me see," RJ whispered, running a hand down his back. "I may have hurt you."

"You're not that big," Aaron said, denying the truth.

"Get on your stomach," RJ said in that firm voice he used during sex, and which made Aaron's toes curl. Whatever resistance he had inside simply melted away. "I'm plenty big, but besides that the anal beads were a lot."

That was true enough.

Constance meowed in protest, but Aaron did as he was told, a new hard-on starting when RJ knelt between his legs and ran his fingers over the bruises from the ruler.

"Wow."

"It's okay. I like it."

"I like it too," RJ whispered. "You're going to have that on your ass for days, Mr. Danvers. How do you feel about that?"

"Good."

RJ laughed. Then he spread Aaron's butt cheeks wide, the morning sun from the windows pouring in with plenty of light to illuminate his most private place.

"That's beautiful," RJ said. "Perfect. No injury that I can see. Does it hurt inside?"

"I'm okay," Aaron insisted. "I promise."

RJ leaned down, nuzzled his ass cheeks, and pressed a kiss to his hole. "For the boo-boo."

Aaron shivered, wishing for a hint of tongue, but RJ didn't do more. Crawling out of the bed before Aaron could stand up, RJ stretched himself out, all tall and lanky, with strong muscles outlined with morning sun. "I'm going to take a piss. I'll feed Constance if you want. Where do I find her food?"

"I'll get it," Aaron said, rising from the bed with only a little wince. His thighs felt like he'd stretched them beyond endurance, which given the positions they'd screwed in, was entirely possible.

He pulled on his robe.

Constance approached with a twitchy tail, and he leapt out of the trajectory of her paw, just barely missing a swipe that would have taken off some skin. "Fine, you sweet bitch, I'm getting it."

"Should have named her Patience," RJ called from within the bathroom where the splash of urine echoed. "For irony."

Aaron scoffed but thought RJ was onto something when he scraped the second half of Constance's can of food into her bowl and she just hissed, turned her back, and walked away like he'd put actual shit in her dish.

"You liked it yesterday!" he said, staring after her. "You ate it like it was nectar of the gods. Don't you hiss at me like that."

"Your Instagram doesn't do her bitchiness justice," RJ said, walking into the kitchen wiping damp hands on his boxers. "It's all sweet sleeping in the sunshine pics and showing her pretty tummy."

"Oh, God, if she ever does that? Shows her floofy tummy? Don't fall for it. It's a trap. A floof trap."

"A floof trap?" RJ grinned, heading over to Keurig and turning it on. Aaron hated the waste of all the little disposable cups, but his mother had given the machine to him last Christmas, and he had to admit that it saved so much time in the mornings, and he wasted less coffee too.

RJ was looking through the little tree of coffee cups, smirking. "French vanilla, cinnamon bun, hazelnut, vanilla nougat…got any plain old coffee? Ah, here we go. Dark roast. Perfect."

"I have a whole case of that beneath. It came with the machine. I don't drink it."

"Write my name on it, then," RJ said. "I'll be glad to drink it for you." He met Aaron's eyes hopefully. "I'd like some more mornings waking up here with you."

Aaron looked away. Truth be told, he'd like that too, but that was a lot to ask. Too much of *everything* was wrapped up in agreeing to something like that. His mom, his job, his family out on the farm, and RJ was leaving anyway. He'd go back on tour. No reason for Aaron to let his body or mind or stupid heart want anything more than another fuck.

Because he did want that. At least one more fuck.

More like ten.

"How long are you in town for?" he asked, crouching down to pull the dark roast box of Keurig cups out and broaching the easiest concern first. May as well set clear expectations now.

"Until the new year."

"Consider this your box until then." Aaron's tummy fluttered. Was he making a mistake? He thought he probably had, until he caught RJ's expression: vibrant, alive, intense. RJ came at him then, wrapping him up against his tall, firm body, holding him tight.

"Thank you," RJ whispered.

"You don't have to keep doing that," Aaron said.

"What?"

"Thanking me for everything."

RJ pulled back, touched Aaron's chin gently, and forced their eyes to meet. "Babe, I'll thank you every time you give me something, because you deserve that gratitude. And as long as we're doing this, whatever *this* is, I'm gonna give you what you deserve. It's part of my honor code."

Aaron swallowed, his dick stirring. "Oh yeah?"

"Yeah."

The sound of the Keurig filling the mug behind them broke the spell, and RJ let him go, gathering the mug of dark roast between his big palms and taking a closed-eyed sip.

"Ah. Perfect," he said again. He leaned his hip against the counter and chuckled when Constance walked back into the room, went to her food dish and started to eat with a little chirrup of joy, like she hadn't just disdained that meal a few minutes before. "She's something else."

"What are your plans today?" Aaron asked, a wad of weird feelings balling up in his gut. He didn't know what he wanted RJ to say, but he wanted to know as soon as possible so he could get on with his own plans. He'd need a distraction if RJ wasn't sticking around, lest he fall into a pit of post-sex shame and post-fight-with-his-mom stressing.

Aaron supposed he could take his father up on his recent request for a visit. That would take up most of his day and would keep him out of his mother's crosshairs, since cell reception wasn't great on the farm. He wondered what RJ might think of the Danvers Farm. It was a pretty piece of land...

"I have a show tonight. Before that..." RJ shrugged. "I need to go into my friend Chip's recording studio and talk to him about a demo I want to make. How about you?"

Aaron was glad he had a ready answer. "I was going to head out to Strawberry Plains to visit my father. He mentioned some sort of gift he wanted to give to me before Christmas, so I thought I'd go see what it is." Disappointment welled up. He hadn't realized how much he'd wanted RJ to stick around for the day, or that he'd planned to ask RJ to come out to his dad's farm with him. Or that he'd wanted RJ to say yes.

"Chip's studio's in Strawberry Plains," RJ said, surprised delight coloring his tone. "Weird, huh? There's not much out that way, but we both planned to go there today." He raised his coffee in a toast and winked. "It's almost like the universe is setting us up."

Aaron raised his brow. "Meaning?"

"How about this..." RJ paused, took another swallow of coffee, and motioned at the coffee cup tree. "What do you like? Cinnamon bun?"

Aaron felt a rush of pleasure. "Actually, that's my favorite."

"I knew it." RJ winked. "Okay, so how about this..." He started the Keurig for Aaron's mug. "We go out that way together. I've got this cushy SUV I've been forced to borrow—long story—and so I might as well use it."

"Oh. Well."

Yes, a part of Aaron had wanted to ask RJ to go out to the Danvers Farm with him. But now that it could actually happen? His gut twisted up with anxiety.

He'd never taken a man out to his father's place before. All or some of the cousins might be around. He'd never explicitly told any of them that he was gay. Not even his dad. Though, Aaron assumed his dad knew. He was sure that his mother had thrown it in his dad's face during one of their incredibly rare and always toxic interactions.

Taking a man out there seemed risky. Especially when it was a man he was just fucking and not in love with. They were country folk, after all. Loving, but traditional for the most part. Casual hookups were not part of their ideal for love of any kind, much less homosexual love.

The Keurig kicked off again.

Aaron took the mug from RJ's hands, taking a deep sniff of the cinnamon bun scent, suddenly unsure if he needed the extra jitteriness of caffeine. "So, what? You'd drop me off at the farm and then pick me up on the way back?"

"I could. Or you could come to the studio with me. It won't take long for me and Chip to figure out what we want to do, or if he's even up for working with me right now given that I'm about three songs short of a four-song demo."

"I've never been inside a recording studio."

"It's small, but good quality. You should come. Chip will like you."

Aaron gulped. "I don't know. I'm not really...out."

RJ tilted his head. "Because you're a teacher."

"That. And a few other things." His mother's reaction at the dance the night before, for example.

"Okay. That's fine. I'll just say you're my friend. No big." RJ shrugged. He glanced up, his hazel eyes raking over Aaron. "I mean, we are friends, right?" He lifted his chin and said more definitively, "We're not just fucking anymore."

"Aren't we? Just fucking?" Aaron's heart started to pound, and he put the coffee cup aside on the counter. He definitely didn't need the extra stimulant right now.

RJ shook his head, slipping into that relaxed certainty he used while they were screwing. "No, babe. We passed 'just fucking' when you started texting me about your day, and then when you slept wrapped around me like a boa constrictor last night. We're definitely in the friends-with-benefits category now, leaning toward outright holiday lovers." RJ grinned, taking in Aaron's body, top to bottom again.

"Oh, shit."

RJ laughed. "Sorry. But it's true." When he caught the expression on Aaron's face, he reassured him, "But don't worry. We're not boyfriends. We're definitely not that."

"Holiday lovers?" Aaron kind of liked the sound of that. The men in the documentaries he'd watched about queer culture of the nineteen seventies and eighties all called each other that: lover. It was so much better, he'd always thought, than boyfriend or partner. He'd always wanted to be someone's lover. It sounded sexy, romantic, and fleeting.

Fleeting.

Well, okay. He could get behind fleeting.

"Lovers," he agreed. "We're lovers."

RJ grinned. "Cool. So we'll go out to Straw Plains together, then? No sense in taking two cars. I mean, really, think of the environment."

Aaron smothered a grin. "You don't have to convince me. I'm in."

RJ swooped over and wrapped his arms around Aaron, his coffee sloshing on Aaron's bare arm, still hot but not scalding. "Great. I just need to grab my guitar from my mom's, and we can get on our way."

"Your mom's?" Aaron blinked. Never mind whether RJ was ready to meet his family, was he ready to meet RJ's?

"Breathe. She's just my mom. And we're just friends, remember?"

"Lovers," Aaron insisted, tasting the word.

"Right." RJ grinned a little soppily. Aaron's inner alarms went off at that, but he silenced them, reveling in the way RJ looked at him like he was precious. "But I get the impression you're not ready to tell people about that part?"

"Oh, no. Right."

"My mom will guess, but she won't say anything. I'll just dash in and get the guitar and then we'll go."

"Can I wait in the SUV?"

"Probably not."

"Are you sure?"

"Eh, maybe I want you to meet my little siblings." RJ laughed. "Since we're lovers and all."

Aaron chewed on his bottom lip. He liked older kids, but he was intimidated by little ones. "We should shower."

"If that's a euphemism, I'm all for it."

Aaron laughed, tugging out of RJ's embrace. "C'mon. Let's get cleaned up."

"I'm gonna get you so dirty first," RJ said. "You're still on my naughty list, you know."

"I hope so," Aaron said, his cock lifting and growing achingly hard in seconds. "Santa needs to show me again how he deals with bad elves."

RJ tugged Aaron toward the bathroom. By the time they left, they'd both come two more times, and their balls were aching and utterly drained.

Chapter Sixteen

AARON WAS RELIEVED when they pulled into RJ's mom's neighborhood to find that it was far outside of his school zone. When RJ dropped the fact that he had three younger siblings, Aaron had lost several minutes entertaining awful fantasies of having to teach them one day. He'd nearly broken out in a cold sweat thinking of looking a young student in the face while knowing he'd done filthy, dirty, amazing things with their older brother. School was for teaching, and hookups and school never mixed. He'd learned that lesson well.

But West Knoxville was firmly outside of his territory. He was safe.

As RJ parked on the pad in front of his mom's house, with the front yard a veritable explosion of Christmas decorations, he let out a low groan.

"What?" Aaron asked, glancing around to see if he was missing something.

"This is the first time I've brought a guy home."

"Oh? Why?"

"Well, my relationships have generally been with other musicians on the road, or people in the music business anyway. Not only short lived, but also not here. Besides, my last boyfriend was a bit of a drug fiend, and I wouldn't have wanted an active user around my family." He shrugged at that, and Aaron made a note to ask more about this ex later.

"And before I went out on the road... Well, I was always out to my mom. She always knew. But this isn't how I grew up." He motioned at the house. "I didn't live in a house. It was just me and my mom. Or more like, it was just me." He frowned and ran a hand over his hair. "Times got rough. For six months we lived in a van. Various run-down apartments. Rooms in strange houses. Trailers. We moved around a lot. Living in a hotel room when I started touring was nothing new. More like old times."

"She couldn't find work?" Aaron ventured, looking up at the nice, middle-class home in front of them.

"More like she had two jobs and a bunch of debt to settle. My dad left it behind as a going away present." Disgust filled his voice at the mention of his father and didn't drop away with this next words. "How can I put this? Okay, so, it was like this: when I was fifteen, I basically lived with a forty-year-old guy for a few months. I told no one. Not even my friends. I'm not sure they know about it even now. But I had a warm bed most nights so long as I sucked his cock, and he gave me plenty of food. My mom was gone so much that she didn't even realize I wasn't living at home."

"I…I'm sorry. You were too young to deal with something like that alone."

"Yeah. Well, I wasn't in love, and I didn't imagine he was either." RJ sneered. "He was using me, but I was using him too."

"You were still just a child."

"I was," RJ agreed. "That part of my life sort of prepared me for this part, though. Living on the road, going from hotel to hotel. Back when I started touring it felt like nothing new. We'd lived in so many dumps growing up that most places the bands stayed felt like heaven." His eyes went dark, like he was seeing something from years before. "My senior year, when I was a student in your class—"

"Oh, God. Were you with that man when you were in my class?" Had Aaron failed to protect RJ when he was his student, writing him off as a scary, potentially dangerous kid instead?

"No," RJ said, putting a soothing hand on Aaron's shoulder. "Like I said, I was nineteen when I was in your class. I was only fucking that guy for a year."

"When you were a *freshman*?"

RJ nodded. "When I *was* in your class, my mom finally got a little stability. We were living in a two-bedroom mobile home then. But one whole bedroom was filled with unpacked boxes because my mom was sure there was no way she could afford it long enough to bother unpacking. I slept on the sofa. That was one of my best years growing up."

"Oh." Aaron looked up at the big house. "So, did you buy this place for your mom and your siblings? With your touring income?"

RJ laughed. "Hell no. I do okay, but I'm not *that* well off. No, my mom married the kids' dad. He's a doctor. They met at a mutual friend's birthday party. She got knocked up. They got married. I like him fine, but it's weird. A whole different world from how I grew up."

"I can only imagine." Aaron's heart ached. He'd failed RJ so much back then, and he knew there was no making up for that now.

"Anyway, yeah." RJ gestured ruefully at the house. "This is where I'm staying for the time being. It's not really my home."

RJ unbuckled his seatbelt.

"I'll just wait here," Aaron said, but two little kids spilled out of the house, running for the parked SUV. "Oh, God."

"They won't bite," RJ said, laughing. "C'mon. It's not that bad. They're just kids."

He opened the door and the little voices rose in a clamor of excitement, both of them shouting, "RJ!" and variations of, "Where were you? Are you staying? Please stay!"

Then a lovely woman appeared at the front door. She was tall, like RJ, and long-limbed like him. Her blond hair was held back in a messy ponytail, and she looked harried despite her attractive face. She crossed her arms over her chest, shook her head, and rolled her eyes.

"At least you texted this time," she called out. Her eyes caught Aaron's where he sat frozen in the car. "Oh. You brought someone home?"

She grew flustered, and then smiled nervously. "I, uh, hello. Welcome."

Aaron climbed out of the car and waved awkwardly. "Hi, I'm Aaron, Mrs…" He didn't know how to end that greeting. RJ hadn't said if his mother shared his last name now that she'd remarried. His own mother had never changed hers.

"Just call me Betsy," she said, smiling widely, her gaze darting from him to RJ and back again. "Come on in, both of you."

"We're just here to grab my guitar and go. I'm meeting Chip at the studio to talk about that demo."

"Oh, right. Of course. Well, you can stay a few minutes, surely. I'll make coffee. The kids saved you those cookies you asked for." She shot Aaron an anxious glance. "You can share them with your…friend."

Lover, Aaron corrected in his head, surprised by the fierceness of his attachment to the term.

Loud rap music played loudly from upstairs, but Aaron didn't recognize it. Betsy ushered him into the kitchen. RJ followed at his heels, one hand on his lower back, reassuringly. The kids ran in past them, the boy making a helicopter noise with his mouth, and the girl yelling, "I'll get the cookies, RJ! We saved four for you." She gave Aaron a skeptical look. "I guess you can split them with your friend."

"That's Perri," RJ said. "And the other one is Beau."

"Ah. I thought you said you had three?" RJ had mentioned that tidbit on the way over.

"I have a stepbrother." He pointed up at the ceiling where the beat of the rap music pounded. "I doubt we'll see him."

"He's in a mood," Betsy said. "I never know what to expect from him these days. When Doug and I married, he was a cherub. Now?" She shrugged. "He's a teenager. I suppose it's to be expected."

"Hormones," Aaron offered. "They make a moody monster of them all. I teach middle schoolers, so I know."

She laughed. "Great. So happy I'll be dealing with it two more times. I'd hoped RJ and my stepson were outliers."

Betsy put Aaron in a chair by the window facing a lovely winter garden. It was well-tended, and he enjoyed the choices that kept the colors popping even during the dreary month of December.

He chatted with Betsy about the garden (it turned out it was maintained by her husband, who was at work). He kept everything relaxed and easy, hoping to erase the occasional speculative look sent his way.

Yes, I let your son fuck me blind last night, Betsy. And, no I don't regret it.

Thankfully, it wasn't long at all until RJ returned from upstairs with his guitar case slung over his back.

"Don't go again, RJ!" Beau called, running to cling to big brother's leg. "You said you'd stay for Christmas! You said!"

RJ ruffled his brother's hair and then squatted to meet his eyes. "I'll be here for Christmas. I'd never break that promise. I'm just going out for the day, that's all."

"But you were gone last night, and you just got home, and we *miss you*," Perri said, coming to RJ's other side and wrapping her arms around his opposite leg.

"I know. I miss you too. But I might not be home again tonight," he met his mother's eye and she lifted a brow but didn't seem actually annoyed. "It depends on how my show goes."

Aaron tried not to squirm with embarrassment. Was RJ's mother now imagining the reasons why RJ wouldn't be home? And RJ doing those things with Aaron? Because *he* was. Fuck. Why did RJ have to be so sexy? Even with two kids clinging to his legs?

RJ went on. "But I'm still here in town, and I'm going to be right here at home for Christmas Day. Got it?"

"Yeah." But neither kid seemed happy, and both shot Aaron suspicious glances like it might be his fault. So much for making a good impression on his lover's siblings. Good thing this wasn't going to last more than a few weeks, tops.

Oh God, had he already decided on letting it go on for a few weeks?

That seemed risky as hell. But could he really give it up any sooner? He didn't think so. Or maybe he just didn't want to.

Lauren would have something to say about that. Maybe she'd be able to talk sense into him. In the meantime, he was going to enjoy this like an elf enjoyed Christmas: feverishly and ready to crash when it was over.

Betsy packaged up the cookies and sent them off with a thermos of coffee. She grabbed them both in firm but awkward hugs on their way out the door.

"Good luck with Chip, hon," she said. "I believe in you."

"I know, Mom."

"I believe in Santa Claus," Beau said from behind his mom's knee.

"So does Aaron," RJ said with a shit-eating grin. "He's on Santa's naughty list."

"Oh RJ," his mother said, rolling her eyes and turning away.

"I'm sorry, Aaron," Beau said, seriously. "I hope you don't get coal in your stocking." His brows rucked with worry.

"It's okay. I love coal," Aaron called out, opening the door to the SUV and preparing to climb inside. "Under pressure, it turns to diamonds."

RJ squeezed his hand before starting the motor, and Aaron waved at the kids as they backed down the drive.

Chapter Seventeen

"LET'S HEAR IT," Chip said, sitting back in the control room of his small studio in the middle of a nineteen-seventies strip mall. He gestured at RJ and his guitar. "I wanna know what we're working with here."

Aaron stood behind Chip, both of them visible through the plexiglass separating the small recording booth from the control room. Chip was a robust, furry guy of somewhere between twenty-eight and thirty-nine. It was hard to tell for sure since he was covered in a beard and a beer belly. But he was a nice guy and had always treated RJ well, even when the Old Skool Millennials were still playing back in high school, and he'd offered ages ago to help RJ with a new demo.

"Gonna puss out on me now?" Chip said, laughing. "C'mon, RJ. Hit me."

RJ licked his lips nervously. He hadn't thought this part through when he'd asked Aaron along. Was he ready to sing the song he'd written just the other day in front of the man who'd inspired it? Christ, he had balls. He knew that. But did he have balls this big? He was about to find out.

RJ cleared his throat, got more comfortable on the creaky stool set up in front of the mic, and started to strum. He let it rise in him, the lyrics starting out quiet and unsure, and then picking up power as he got to the bridge. He crested with the chorus and dropped back into a verse with ease. He opened his eyes, his gaze landing first on Aaron, and he let himself smile, allowing himself to project the song lyrics at the man himself.

Aaron swallowed visibly, broke eye contact, and stepped back into a shadow behind Chip, arms crossed protectively over his middle. RJ sang on. He had no choice. No matter what Aaron thought, he was halfway through this thing now, and he had to see it out.

When it was over, Chip whistled. "Got more like that?"

"A couple," he lied.

"Okay. We'll book it for next week. I kept those days blank on my schedule 'cause I thought I'd spend that time with Anna, considering she's done with classes and all, but she's a bitch so..." He shrugged.

RJ cocked his head. "There's a story there."

"Fine. *I'm* the asshole. But whatever. My girl's spending the holidays with her mama in Tampa, so it doesn't matter anymore. I'll book you in."

"I can pay for the hours. Your usual rate."

"Good for you. Because I'm not giving you a friend's discount."

"Fair enough."

Chip rose and stretched, his beer belly popping out from beneath his vintage Metallica T-shirt. "If it all goes well, you should have something good for your agent to hand around. Who knows? Maybe next year you'll be a rising star on the alt-rock scene."

RJ huffed a laugh. "I just want to make something of my own. Screw the rest of it."

"If only that was how it worked, bub."

"There's always Spotify," RJ said, mentioning Casey's idea from the rehearsal the night before. His friend had mentioned the streaming service, pointing out how times had changed since the last time RJ had tried his hand at making his own music.

"It's like self-publishing Joel's horror books," Casey had said. "You don't have to get anyone's permission to make music now."

Casey was right. RJ had other options aside from the traditional route.

"Sure, sure. It's a new world of opportunities to make pennies," Chip said sarcastically.

Aaron still lingered in the darkness of the corner, one arm hanging low, the other crossed over his waist. He didn't meet RJ's eyes even when he came into the control room and made further plans. He also walked a few steps behind RJ and Chip when they all went back out to the lobby to say their goodbyes for now.

Aaron was dressed sweetly casual today in soft, faded blue jeans, a long-sleeved, green Henley shirt, a loose, forest green jacket, and a pair of black, high top converse. His ass was still magnificent, but RJ also knew it still hurt. He'd practically winced when he sat down on the folding chair in the control room before leaping up to stand again, and then skedaddling to hide in the shadows behind Chip.

Was it RJ's voice that had scared him? His lyrics? What had pushed Aaron to want to disappear? RJ supposed he'd have to wait until they were in the car to find out.

Grabbing his own jacket from the coat rack by the door and slinging his guitar over his shoulder, he shook Chip's hand and watched as Aaron did the same. Then they were in the blacktop parking lot, approaching the shining, stupidly big SUV together.

Aaron suddenly reached out and took hold of RJ's hand and twined their fingers together. RJ almost asked why, but he bit the question back and didn't mention that Chip could surely see them from the windows of the lobby. He just gripped Aaron's fingers in return until they got to the car. Then he used his fob to unlock Aaron's side and let him in first.

When their hands broke apart, Aaron smiled at him.

"It was a good song," Aaron finally said once RJ had climbed in behind the steering wheel. "Was it…. Am I overthinking it or is it about…" He blushed. "Never mind."

"It was about you and that magical ass, Mr. Danvers."

"Really?" He blushed even more, dimples blossoming, and RJ's heart clenched at the sweetness of it. "I thought so, but that seemed egotistical.

I second-guessed myself."

"You should be proud. It's the first song I've written in over a year. The well was dry. Then I got to unwrap that sweet butt of yours, and suddenly I'm chock full of inspiration."

Aaron chuckled. "Well, as my kids at school say, don't get all extra about it." His blush extended down up to his hairline now, and his dimples kept popping. "But, still, I've never had a song written about me before."

"I admit, when you went to go hide in the corner of the studio, I was surprised." RJ played up his ego rather than reveal how vulnerable he'd felt. "I expected a full-on swoon when you heard it."

Aaron shook his head. "I don't swoon. I just got really embarrassingly hard watching you play, and I had to hide myself so Chip didn't see it. I didn't even know that was a thing that could happen."

RJ whooped, laughter shaking him as he pulled out onto the highway toward the address Aaron had plugged into his GPS earlier. He didn't know what to expect for the rest of the afternoon, but he was excited to go meet Aaron's dad.

RJ wondered how Aaron planned to introduce him. He knew it was too much to hope he'd introduce him as his holiday lover. But a guy could dream.

AS THEY DROVE deeper into the countryside, heading toward the gray Holston River and the winter-brown farmland that ran along it, Aaron finally spoke again. "This is all Danvers family land now. Starting about here. It used to go out even farther, but a lot of it was sold to pay my grandfather's estate taxes, and then to provide the monetary inheritance for us kids that didn't want to take a house out this way."

"Take a house?"

"Yeah, there are houses all over the property. Some old, like from the eighteen hundreds, and some newer. The cousins who stayed all took one. It's the way it's been for generations now. I wasn't the only one who left." Aaron shrugged. "Though that wasn't really my choice."

"Oh?"

"The divorce. My mom got custody."

"Why's that?"

Doug was divorced from his first wife (who claimed that was all Betsy's fault, but RJ stayed out of that discussion; he didn't want to know), but Carter spent one week a month at his mom's, and three with Doug and Mom. Mainly because Carter's mom's job required a lot of travel. But RJ knew it was unusual for parents not to get fifty-fifty custody anymore. Of course, when he and Aaron had been kids times were different. Heck, times were always different.

"Mom moved into Knoxville proper, became a teacher first, and then a principal. She insisted I attend her school. My dad couldn't easily get me into Knoxville and back every day for classes, not from all the way out here anyway, and especially not with his farm duties. Plus, my mom was...the mom." His voice took on a flatter note. "The judge agreed with her that I needed consistency with my schooling. So, that was that."

"Ah. And your grandfather died when you were a kid?"

"No. I was grown. And when he died, I could have taken land out here, but I didn't." Aaron gestured toward the green rolling fields. "Don't get me wrong. I love it, but being a farmer isn't for me. And you can't live out here on the family farm and not participate in some way. It's just not done."

"Interesting."

"Yeah, all of my cousins chip in. Plow fields, sow and pick crops, or they deal with cattle, pigs, horses, and goats. Gather eggs from the free-range chickens. Mend fences. Read up on the latest and greatest family farming techniques. None of that is really of interest to me. I've never been into getting dirt on my hands."

"Prissy."

"Tidy." He nudged RJ with an elbow. "Also, my job's in town. I don't want to drive all that way every day either, so I can't blame my dad for not wanting to do it back when I was a kid."

"Yeah."

There was more to the story of the divorce, RJ could tell. But that kind of personal information was always a tender thing. RJ didn't push.

Speaking of tender.

"How's that sweet ass feeling?" RJ asked. The roads out this way were rough at times and Aaron was holding himself a little stiffly.

"Bruised. But I'm fine." He smiled shyly at RJ. "Don't worry about me."

"I'll worry about you, and I'll thank you, and I'll spank you all I damn well want. You can't stop me, Mr. Danvers."

"I don't want to stop you."

RJ reached out and took Aaron's hand again, feeling the rightness of the slim fingers fitting between his own. It was like a shock of joy to the heart, and he didn't want to let go. But at the next curve, he needed both hands on the wheel, so he did.

"This driveway, up ahead," Aaron said quietly. "This is my dad's place."

The bare, brown trees rolled past them as they approached, and then suddenly dropped away, opening up a vista of brown and light green rolling hills, several barns to the left, a farmhouse up ahead, and the sparkling river delineating a boundary behind it all.

"Wow."

"Yeah. My dad got one of the best pieces, but that was way back before Papaw died. Uncle Jokey got another good strip by the river." He indicated with his thumb. "That way."

"Uncle Jokey?"

Aaron flushed a little. "My family's got a thing for nicknames. I guess I should tell you now. My dad's name is Rutger, but they call him

Rutty. I'm Cracker."

"Cracker? Like the insult?"

Aaron laughed. "No, like a saltine. I ate a whole sleeve of them in my bed when I was a kid and then cried because the crumbs were all itchy and I couldn't sleep that night. I've been Cracker to my family out this way ever since."

"Makes my mom's 'hon' seem completely tolerable."

Aaron snorted gently. "Yeah. Well, here, pull up by the barns. Watch for the goats."

The farmhouse was beautiful. Freshly painted white with black shutters, and fresh, green wreaths with red bows hung over each window. The front door was graced by a thick, woven, pine garland also punctuated with several bright red bows. Festive. Pretty. RJ wondered if Aaron's father had picked them out.

"Cracker!" Aaron's father was a tall man, broad in the shoulders, with a face that had clearly seen a lot of sun over the years. RJ estimated that he was probably only in his mid-fifties, but on first glance he came across as older given his cotton-white hair and sun-deep wrinkles.

He strode down from the wraparound porch at the house, wearing actual cowboy boots and a plaid shirt tucked into jeans, all strapped into place with a belt buckle the size of Texas.

"Cracker, who've you brought with you?" he asked with a wide smile. "Hi, I'm Rutty."

Aaron groaned almost sub-audibly, but RJ heard it anyway, attuned as he seemed to be to all of Aaron's noises. "This is RJ Blitz, Dad. My...friend."

Rutger Danvers registered that slight hesitation all right. His smile sharpened and his eyes dug into RJ with an intensity beyond curiosity. It wasn't hateful at all. RJ had seen hateful, was familiar with its gleam, and this wasn't it. But it was definitely protective, and RJ could respect Rutger for that. This man loved Aaron, and why shouldn't he? Aaron was his son, plus Aaron was utterly amazing.

Oh crap.

He wasn't falling for Aaron was he? The last time he'd thought any-one was amazing was his ex, lead singer of Pearl Necklace, stage name: Pan Soldier. After they'd been fucking for a few days, RJ had looked over at him, sprawled out boneless and submissive on the bed, and felt that awful squish of affection in his chest. Helplessly, he'd thought, "This guy's amazing. This guy's worth the fall." How wrong he'd been.

But Aaron was nothing like Pan. Obviously. And aside from being in the closet, and running a little hot and cold, and really not being the kind of person RJ should ever start a relationship with for so many reasons (but especially because RJ couldn't stay and be a domestic partner to a *teacher*, for fuck's sake)…Aaron *was* amazing.

So Papa Danvers was right to be worried for him. RJ was a dick who had only come into his son's life to fuck him silly for a few breathless weeks and then hit the road.

So, yeah, glare at me, stare me down, Rutty. Fair's fair.

"Good to meet you, sir." RJ put out his hand and they shook. Again, Rutty seemed to be testing RJ out in some way, but he didn't hold his hand longer than any other man would.

"Nice manners. You a country boy?"

"Knoxville proper, actually. Through and through."

"Too bad. Not that Knoxville's a terrible place to be from. There's just something about a country boy that you know you can trust."

"Dad…" Aaron hissed in warning.

Rutty grinned. "You boys want some coffee before we head out to the barn to see that thing I found for ya, Aaron?"

Aaron shook his head. "We had plenty of coffee in the car, actually. RJ's mom sent some along this morning."

"In fact," RJ said, with an embarrassed chuckle. "Speaking of all that coffee, is there a restroom I could use?"

"Heck yeah. Come on inside."

Following Rutty into the hallway of the farmhouse, RJ blinked in amazement. It was set up beautifully with old, burnished wood floors and wood-burning stoves in every room. Rutty led them toward the kitchen, which boasted glossy, brick floors and wide windows that looked out on the river. It was from there that RJ was pointed toward the bathroom down a back hallway.

The entire house was tidy, and so was the bathroom. RJ wasn't sure what he'd expected from a solitary farmer, but it wasn't this. Quickly, RJ did his business and washed up. As he stepped back out into the short hall that led to the kitchen, he heard Rutty's deep voice. "He's a handsome one, Cracker. So you're sleeping with him?"

Aaron squawked and a crashing noise followed.

"Now don't go droppin' the plates. I asked you to help me put them away, not break them." Then Rutty laughed gently. "Look, son, I've known you were gay since you were a young'un. Just because you never saw fit to come out and tell me directly to my face doesn't mean I didn't know."

"Dad, I…I'm sorry. I should have told you."

"Yeah, you should have."

Aaron voice shook slightly. "I wasn't sure how you'd take it and—"

"I don't give a shit. That's how I take it. You're my son and I love you."

Aaron grunted oddly, and RJ held back, waiting a minute before striding out into the kitchen. Aaron was in his dad's arms, accepting a giant, warm hug. They broke apart as RJ came in. "Nice wallpaper," RJ said, gesturing with his thumb back the way he'd come. "In the bathroom, I mean. Floral. Pretty."

"My mother chose it in the nineteen forties. It's aged well. So've the rest of her choices."

Aaron went back to putting the plates from the drying rack into a cupboard, and Rutty gripped him by the neck and shook him gently. "Never mind that now. I'll get it later. Let's head out to the barn. Candace found something of your gran's in the basement out in that old house she and her husband are wanting to fix up. They want to use it as some Airbnb or somethin'. Anyway, she said you could have it. We both figured you'd want it for sure."

"Well, put an end to the suspense. Tell me what it is."

"Nah, let's go have a look." His dad grinned. "It's best when you see it."

As they sauntered out toward the barn, goats and dogs milled around the yard, playing together. In the fields leading down to the river, there were cows huffing in the chilling air, and everywhere RJ looked there were chickens squawking, scratching, and pecking around.

"This is a working farm, sir?" RJ asked, keeping his best foot forward, using all the Southern manners his mama had instilled in him long ago.

"For over a hundred and fifty years," Rutty said. "Been a Danvers farm from the start. Used to pass down just to the boys, but the girls get included now, if'n they want. They don't all want." He nodded at Aaron. "Even the boys have better things to do these days than plow and feed cows." He winked at his son. "That's not to say I'm not real proud of my teacher here, because I am."

Aaron winked back at his dad but didn't say anything.

Rutty turned his speculative gaze on RJ again. "What do you do, son?"

"I'm a guitarist. I tour with bands. Play music." RJ smiled. "It's a lot less admirable than shaping young minds or working on a farm, but I love it."

"So long as you love a thing, you should do it," Rutty said, nodding firmly. "It's the only way to live."

They'd reached the barn then and Rutty beckoned them inside. The scent of hay, horseflesh, and manure was familiar from a summer RJ had spent mucking stalls at a local riding school for extra cash as a teen. A horse stamped its feet in a stall nearby and Rutty called out, "I'll let you out soon. Have some patience, darlin', the vet says you have to take it easy a few more days." He grabbed a handful of what looked like a combination of raisins and some kind of oats and fed it to the horse out of his palm.

"Can I pet him?" RJ asked.

"This is Iris, and she's a lady. But you can certainly pet her," Rutty said.

RJ stepped forward and ran his hand over the horse's neck. She turned to gaze at him with big eyes, but then went back to nuzzling Rutty. RJ patted her some more, enjoying the texture of her hair.

Rutty gestured toward a stall with the door open. "It's in there. Go on. Have a look."

"Better not be a pony, Dad," Aaron teased. "I'm past wanting one of those."

Rutty laughed and continued to pet the horse in front of him. "Nah. It's something better."

Aaron stopped dead outside the stall and stared with his mouth open. "No way! Where'd you say this was?"

"Candace's basement, believe it or not. It's held up well, hasn't it?"

Aaron whistled. "You can say that again. It's gorgeous. Just like I remember."

RJ abandoned the horse to go see what had made Aaron's eyes go wide as saucers. It turned out to be a six-foot-tall, silver aluminum Christmas tree. It looked vintage, not like the new ones he'd seen in Costco. He knew the silver style had come back into fashion, if his shopping excursions with his mother the week before were any indication of current fake Christmas tree fads.

"This was my Grandma's," Aaron said, noticing that RJ had crept up next to him. "Her Sapphire Regal, she always called it. Every year she used to put it up, and then she'd tell me, 'The others can have their Douglas firs and Scotch pines, I'll have my Sapphire Regal.' She loved how it glittered with the colored lights on it."

"Couldn't find the box for it. It was put together like that beneath a couple of blankets," Rutty said. "Truly shocked it's still so nice. Good thing that basement's always been dry as a bone and rodent free. Thought you'd want it."

"I…well, I guess I do." Aaron sounded surprised by the fact.

"We found some of her old ornaments too. That box there in the corner of the stall. Candace kept some for herself, and I took the one I liked best when I was a boy. Left the rest for you. Don't tell the other cousins. By the time they all chose out what they wanted, you'd end up getting nothing but half of a bulb to share with one of Blinker's boys."

Aaron snorted. "I'll keep my trap shut. Besides, they all have plenty of Grandma's things."

"That's God's honest truth."

RJ watched Aaron carefully as he drew closer to the silver, glittering tree. His smile softened, and he touched it carefully. "I'm not sure how to get it home, though."

"It'll fit in the back of the SUV," RJ offered. "We'll just lay the seats down, wrap it up in those blankets again, and it'll make it just fine."

Aaron grinned. "Isn't that convenient? That I'm out here with you, and you're borrowing that SUV, and this will just happen to fit? I think you might be onto something when you said the universe was setting us up."

"If that's the case, I'll get my suit out and start prepping for a wedding," Rutty said with a laugh. "Ain't no use fighting the universe…or as we call it out in these parts: God."

"Never mind my dad. Christianity's in the water here."

"I'm a Christian," RJ said, shoving his hands into his pockets and rocking back on his heels.

"You are?"

"Sure." RJ shrugged. He never went to church, and half the folks he knew from the church his mom had attended when he was little would turn their back on him for a million reasons, but he still believed. For one thing, he liked believing, for another…well, it just felt right.

"Okay," Aaron said. "I'm…uh, not exactly not-a-Christian."

"Undecided then." RJ smiled. "Keeping your mind open. I like it."

Aaron smiled and nearly rolled his eyes, but then he said, "Yeah, Dad. I want to take it home." Then he winced. "Oh, hell. Constance is going to wreck it."

"We'll figure something out," RJ said. "And maybe she won't mess with it. Like, as a gift to you. A kindness."

"Constance isn't kind," Aaron said, contemplating the tree with one hip cocked, his lips twisting up worriedly.

RJ pulled his phone from his pocket and quickly googled: *how to keep cats away from a Christmas tree?* He held out the phone to Aaron. "Look, babe, there are like twenty sites that give suggestions. This one says to put orange peels under the tree skirt because cats hate the smell of oranges." He paused. "Do you think that's why they used to hang oranges on the trees back in the old days? So Victorian cats stayed away?"

Then he clicked another site. "This one says you can spritz watered-down lemon juice around it to the same effect. Not sure how that might affect the aluminum, though."

RJ looked up from his phone to see Rutty examining him closely, a warm expression on his face. "Listen to your boyfriend, son. He's got it covered."

Aaron coughed and blushed. "He's not my—"

"Lover," RJ corrected. "We're not using boyfriend. We're going with lover."

Rutty hooted and laughed until his eyes started to water.

"What?" Aaron said, his entire face going red. "What's funny?"

"Oh, law. Just thinking about Christmas Eve and introducing this handsome man to the family as your *lover*."

Aaron looked at his dad like he'd gone mad. "First, no way you're doing anything like that. Second, he's not going to be here on Christmas Eve."

RJ felt oddly hurt by that comment, but he couldn't say just why. They'd fucked for a few nights, were clearly going to continue fucking for however long his break from touring lasted, but being invited to family holidays was a big deal, like a real commitment kind of deal, and—

Rutty interrupted RJ's thoughts by saying, "He sure as hell is! You've finally brought a boy home and he's going to be treated just like everyone else's, ah, errr...*lover*—" He cut up laughing again, but after a few guffaws got it back together enough to wheeze, "I'm going to make sure of it." He turned to RJ, still wiping at his eyes. "Supper's at five thirty. Don't worry about bringing presents. But a bottle of whiskey's always good. Maker's Mark is my favorite."

"Dad, that's not—" Aaron started, but Rutty turned and walked from the barn, shaking his head and raising his hand to the sky.

"I won't hear it, Cracker. He'll be here."

RJ stared after Aaron's bear of a father in shock and then he started laughing too. "Lover," he said, and sputtered.

"What were you thinking telling him that?" Aaron fussed.

RJ giggled. "He's going to introduce me to your aunts, uncles, and cousins as your *lover*."

"Well, he's not, actually, because you aren't coming." Aaron crossed his arms over his chest and gazed at the shining square of light illuminating the way out to the barnyard. A goat ambled in and bleated, kicking his feet up and down, before finding a little pile of hay and chowing down.

"What if I want to come?" RJ said a little petulantly. "I've never been to a big family shindig before. My family was just me and my mom growing up."

"But now it's you and your mom, and the kids, and your stepdad, and other people surely?" Aaron turned to him, confusion sliding around his face.

"I don't know what it'll be like. I've never spent Christmas with them since they married." RJ ran a hand through his hair. "I haven't really wanted to."

"You promised your brother and sister—"

"That I'd be there on Christmas Day. And I will. But I didn't say anything about Christmas Eve." He paused, raising a brow. "If you don't want me to come, Mr. Danvers, just say so."

Aaron swallowed and looked RJ up and down. His shoulders dropped. "I don't know. It's all so sudden. We barely know each other. Last week you were just a former student of mine. Now you're..." He fidgeted and looked up at RJ through his lashes.

"Now I'm the guy who's made you cry with pleasure."

Aaron closed his eyes and swallowed. "Yeah, and that's exactly why this is all too fast. That's what we've been doing. Not whatever it is my dad thinks we're up to."

"Oh, I think he's pretty sure we've been doing that."

"You know what I mean. He thinks we're an item. Two men making a go at something real."

RJ had an urge to say they *could* be those guys. But they couldn't. They would never be. How fucked up was that? And how much more fucked up that RJ's stomach hurt over it? Aaron was right. They'd really only known each other for less than a week.

"Let's talk about it next week, maybe," Aaron said, obviously compromising for show only. He ran a hand into his hair, conflicted distraction laying over his pretty features. "You know, if we're even still doing this next week."

RJ turned back to the Christmas tree in the stall. The shining joy of it spattered light all around the wood enclosure. He'd let all of this get to him. The heat of the sex, the sweetness of Aaron's hand in his own, and the thrill of Rutty's easy acceptance. He'd let his mind and heart go too fast. He looked foolish.

"Fair enough, Mr. Danvers," RJ said, putting his chin up. He hoped Aaron didn't notice the hint of lingering, irrational hurt under his false cheerfulness. "What do you say we load this tree and these ornament boxes into my car?" He pulled out his phone and glanced at the time. "Yeah. Wow, it's almost two. I should probably be getting back to town soon. I have that show tonight. I should prepare for it."

Aaron stepped closer and touched his arm. "RJ, I'm sorry. I didn't mean to hurt you. It's not that I wouldn't be proud to tell my family about you, but we just aren't there. I don't think either of us plans to ever be there. Am I right? You're leaving soon. I'm not out at my job and don't want to be."

RJ stared down at him. There was a lie in that, about not wanting to be out at his job. RJ sensed it. "And why is that?"

"Why is what?"

"Why are you closeted in your job? Is the school homophobic?"

Aaron scrubbed his hands through his hair. "Christ, it's such a long story. Can I tell you later? I'm not blowing you off, but, like you said, we should get going soon."

Rutty walked back into the barn with some big, old blankets hefted over his shoulder.

Aaron cast his voice lower. "Besides, now isn't the time or place for this tale."

RJ nodded, swallowed down his unfair and ugly hurt, and plastered a smile on for Rutty's sake. "Let me help with those, sir. We'd love to stay longer, but I've got a show in town tonight, and I need to be getting back."

Rutty clapped him on the shoulder. "Sure thing, son. But don't be a stranger. Now that Aaron's brought you, I want to see you again soon. Like, say, on Christmas Eve."

"Dad, stop, please."

After they'd figured out how to lay the seats down in the Lexus, laid out protective blankets, and loaded in the blanket-wrapped tree, Rutty said to Aaron, "You can keep all those quilts. My Aunt Gladdy made about a hundred before she died. I don't need more than a couple. If

166

you don't want 'em, give some to your mama. Just don't say they came from me. Make it a gift from you somehow." He shook his head and let loose a bitter sound. "That woman would vomit up a beautiful steak dinner if she found out that I was the one to grill it."

Aaron nodded with downcast eyes. He'd been solemn ever since their short private discussion, but he seemed to summon a small smile for his father. "Thanks for everything, Dad."

Rutty glanced between them, and RJ gave the man a stiff smile, hoping it looked less awkward than he felt right now. Rutty lifted a brow. "Ah, Cracker, c'mere."

He tugged Aaron aside, and RJ pretended that he couldn't hear every word, continuing to tuck blankets around the tree in the SUV and keeping his back turned. He winced a little at what he did hear, though.

"I don't know what was said or done in the little bit o' time since you first showed up here looking like a light had been turned on in your soul. I don't know what happened to make that light turn off again. But, please, son. Don't be like your mother. Don't ruin perfectly good things just because they aren't what you planned."

"Dad, that's not—"

"Just think on it." Rutty hugged Aaron and then pulled away, starting to lumber back up to the house. "Good to meet you, RJ. Thanks for coming out."

"Thanks for the warm welcome," RJ said, waving as he and Aaron climbed into the SUV and put on their seat belts. "Your dad's nice."

"Yeah," Aaron agreed.

RJ started the car and decided to risk a question. He'd already spilled some of his darkest history earlier in the day. It could be Aaron's turn if he was willing. "So, I didn't mean to overhear, but what was that about your mom?"

They circled around in the yard, heading back down the bumpy driveway, avoiding goats and dogs. Aaron groaned. "It's another long story, sort of connected to the first long story."

RJ glanced at Aaron. His dad was right. Whatever light had been shining in him when they'd arrived was definitely dimmed now. Aaron was just as handsome as before. Maybe, in a weird way, even more so, with his expression so solemn and his vulnerability leaking out all over the car. RJ wanted to hold him close, soothe him, and force the layers of his brittle, protective shell to split open. Force him to let it all go.

RJ took another chance, because Aaron Danvers brought out the risk taker in him. He cleared his throat and prompted, "A long story, huh? Well, it's a long ride back home."

Home. Wow. How was it that Aaron's little loft had come to mind when he'd said that word? He'd only been in it twice, and it wasn't exactly the coziest of places. RJ could think of a hundred improvements to make for comfort: a few cat-safe house plants here and there, colored curtains that billowed and shifted the light, and warm, soft quilts to huddle under on the sofa. Hey, at least the last item was covered now, what with the quilts around the tree in the back.

But Aaron's apartment wasn't his home. So why had it come to mind instead of Mom and Doug's place?

"All right," Aaron said, a little resentfully. "Let me figure out where to start. What harm can it do to tell you?"

RJ hoped it wouldn't do any harm at all. But he couldn't be sure. Aaron was pricklier than ever as he started his story.

"My mom is the principal of the school where I teach. But I guess the story begins way before that. It starts with the divorce. I was ten."

RJ listened and as he did, he clenched the steering wheel harder and harder. His mother had been neglectful, sure, but only because she'd had no choice. Aaron's mother was outright mean, and for no real reason RJ could discern. She was blessed with Aaron for a son—a beautiful man, a good person, and an excellent teacher. What was wrong with Aaron's mother that he wasn't her pride and joy?

RJ hadn't ever despised a person he'd never met before, but the more he listened, the closer he came to just that.

Chapter Eighteen

RJ'S VOICE HELD daggers as he whispered, "Wait, wait. She actually said, 'Don't embarrass me, Aaron'? *That* was her motherly advice the first day you started work in her school?"

"Yep."

They were back at the loft. Aaron's story about his parents' ugly divorce, the custody fights, and his own difficult relationship with his mother as a teen, and now as an adult, had taken the entire ride back to Knoxville to impart.

He'd divulged the finer details of her role in Aaron remaining closeted at school as they'd carried the tree inside and unwrapped it, though he'd avoided mentioning the humiliation of Coach McAllister. And he'd kept right on talking as they mixed up a formula of vinegar, baking soda, and hot water to clean Grandma's ornaments.

Constance sat beneath the tree staring up at it in awe, but so far hadn't tried to climb it. Thank God.

"And yesterday was the worst conflict I've had with her in years. Maybe ever," Aaron said. "I've tried to put it out of my mind, and thanks to you and the whole naughty elf game, I was pretty much able to do it. But then you asked about why I was still closeted, and my dad brought my mom up, and so it's all come rushing back in. The anger. The shame."

"What happened yesterday?"

Aaron sighed, polishing a silver and gold bulb. "During the dance, she pulled me aside and told me off for flirting with a parent." He rolled his eyes. "Obviously, I was *not* flirting with a parent. Just talking to a dad about his son, a young man who's struggling right now."

"So not only did she accuse you of something you would never do—"

Aaron scoffed. "I'm not a saint. I won't say I've never accidentally flirted with a student's dad. But never on purpose. And the time it happened, he started it."

RJ raised a brow. "Sounds like another story there."

"An embarrassing one. Never mind."

"What I was saying is that she accused you of something you weren't doing, and she also interrupted a potentially important conversation about a student."

"Exactly!" Aaron applied more baking soda and vinegar solution, making the bulb shine. "She also said other things." He flushed a little. "I'm embarrassed to repeat them."

"After what I told you about my teen years, you can tell me anything."

"I'm sorry about that, by the way." Aaron put the bulb aside and took hold of RJ's hand. "I should have been there for you. I was your teacher, and I had no idea. I wish you'd come to me. I could have helped you."

"Could you have? Really, Aaron? What would that have looked like? Placement in some kind of foster care? Believe me, I consider myself lucky."

"How?"

"What happened with me wasn't great. But at least I was getting off with an older guy I actually *chose* to screw and not being molested by someone who was supposed to care for me. Or being passed from loveless home to loveless home. And, like I also said earlier, I was a freshman when I was with that guy. All that was over by the time I saw you for the first time my senior year." RJ's eyes went darker. "I'll never forget how you came in that first day, looking so sweet in that sports coat and bow tie, and your hot ass all—" RJ let out a low whistle.

"You're really fixated on my ass."

"Spent an entire school year staring at it. I like your dimples too. They make me want to eat you alive." He raised a brow. "But don't think I didn't notice how you deflected the topic of conversation away from the stuff about your mom. What else did your mom say? It's better to get the poison out than let it fester."

Aaron took a deep breath. Then he spit out the insults his mother had sent his way, calling his sexual behavior illicit and dangerous, without accepting any of the blame for that. "How can I give myself to someone, heart and soul, when I'm not allowed to be open and honest about who I am? Not only at work, but in my mother's home? She's set me up for this life, and I don't know how much longer I can keep living it. I want more."

"You deserve more, babe." RJ stared at him with solemn, hazel eyes. "You're a lovable man. And you *deserve* to be loved. Don't let her take that away from you."

Aaron's heart fluttered, and he ducked his head, putting a few more ornaments in the aluminum tub to soak. "I wonder sometimes."

"What do you wonder?"

"If I do deserve it?"

RJ moved closer, took Aaron's chin in his hand and tipped it up. "What deep, dark secret haven't you shared with me, Mr. Danvers? Hmm."

Aaron licked his lips, his gut quivering and his cock filling slightly. "I…don't know. But there's got to be something."

RJ's gaze bore into him. "What's the worst thing about you? The thing you'd be completely mortified if anyone found out?"

Aaron's breath caught, and then he whispered, "Like I'd tell you."

"Tell me, Mr. Danvers, or you're going back on the naughty list."

Aaron huffed a half-aroused laugh. "That's a threat? If last night is what happens to people on the naughty list, why would I ever want off?"

"Because what happens to people on the nice list is even better. It comes with handcuffs and hours of edging."

"Oh, fuck."

RJ laughed. "So tell me, what's the worst sin you've committed?"

"I'm a slut."

"Mm, I love sluts. What else?"

"I let a former student spank and fuck me."

"So hot. What else?"

"Oh, Jesus."

"C'mon."

"I hate my mother."

"Yeah. I know you do. But you love her too." RJ stroked his hand over Aaron's cheek, probing one finger into a dimple when Aaron smiled. "Good work, Mr. Danvers. You've been promoted to the nice list now. When do you want to collect on the handcuffs and edging? Spoiler alert: not tonight. I have a show. Plus, I need to get some handcuffs first. Though duct tape could work, if you have that around."

Aaron laughed. "Jesus, RJ. You're ridiculous."

"But you like me."

Aaron grinned, heat rising up his chest and into his cheeks. "Yeah. I do."

"Tell me more." RJ sat back and broke the tension between them. "What do your friends think about all of this with your mom?"

"*Friend*," Aaron said. "Only Lauren knows the truth about me."

"Who's Lauren?"

RJ was a surprisingly good listener. He didn't try to fix things, he had appropriate responses even if it was just a sympathetic sigh, and he asked relevant, insightful questions that expanded on what Aaron was relating. He made it easy for Aaron to talk and keep talking. It was only now that they were almost done with washing the ornaments that Aaron realized he'd talked for nearly three full hours.

"Oh, man. What time do you have to leave to set up for the show?" Aaron asked, cutting off whatever it was RJ was going to ask him next.

RJ pulled out his phone, typed something into it, and said, "Joel and Casey will bring my stuff with them. So, I just need to be at Scruffy City Hall by seven, and the show starts at eight." He smiled. "You'll come?"

Aaron looked at the ornament in his hands, a fragile, clear glass bulb with a lonely snowman inside. "I don't know. I should decorate this tree."

RJ took the globe from his hand and set it back into the box of now mostly clean ornaments. He took Aaron's fingers in his own. "I'd like you to be there."

"RJ…" Aaron shook his head.

RJ sighed. "Okay. That's fine." He shrugged and stood up. "Well, I guess I should go to Mom and Doug's, clean up a little. Give you some time alone."

Aaron nodded glumly. He didn't want RJ to leave, but he wasn't sure it was a good idea to just keep on hanging out together without a break to process things. They'd been so entangled over the last twenty-four hours, and somehow so much had happened and been said that it felt like they'd been together for a week straight. Aaron did need a little space to breathe, screw his head on, and decorate his Grandma's tree. Alone.

As good a listener as RJ was, and as arousing as the naughty vs. nice list talk had been, this was a special thing for him, having his Grandma's tree here in his apartment. He wanted to listen to Christmas music, decorate it, and remember her and all of his childhood Christmases.

"Don't forget to put the lemon and orange peels around the bottom of the tree," RJ said, pulling on his leather jacket and zipping it up. He didn't look or sound hurt, but still Aaron felt the distance expand between them, the awkward space that had opened up when he'd declined to go to the pub with RJ tonight.

"I won't forget. These ornaments are too precious to risk."

RJ nodded. "Good luck." He leaned in and kissed Aaron's forehead. A warm, proprietary kiss that Aaron felt all the way down to the soles of his feet. "Text me when you're ready to see me again. I'll be waiting."

Then he left.

Aaron stared at the door for way too long, his mind a complete blank but his body full of yearning. Then he headed for his stereo, found his old vinyl record of Nat King Cole's "The Christmas Song," and let the soothing sounds of his Grandma's favorite singer fill the space.

While Constance slept on the sofa, Aaron began to decorate the silvery Christmas tree alone.

Chapter Nineteen

RJ WAS JUST as sexy onstage as he'd been the first time Aaron had spotted him up there not even a week ago. Knowing what was beneath RJ's white, V-necked T-shirt and his comfortable-looking blue jeans didn't detract in the least from the erotic visions buzzing in Aaron's head.

Tonight, RJ wore another jingle-bell tipped reindeer antler headband. Someone had fashioned more tinsel wrist cuffs for him, and he sang a jazzy-blues version of "Frosty the Snowman." By all rights, he should have appeared absurd.

Instead, his natural grace and complete personal comfort in his body made it impossible for Aaron to tear his eyes away. And he didn't think he was alone. By the time he'd found a seat in the corner of the bar, he'd overheard two different groups of women angling to approach RJ during a break or once the show as over.

Good luck with that, honeys.

He'd dressed in a pair of slacks that he knew clung to his ass just right, a sports coat, and a tight, red and green Polo shirt that gripped his biceps in a way that made them look bigger than they really were. Though he'd have to take his sports coat off for anyone to see that.

Aaron shouldn't have come. He knew that deep down. Or rather, he shouldn't have come if he didn't plan to fuck RJ tonight, and probably tomorrow, and definitely for the rest of however long RJ stayed in town. And he really shouldn't have come if he didn't want to get his heart broken when it was over. Because that was what he'd figured out while he was putting his grandma's ornaments on her beautiful, sparkling tree: he was already falling for RJ Blitz.

Even his dad had seen it.

Maybe it doesn't have to be over when he goes.

He shook the thought away. Hope like that would make this hurt so much more when it was done. Better not to indulge in it at all. He shouldn't have gotten so sentimental over the word "lover" or taken RJ out to meet his dad. He shouldn't have told him all his fucked up, emotional baggage and let him into his life like that. He shouldn't have started to care about RJ, dammit.

Fuck, Lauren was *right*. He shouldn't have fucked a former student at all.

And yet...

Once he'd finished decorating the tree, he'd glanced at his phone and realized that RJ was on the stage performing at that exact moment, not even a mile away from him. A five-minute walk at most. Aaron hadn't been able to keep away, hadn't wanted to even try.

So, he'd tucked orange and lemon peels beneath the tree skirt he'd fashioned out of one of Aunt Gladdy's quilts, satisfied when Constance ran away from it like a vampire from garlic. Staring happily at the finished tree, he came to a realization. If he'd put the Christmas tree in a box, and all the ornaments too to keep them safe, then they might as well have remained lost to the world in Candace's basement forever.

If he returned home to find the tree overturned and the ornaments smashed, he knew he'd cry. But he also knew life would go on. No matter what disaster happened, life always went on. So why not enjoy what he had while he had it?

It was the same with RJ.

Aaron would no doubt cry real tears of pain when *whatever this was* crashed and burned, but so what? He'd have felt cared for and been, for a short time, someone's lover. Not just some guy's hookup or an easy hole to fuck. *Lover.* So, he should enjoy it while it lasted.

As he'd added his Grandma's angel on top of the tree, he'd resolved to stop pushing RJ away. So here he was at Scruffy City Hall again, a little nervous, a little stupid, and a lot turned on. He sat his bruised ass on the barstool and watched RJ play and sing, admiring the way he closed his eyes and let his gritty baritone rush out. RJ looked vulnerable like that and yet powerful too. Christmas carols had never been so sexy.

When the bartender swung by to get Aaron's order, he motioned the man closer. "Do you have a girlfriend with a kid that goes to Pineview?"

The man tilted his head. "What's it to you?"

"I'd appreciate it if you told your girlfriend, or whoever, that what she sees while she's here visiting you at work really ought to be kept to herself."

"Oh yeah?"

"Yeah. Or I might need to have a word with the manager about how his bartender's woman is causing problems for paying customers at their place of work."

The bartender looked like he couldn't decide if he should get pissed off or not, but then he shocked Aaron by saying, "Sorry. It's not what it seems. I promise."

"Oh? What was it then, if not your girlfriend gossiping about me in a way that could affect my career?"

It was hard to hear over the music, so the bartender leaned close until he was practically yelling in Aaron's ear.

"I'm bi," he shouted. "I saw you in here the other night and thought you were hot. Then you went home with *that* guy," he nodded up at RJ, "and I realized that, even if I wasn't with my girlfriend, you're way out of my league."

"Wait? *What?*"

The bartender leaned closer and yelled, "I told my ex I thought you were hot, and she lost her shit and dumped me." He shrugged. "Can't say I'm sorry I found out she was a bigot, though. Good riddance."

Aaron blinked. Hot? The bartender had thought he was *hot?* And then told his girlfriend about it? That was…psycho. Who does that? He didn't know what part to latch onto first, so he just said, "Whiskey up. Maker's Mark." Because that was his brand too, not just his dad's.

"Sure thing."

The set continued with RJ oblivious to Aaron's presence. He mostly sang with his eyes shut tonight, which was different from when Aaron had seen him the first time. But the performances were just as entertaining, touching, and impassioned. The rest of the band seemed looser, more confident, and less like they had something to prove.

The pianist was clearly fucking the drummer given the looks they exchanged, and the bassist had his eyes on his boyfriend in the audience the whole time. But they were all talented enough to keep the songs on track despite their constant flirting. The entire group wore outfits with homemade holiday sparkle added, just like RJ. They all looked festive as fuck.

Aaron rolled his eyes at himself. He was a composition teacher. He should be able to come up with better descriptions than curse words. Normally, he'd insist on it and berate himself for being too lazy to do better. But tonight, waiting and aching to be noticed by RJ, some part of him liked the commonness of the curses, the crassness. He liked not being too fussy to use them. He liked what that meant about him.

Aaron could toss off the reins. He could be wild and free. He hadn't shown that side of himself to enough people before. Not even to himself. He needed to change that.

He'd let RJ spank this fun, dirty, naughty feeling out of him later.

Aaron bit into his lower lip just imagining the jolting rush of RJ's hand connecting with his ass. He didn't know if he could handle another spanking, though, given the lingering bruises from the ruler the night before. But he'd like to try. His ass ached from where he sat on the hard, wooden barstool, but the nagging discomfort just made him feel squirmy and hot inside.

"Buy you a drink?"

Aaron looked up to find a tall guy with salt-and-pepper hair and a well-trimmed goatee gazing down at him with a cocky smile. Though there was also a hint of worry in his blue gaze, obviously a tad unsure about whether he'd picked the right target for his come-on.

Aaron looked up to find a tall guy with salt-and-pepper hair and a well-trimmed goatee gazing down at him with a cocky smile. Though there was also a hint of worry in his blue gaze, obviously a tad unsure about whether he'd picked the right target for his come-on.

He hadn't, because Aaron wasn't going to fuck him tonight. But he *had* correctly guessed Aaron's orientation. Frankly, Aaron was starting to feel a little paranoid about his ability to pass for straight.

Why?

Don't embarrass me, Aaron.

He put his chin up and smiled at the guy. Fuck his mother. There was nothing embarrassing about being gay. Or there shouldn't be. He *refused* to let there be. With a slightly seductive tone, he accepted the guy's offer with a coy, "Sure. Why not?"

In one way, it was a dick move because nothing was going to come of chatting the guy up, but so what? Accepting a drink wasn't a contract, and he was feeling good tonight. When did he ever feel this proud of himself? Only when he was about to get fucked by RJ Blitz. And he had a feeling that was still going to happen, no matter how many drinks he accepted from goatee guy.

The man smiled, and Aaron took a good look at him. He wasn't ugly despite the stupid little beard, but he was no RJ. He had tattoos, a few earrings, and now that he was sure he hadn't made a mistake, incredibly kind blue eyes. Normally, Aaron would be spreading his ass cheeks for him in the Scruffy City Hall's bathroom stall in less than half an hour's time. But not tonight.

The bartender deposited Aaron's whiskey in front of him, and the guy motioned for it to go on his tab.

Aaron put his hand out too. "No, I'll get this round."

Maybe he was a dick to have accepted at all, leading the guy on that way, but he wasn't enough of a dick that he was going to let the guy waste his money as well as his time.

The guy looked dissatisfied, clearly sensing the writing on the wall, but he pulled up the stool beside Aaron and tried to start a conversation over the noise of the music.

"The name's Trevor," the guy said, with a twist to his handsome mouth. "You?"

"Aaron."

"What brings you out tonight?"

A slow smile crept over Aaron's face. He nodded toward the stage. "I'm here to see my lover's band."

Maybe it was the whiskey, but he gave up fighting it. He *really* liked having a lover. Pride flowed through him like a rushing river, smoothing the fear in his pounding heart. Especially a lover as talented and hot as RJ Blitz.

"Oh. Uh, okay." Trevor turned toward the stage and blinked. "Which one is your, um, lover?" He sounded confounded, like the word itself was foreign to him.

"The hot one."

"I meant, girl or guy?"

At that moment, RJ's eyes opened and, like he'd suddenly felt Aaron's presence, they landed directly on him. Aaron raised a glass. A smirky smile twisted RJ's lips, but he didn't miss a beat of the song. His eyes took on a gleam.

"That one," Aaron said, lifting his chin toward RJ. "In the reindeer antlers."

"Hot damn," Trevor said, laughing. "You had me all confused. Normally, I can spot a member of the family pretty easily, but you gave me a scare just now."

"Oh no, you had me pegged from the start," Aaron replied a bit flirtatiously, feeling RJ's eyes on him and liking that. He touched the man's forearm. "If I weren't here to watch my lover, I'd absolutely be the man to buy a drink." He watched Trevor's eyes widen. "Unfortunately..." He shrugged.

"So, you're saying another night when he's not around I might have a chance?" Trevor grinned, eyes crinkling handsomely at the corners.

"Maybe."

No reason not to flirt. When this fling ended and RJ left town, Aaron would need an option for getting off. So long as Trevor wasn't a student's father or stepfather or uncle or brother or cousin…

A weird twist in his stomach made his smile falter. He took a fast sip of his whisky to cover it up. The truth was, he didn't want this man as a future option for sex. He didn't want him *ever*.

Shit. What had RJ done to him?

Aaron glanced toward the stage again and found RJ watching him closely, an expression on his face Aaron hoped might be jealousy. His twisting stomach unclenched into a whirl of excited butterflies. He wondered how a naughty elf might be punished for flirting with a hot man who wasn't Santa. Aaron's blood rushed wildly, and he smiled up at the man beside him.

"Trying to make him jealous?" Trevor asked, glancing toward the stage with a laugh.

"Why not? Might make for a fun night later."

Trevor laughed heartily and leaned closer. "Is that how it is with you two?"

Aaron shrugged. He didn't know how it would be. He hoped it'd be good, but who really knew? He was pretty excited to find out.

Trevor grimaced. "My ex was a real dick when he was jealous. No fun at all."

Aaron met RJ's gaze again. He wasn't singing now, just strumming some steady chords while their pianist took a turn being the one to carry the melody. RJ lifted a brow at Aaron, a warning or scolding, maybe both, but his eyes sparkled with a dangerous humor.

"I think it'll be okay." Aaron patted Trevor's cheek, feeling his smooth goatee beneath this thumb. "Thanks for sharing a drink with me. It's been fun chatting."

"Is that a dismissal?"

"It's a 'see you another time' Maybe."

Trevor laughed even harder, and Aaron slipped from his barstool to move closer to the stage, and closer to the man who was going to take him home tonight. And, with any luck, break him apart on his dick.

He couldn't wait.

RJ KEPT AN eye on Aaron throughout the rest of the show. The little shit was definitely trying to make him jealous with the slick-looking older guy at the bar. Which was hilarious. Mostly because it was working.

He didn't know what kind of game Aaron was playing with him— hot and cold, pull and push—but he didn't mind it. It probably had to do with all that shit Aaron had told him about his mom earlier in the day and the divorce, and maybe it had to do with his father too. Though RJ hadn't quite worked that out yet. But whatever the case, RJ dug it.

Maybe it was the caveman in him, but he enjoyed the chase. Especially when his prey wasn't really trying to get away but was simply making sure that he would definitely be caught. Because Aaron really obviously wanted RJ to catch him.

RJ grinned when Aaron abandoned his flirtation with the dude at the bar and brought his sexy ass closer to the stage. Something had changed in him tonight. Aaron was on fire with a wild light that RJ hadn't seen in him outside of the bedroom. His eyes glowed, and he stared up at RJ with a defiant, challenging bravery that made RJ's dick hard. Good thing he held his guitar slung slow.

Aaron sipped his whiskey, shimmying his hips every once in a while, and gazed up at RJ with eyes that were nearly as adoring as the ones Casey always had turned on Joel twenty-four-seven.

But there was something else in them too. A kind of mischievous gleam that hooked into RJ's heart, tugged, and ripped it open to expose a hitherto unknown treasure trove of glee and affectionate anticipation.

Mr. Danvers was a hell of a tease.

But he wouldn't be teasing for long.

When the set was over, RJ cleared out his stuff, loaded it out to the van, and said bye to his bandmates alone. Aaron had disappeared into the crowd as soon as the last song finished and seemed to be avoiding him now. All the better for the chase, RJ supposed. It was clear Joel and Becca, and even Madison, had noticed Aaron in the crowd and wondered why he wasn't glued to RJ's side now that the show was over.

"Cold feet?" Madison asked with a raised brow, bumping against RJ with her pointy shoulder.

"Too late for that," RJ said.

She grinned. "Ah, so he's already jumped in with both of 'em?"

"You could say that."

Becca smirked. "More like he's realized he's bitten off a bit more than he could chew."

"Nah. He's playing a game."

Becca laughed. "What game is that? Cocktease?"

"Basically." RJ waggled his brows and located Aaron near the bar, chatting up another guy. Christ, he was asking for it, wasn't he? "Let's just say he's trying to get on my naughty list."

The girls burst into gales of laughter, but Joel blushed, and Casey winked at RJ before flinging his arm around Joel's shoulder and ruffling his hair. Guess RJ knew who the sexually shy one was there. Not that he hadn't already guessed. For all Joel's ramblings about girls back in high school, they'd all been a cover for his deep, secret homosexual urges. Apparently, he still wasn't entirely open about discussing them yet.

After loading up the van, a few fist bumps, and making plans for rehearsals the following week, RJ headed back inside the pub to collect his naughty elf.

He found Aaron's perfect ass up on a barstool, looking round and delicious, while his dimpled cheeks shone up at yet another hot guy around RJ's size and build. Fuck that.

"'Scuse me," RJ said, stepping in between them to wrap his arms around Aaron's waist and lift him from the chair.

Aaron's surprised laughter should have cut off any protest from the chump Aaron had been playing as part of his game. But the dupe muscled in anyway, asking Aaron, "This guy bothering you? I can deal with him if you want."

"No," Aaron answered, drunken laughter bursting free. "He's my lover. Isn't that a phenomenal word? Loverrrrr." He practically purred it, like a cat. After patting RJ's chest, Aaron rested his head on RJ's shoulder and grinned with delight. "He's going to take me home now. Bye."

The guy scoffed but moved aside. RJ swooped Aaron up and carried him bodily from the pub while Aaron giggled and clung to RJ's shoulders. He was heavy, and it wasn't easy, but there was something to be said about literally sweeping a man off his feet, and Aaron's glowing eyes made the strain worth it.

As they burst through the front doors out into Market Square, RJ dropped Aaron's feet to the sidewalk with a huff of exertion but didn't take his arm from around Aaron's waist. The Christmas lights and decorations sparkled in the night, and the music from the skating rink filled the air. "What were you doing in there? Trying to make me crazy, Hermey?"

Aaron laughed. "Hermey? Who? What?"

RJ bent close and whispered in his ear, "The naughty elf who wanted to be a dentist. Remember?"

Aaron's smile grew wider, and his dimples dug in even deeper. He shot a coy glance up through his lashes. Oh, he was really playing his game tonight. Flirty, naughty, asking for it. "That's right. He was a very bad elf." Aaron pressed closer, heat from his body blazing against RJ's side. "Like me."

RJ wrapped his arm around Aaron's shoulders, the sports coat stiff under his palm. His own leather jacket kept the cool night air from chilling him deeply, though it stung his cheeks and chin. He directed Aaron toward the apartment, his blood pumping and plans unfolding in his mind for all kinds of kinky ways to make Aaron pay for teasing him tonight.

"Why were you flirting with asshole guys like that when you can get a good, hard spanking from a nice guy like me?" RJ hissed in Aaron's ear. Their breath puffed from their mouths in soft clouds, and Aaron's laugh was a stream of them.

"Because guess what? I'm allowed to have both," Aaron said, still sounding quite drunk. He tilted his head to the side as RJ moved behind him, wrapped his arms around his waist, and kissed the side of his neck. They walked together that way, a bit awkwardly, until RJ moved back to Aaron's side again.

"You're a tease, Mr. Danvers," RJ muttered. "Push, pull. Hot, cold."

Aaron's shoulders shook with laughter, but he didn't deny it.

RJ added, "I liked you being there tonight." He put his arm around Aaron's shoulders again, nuzzling his ear, as he whispered, "I even liked you flirting with those assholes."

"Did you?"

"Knowing I'm going to take you home? Yeah."

Aaron glanced up at him, his eyes shining. "You were so sure?"

RJ narrowed his gaze. "You know there was never anyone else you were going home with tonight."

Aaron shivered against him and angled his body in to snuggle closer. "I know."

RJ unzipped his leather jacket and pulled Aaron close to his chest, kissing the top of his head as he tried to wrap the leather around the both of them. The fizzy, thrilling rush of whatever was happening between them—and whatever else was going to happen tonight—propelled them through Market Square.

"Mr. Danvers!"

Aaron stiffened in RJ's arms. They stumbled to a halt, and then

Aaron slowly turned to the patio area outside the Tomato Head restaurant. RJ didn't release him and was surprised when Aaron didn't shrug him off or leap out of his embrace in a panic either.

"I knew that was you, Mr. Danvers." A young man, probably a college freshman by the gawky look of him, so not that much younger than RJ to be honest, slipped from the crowded patio full of people eating pizza.

Wearing a black apron around his waist, the guy looked like he was on the waitstaff there. He had a hippie, maybe-he'd-showered-this-week-maybe-not look about him. Typical for the Tomato Head servers. The kid smiled widely at Aaron and put out his hand.

"So good to see you, Mr. Danvers. It's me, Ephraim Freemont?"

"Right. Of course. Sorry. It's been a few years. I remember you now. It's wonderful to see you."

"It's great to see you too. I won't keep you. I just wanted to say hi."

"Hi." Aaron smiled and stepped away from RJ a bit. He put out his hand to Ephraim to shake. Ephraim clung to Aaron's hand longer than necessary, and seemed tempted to go in for a hug, but restrained himself.

Grinning, he looked toward RJ. "Yeah, so, uh, I saw you walking here with your boyfriend and I just wanted to tell you I'm proud of you."

Aaron tilted his head, bright eyes dulling slightly. "Thank you? For what?"

"For being out now. That's awesome. So many kids need to see that, you know? That teachers can be out, that people they look up to and admire are gay." Ephraim lifted his hand for a high five. Aaron gave him one but looked more confused than anything.

"Ephraim! They need you in the kitchen!" Another member of the waitstaff called to him.

"See you, Mr. Danvers. And thanks for being brave."

Aaron stared after the kid for a minute, and then turned to RJ with a stunned twist to his features. "I don't understand."

"You're his hero. For tonight anyway." RJ shrugged. He was used to being someone's temporary hero. Admittedly rarely for being gay, more often for being the guitar hero of their dreams. As a teacher, Aaron couldn't be entirely unaccustomed to the feeling, could he?

"I don't know about that." Aaron started off toward his apartment again. The teasing, fun spell between them felt suddenly irreparably broken. RJ didn't know whether to thank Ephraim for the truth bombs exploding in Aaron's mind right now or smack him for ruining what had been a very long set-up to a very fun game.

RJ walked beside Aaron, but reading the signs Aaron was giving off, he kept his hands to himself for now.

"I don't want to hide," Aaron said, as they crossed the street and entered the light-filled path of Krutch Park. "I'm not embarrassed to be gay," he said urgently. "Or I guess, well, I *shouldn't* be."

"No," RJ agreed, reaching out for Aaron's hand and tugging him to stop.

They faced each other with the Christmas lights brightening their faces. Other walkers passing them on the path. RJ tightened his hold on Aaron's hands and waited. He could feel the words bubbling up in Aaron. He just needed to wait and hear them out.

"Tonight felt different for me," Aaron said slowly, glancing down at the ground before meeting RJ's eyes again. "Tonight, I pretended that I didn't have to hide. I didn't quite believe it, but I pretended it was true."

"You were gorgeous, babe," RJ said softly, not wanting to be over-heard by the passing families. He wasn't ashamed either, but this moment felt fragile. "The men flocked to you."

Aaron nodded, eyes distant, remembering. "I felt gorgeous. I wanted them to see me, RJ. I didn't hide."

"No, you shone. Like a star. Brightest light in the room."

Aaron shook his head, a shy smile blooming. "That was you."

"No, Aaron. That was you."

Aaron snorted, but suddenly moved closer to RJ, burying his head against RJ's chest. RJ wrapped his arms around him, and they held each other in the park.

Families passed, couples old and young, and still they held each other in silence, letting the mild, winter night cradle them both.

When they made it back to the apartment, RJ walked a circle around the utterly fantastic silver tree. "Where'd you get the lights?" he asked, admiring the way the colored strings reflected off every silver needle, sending spangles of magical, holiday color everywhere.

"Ran down the street to Mast General. They wanted an arm and leg for them, but it beat driving out of the city to Wal-Mart." Aaron refilled Constance's water bowl and went to scoop the litter by the back door.

RJ stared at his bent-over ass and licked his lips.

They hadn't quite achieved the same level of sexual promise that had been lost when Aaron's former student had called out to them, but RJ knew they'd recapture it sooner rather than later.

"Constance is staying away from it?"

"She thinks it's evil." Aaron smiled. "The citrus is doing the trick."

"Good." RJ sat down on the sofa, glad to see a cozy quilt laying across the back. "Mind if I kick my shoes off and get comfortable?"

Aaron smiled over his shoulder at him as he shoveled some clumps of litter into a bag. "Go ahead. I'll be there in a minute."

While Aaron finished up and washed his hands, RJ settled back on the sofa, shoes off, quilt over his shoulders, and a slow, steady thrum under his skin. He could get used to this. He wondered if Aaron had any snacks around. He wasn't usually munchie after a show, horny being the operative word for his post-show yearnings, but he wasn't ready to rush anything tonight. They had time. Tomorrow was Sunday, and he was pretty sure Aaron wouldn't be waking early to head to church. They had the whole night to spend together.

As Aaron dried off his hands, he turned to the fridge and called over his shoulder, "Lemon seltzer water or regular tap water? That's what I've got at the moment. Sorry, I should have picked up some beer. Or wine."

He scratched at the back of his head. "Or maybe some liquor. I don't really drink at home."

"Lemon seltzer water is fine."

Aaron poured them both a glass and brought it over along with a bag of corn chips and a bowl of salsa. "I'm starving. Dancing and flirting make me a hungry boy," he said, and RJ wasn't sure if he was glad that flirtatious tone was back, or disappointed that Aaron was signaling that serious discussion was now shelved in favor of advancing toward sex.

RJ put a chip in his mouth, crunching as he watched Constance stalk over to the tree, hiss at it, then flee again. "She really hates it," he observed.

"Perfect."

"So, why'd you come tonight? I thought you needed some time alone."

Aaron dipped his chip in salsa, chewed it thoroughly, and swallowed before answering, obviously weighing what he wanted to say.

"I could tell you that I got horny again, which wouldn't be a lie. We're good together. In bed, I mean." He glanced up at RJ. "And maybe out of bed. I don't know. But…" He swallowed hard and darted his eyes toward the Christmas tree again before pulling his gaze back to RJ. "I decided I'd like to find out." He put out his hands. "Look, I know you're not staying. That you're not looking for anything long term. But like I said earlier tonight, I've never allowed myself to have anything real. This"—he gestured between them—"is real. It's messy and complicated and not going to last. But real."

RJ's tongue felt stuck to the top of his mouth, so he just nodded and was grateful when Aaron went on talking without requiring a real response.

"I don't expect anything out of you. I promise. But if you want… If you feel the same, I mean." He blew out a breath, obviously trying to get his words in order. "If you'd like to see what happens between us whenever you're in town, I'd like that too. Because I genuinely like you, and I think…" He blushed. "I think you could be good for me, RJ. An inoculation against the fear of letting myself have what I want. Fear that I don't deserve it."

"Oh, babe," RJ murmured, reaching out to touch Aaron's cheek. He slipped his hand around his neck and tugged him close, holding him against his chest. Aaron melted against him, the tension that had filled him as he'd spoken releasing with a heavy sigh of relief. "You deserve everything good." He almost stalled out then, wavering between promises he'd never be able to keep, a future he didn't believe possible, and the undeniable urge to open his heart a crack and be even half as brave as Aaron was being right now.

His hesitation lasted a breath too long, because Aaron pulled away and wiped at his eyes. "Don't feel obligated, RJ. If you just want to fuck and move on, that's on the table too. I'd never ask more from you."

Though he kind of just had, hadn't he? Aaron had balls-out said he wanted to see what they might be, and RJ was being a coward right now. No ifs, ands, or buts about it. Casey and Joel, and definitely Becca, would call him out so hard if they were here.

Gazing into Aaron's eyes, he no longer knew which way was up, and yet he knew what he wanted to say. Hadn't he promised himself during that sunrise on Montmartre to be honest with himself, to live a better life, and to not run away from the things that scared him? Like making a new demo, and visiting his mom, and…and…maybe something that could become love.

"I don't feel obligated, and I do plan to fuck you until you can't walk straight, Aaron," RJ said, carefully. "But there's no—"

"No way this would work. I know." Aaron began to pull away.

RJ tugged him right back into place. "You didn't let me finish. I was going to say there's no doubt I haven't felt like this in a long time. And the last time I did, well, it was a disaster. I've been in love before—"

Aaron's eyes widened.

"Don't freak out. This isn't a declaration. I'm just saying that I've

been in love before and it ended really badly. So, like you, I'm skittish."
He pushed away his pride and admitted, "Maybe even afraid. But it's for
a different reason than you. My last lover was a drug addict. I lost him to
the drugs."

"I'm sorry."

"Yeah, well." RJ held himself stiffly, trying not to let those old feelings out. They had no place here with Aaron and his earnest, sweet eyes.
Aaron who didn't even keep alcohol in his house, much less pills and
heroin. Christ, *Pan*... even if they'd never have worked out long term
for other reasons, RJ wished him clean and healthy.

"Anyway, what I'm trying to say is that admitting that I want to see
where this goes? It's a big deal. Understand? I'm not just saying it to
make you happy or to get out of an awkward conversation. I'm saying it
because I truly want to know where this could go too."

"Are you sure, because—"

"Aaron. Stop. Listen to me. I want to try with you. You want to try
with me." RJ brushed his fingers over Aaron's cheek again, slipping his
fingers into the soft hair by his temple and bringing him close enough to
kiss. "I'm not a patient man. So, let's start now by trusting each other to
be honest."

"You honestly want to date me?"

"I'm your lover, aren't I? Let me love you for as long as I can, or as
long as you want me to."

"That sounds a lot like a declaration," Aaron said breathlessly.

"I guess it is, in its way. A declaration to love you until I go, or until
you want me to stop."

"I've never been loved before," Aaron said. "I've been fucked a lot.
But never loved." He sounded so vulnerable, absolutely terrified, and his
hands shook as he reached out to grip RJ's shirt. "Even if it's just for a
few weeks, it could be interesting."

"It could be phenomenal," RJ said, feeling suddenly certain that
given full permission to love Aaron for the next few weeks, he could love

him so well that he'd never accept anything less for as long as he lived. Aaron needed that, deserved it. Loving him like this would be like a protection spell: it'd keep him safe forever.

RJ tugged Aaron into his lap, kissing his mouth and gripping his ass. Aaron gasped and wriggled. Chips and salsa were left uneaten as they pulled off their shirts and lost the fearful awkwardness of the conversation in hard kisses, greedy bites, and tingling nipple play.

Aaron's mouth was a dirty thing, making RJ twist and gasp with his teeth and tongue on his nipples. He'd never enjoyed having his nipples tweaked before, but the rough play was tantalizing and urgent. Just what he needed to seal their reckless agreement to have feelings—albeit short-term feelings—and show them to each other.

Pushing Aaron away from his red, aching nipples, RJ worked to get him undressed. The lights from the tree spangled over Aaron's pale skin.

"Good God, Mr. Danvers," RJ breathed, shoving Aaron's jeans down to reveal a black, lacy jockstrap. "You *were* planning to get laid tonight, weren't you?"

"By hook or by crook."

"Lucky for me those other guys weren't worth your time, huh?"

"Lucky for *me* you know how to discipline an elf gone rogue."

"Are you rogue, babe?"

Aaron lifted his mouth up for a kiss. "I think so. Maybe I'm freed."

RJ rubbed their noses together as Aaron closed his eyes and trembled against him. "Santa's a slaver, you know," he whispered. "Keeping all those elves, forcing them to make toys."

"RJ, just fuck me."

"You don't tell me what to do, Mr. Danvers." He palmed Aaron's hard cock pressing against the soft, lacy material, and then took handfuls of his fleshy ass, exposed and cold in the chilly living room. Aaron whimpered, likely from the bruises left behind by the ruler the night before.

RJ grinned. Time to leave a few more.

Chapter Twenty

S UNDAY TURNED INTO more of the same: sleep, more sex, and heading out into the city to grab breakfast and lunch at various establishments rather than make it themselves. That aspect of the fling was eating into Aaron's budget, but seeing RJ across from him in his favorite restaurants did something to him. It left him feeling proud.

"I don't want to go," RJ said, his things packed up as the flat, afternoon light coming in through the windows.

"It's been amazing," Aaron agreed, leaning against the kitchen counter by the Keurig, a mug of watery hot chocolate in hand. "I've never been fucked so many times, and in so many ways, in all my life."

"It was an honor," RJ said, grinning and slinking up to kiss Aaron's neck. "I don't know how I'm gonna top what we've already done. But I'm going to find a way. Just you wait."

Aaron smiled, blushing. "The only thing that would have made it better would be…" He trailed off.

"What?"

"It's nothing."

RJ raised a brow. "Do I need to swat that pretty ass?"

"Promises, promises," Aaron murmured. "It's just…it's fine. We're fine."

"I know we're fine, baby, but I want to hear what would be better than you nearly going comatose from coming so hard."

Aaron laughed, though RJ's description wasn't far from the truth. "It's just…when's the last time you were tested?"

"HIV? Or everything?"

"The works."

"Why?" RJ's smile went sly and filthy. "You want some come play in your life, Mr. Danvers?"

Aaron blushed harder. "Fuck you. Maybe I do."

"I can make that happen. Probably." He cocked his head and stole Aaron's watery hot chocolate from his hand, taking a sip. He grimaced. "But what about you, Mr. I Fuck Strangers In Bathrooms? When were you last tested?"

"After my last hookup. Six months ago." Aaron stole his coffee back.

RJ gaped. "What the fuck, Aaron? That long? You can't do that to yourself, baby. You need sex."

Aaron laughed. "Okay, well, what do you want me to say? I'll fuck strangers in bathrooms much more often after you leave?"

"No." RJ's brows rucked together. "I mean...I don't know what I mean. I thought this, us...I thought we'd agreed to see where it went while I'm here. That we'd be, at the very least, practice for you to move on to something better than hookups? Something that would last?"

"Something that lasts isn't easy to find," Aaron said reasonably, putting the hot chocolate aside. "I think we're getting sidetracked in this conversation. I just wanted to know if we could skip the condoms. On my side, we're good to go. What about you?"

"Tested when I first got in town, along with a full physical. I'm good to play, too." RJ's lips twisted up into the sexiest smirk imaginable, and Aaron went a little weak in the knees. "I need to go home and help mom with the kids until her husband gets home at six, but I could come back later tonight? Yeah?"

Oh, fuck, Aaron wanted to say yes. He wanted to play with RJ's come, paint his nipples with it and let RJ suck it off, and have it spurt up inside him when RJ shattered in pleasure, but...fuck. He wasn't a teenager anymore. He had some responsibilities. Plus, there was school in the morning. The last day. And his mother. Ugh. "I need to catch up on my grading." He needed to stew a little over what he'd say to his mom too. There was no way he'd be lucky enough to get out of a confrontation tomorrow.

"What if I come over and work on my music while you do your work? I need to have a few more songs for Chip. It's too chaotic to concentrate at Mom and Doug's house."

"Why do you always call him Doug?"

"He's not my dad, that's for damn sure," RJ said tightly.

Aaron rubbed a hand on RJ's arm, the cool leather of his jacket under his palm. "Right, but you say it like he's a stranger somehow. Something about your tone."

"He is. He and Mom got together when I was touring, and I met him on their wedding day. He's fine. She's happy. But I'm not part of that family, no matter what the kids or Mom say."

"Because of Doug?"

RJ shook his head. "Because this time around she deserves to have a family where everything is normal."

"You're her son. She adores you. Even I saw it the other day."

"I know. It's complicated."

"Is it?" Aaron frowned. "I mean, my family's complicated. Yours seems like it's just there for the taking. But you're acting like you don't want it. You told me the night we met outside of Scruffy City Hall that you'd come back to Knoxville after that sunrise on Montmartre to make a change with your mom. And yet..." He shrugged. "Here you are. Avoiding her."

Oh God, don't let RJ see what a hypocrite he was being. Aaron swallowed hard.

"Is this your way of saying you don't want me to come back here tonight? More push and pull?"

Aaron smiled gently. "No, believe it or not, I'd rather you were here with me." He stiffened his resolve. "But I think you should spend some time with your family. They're why you came home."

RJ couldn't seem to find it in himself to argue with that. "Tomorrow night, then?"

Now that Aaron could agree to. Whatever happened with his mom in the morning, he'd need a good, hard, spanking as a distraction. Hopefully his ass would be healed up enough by then. And how lucky was he to have RJ on hand and eager to deliver just what he needed most? It was too good to be true.

They kissed goodbye at the door and no sooner had it closed behind RJ's back than Aaron groaned, wishing he hadn't sent him away and instead insisted on another night together.

His phone buzzed.

Gonna be a long 24 hours. Miss you already.

Aaron's heart flipped over, and he sent a kiss emoji back and hardened himself for the night of grading and mental Mom-arguing ahead. No matter what, tomorrow he was going to take charge of the situation. He wasn't going to give his mother a chance to rake him over the coals. Though the largest part of his plan was to simply avoid her.

The last day of school before Christmas break was always hectic. With any luck, he could make like a snowflake and melt into the scenery. And if not, then he'd just have to be courageous and take his licks like a man.

Like he took the swats of RJ's hand.

BY MID-DAY, THE plan to avoid his mom was going well. Avoiding Lauren was another story.

"You have that look again," Lauren said, gazing at him thoughtfully over her coffee mug. She leaned against the door to his classroom, having appeared there like the Ghost of Christmas Present at the start of his free period. Her green, red, and white plaid skirt stopped just above the knee, revealing a line of skin that was a bit risqué by her standards.

Her red sweater was tight over her bosom, and she looked like she might even be wearing lipstick. Festive.

Aaron motioned her in. She shut the door behind her and crossed to him, eyes glittering with disapproval. "Please tell me you hooked up with some Grindr stranger and not our former student again."

Aaron wondered what it was about his face that seemed to give away to everyone the fact that he'd gotten fucked again. He didn't have any beard burn, and he'd gone to bed early in hopes of recovering from his weekend-long tryst, but still… The kids had all given him funny looks again this morning when he'd walked in, along with a few giggles, hisses, and ridiculous ewwws and oooohs. He'd ignored them, of course, but what was different about him after being with RJ? How did everyone know?

"It wasn't a Grindr hookup, no," Aaron hedged.

Lauren wasn't an idiot, and her brow arched above a decidedly sour expression. "Why, Aaron? I thought we decided not to go any farther down that path? You're already in the doghouse with your mother. Or so I heard. Word gets around when you throw a hissy fit at a dance and stomp out on the principal."

"I didn't throw a hissy fit. I'm not the drama queen for fuck's sake. She is."

"I know, I know, but while I want to hear about your mother—why didn't you call me by the way? I had to hear about it from Jennifer Jenkins, and you know how she distorts things?" She pulled up a chair and sat down by Aaron at his desk. "Never mind—we really need to discuss this mess with your student."

"Former student. Very much former."

Lauren snapped her fingers in his face. "Aaron!"

"What? I didn't call you after the fight with my mother because I had a date."

"With RJ Blitz?"

"Yes."

"Why?" She squeezed the bridge of her nose and put her coffee mug down on his desk beside his page-a-day calendar. It offered a decidedly pointed quote by Pema Chödrön declaring that we already had everything we needed.

"I don't know, because I wanted to, and don't you think it's about damn time I do something *I* want to do for a change? For me? Because I *want* it?"

Lauren stared at him and said slowly, "Your mother is going to lose her mind."

"I don't give a shit."

Lauren blinked, stood up, paced away from him, and then came back to sit on the edge of his desk. "Who are you? What have you done with Aaron?"

"Cute. Look, I didn't mean to see him again. But he texted me on Wednesday—"

"Wednesday! That's the day we talked about it and you swore him off!" Her eyes were round and vehement.

"I know, but he texted a very civilized message and I ended up replying." Aaron rubbed a hand over his face. His cheeks were hot to the touch. "So we had a little back and forth then."

"Aaron…"

"Then, Thursday, after the humiliating elf gig at the pep rally—"

Lauren sighed sympathetically. "That really was too much. Your mother took that whole thing too far. I'm sorry. I feel like I should have done more to put a stop to it. Volunteered myself or something."

Aaron waved the thought away. "I think she wanted to avoid any sort of 'sexy elf' issues that may have come up by having one of the women teachers dressed up in front of the boys." Aaron knew he really should admit that it wasn't his mother's fault that he'd stood up in front of all of his students in an elf costume, that it was his own damn idiocy, but he couldn't bring himself to say it.

Lauren looked pleased that Aaron thought she was hot enough to bring the threat of "sexy elf" to the middle school pep rally.

Aaron added, "So I was having a rough day."

"You should have called me."

"I know, but he texted me before I could."

Lauren tilted her head and gave him a narrow-eyed once-over. "Why'd you even give him your number?'"

"Christ. I'm allowed to give the men I fuck my number, Lauren."

"I know, I know, this is just…" She grabbed her coffee, closed her eyes, and sipped it again, seeming to get herself together. "Go on. I'm sorry. I'm listening."

"So we texted Thursday. That's all."

"Sexted?"

"Maybe."

Lauren moaned. "He's a former student, Aaron! What were you thinking? After everything before? With Coach McAllister? That was such a close call for you. And now this?"

Aaron rubbed hand over his face again, his cheeks even hotter, and leaned back. "For God's sake, he's a grown man who's fucked his way across half of Europe and all of America from what I can tell. He can make up his own mind whether or not to fuck a former teacher. I have no power to lord over him now. He received his entirely well-deserved C-minus from me ages ago. There's no changing it and I wouldn't even if I could."

Lauren moved from his desk to the chair again, crossed her legs, and glanced over her shoulder to make sure the door to Aaron's classroom was still firmly closed. "I know all that, and it's all true. But Aaron it just isn't done. Former students are…off limits. Taboo. It's just…hinky."

"Normally, I'd agree. But this is different."

"How?"

"He's more experienced than I am. He's a man."

"He's the man?"

"Don't even go there. Not even as a joke."

Lauren held her hands up in surrender. "Fine, fine. Sorry. We've been close for how long now? Since grad school, right? I just don't want to see you make your life harder than it already is. You struggle so much dealing with your mom, and not being out at school, and all the rest. The McAllister mess just made everything worse. You have that ding against you and…Aaron, I just want you to be happy."

"My life is good. I am happy," Aaron said. "I'm a homeowner, my cat loves me, and I have you as my friend." And RJ in the sack, for however long that lasts.

"And I'm just trying to watch your back. I don't want you to get hurt."

"I know. But you don't need to worry about that."

Lauren cocked a brow skeptically.

"RJ's just in town for the holidays. There's an expiration date on this affair, Lauren." Not exactly true anymore, after what they'd agreed to the day before, but he didn't know how to explain that. RJ would leave and it would likely end anyway. This explanation was easier.

Plus, he wasn't sure there was an expiration date on his dissatisfaction with staying in the closet at school to soothe his mother's sensibilities. If this weekend had proven anything, it was that by denying himself what he most wanted in life in order to keep from losing his job and his mom, he wasn't actually saving anything. Much less himself.

"So, he's bored and you're just a bit of fun for him? Meaningless sex? That's all?" Lauren asked.

Aaron blinked up at her in shock. "Is that what you think of me? That the only thing someone would want from me is meaningless sex?"

"What? No! You said—" Lauren broke off. "Aaron, *you* said this was going to be over after the holidays."

"It doesn't make it meaningless. Not to him. Or to me."

Lauren's head tilted. "Okay? I'm sorry? I didn't mean to upset you."

"It's *not* meaningless sex." His gut churned at the thought that what he'd done with RJ, what they shared could be considered meaningless by anyone at all. Much less RJ. God.

"Okay, I believe you. And isn't that why this is a problem?"

"No." Aaron wasn't hearing anymore. He was done with this conversation. He glanced at the clock, willing his free hour to be done. "I have some grading I need to finish. We'll discuss this more another day."

"Aaron, I didn't mean to hurt you. I never want to hurt you." Lauren's voice had gone soft and tender.

"I know."

"It's just that I don't understand. You made it out like a hookup, then you said it was going to be, I don't know, a fling? Something with an expiration date. But now..." She took hold of his hand and he met her gaze again. "Please. I know I said the wrong thing. Just explain it to me. I want to have your back when the shit hits the fan. Because, hon, if this gets out, and you know that it will, it's going to be a zinger. With your mother if no one else."

Aaron pulled his hand away, the dull angry panic still racing inside him at the suggestion that his hours with RJ had no meaning. "I don't want to talk about it now. I have these papers." He indicated the stack he was only halfway through. The sooner he finished them, the sooner he could submit the grades, and the sooner he could climb into RJ's lap and be held again. The sooner he could prove it meant something even if it wasn't going to last.

"Don't see him again," Lauren urged as she stood up to leave.

"Are you serious?" Aaron didn't have the willpower for that.

"Get yourself a nice stranger from Grindr tonight to blot out the memories and move on from this. He's not worth it."

"Not worth—"

The speaker crackled. "Aaron Danvers, please report to the principal's office. Aaron Danvers, report to Principal Shock's office."

"You'd think I was an actual child," Aaron said, shoving back his chair. "Summoning me the way she would a sixth grader she wanted to humiliate."

Lauren followed him out of the room, her mug gripped in both hands. "I know you're mad at me right now, but I'll be here for you. After." Lauren squeezed his shoulder with sympathetic eyes. "Go on."

Chapter Twenty-One

"CARTER WARD WAS in my office earlier this morning."

Aaron blinked at his mother, his stomach knotting up at her severe and uncompromising expression. He took the seat across from her desk. It didn't have any fresh stains as far as he could tell, but he didn't look too closely. He'd expected her to start in on him about their "discussion" at the dance the other night, and maybe she was warming up to it by mentioning Carter's visit to her office, but maybe not.

Swallowing hard, he asked, "Is he okay?"

"He's fine. But he had some interesting news for me."

Aaron wiped his palms on his pant legs. "What's that?"

"He said you're sleeping with his brother? A former student of yours, no less."

"Wait, what? Carter Ward's brother…" In a flash, pieces of his conversations with Carter, Carter's dad, and RJ all came together. "Oh, my God." Aaron choked on his own spit.

By the time he finished coughing and sputtering, his mother had stood up, put both hands on her desk, and leaned toward him, eyes radiating fury. "What did I tell you, Aaron, when you started here?"

"Not to embarrass you."

"And what have you done?"

Aaron stood. There was no way he was giving her the higher ground. This way, they had to look at each other face-to-face.

"What have I done, Mom? First off, what I've done is none of your business as the principal of this school."

"It is! There are ethical violations at play here, and we know from the past that you are not above violating those for your pleasure!"

Aaron sucked in a breath, gut-punched by her words. "No. That's not true. And I owe you no explanation. But since you're my mother, not just my principal, I'll tell you what I've done. I've started seeing a grown man who, as I've only just now discovered, happens to be the stepbrother of a current student, and who I knew from the start had been a student of mine five years ago. This man was a senior then, and *nothing* happened at the time. I barely interacted with him at all, which says more about my teaching skills than my morals."

His mother's eyes narrowed, and she spit out a question. "How long?"

Aaron tilted his head in confusion.

"How long have you been sleeping with this man?"

Swallowing hard, Aaron whispered, "Not long. It's very new."

"Then put a stop to it."

"Why?"

"You know why, Aaron." She pointed at him, her sharp nail coming close to his face as she leaned across her desk. "Parents will get wind of it and think you're a pervert. And what will I say to that? It's bad enough that you're *gay*, hard enough to defend that choice to even my friends, but to parents? This will look as if you're a child molester, a child *groomer*, and I won't be able to say you aren't. What? What are you doing?"

Aaron's cheeks burned like he'd been slapped. He sucked in a breath, ready to say something—he didn't even know what—but instead turned and walked out of the room. Rita and Jolene stared after him, buffing their nails and reeking of peppermint. The Christmas tree in the office corner with the art class decorations blinked in multicolor spasms.

"Aaron!" his mother called, her high heels clacking as she came to her office door. "Aaron Danvers, come back here! Now!"

But he didn't. He didn't go back to his classroom either. He went outside and used his phone to call an Uber because he'd left his car keys in his desk. He couldn't breathe if he went back in that building. He only had to wait three minutes to climb inside the dark car.

He'd always believed his mother in the past. Believed her lies about just needing some time to accept him, about not caring that he was gay but rather how hard being gay would make his life. But in the end, the truth was she not only cared more about what people thought of her than about his happiness, but actually believed he was the kind of man who couldn't be trusted around children. One thoughtless sentence had driven that home.

This will look as if you're a child molester, a child groomer, and I won't be able to say you aren't.

The Uber took him back to his apartment, and he used the key he'd hidden beneath his neighbor's never-used grill to get into his apartment, grateful for the waiting, comforting purrs of Constance. He'd have Lauren bring his keys, satchel, and the final papers home for him to grade. He was done for the rest of this semester. There was the entirety of the day left, sure.

But as far as he was concerned, he didn't need to be there for it. Any substitute, even a last-minute one, could handle it as well as he could. Everyone knew the last day before break was for watching movies and eating cookies anyway.

Aaron wasn't willing to talk to anyone right now, what with his throat still tight with unshed tears. So he texted Lauren with his requests and sent a message through the school email to Rita letting her know that he would be invoking a sick day and would not be returning until next semester.

Then he crawled into the bed where only twenty-four hours before he'd rested peacefully in RJ's arms. He stared up at the ceiling trying to understand the extent of the bomb he'd just set off in his life. When his anger ran out, he was left tired and threadbare, so he rolled onto his stomach and fell asleep.

RJ SAT DOWN in the lounge chair across from where his mother was folding laundry, still thinking about Aaron's request that they fuck bareback. He wanted to, desperately, and yet...*fuck.*

"Mom, I think I'm in trouble."

She put aside a small swimsuit of Beau's and pushed her blonde hair behind her ears. "RJ, what on earth have you done now?"

"I've fallen in love."

His mom blinked at him from over the many, many, many pairs of underwear she'd folded and had put into carefully sorted piles on the couch. They came in all shapes and sizes for the family. "Excuse me?"

RJ ran a hand over his close-shorn hair and sighed. "I've fallen in love."

"With that young man you brought by the other day? Aaron?"

"Yes." A helpless grin spread over his face, and his mother's skeptical expression melted into a silly grin of her own, which she promptly schooled into something much more parental.

"Oh, hon. Don't you think it's a little too soon? You just met him."

"Yeah. It's definitely too soon," RJ said, deciding to leave aside the clarification on just when he'd met Aaron for another day. "But I also know for sure." He lifted his hands and let them fall again. "I'm in love."

His mother pondered him uncertainly. "That's...that's...well, then I'm happy for you."

"No, Mom, it's terrible. I'm in awful trouble."

She cocked her head. "I don't understand."

RJ groaned and wiped a hand over his eyes. "Because we've agreed it's just a temporary thing. Until I leave on my next tour."

"So... Aaron doesn't feel the same way about you?" She sounded sad and a little angry, like she might go yell at Aaron for failing to love her son. It was sweet.

RJ considered Aaron's confession, when he'd admitted that he wanted to see where this might go, that he wasn't willing to call it a hookup and be done. "I think he might, actually. But he won't see it that way. He's skittish. And even if he does admit to his feelings, it won't change anything."

"Now you've really confused me." She crossed her legs on the couch, barefoot and comfortable. "How does loving each other not change anything?"

"I mean it will change *everything*," RJ corrected. "That's what makes it trouble. But it won't matter. It won't make any difference in the long run. We'll fall apart like everyone does, and us faster than usual, because, you know...me."

"You?"

"I'm a bad risk." RJ shrugged. "I wouldn't put any bets on myself, why would Aaron?"

"Hon, you're saying that like...like..." She tossed her hands up. "What on earth *are* you saying? You're speaking in riddles now. Just get it out. Tell me what you mean."

RJ chewed on his inner cheek, considering. He almost said never mind and walked out of the room, almost made an excuse about just being tired and needing to go write music or practice just to get out of the conversation. But then he remembered Aaron that morning calling him out on his bullshit about his family, about not fitting into it. He never would if he didn't let them into his life, now would he?

"I don't really believe in lasting love, Mama," he finally said. "I mean, I believe in *love*. I've fallen into it before—with Pan—and that ended with me not able to get away fast enough from the shit show we'd become together. And then there was you and Dad—"

"Oh, RJ."

He winced. "And then you and Dad *again*. The second time was the real kicker, you know? That's when I knew that love couldn't last. And I'm not blaming you. I just know it's true. Things fade, people get tired of each other, the bloom goes off the rose—"

"That's not what happened between me and your father, and that's not what happened with Pan either," she said tightly. Pushing her hair behind her ears again, she leaned forward and caught his gaze in her own, making sure he didn't look away. "Don't lie to yourself about the past, because that'll only poison the future. I spent years lying to myself about your dad, and you're right, it did nothing good for either of us. But I had to stop eventually, and as soon as I did, Doug came along."

RJ's lip twitched. He didn't do it on purpose. He'd swear to it in a court of law. Still, his face betrayed him.

"What? You don't like Doug?"

"I like him. He'll be a good dad to the kids even after, I mean, if…" He swallowed hard. "He does right by Carter, so I know that he'll do right by Perri and Beau, too. That's all I can ask."

She blinked at him, her eyes growing bright with tears.

RJ felt sick. What had he said so wrong?

"Are you… Did you just… Randall James Blitz, are you saying you expect Doug to *leave me*?"

RJ threw his hands out, blocking her words. "No! Of course not. I mean, you could leave him for all I know."

"I am *not* going to leave him!" She threw a pair of folded socks at RJ's head.

"I didn't say…!" He dodged a second pair. "Mom, I'm trying to tell you that I don't believe—"

"That you don't believe in love. I get it." She wiped at her eyes before furiously piling the stack of underwear she'd folded onto another stack. RJ'd had no idea folding laundry could be so aggressive. "Because of me. And my choices. And—"

"No. That's not it at all!" RJ exclaimed. "You're twisting this all around and backwards." He let out a slow breath, trying to keep this conversation from going further off the rails. "I just see the way the world works. Love doesn't last. People divorce, or cheat, or live in bitter resignation with each other. It's always the same. It's human nature. It's not about you, or Doug, or even about Dad—"

"It's definitely about your dad," she said bitterly.

"It's not about Dad! It's about love!" RJ jerked his hands over his hair. "And how I don't believe in it. And that sucks, because I'm in it, and it won't last! And everyone's going to get hurt!"

His mother stared at him, utterly bewildered. Her eyes glittered with more tears. "I don't know what you thought you said just now, RJ? But all I'm hearing is how I'm a terrible mother who failed you completely in the most important thing a mother can teach: love. And I don't even know what to say about that. Except that I'm sorry. I'm *so* sorry. If I could go back and do it all differently I would."

RJ covered his face, his stomach curdling. He whispered, "You should have aborted me."

"For fuck's sake, shut your mouth."

"No, I'm serious," he said, lifting his head and speaking the truth for once. "You wouldn't have spent those first years with Dad then. You'd have gone to school and gotten a degree. Had a career. And, if not for me, later when he came back, he'd have had no way to get back in with you. No reason to ask you to let him back into your life without me as his pawn."

"RJ, I love you," his mom said, tears slipping over her cheeks. "Please, stop saying this... Just stop."

"I'm only saying I wouldn't blame you if you ever wished you'd ended it before it began."

"Abort you? I don't wish that," she choked out. "I certainly don't blame any woman for making that choice, but it *is* a choice. And I chose to keep you. I look at you here with me right now, and I can't imagine my world without you in it." She wiped at her eyes. "I know you don't see it that way. To you, I was never home, and we never had money, and when your father came back with all those sky-high promises, I fell for it and I let him hurt you—"

"He never laid a finger on me," RJ spit out.

"I know. He laid fingers on me. Fists."

They stared at each other. She'd never admitted that out loud. RJ had guessed it, had thought maybe, and had sometimes seen bruises, but there were always excuses. His father had been a piece of shit in enough other ways that adding physical abuse to the list hadn't been necessary to hate him. Not really. But now that he knew—

"I'm so sorry, Mama. I would have stopped him if I'd known."

"And that's why I didn't tell you. I didn't want him turning it on you. When he left again, it was such a huge fucking relief." She gusted a sigh. "I only wish I had been able to get therapy for you back then." She tilted her head. "Do you want to go now? To therapy? Doug could—"

"No, Mama. I'm fine."

"You're not fine!" She flung her arms wide. "You fly all over the world, trailing after bands, and you barely call home, and you don't text or write, and you don't know how to love, and—"

"I know how to love, Mama," he whispered. "I don't trust it to last. It's different."

"It's not!"

"It is."

She blew her hair out of her face. "Oh, for fuck's sake, RJ, we aren't children. Let's not be ridiculous here. Love is trust. Don't you get it?" She reached out and grabbed his hand, squeezing hard. "Love *is* trust."

Chapter Twenty-Two

*C*AN YOU COME *over?*

That was all the text said, but it was all RJ needed. He'd practiced with the Old Skool Millennials at Joel and Casey's place after his long talk with his mom had finally ended with her sobbing in his arms and him crying a little too. They'd said a lot of scary things to each other, but they'd made it through. It was more than he'd expected when the conversation had started, but a pretty big dent had been made in the mountain of things kept unsaid for far too long.

The band had added a few more songs to their repertoire for the shows this week, so he was able to get his mind off things during the rehearsal itself. But no sooner had he climbed back into the SUV than his mind had gone racing back to Aaron, and then ping-ponged around the conversation with his mom.

The text was perfect timing.

Yes. I'm on my way.

That was all he sent back, but it said more than maybe even Aaron knew. *Yes, I'll drop everything to come to you.* Because he was in love.

And he knew from experience how precious and fleeting that feeling was, so he'd indulge it while it lasted. He'd do anything for Aaron right now. One day in the future, probably before he even left for his next tour, they'd fight, or figure out each other's flaws, and the shine would wear off. They'd part ways, hopefully amicably, but maybe not, and so it would go. But for now, he would indulge his lover's whims, and happily.

Besides, going home felt too awkward right now. After everything he'd admitted to his mother, and she'd admitted to him, a little space would be good for them. And absolutely no space at all would be perfect with Aaron. They could lose themselves in all the sweaty, cummy potential of their bodies. Zero space between them.

But when he arrived at Aaron's apartment, any ideas he might have had about sex flew out the window. Aaron opened the door wearing a pair of soft sweatpants that hung off his narrow hips, a worn-out T-shirt with a stretched collar exposing the line of his neck, and the saddest pair of eyes RJ had seen in a long time. Sadder even than his mother's during their difficult talk. There was a deep hopelessness in Aaron's gaze that had been absent from his mom's, a lack of fire.

"What's wrong?" RJ asked, taking off his leather jacket and hanging it up on the rack beside the door before following Aaron into the living room.

The silver tree still sparkled, but the colored lights weren't turned on, and it looked a little dimmer than it should. Like Aaron.

"Something happen at school today? Your mom?"

Aaron patted the couch beside him, and RJ took the spot. He took hold of the back of Aaron's neck to drag him into what looked like a very necessary hug. But Aaron dislodged his hand, pulling it between his own to hold in his lap. One knee up on the sofa, and the other bare foot on the floor in a half cross-legged position, Aaron stared quietly down at their joined hands.

"Your stepbrother is a student of mine."

"Carter?" RJ blinked in confusion. "Why didn't you say... Oh, you didn't know." Aaron nodded. "Until today." Another nod. "How?"

"Doug and Betsy's house isn't in my school's zone. I assumed I was safe. You know what they say about assumptions..." Aaron winced.

"Ah. I think he still goes to his old school from before the divorce. Over near where his mom lives." RJ groaned. "Which, yeah, probably zones him for Pineview. Fuck."

Aaron swallowed, wiping his fingers over his tired eyes. "That makes sense."

"So what happened?"

"He went to the principal—my mother—about it."

RJ tried to figure out what that meant. "I don't understand."

"He somehow knows we're seeing each other. He told her."

"He turned you in? For seeing me?"

"I have no idea what he said to her. It all blew up too fast for me to even discern what Carter's motivations were." He blinked rapidly. "It was just…kerblewy. She accused me of…things. I lost my temper. She lost her temper. I stormed out. I…I left school. In the middle of the day. I've never done that before."

RJ shifted so that he was mirroring Aaron's position on the sofa, never pulling his hand away, letting Aaron clench it for comfort. "Okay."

"It's not okay, RJ."

"Why not?"

Aaron looked down at their hands and his shoulders sagged. "I didn't tell you everything about my past. When you asked me why I switched schools and what was going on with my mother, I left out a key piece of my history."

"Why?"

"Because I was ashamed." He actually trembled but when RJ reached out to comfort him, he drew back, still clinging to RJ's hand, though.

"Tell me."

Aaron shook his head.

"Tell. Me." RJ tried the dom voice, and just like that Aaron softened, surrendered.

"As teachers, we're bound by a code of ethics. There are certain things we can lose our careers over."

"Like?"

"Our code of ethics says that teachers must demonstrate strong character traits, such as honesty, lawfulness, respect, decency, and unity."

"That sounds pretty vague to be honest."

"Maybe, but I've already been written up once by my former school and by the Superintendent of Schools for violating the code of ethics with regards to decency."

RJ went very still. "Because you're gay?"

Aaron shook his head. "No, because I fucked the gym coach at Taylor High while he was still married."

RJ nodded his head slowly. "Coach Ingles or Coach McAllister?"

Aaron blinked at him, tears rising in his eyes. Shit, why did RJ keep doing this to people he cared about? Saying things that obviously hurt? "McAllister," Aaron whispered. "On school property. Twice. We got busted by another teacher."

RJ stayed silent, hoping that was the better choice, and squeezed Aaron's hand to encourage him to go on.

"I didn't know he was married. I barely knew anything about him. We hooked up via Grindr, and we both just had torso pics up. He listed things I'm interested in." Aaron blushed. "He promised to be rough with me. I wanted that."

RJ nodded again, though the idea of anyone else blemishing Aaron's skin pissed him off.

"We met up outside of school the first time. Recognized each other. Fucked anyway. And then at school..." He shrugged. "He enjoyed humiliating me. Fucking me over the desk in his office. Taunting me about what his football players would think if they saw him pounding their queer composition teacher."

RJ swallowed the groan that rose up. "Did you like that?"

Aaron shrugged. "I couldn't afford to be picky. He fucked like he meant it. That was enough to lure me back for another round. Again, in the coaching staff office. Coach Ingles came in late to make some copies for his class..." Aaron smiled bitterly. "I was fired the next day."

"And McAllister?"

"Can't lose a winning coach, you know."

"He got to stay?"

Aaron nodded. "Everyone knew I'd been let go for violating the code of ethics. They all assumed I'd done something terrible. There were rumors of all sorts. I was told by the principals of other schools not to even bother applying in Knoxville. To move on. But I'd just bought the apartment and I know that fucking on school property was wrong, but..." His voice broke. "I swear I didn't know he was married."

"I know," RJ said. Though it wouldn't have mattered to him if Aaron had known. It fit his narrative about love anyway. It didn't last. Of course, Coach McAllister was boning Aaron instead of his wife. That's the way relationships worked in the end. He was just pissed that Aaron had been hurt.

"My mom was my only option. She took me on. Made me promise...all that stuff I told you about already. But this is why. The real reason. Because I'm not a good man and I've done bad things. I can't be trusted."

"That's absurd."

"You'd think so, but she as much as said today that she wouldn't be able to defend me if people found out you were my former student. That they'd accuse me of being a pedophile and she—" Aaron's voice broke off, his throat working. He shook his head and tears rose in his eyes again. "She said she couldn't refute it."

RJ breathed through the rush of red in his eyes. He wanted to find the woman and shake her, shout her down. But that was ridiculous. He couldn't change a homophobe's mind by screaming at them. He'd learned that years ago during his one and only bar fight in L.A.

"So Carter told your mother—the principal—that you and I were dating, and that you'd been my teacher."

Aaron nodded.

"Okay. What happens now?"

"I don't know. I suppose..." Aaron took in a shaky breath. "We should stop seeing each other."

RJ scoffed. "I don't think so."

Aaron looked up at him, lashes wet with tears. "We have to. I'll lose my job, and I don't know if I'll be able to find another one. I was thinking of leaving, looking for something else, but with two ethics strikes against me, no one will hire me. And what about Carter? What this could do to him?"

"You're not going to lose your job, Aaron. And Carter needs to pull his head out of his ass."

"Excuse me?"

"I'm just saying that I don't know what's going on with Carter, but whatever it is, I refuse to let it cost you your job. If you still want to work with your mother, that is. I don't see why you do, honestly."

"I don't want to work with her anymore? I don't think so, anyway. I love working with Lauren, but everything else about the job is just so toxic." Aaron frowned. "What do you know about Carter?"

"Not much. He's not around me often. I don't know if it's because I'm gay or what, but he doesn't seem comfortable with me."

Aaron nodded slowly. "I think the first thing we need to do is have a meeting with your mom and Doug, and then maybe Carter, after they understand the situation."

"Okay? But why?"

"I can't say much because I don't want to break anyone's trust, but if Carter's upset because I'm dating you—for any reason—then it needs to be sorted out, and the quicker we do that the better off for him."

"And what about what's best for you, baby?"

"I'm at a loss," Aaron whispered. "My behavior was unprofessional, but I don't regret it. So was hers, not that it excuses me. Like you say, I can't keep on this way. I know you and I aren't a forever thing, but I want to find that someday with someone. And I believe you when you say I deserve to have that." He looked up shyly. "But so long as I work at the same school as my mom, there's just no chance. I think, no matter what happens with Carter, it's time I start looking for another job."

"Is that really the solution? Maybe your mother's the one who should leave. Think about the other teachers working under her. She must have others who are LGBT on staff."

"Yes, but they aren't her son. It may be hard to understand, but my mother can actually be pretty accepting of LGBT people, supportive even, so long as the person in question isn't me."

"That's bullshit."

"I know. But she's gone to gay weddings and sent flowers to sick partners. It's just me that she holds to this standard."

"The straight standard?"

"The 'everything you do must fit this mold I had in mind for you when you were born' standard. But there's always some part of me that doesn't fit, like my choices with Coach McAllister, and now you. She's always trying to shove those parts of me back in the mold, and another part pops out the other side. It's an endless struggle. I think...I genuinely think we'd have a better relationship if I saw less of her, if I worked in another school, or, hell, another city. Another country even."

RJ touched Aaron's cheek, missing the dimples that played there when he smiled. "What's the first step in doing that?"

Aaron huffed. "Accepting that I need to do it. Then putting out feelers for open positions. Checking listings. I've been curious about overseas opportunities. I hear winter is really cold in Finland, though." The dimples appeared and RJ's heart clenched.

"Would you really want to go so far? Leave your apartment?"

"I could rent it out while I'm gone. I've never been anywhere. It could be a fresh start for me. No more pretending or playing myself down. Just being fully Aaron. Like I was Saturday night at Scruffy Town Hall. Like I am when I'm with you."

"What about Constance?"

Aaron's eyes softened. "She could come with me. I have a cat carrier for things like that. I just want to be free."

"Speaking of free." RJ reached into his jeans pocket and pulled out the already-worn-at-the-creases piece of paper with his results from his doctor visit earlier in the month. He'd looked at it far too often since he'd printed it out, imagining what it meant for the ways they could play now. "Proof. STD-free." He passed it to Aaron. who flicked his gaze over the results, the corner of his lips lifting slightly.

"Wow." He met RJ's eyes. "So, we could? Without a condom?"

"Yeah."

"I've never..." Aaron bit into his lower lip. "I've never actually played that way before."

"Me either."

"Really?"

RJ shook his head.

"Why?"

"Never had anyone I trusted enough."

Love is trust, he remembered his mother saying. Maybe he'd never loved Pan at all then, since he'd never trusted him as far as he could throw him. Maybe what they'd had was something else similar to love—infatuation, or maybe a word in another language. English was limited in its words for feelings around romance, affection, and sex.

"I'd be your first?" Aaron whispered.

"Yes." *And maybe my last.*

RJ tried to harden the melting softness that Aaron brought out in him, wishing that he could imagine ever wanting anyone but this man again. But he couldn't. No doubt time would make a fool of him. But would it be so bad if he just let it?

"Winter break starts officially tomorrow," Aaron said hesitantly, looking up at RJ with a strange expression. "Even if I hadn't left early today, I don't need to go in."

"Is this your way of giving me permission to ditch my family to stay here with you?"

"No," Aaron said, laughing a little, a hint of light returning to his eyes. "I guess I'm just saying that I'll be bored out of my mind looking for new teaching positions all day for the next few weeks, and stressed thinking about the implications of that fight with my mother. And, at night, if you can get away, I'd enjoy having something else to do with my time."

"Like me."

"You."

"It'll be my pleasure to entertain you." RJ took the slip of paper with the results from Aaron's hand and put it on the coffee table. "Do you want to play a little now? Take your mind off everything?"

"All right." Aaron's breath came faster.

"Start by taking off those sweatpants. Leave the T-shirt." He leaned in and whispered in Aaron's ear, "I'll make you forget." He hardened his voice. "Get on the floor. Elbows on the coffee table. Ass up."

Chapter Twenty-Three

S HIVERING AT THE command in RJ's voice, Aaron did as he was told. As soon as he was positioned, RJ walked around him. "Eyes on me," RJ said when Aaron blushed and looked away.

Constance let out a sharp meow and ran out from under the sofa to dash down the hallway toward the bedroom. RJ put his hand on Aaron's head, ruffling through his hair soothingly before gripping and yanking his head back, meeting his gaze. "Eyes on me," he said more firmly.

Aaron licked his lips and complied, barely even blinking when RJ released his hair and stepped back. He touched the buckle of his brown, braided leather belt. "I found this in a box of stuff from high school. There was a poem in there too. I should have brought it."

Aaron opened his mouth, but RJ swooped in and covered it with his palm. "Do you want to play hard tonight?"

Aaron nodded. *Oh yes.* Excitement drummed through him.

"Safe-word hard?"

He nodded even more enthusiastically.

"Good. Me too." RJ stroked Aarons lips with his fingertips, lifting a brow slowly. He undid the buckle on his belt, slipped it through the loops, and held it out. Aaron stared at it and swallowed hard.

"Listen carefully. Your safe word is Hermey, got it?"

"Hermey," Aaron repeated.

"Good. You say that, and I'll stop immediately no matter what we're doing."

Aaron nodded.

He lifted the belt. "I intend to use this. Do you consent?"

"Yes."

"Do you want to come in me? Or do you want me to come in you?"

Aaron lifted his chin defiantly. "I want both."

"Mmm. I like to stay in charge though, if that's okay with you. Just call me a bossy bottom."

Aaron licked his lips. "That's fine. I like it when you…" He took a shuddery breath, and his eyes closed again. "I like it when…" He couldn't seem to get the words out.

"You like when someone else cares enough to take control, don't you, Mr. Danvers? Makes you feel safe." There was a long pause before RJ quietly added, "Loved."

Aaron shuddered, his heart racing. *Yes. Oh, yes.*

RJ smiled wickedly. "Is there anything you need to tell me? Hard boundaries I should be aware of? Speak now or forever hold your peace—unless you invoke your safe word, of course."

"I don't like watersports." Aaron had only had one guy try that with him once years ago, but it left him feeling degraded, and not in a good way. "And no bruises on my face."

Heat flashed in RJ's eyes, some sort of possessive lust that Aaron felt like a punch to his heart. He gasped for air, his asshole feeling exposed and achy at the same time, even though it was, as yet, untouched.

Fuck, he wanted whatever RJ was going to dish out. He'd take any-thing—anything at all. If RJ pushed, he'd relent on the hard boundaries too, he could feel it. He wanted to give himself over to RJ's care. Surrender entirely. Stop living by anyone's rules but RJ's. Give up the hard choices. Just for a few minutes. Just for tonight.

"Right. Done," RJ said, bending his belt in half and using the folded end to stroke Aaron's cheekbone. The braided leather scraped along his skin, rough and a little threatening. "The rules. Number one: no talking except for your safe word. That means no arguing, no suggestions, no complaining, and no begging. All I want from you now, Mr. Danvers, are your honest noises or silence." He stroked the belt over Aaron's back, letting it run its whole length, seductive and menacing at the same time. "Though I prefer noises, just so you know."

Aaron swallowed and nodded.

"Number two: submit and obey. Do what I tell you to do. It'll be harder than it sounds, but I promise it will be worth it."

Aaron nodded his assent again, though his heart kicked. What might RJ ask of him? His hands went sweaty, and he squeezed his asshole, trying to get a grip on the rush of excitement and fear flooding him.

"That's it, Mr. Danvers. Two very hard-to-follow rules. But I believe in you." RJ reached out and took hold of Aaron's hair again, slipping his fingers through it soothingly. "I'm going to take you so high tonight. You're going to fly like one of Santa's reindeer."

Aaron let out a shaky breath and said nothing, assuming the rules were already in place. RJ kissed his forehead, his nose, and then his mouth. Chaste kisses, a little wet from where he'd licked his lips, but lacking in the open-mouthed passion RJ usually went for immediately. Then he straightened.

"We'll warm up to the belt," he said, putting it down beside Aaron's head on the coffee table, right where Aaron would see it. RJ undid his dark jeans, shoving them open enough for the slick head of his cock to poke out from the top of his boxer briefs. Aaron's pulse pounded as he watched RJ roll up the sleeves of his T-shirt, further exposing his strong arms. With a grim smile, RJ shook out his hands. His long fingers danced in front of Aaron's face.

"Hold still," RJ said. "I'm going to make that sweet ass shake, Mr. Danvers."

Aaron took hold of the edge of the coffee table, the rug making his knees ache already. He wondered if he was allowed to use gestures to request a pillow, or if all communication was discouraged.

RJ's hand came down on his ass, blotting out the query with a rosy smear of pain. Aaron was still a little tender from the night with the ruler, though the redness and bruises had faded entirely. He gasped, tucking tail and tossing his head back, exposing his throat.

"Mmm," RJ said. "I love how you react." He pressed on Aaron's lower back, pushing until Aaron untucked his butt and stuck it back out again. "Hold it just like that, Mr. Danvers." He leaned close and whispered menacingly in Aaron's ear, "Or else."

Aaron didn't have time to wonder what threat underlined the words because RJ swatted his butt again, this time in a rhythm of slap-stroke-slap, alternating cheeks and building in intensity. Aaron squirmed, ducking his head down to press his forehead against the coffee table, shoving his ass back even though the rising pain had him gasping and grunting with each swat.

Sweat broke out on his shoulders and chills shivered down his spine. Still RJ continued on, steady and smooth, each slap burning deep into Aaron's flesh until all he could think about was grabbing a breath before the next one landed. The rest of the world and its worries evaporated in the pain.

"Nice work," RJ said, ending with a slow stroke on Aaron's stinging ass cheeks. "Let me just…" He squatted down behind Aaron, palming his burning cheeks and spreading him open. "There. Mmm."

Aaron shivered as RJ licked his asshole gently, almost imperceptibly, the exact opposite of the feeling of the harsh spanking. He had to slow his breathing and concentrate just to sense the slick, tingly teasing of his rim.

"Mmm," RJ said again, releasing Aaron's ass cheeks like he was putting away a treat he planned to finish later. "I love the way you tremble when I do that."

Aaron hadn't even realized he was shaking, but of course he was. Not just from the tender rimming, which hadn't lasted nearly long enough, but also from the spanking itself. His cock was hard, straining up against his stomach and leaking pre-come into a tiny puddle on the rug beneath his knees. He looked up at RJ, hoping his eyes conveyed his need for more assplay. He needed RJ's tongue and fingers. He craved prostate stroking.

"So naughty," RJ said. "My little slut."

Aaron shivered.

"Mmm, you like to be called names, Mr. Danvers? Slut, whore…what else?"

Aaron opened his mouth to answer, then snapped it shut when RJ pressed a finger to his lips. He nodded instead.

"My slut," RJ said fiercely. "This hole? Mine. This body? Mine."

Aaron shuddered, shocked by the way his cock throbbed at those words and his asshole pulsed in need. Being RJ's felt good. He'd never been anyone's before, much less anyone he trusted.

RJ picked up the belt, and Aaron tensed, another rush of adrenaline firing into his bloodstream, leaving him lightheaded and panting. "I bought this belt at JC Penney when I was a senior in high school," RJ said, holding it out in front of Aaron's face. "I wore it not because it was fashionable, but because I didn't have enough money to buy pants that fit."

Aaron eyed the belt before looking up to RJ, who was staring at it with a thoughtful expression.

"I wore this belt in your classroom, Mr. Danvers. Do you know how many times I thought about how hot it would be to bend you over that pristine fucking desk of yours and use it on you?"

Aaron bit his lip, gazing up at RJ beneath his lashes, hoping to let him know that he was more than amenable to RJ using it on him now.

"Back then, I bet you never imagined that you'd be all naked on your coffee table, letting RJ Blitz spank you, did you? You never saw this coming."

Aaron shook his head, sweat slipping down from his temples and his cock twitching where it ached between his legs.

"I did," RJ said. "I thought about this for years. Does that scare you?"

Aaron figured it probably should. RJ was still pretty much a stranger to him, yet he couldn't help but trust him implicitly, to love being here with his ass burning from RJ's hand and his hole slick from his tongue. He shook his head.

RJ smiled. "Good." He kissed Aaron's forehead, then showed him the belt again. "But I'm going to scare you a little bit now. Safe word is Hermey."

RJ moved behind Aaron, pushed him chest-down against the coffee table, and pulled his arms out behind him, capturing both wrists in one big hand. Aaron's heart stuttered in his chest, and the strain in his shoulders burned. For one brief second, he considered saying the word, because RJ was raising the belt up, and…

"Fuuuuuuuuuuuhhhhhh!" he screamed as the belt made contact.

"No words," RJ said between the strikes. "Unless you want to use the safe word."

Aaron could barely remember his own name, much less the safe word as the braided leather fell on his already-stinging buttocks. He squirmed, but that pulled at his shoulders and made RJ's belt land less strategically and thus more painfully.

He tensed all over, straining his muscles to hold as still as he could. With his eyes wide and a cry that bounced from the brick walls of his apartment, he endured RJ landing the belt on him nine more times.

He only knew for sure because when it was over and he was gasping for breath between tears, RJ leaned close and murmured, "Twelve. Unbelievable." He kissed Aaron's shoulders and the side of his face. "That's my sweet Mr. Danvers."

RJ rubbed Aaron's shoulders and back, massaging the tension from his muscles. When Aaron was flat on the coffee table again, hiccups of sobs jolting from him, his attention torn between the pleasure of the massage and the pain radiating from his ass, RJ said, "I'll be right back. Shh, wait here for me."

Aaron wanted to raise up and watch RJ go, but he was too shocked to move, tears slipping from his eyes even though he didn't feel like crying. If anything, he felt like begging—for what? He didn't know. For more, maybe, though he wasn't sure he could handle that. For a fuck, definitely, but he didn't want the evening to be over yet. He had a feeling they were only beginning.

RJ's footsteps neared again. Aaron saw his black boots and jeans stepping toward him before RJ squatted down and his face filled Aaron's view. "You might need to bite down on this," RJ whispered, putting a cool, wet washcloth in his mouth. "This is going to sting."

Aaron struggled to sit up, not sure if he wanted more, but RJ pushed him back down. Aaron didn't spit the washcloth out, and he didn't say Hermey, but his heart pounded wildly, and he saw spots as fear roared through him.

RJ smoothed reassuring fingers over his back and down to his hips, avoiding the most painful places. "You're still so hard, Mr. Danvers. My pain slut. Mine and no one else's." He kissed the hot spots on Aaron's ass with a tenderness that made Aaron's thighs quiver. "Has anyone else ever taken you this far?"

Aaron grunted around the washcloth and shook his head.

"I don't want anyone else to ever see you like this," RJ said darkly. "This is too beautiful." He slipped his hands around Aaron's hips, combed his fingers through Aaron's pubic hair, and gripped his cock in one hand and his balls in the other. He squeezed Aaron's balls lightly, making him catch his breath and go very, very still.

"Mr. Danvers, I know this has already been a lot for you, but if you trust me and give in—if you don't fight, I'll take you somewhere you've never gone before."

Aaron looked over his shoulder, caught RJ's determined, lust-filled expression, and felt faint. He swallowed, cool water from the washcloth slipping down his throat. He turned back to the coffee table, planting his right cheek on the wood and biting hard on the washcloth.

"Oh, fuck yes," RJ said, squeezing Aaron's balls harder, so that it hurt enough to squeal before releasing them aching and tight between Aaron's legs. RJ hummed with clear pleasure, perhaps at how hard Aaron was. "This is the difficult part now, baby. Hold tight and trust me. It'll be worth it."

Aaron shivered and gripped the edges of the coffee table, the wood cool and solid beneath his fingers.

The belt started up again, and this time it didn't stop. Each strike was not quite as hard as the initial belting had been, but the cumulative strikes were like wildfire bursting into flame over and over. Aaron squirmed, he moved, he jolted, and when RJ pushed his head against the table with one hand and stepped on his calf with his heavy boot and *held* him down for the shocking pain, Aaron collapsed into it.

A dizzy, warm, open space grabbed him and took him higher and higher, flying him into an aching bliss he'd never known possible. The pain was still there, but it was necessary, and he stopped fighting, taking it eagerly and crying like his heart was broken. He never wanted it to stop.

Abruptly, RJ pulled back, the sudden end to the strikes making Aaron scream, "No!"

His sweaty skin prickled, his nipples ached, and his cock was throbbing like a wound, but he wanted more—he needed RJ to hold him down and force these scary feelings from him. He loved when RJ held the reins on his body. He *needed* it.

"Shh," RJ soothed. "You're all right. I've got you." He kissed Aaron, his tongue sliding in and soothing the panting sobs. "I've got my sweet baby boy."

Aaron grabbed hold of RJ's shoulders, gripping his T-shirt and tugging himself against RJ's body, hungry for his kisses and desperate for his arms around him. RJ gave him what he wanted, sliding his hands down to cup Aaron's flaming ass, squeezing and making him cry out into RJ's mouth, making his cock jerk a spurt of pre-come against RJ's jeans-clad thigh.

"That's right," RJ said. "I've got you, baby. You're safe." He nuzzled Aaron's neck. "Did you fly?"

Aaron nodded, his throat clogged with tears and fear that he was still flying, that he'd crash land, and that he'd never fly again. Not if RJ left. Not if this ended.

RJ kissed Aaron's throat. "Take off your T-shirt. Get on your hands and knees. Crawl to the bedroom, Mr. Danvers. I want to see your red ass move."

Dazed and tender everywhere from lips to nipples to smarting ass, he clung to RJ for a moment longer. Shame and arousal prickling him in equal amounts, Aaron did as he was told. RJ followed behind him, commenting on his ruddy ass and the bruises he could see forming.

"Baby, you're not going to forget tonight, and neither will I. Come Christmas you're still going to have my marks on you."

Aaron shivered, his cock dripping as he made his slow, crawling way to the bedroom. He yelped when RJ's hand landed in his hair and pulled him to a stop on the rug by the bed. "Stay there."

He panted on the floor by the bed, his knees aching. RJ rummaged in his closet and emerged with a long, dark tie. He placed it over Aaron's eyes.

"Remember your safe word?" RJ asked.

Aaron nodded.

"Good." He knotted the tie behind Aaron's head, and Aaron shivered in the darkness. He hadn't been too aware of using his eyes since he'd had them screwed shut for the most part while being spanked and belted, but now that he couldn't see, even if he wanted to, he felt more vulnerable than ever.

"First things first," RJ said, and Aaron heard the sound of RJ's shoes clomping to the floor and clothes coming off. He wished he could see RJ's body, but he held still, ass hurting like he'd never known possible and his cock aching like hell. He wanted to come, but he wanted to make this last for the rest of his life too.

"Get on the bed," RJ said. "On your back."

It was harder than it should be to get onto the bed without being able to see, but he managed it, though less than gracefully given the small huff of laughter RJ let out. Aaron settled on his back, letting out a small shriek of pain as his sore ass touched the sheets.

"Hands up to the headboard," RJ said from beside the bed, where Aaron could hear him opening drawers. He winced when he heard RJ's chuckle.

"Oh, baby, this is a nice set of toys you have here."

Aaron opened his mouth to answer but remembered the no-words rule when RJ's finger descended on his lips.

"I think I'll have fun with these. Now, what did I say? Hands on the headboard, slut."

Aaron shivered and thrust his hands up to touch the wooden head-board behind him.

"I don't have restraints," RJ said. "But I want you to imagine I do. Pretend your hands are stuck there. No matter what I do, don't take them off."

No touching now too? No words. No touching. He was just sup-posed to, what? Lie back and take it? He shivered again. *Fuck yes.*

"Good," RJ murmured, taking hold of Aaron's throbbing dick again and squeezing it. "I see you like that idea a hell of a lot." RJ rubbed Aaron's slick pre-come around the sensitive crown, making him moan and squirm, which only rubbed his sore ass against the sheets, making him tear up and somehow nearly come.

RJ dropped his cock. "Oh no, not yet. If you come before I say you can, I don't think you'll enjoy the punishment."

Aaron didn't know what to make of that threat, but he held very still, taking in steady breaths.

"Now, let's see how you like this," RJ said. "I already know I'm going to love it."

RJ WAS INSANELY hard. He was sweaty and desperate, and he wanted to fuck Aaron, but he had bigger plans than that. Including slicking up the big fat toy he'd found in Aaron's drawer and sliding it up Aaron's hot, quivering ass.

"That's so good," he encouraged as Aaron squirmed and moaned, obviously struggling to get the full girth of the ridiculous thing inside. Either he didn't use it very much or he'd never used it at all, because Aaron was a shocked, sweaty mess when RJ finally pushed the base flush against his trembling ass cheeks. His cock was so hard it was nearly purple and pre-come slipped down the sides of his stomach as he strained in pleasure.

"That's gorgeous," RJ murmured, slipping up to kiss Aaron's red, panting mouth and whisper encouragement in his ear. "You're stretched so wide."

Aaron whined and turned to RJ, his expression one of wrecked pain and pleasure mixed together, his tongue outstretched begging for a kiss. RJ gave him one and sank into a sweet exchange of spit and tongue strokes, pressing his hard cock against Aaron's hip as they kissed and squirmed together.

"That's enough of that," he said, pulling away and laughing at Aaron's soft noise of disappointment. "Don't worry. You'll like the next part. I promise."

He was torn between some nipple torture, which he thought Aaron would really get off on, and getting his own needs met sooner rather than later. He decided on the latter. He'd already gone above and beyond in fulfilling some of Aaron's kinks, so he might as well get in a few of his own.

RJ reached for the lube and prepped himself while Aaron waited, breathing hard, his skin splotchy red and the giant dildo in his ass, his legs splayed. RJ straddled Aaron's hips and without preamble or warning, gripped his straining cock and guided it straight to RJ's lubed and marginally stretched asshole.

Aaron lifted his hips to meet RJ's descent, his mouth open in pleasured shock, a low, "Ooooooh fuuuuuuuuuuuuhhhh," slipping out of him, the lack of a consonant at the end the only thing that kept it from being a violation of their rules for the night.

RJ slipped two fingers in Aaron's open mouth, further distorting the sound, and hinged them into his cheek, tugging slightly like on a horse's bit. "Stop moving."

Aaron shuddered and stilled his hips. RJ wasn't a size queen since he wasn't really much of a bottom at all, so he was happy with Aaron's nice, average dick. But he needed Aaron to let him be in charge of the fuck.

"Good boy," RJ murmured, rubbing his fingers against the slick skin inside Aaron's mouth, thinking of how it felt so similar to the slickness in Aaron's ass and the slickness in his own. Slickness that Aaron was now feeling on his bare cock. For the first time ever.

RJ almost regretted the rules then. Aaron's whole body was taut like a bow, and his breath came in harsh, emotional pants. Yet the rules kept whatever he was feeling—whatever this meant to him—locked up inside. But he wasn't going to change the game now.

RJ pulled his fingers from Aaron's mouth, bent forward to kiss his lips, and groaned as the movement shoved Aaron's cock against his prostate. That too-much, too-good sensation that he'd never been sure he truly liked shocked him to the core.

Aaron held so still, letting RJ kiss him, a shocked silence filling the space where before there had been so much variety of noise: cries, whimpers, sobs, stifled curses, and moans of pleasure. Now there was tense, blaring stillness. And then...

"Please. Let me touch you."

Aaron broke the rules. Ah, RJ's sweet, angel slut of a teacher had broken the rules.

"No," RJ said firmly, rising up and sliding down so that Aaron groaned and shook beneath him. "You broke the rules, baby. I'll have to punish you now. I'm sorry."

Aaron quaked, his muscles jumping and twitching from his thighs to his stomach. Even his arms jerked and trembled where he held them stretched out to touch the headboard. The toy was still shoved inside him, and RJ could imagine how overwhelmed Aaron was. Just having Aaron's cock inside him was intense, especially the raw heat of no barrier between them.

RJ gripped Aaron's nipples and twisted, pinching hard enough to make him yell as he rode Aaron's cock up and down. He watched as Aaron struggled not to let go of the headboard while trying not to come and not to cry with pain.

"Oh, baby, you're the sexiest thing I've ever seen," RJ said, his cock slapping against Aaron's stomach and then bouncing up to slap against his own. Each jolt of flesh on flesh was a sweet pleasure, yet he wasn't close to coming. Not yet. He never could come with a dick in his ass. Other men loved the prostate action, and he loved watching them get off on it—especially Aaron—but for him, it was always too much, and he couldn't get there no matter how hard he tried.

He tried harder.

Driving Aaron to sobs as he rode him, RJ had no doubt Aaron would be begging if he wasn't entirely incoherent. He finally relented, knowing what he wanted even more than he wanted to torture Aaron with pleasure and pain.

RJ left off twisting Aaron's nipples and bent low to whisper in his ear, "Come for me, Mr. Danvers."

Aaron shuddered, his pale chest blotched red from lust, sobs, and pain, his mouth ruddy and slick with kisses, his cheeks wet with tears. His cock grew harder in RJ's ass, and he let go of the headboard, gripping the sheets and screaming as he convulsed before tearing off the tie to stare at RJ with ecstasy-wild eyes. Hot pulses of Aaron's come emptied into RJ.

Staring into Aaron's beautiful face, so earnest and desperate, RJ's heart burst with affection. They'd trusted each other with their bodies, passion, and truth. And their trust. Yes, this between them, was the epitome of trust.

And love...love was trust.

AARON DIDN'T KNOW how much more he could take. He was overwhelmed with sensation and had just shot deep into RJ's sexy, lithe body. He'd never felt anything like the hot, velvet, slippery heat of RJ's ass. He'd never imagined he could feel so sated and adored as he did after being hurt so good and then ridden like an animal.

But it wasn't over, apparently, even though he was a limp ragdoll of too much sensation. RJ was down between his legs, removing the giant plug that had stimulated his prostate through the whole, beautiful ordeal, and Aaron was too shaky and dazed to know where pleasure started and pain began.

As RJ rose up, his cock slick and hard, he pushed Aaron's limp legs up to his shoulders and slid right into him. Aaron moaned, his dick somehow twitching and growing slightly hard again as RJ settled in with his cock buried deep inside.

"Holy fuck," RJ whimpered. "That's...oh, fuck, baby. It feels so good being inside you like this."

Aaron's ass convulsed on RJ's cock, his nipples pinging with an echoing pleasure as if connected somehow. His heart raced with joy. RJ was inside him, raw and bare, skin on skin. Aaron shivered, excited and desperate to fully know what this all meant. Because there was no denying it. This penetration, this bareness, meant *more*. He didn't know if he was allowed to talk yet, and he knew for sure he couldn't take any more "punishment" tonight. He needed to be held. He wondered if he was allowed to ask for that.

RJ said softly, "I'm safe wording for you now, okay? Hermey."

Aaron blinked at him in confusion, shivering when RJ rolled his hips, setting up a beautiful, slow pace.

RJ nuzzled his ear. "The rules are done now. The game is over. It's just us again. RJ and Aaron. No more Mr. Danvers and his dirty former student. Just me and you, baby. Just me and you."

Aaron nodded slowly, warmth spreading through him so solidly that it was almost like a blanket covering them both, blocking out everything but the sweetness in RJ's gaze as he stared down at him and the rightness of his cock pushing and pulling inside, and the soul-shivering bliss of his prostate being stroked, and the way it was building, building, building up inside...

"I'm going to come," Aaron gasped, shocked to think it was going to happen again so soon.

"Then come, baby." RJ kept himself to a steady pace that made Aaron's insides thump with pleasure.

It broke over Aaron, the shouting, shaking, anal-orgasm pleasure that he'd rarely experienced. It pounded him with pleasure, leaving him soft and open and aching for more.

"Oh, holy shit," RJ murmured. "Aaron, you with me?"

Aaron nodded, his eyes rolled up in his head. He was with him—that was the only place he could ever be, right here, legs on RJ's shoulders and his body an instrument for RJ Blitz's cock.

"Let's do it again," RJ said, and Aaron didn't need the rules to not speak now, he was already tipping over into another shuddering wave, feeling as though his very cells were shattering and realigning and shattering all over again.

RJ held him close, pumping in and out, kissing his neck, murmuring things that Aaron didn't understand. Then, just as another beautiful and terrifying jittering grip of bliss left his body, RJ rose up, fucked into him hard and fast, and yelled.

His expression was ecstatic as he stared down at Aaron, his body rigid for a long moment as his orgasm clutched him. He groaned and twitched, pumping hot, slick heat into Aaron's body.

Aaron held RJ close, tasting his sweat and spit and holding his pleasure cries in his heart. "Don't leave me," he whispered. "Don't go."

RJ collapsed against him, face buried in Aaron's neck and dick thrust deep inside. Aaron's legs slipped from RJ's shoulders to wrap around his waist and hold him. The pleasure echoed between them, shivers and trembling taking them both in turns until finally, RJ heaved himself up and off—then carefully out.

Aaron moaned, feeling empty inside. RJ lay down beside him, staring at his face in wonder. He shoved Aaron's legs apart and pressed his hand down, slipping three fingers inside.

Aaron grunted, shocked at the sudden, fast intrusion, staring in utter amazement as RJ removed his fingers, dragging some come with them. He held it up for Aaron to see.

"My come," he muttered. "My slut." Then he pressed his fingers back inside, pushing the come with them. "Mine, Mr. Danvers. Got it? This is mine."

Aaron swallowed and nodded. He had no idea what he was agreeing to now, but he only knew that he'd never trusted anyone the way he'd trusted RJ tonight, and he'd never been so amply rewarded.

"Yours," he whispered. "All of it."

RJ smirked, satisfaction reflecting in his eyes. "That's what I like to hear." He kissed Aaron's mouth before curling around him. "Thank you, baby. This night has changed my life."

Aaron clung to RJ, shaking and scared, because it had changed his too. All he wanted now was to be RJ's elf, or slut, or boy or *lover* forever.

This Christmas fling had turned all too serious.

Chapter Twenty-Four

THE NEXT MORNING, RJ woke smiling. He rose before Aaron and went out to the kitchen area. Remembering where Aaron kept Constance's food, he placed a bowl of it out and watched, amazed, as Constance ate it without complaint for a change.

He poked in the fridge to see what was there for breakfast. He wanted to make something nice for Aaron as a reward and thank you for his amazing submission the night before. Just thinking of it sent shivers racing up and down RJ's spine, and a puff of pride filled his chest.

He'd played at domination a few times with Pan, but it had never felt entirely right. Pan was never truly into it, only pretending to submit and playing the part like a bad actor in a porn movie.

Then there'd been the training he'd received in a club in Berlin, obtained during his many off-hours from the monthlong studio recording session he'd been hired for at the famous Hansa Tonstudio. While the album took longer to make than he'd liked, RJ had found it fascinating to kill time studying BDSM both by reading and by attending a nightclub that specialized in it.

Pieter was a Dutchman living in Berlin for his day job as a mixing engineer, but at night he wore leather and dominated men at Schmerz, a club for learning pain and pleasure. After discovering RJ's interest in domination while shooting the shit between takes in the studio, Pieter had taken RJ under his wing for three and a half fun weeks, demonstrating and allowing RJ to practice with a few of his subs.

RJ hadn't really had a chance after that to explore the way he'd always craved, but he appreciated, he supposed, that Pan had let him try.

Aaron, though. It was beyond his high school fantasy to actually have the man he'd wanted for so long naked and trusting, hurting and pleasured at RJ's discretion, to know that Aaron wouldn't say no.

RJ pulled eggs out of the fridge, along with bell peppers, onions, mushrooms, and a can of some sort of artichoke and olive dip that looked like it'd go well in an omelet. Humming under his breath, he set about making breakfast, remembering details of the night before with lightning-strike clarity.

His cock thickened as flashes of lustful images came to mind: Aaron on the coffee table, chills racing over his exposed flesh as he accepted RJ's comforting hand, having taken the braided belt so well.

RJ made a mental note to check Aaron's ass and apply arnica from his bag, and possibly cold cream, if Aaron had any. There was no doubt there would be marks this morning. He'd stayed as in control as he could, but watching Aaron surrender and unravel had made him so hot that he'd probably struck him a few times more than he should have.

He shouldn't feel so proud about that. And yet, knowing the marks would be there on Aaron's flesh for days, proof of the trust they'd shared (*trust is love, RJ*)... He couldn't imagine anything sexier or more beautiful in the world. Falling in love was dumb. And yet...

Here he was.

As he plated the omelet and grabbed glasses for orange juice, he recalled the way he'd managed to piece himself back together last night in order to make sure Aaron was safely brought out of subspace. Before tucking Aaron into bed and letting him sleep the sleep of a properly dominated sub, he'd watered and fed his lover (with both food and praise) and checked him for injury.

Only then had he let himself collapse beside Aaron and sleep curled close by his side, his entire body thrumming with barely satisfied lust and tender feelings. It'd been hard to sleep, despite being exhausted. He'd helped Aaron fly into subspace, but he hadn't been prepared for flying high as a kite himself from the thrill of dominating a man like Aaron Danvers.

The way he'd just given himself over. Christ.

RJ strove to keep his mind from drifting off into the memories as he found a platter to act as a tray and placed the omelet and two glasses of juice on it. He added a few napkins, wished he had some flowers, and instead grabbed a glittery bird ornament from Aaron's silver spangle tree to add a splash of color to the presentation. He carefully balanced it as he walked down the hallway to the bedroom.

Aaron was resting on his side, gazing out the window toward the church behind the apartment building. His brows were rucked low and his lips twisted down, and when he stiffened slightly, giving away that he'd heard RJ's footsteps, he didn't look toward him or offer up a morning greeting or smile.

RJ's stomach tensed, and the easy delight of the morning seemed to flee. He sat the platter on the dresser near the doorway and crossed to crouch in Aaron's line of sight. Blinking, Aaron shifted his gaze from the window to RJ's face, but his expression didn't change.

"What's wrong?"

"Nothing."

"Talk to me," RJ ordered, using his dom voice, satisfied to see Aaron's resistance crumble easily again.

Aaron shifted to sit up, hissing a little and squeezing his eyes shut briefly. RJ fought back the urge to ask if he was all right. He'd need to check him over soon, but he didn't want to do anything to prevent Aaron from talking. He was afraid if he did that Aaron might not open up again.

"No hiding?" Aaron asked. "You want the whole truth?"

RJ sat on the bed next to him and took hold of Aaron's hands. His throat felt tight and his skin tingled with fear. "Yeah, tell me the whole truth, Aaron."

"I think I've lost my mom."

Relief, wrong and yet intense, rushed over him. He'd been prepared to hear that he'd gone too far, that Aaron hated what they'd done, or any number of things that would turn last night from a thing of beauty into a hellscape. Aaron was upset about his mother. Maybe RJ couldn't fix that, but at least Aaron wasn't despondent over their encounter.

"And I'm scared of what we did last night."

Well, fuck.

RJ's stomach dropped. "I'm sorry."

Aaron shrugged, gazing toward where RJ had placed the platter with breakfast and the bird ornament. "It's okay."

"It's not okay if you're scared of me or of what we did."

"It's not that," Aaron said, swallowing hard. "It's that I'm scared of what it means when you go. When this is over. What I'll go back to…"

He looked up at RJ with sweet, earnest eyes, and the pain RJ saw in them made his heart ache. He wanted to reach inside and take all that away from Aaron, wash it clean with affection and kisses and fierce hugs that could squeeze the pain away. "I don't want more shitty bathroom hookups or strange men in hotel rooms who're just passing through, and I don't want to know what it means that I let you do those things to me, and that I want you to do it again…" He broke into a soft sob, and RJ scooted closer, searching his memory of what Pieter had said to do if he messed up and broke a sub's heart.

But Mr. Danvers wasn't any sub. He was Aaron. He was perfect. He was the dream made real.

RJ wrapped his arms around Aaron. The naked skin of his back felt soft under his hands. "Are you sure you wanted it?"

"I loved it," Aaron said, head snapping up. "Don't get all insecure on me now. I need you to"—he waved his hand around—"know what you're doing. You do know what you're doing, don't you?"

"Some. I've studied it a little. Practiced on a few guys."

Aaron stiffened slightly.

"What's wrong?"

"It's stupid. But I guess I hoped… I mean, it's good you know what you're doing. We should be sane and safe and all the rest."

"Consensual," RJ supplied. "But be honest with me. What's wrong?"

"I don't like the idea of you doing that with anyone else. Dumb, huh? It's good that you knew how to do it right. I really lost myself last night and you could have done anything, and I wouldn't have stopped you—"

"Oh, baby, the things you say."

"But I hate the idea that you've ever taken anyone else flying like that."

"I don't think I have. I got some practice in with some subs at a club in Berlin a few years ago, and I had a boyfriend that I tried to play with, but he wasn't interested."

"Pan?"

"Yeah. He wasn't…like that. He was a bossy, dramatic bottom who liked to pretend to let me be in control. But true submission to another person was beyond him. He could only submit to his drugs."

"I'm sorry."

"I'm sorry for him, but not sorry that it didn't work between us. Otherwise, I wouldn't be here with you, and what you gave me last night was the most beautiful gift I've ever received. I can't imagine anything better than the way you just…gave yourself to me. Thank you."

Aaron licked his lips and scooted closer, neediness rolling off of him. "But you did all the work. I should be the one thanking you."

"You can thank me if you want, but the rush of having you like that was beyond words."

"I love you." Aaron's eyes flew wide as he clapped a hand over his mouth. "No, I mean—"

"I love you too." RJ smiled sadly. "We're gonna crash and burn harder than anyone could imagine."

Aaron wrapped his arms around RJ too. "Make it all stop so that we don't get hurt."

"I don't think either of us really want that or we wouldn't be here now."

"What do you mean?"

RJ chucked up Aaron's chin. "You confronted your mother. You wore a lacy jockstrap out the other night to flirt with men in front of me. You walked out from work. You didn't use your safe word last night." RJ shook his head. "Mr. Danvers, I think you want to get hurt. And I want to get hurt too. At least it means we feel something."

Maybe we don't have to get hurt. Maybe it could actually work somehow.

Squashing the rogue blaze of hope, RJ trailed his fingers down to Aaron's ass. He squeezed, and Aaron trembled in his arms, his newly sprung erection pressing against RJ's thigh.

"Last night, with you? I felt free," Aaron said, his breath puffing against RJ's collarbones. "I didn't think of anything or anyone except us. I was completely in the moment. Do you know how often that happens for me?"

"Not often?"

"Try never. As for my mom, I didn't have a choice." Aaron dug deeper into RJ's arms. "Carter told her about us. I don't know if I'd have confronted her otherwise. But telling her the truth and not holding back? Walking out on her? I felt like a man out of prison for the first time in years." He huffed a laugh. "But this morning..." He shook his head.

"This morning?"

"I don't want to lose my mom."

"Oh, Aaron," RJ rubbed his cheek against the top of Aaron's hair, breathing in his scent. His hands went back to that ass like always, holding it, gratitude that he was allowed filling him up. "Let's go out to the living room. Constance is surely plotting my death and you need to eat something."

Aaron wiped at his eyes and pulled back. "Yes. I need to get myself together."

"It's not that. I just want to make sure you're taken care of. I have to go out to Chip's studio today. We're going to start putting down the first few tracks. The one you heard, and a few others I'm playing with."

"And we need to talk with your mom and Doug," Aaron said.

RJ wrinkled his nose. "I guess we do? But it just seems so awkward."

Aaron pulled entirely free from RJ's embrace, giving him a stern look. "Dating a student's relative is something I always tried to avoid."

"Well, we've mainly just been screwing, but…"

Aaron rolled his eyes. "You said the second time we were together that we were more than a hookup. You said we were lovers."

"We are."

Aaron nodded, poking at RJ's chest. "That's not something I ever meant to be with a former student or a relative of a current one."

"I know. I can't say I'm sorry, though."

"No, me either," Aaron said thoughtfully. "C'mon. Let's call your mother. We should get it over with."

"Yes. I guess we should." He stood up and retrieved the tray. "But first, breakfast."

DURING THE DRIVE to his mother's house after a great session at the studio with Chip, RJ tried not to dread what was coming. He failed miserably. Carter was out with his mother and Perri and Beau had a playdate, so RJ had told his mom that he and Aaron were coming over to talk to her and Doug without telling her why.

RJ was happy to see Aaron's car pull up to Doug and Mom's house just as he came around the corner. He met Aaron on the sidewalk leading to the front door. Aaron was dressed nicely—the way he did for the classroom—and that meant his ass was on adorable display in

242

lightweight trousers beneath a tucked-in button-up shirt covered in a soft rose print. He looked edible.

"Nervous?" Aaron asked as RJ took his hand.

"I guess. I've never done anything like this before. I don't know what to expect, or what might happen."

Or if you'll bolt if things go badly.

He didn't even know what "going badly" might look like.

Aaron squeezed his fingers, looking all teacher-like and adult. RJ wanted to kiss him. "It'll be all right. It's just necessary is all. Come on. Let's get it over with."

RJ opened the front door and felt disoriented by the lack of small feet pounding down the stairs and enthusiastic greetings and hugs. He hadn't really been in the house during the day when the kids weren't home. It was unnerving.

Even more unnerving was the look on Doug's face when RJ brought Aaron into the living room. Mom and Doug were waiting there in their easy chairs with coffee mugs and worried expressions, and Doug's only grew doubly so when Aaron came in.

Everyone stood awkwardly beside the coffee table until RJ gestured at Aaron and said, "Doug, this is—"

"Mr. Danvers. I know. He's Carter's favorite teacher."

Aaron smiled and took Doug's outstretched hand. "It's good to see you again, Mr. Ward."

"Oh, no, call me Doug, like I told you before." He blinked between them and took the bull by the horns. "RJ, what's going on? Why is Mr. Danvers here?"

"They're dating," Mom interjected. "Remember? I told you RJ was seeing someone." She motioned at Aaron. "This is the someone."

"Oh." Doug looked between them with some confusion, but then shrugged. "I see. Let's all have a seat."

Mom and Doug took the lounge chairs, and RJ and Aaron sat on the couch. Aaron held himself quite stiffly, all prim and proper now that he had parents as an audience. Nothing like the man in RJ's arms the night before.

Doug cleared his throat. "So, you wanted to meet with us, Mr. Danvers, because you were concerned about this?" He gestured between RJ and Aaron. "Since you're Carter's teacher?" The guess was close but not quite the issue, and RJ opened his mouth to say so, but Aaron beat him to it.

"Actually, I only found out that RJ was related to Carter by marriage just yesterday morning when the principal called me to her office to inform me that Carter had come to her to complain about me dating his stepbrother. I had no idea Carter even knew we were seeing each other, since as I said before, I didn't know Carter was related to RJ."

Doug tilted his head, obviously confused. He took a sip of his coffee and seemed to realize he'd been less than hospitable. "I'm sorry, would you like coffee?" he asked, lifting his mug.

"Good idea," Mom said. "This sounds like it's going to take a little time to fully understand."

"I'm good. Thanks." Aaron wiped his hands on his pant legs, a move RJ recognized as nerves, so he put his arm around Aaron's shoulder and gave a reassuring squeeze. Oddly, Aaron shrugged him off with a strange smile and a cough.

"I'm fine too, thanks," RJ said.

"All right. So, let me see if I understand so far. Carter complained to the principal? About the two of you dating?" Mom asked. "Why would he do that?"

"I think something about me dating his stepbrother has made him uncomfortable," Aaron said. "Going to the principal is a fair thing for a student to do when they have a problem with a teacher's behavior." Aaron put up a hand. "I want to make it clear, Mr. and Mrs. Ward, I don't have a problem with Carter and I'm not hurt or upset with him." He gave a sweetly dimpled smile. "I hoped we could all work together to help Carter be more comfortable with whatever happens between RJ and me going forward. I won't be his teacher forever, but RJ will be his brother for the rest of his life. We need to find a way to help him feel all right about things."

"Carter doesn't like me," RJ said, hoping he didn't sound as butthurt as he felt about it. If Aaron could be this mature about it all, then he could too. "I admit I don't know why he even cares that I'm with you. He can barely stand to look at me." RJ winked. "He must think you're too good for me, Mr. Danvers." Aaron's eyes went wide and RJ had to hold back a chuckle. "I mean, Aaron."

"How… Oh, heavens, I might regret asking this," Mom said, looking between them carefully. "But how did you two meet? One of those apps, I'm assuming?"

"No," Aaron said and looked to RJ.

"Aaron was my teacher," RJ said.

The room went deadly silent. Betsy looked at Doug, and Doug looked at Betsy.

The moment hung dangerously before Aaron jumped in, waving his hands to dispel whatever it was they were thinking. "It was forever ago. My first year teaching. I taught high school back then, English Comp, and RJ was a senior."

That seemed to make it worse.

"Nothing happened!" Aaron said, babbling. "Not back then. I barely noticed him. He was weird and gawky, and stared at me too much. I gave him a C. It was a generous grade."

RJ couldn't stop a chuckle. "C-minus." But his mother was still pale, and Doug didn't look comfortable either. He decided to nip it all in the bud. "Hey, I'm not saying I didn't think Aaron was attractive back then. But he was my teacher and nothing more. When I ran into him after a gig last week, we got caught up. Turns out I'm an adult now and so is he." RJ raised a brow pointedly.

Doug cleared his throat again and looked at Mom. Whatever passed between them seemed to result in a kind of reluctant acceptance.

"I see," Mom said, finally. "It's a little awkward, isn't it? On the surface, it doesn't look that good."

"But nothing untoward happened while RJ was in school, Mrs. Ward," Aaron said. "I promise."

"Of course," she said, reaching out to touch Aaron's arm briefly. "I believe you, Aaron. We both do. Don't we, Doug?"

"Yes," Doug said, but his brows were still furrowed. "But I still don't see why Carter would care about any of this? Why would he want to get you in trouble with your principal?"

"Remember our conversation at the dance the other night?" Aaron asked.

"Before the principal intervened, yes. We were talking about my concerns that Carter might be…" He trailed off and looked guiltily at Mom. *Great. Keeping secrets already. The beginning of the end.* "I should have told you about this Betsy. I just didn't know how to bring it up."

"Bring what up?"

"I think Carter might be gay."

"Oh?" She blinked. "But RJ's gay and you know I totally accept him. Why would you think I'd care?"

"Because…" Doug swallowed hard. "Well, honey, I'm bi. And I think he got it from me."

Doug was bi? RJ blinked in surprise, trying to make sense of that. He'd never thought…never imagined. But wait. "Got it from you?" RJ scoffed. "It's not exactly helpful to think of sexuality that way. It's not a disease you catch or inherit."

"You're bi?" Mom asked softly.

RJ's stomach flipped over. The hint of betrayal in his mom's voice pushed a protective button inside, and he wanted to insinuate himself between Doug and his mother to protect her.

Doug reached out for her hand, but she didn't reciprocate his squeeze. "I am, yeah."

"You never said…" She blinked at him. "Why?"

"I didn't think it mattered. We're together and monogamous, so..."

Aaron shifted uncomfortably, and Mom noticed. She pulled her hand back from Doug and shook her head, the hurt not entirely gone from her eyes. "This is a conversation for another time. It's not really the boys' business, is it?"

"I'm sorry, Betsy."

"It's fine. We'll be fine." Mom smiled a little tightly. "What do we need to do about Carter?" She turned away from Doug in a way that made it clear she wasn't done being hurt by his withheld information and focused on Aaron. "If he's trying to hurt your career because you care about RJ..." She shook her head. "Why would he do that? It doesn't make sense." She turned back to Doug. "You think he's gay, so why would he want to hurt his gay teacher?"

Aaron took a deep breath, and all eyes shifted to him. "He came to me the other day, right after I'd first met RJ again. There was no way he could have known about that. Anyway, he told me that day that he had a stepbrother who'd recently moved in and he wasn't comfortable with it. At the time, I admit I was worried that the stepbrother in question was doing something inappropriate, but now that I've discovered it's RJ he was referring to, and I've spent the last week with him, I understand there must be something else going on."

"We probably won't know for sure what that is unless we talk to Carter," Doug said. "Alone. As his parents."

Mom glanced at her watch. "The kids will be home soon, and Carter will be dropped off shortly. I think it will be best if you're not here, Aaron, when he comes." She pinned RJ with her eyes. "And I think it will be best if you are."

"Why?" RJ asked.

"Won't that embarrass him?" Doug said at the same moment.

"We can send RJ upstairs if Carter is uncomfortable talking with him around, but I think RJ should be the one to help him understand what's happening with Aaron. And keep it PG, RJ. This is a thirteen-year-old, and he doesn't need to understand anything other than you have feelings for his teacher. What kind of feelings can be left to his imagination."

RJ shrugged. "I can do that."

Doug stood and so did everyone else. He put out his hand. "Aaron, we're grateful for you coming by to clarify things for us. We're sorry if Carter has caused problems for you with your job."

Aaron shook his hand firmly. "I'd like to say there's no problem at all with my job, but truth be told, my principal is struggling with the information that I'm dating a man, much less seeing a student's brother. Amongst other things."

"I'm sorry to hear that. Is she fair to queer children?" Betsy asked, clearly concerned. "Should the school board be made aware?"

"She's good with everyone but her son," Aaron said with a grimace. "Which just happens to be me. Apparently, it's all right for anyone else in the world to be gay, but not her kid. It's a specific kind of bias, and one I'm aware she isn't alone in having, and yet that doesn't make it less painful when the kid in question is yourself."

Mom looked as if she wanted to pull Aaron into a hug. "I'm sorry. I admit that when RJ came out to me, I didn't handle it as well as I'd have liked—"

"You handled it great."

"Are you kidding me? I forbid you from seeing your boyfriend."

RJ shrugged. "He was twice my age and using me for sex. It was a good idea to forbid it. I just wish I'd obeyed."

Mom rubbed her forehead and sighed. "You were a stubborn boy. And you're stubborn now too." She smiled at Aaron. "I hope you understand that my son is a bit of a pill, but a good person. He's worth the bitterness."

"He's sweet to me," Aaron said, taking RJ's hand again. "I'm just sorry if the two of us seeing each other has made things hard for Carter. He's a great kid. I would never want to make him uncomfortable by lov—" He flushed. "By caring for his stepbrother."

Mom's eyebrow popped, and RJ's heart tripped at Aaron's verbal slip.

"I should go now," Aaron said. "I have some things I need to finish."

"I'll walk you to your car," RJ said.

Outside, as Aaron climbed into the driver's seat, he pulled RJ close to ask in his ear, "Later will you show me again what happens to bad elves?"

RJ kissed his cheek and whispered, "How about I show you what happens to good ones?"

Chapter Twenty-Five

"**I** CAN'T BELIEVE you had me sneaking in and out of the school like a thief," Lauren said, slipping into the passenger seat and buckling in. She wore a pair of jeans and green shirt beneath a black cardigan. More relaxed than her usual teacher-wear.

She passed his briefcase over and a small tote of other personal odds and ends. "I've never gone back in after it's been shut down for winter break. It was spooky."

"Was she in there?"

"Yeah. In her office."

Aaron shook his head. "She never takes a break. Even when I was a kid, I had to hang out in her office with her during winter break unless Dad came to get me." Aaron groaned. "I just can't deal with her right now."

Lauren smiled sadly at him. "Christmas is in nine days, hon. How are you going to get around that?"

"Ugh. Don't remind me." He put the car in reverse and backed out of the parking space. "Thanks for getting this stuff from my classroom. Where do you want to eat?"

"Full Service sounds good to me." Lauren pulled a lip gloss from her purse and applied it, offering some to Aaron, but he declined. "Too cold to eat at the picnic tables, of course, but I've been dying for their banana pudding."

Aaron didn't argue and turned out of the school parking lot and headed west toward the local barbecue chain. It only had a handful of outdoor picnic tables and a drive-thru window, but it was his and Lauren's favorite spot. In the spring, summer, and autumn, they ate at the picnic tables, but in winter they'd usually find a place to park with some scenery and eat in the car. They didn't care so long as they were with each other.

After going through the drive-thru, Aaron drove them on backroads to Concord Park, where they could watch the winter sunset skip around on the lake. Aaron relaxed into the seat, eating his sauce-covered pork and jalapeños, listening to Lauren chat about her Christmas plans with her mother. As they ate, he fielded questions about what gifts he'd gotten for his father's side of the family and offered advice on what she should get her dad's new wife.

Just as the Christmas lights were blinking to life on the houses around the edges of the lake, they grew quiet together. Wadding up the trash and stuffing it into the paper bag, Aaron knew the time had come for the probing. He decided to suffer it with dignity if he could.

Sure enough, as soon as Lauren had squeezed hand sanitizer onto both of their palms, she asked, "So there's been nothing since yesterday?"

"With my mom?"

"Yeah."

Aaron shrugged. "Nope."

"But you've talked with her?"

"Uh-uh."

The glowy, post-sunset light barely illuminated the interior of the car, but he didn't need it to know what her expression was when she said, "Aaron…"

"Look, why should I be the one to call her?" He tried to keep his voice calm, but he knew it was tight with anger. "She should be calling me. If I were any other teacher, she would have reached out by now."

"To fire you, maybe."

"Maybe. But it'd be something at least." He snorted. "She'd have made contact. As it is, she's playing chicken, waiting for me to be the first to break."

After a quiet moment, Lauren brought it up again. "What about Christmas?"

"I don't know. If she doesn't reach out by then, I guess I'll spend it alone."

She clucked her tongue. "Rutty would want you out at the farm, I'm sure."

"He would. But I don't know if I'd want that. Seems like it would be the sort of thing she'd hold against me forever." He laughed under his breath. Like this thing with RJ—with having a former student—*no, be honest*—with having a former *male* student for a lover wasn't already something she would hold against him forever?

"She wouldn't want you to be alone on the holidays."

"Wouldn't she?" Aaron was sick of making excuses for his mother. "She wants me to be alone every other day of my life."

Lauren shifted uncomfortably but obviously couldn't argue with him about that.

"What is her damage? Why is she like this? What is she afraid of? Being disowned? Of her mother not loving her anymore?" His voice shook. "I'm the one with everything to lose. But what's the point? I've lost it all anyway."

"Your mom is a control freak."

"Exactly. She wants to control me and her reputation. And we both know which one she cares the most about."

"She does. It's true." Lauren's voice was firm from the shadow of the passenger seat. The overhead light flipped on, and Aaron looked at her beneath the harsh glow of it. "She's a pretty terrible mother, I'll give you that. She may love you, but her version of love is abusive."

"Fuck her love. I've been the bigger person with her since I was ten. I'm fucking sick of it."

Wow. He couldn't believe he'd let that rip in front of Lauren. It wasn't something he'd admitted to anyone but RJ. Maybe that's what came of lifting that Band-Aid off. Now he was a throbbing, open wound.

"I can see that." Lauren reached out and touched his cheek. "I'm so sorry you're hurting."

Aaron turned away. Silence reigned for a moment. "Lauren, it's more than that. Think about it. Your mom's annoying, yeah, because she's always trying to set you up with a nice guy from her church, and she calls every other night to update you about the latest events on *Days of Our Lives* even though you haven't watched the show since you lived at home. But your mom isn't telling you not to be yourself, to hide who you are, to deny yourself joy and love and physical affection and a fucking future. She's just annoying. Not toxic."

"You're right. But Helen is a bigot. A controlling bigot." Aaron flinched hearing his mother's first name. It made her sound so human. Like any other person. Not this powerful figure he'd seen her as since childhood. To Lauren, she was just Helen. To him...so much more.

Lauren went on. "And you've *let* her control you, Aaron. You might not want to admit it now, but sometimes you even seemed to prefer her telling you what to do. At the very least, in the past, you didn't seem to fight it much."

Aaron blinked. A flash of RJ saying, *"I think you want to be hurt"* crossed his mind, along with a sharp memory of the way RJ had taken control of him the prior night and how much he'd liked it. How right it had felt to surrender to him.

Lauren was oblivious to the course of his thoughts. "Of course her worst side is going to show itself when you start to resist her."

"Do you think I'm a pushover?" Aaron asked softly. "Am I too soft?"

"You're soft, Aaron, but that's a wonderful quality to have."

"How? You're right. My mom always controlled me. And I let her. Sometimes I even liked that I didn't have to be in charge of my life. And last night..." He flushed. "Never mind."

"What?"

"It's not—"

"Last night…"

Aaron wanted to turn off the overhead light in the car and hide in the darkness, but he pushed on ahead. "RJ and I played a game, and I…let him take control." He felt his fair skin grow hot, Lauren's eyes on him, but he didn't look at her. "I liked that too. It made it easier. Better somehow. It wasn't fun." Aaron paused, and at Lauren's worried expression clarified, "I mean, it wasn't not fun either. It was *right*. It felt necessary? And compelling? I don't know." He scrubbed a hand over his hot face. "Maybe I'm a pervert like my mother says."

"Like she says? Excuse me, but *what the hell?*"

Aaron groaned. "I hadn't wanted to tell you before."

"Tell me now." Lauren steamed silently as she listened to the horrible things his mother had said, and then she whispered, "Fuck her, Aaron. *Fuck her.*" She hissed and then murmured, "Sounds like I need to do some job hunting, too."

"Lauren—"

"No! I've let her push you around too long and not said a word because I thought you wanted it that way. But I was wrong. You don't. And I won't stand by and—"

"You love your work. You love the kids."

"So do you!"

"I know, but…I feel like something has to change. Like maybe everything has to change. For me."

"Wow. I can't say that I disagree, but I never thought I'd see you embrace a thought like that."

"I know, I've been slow." Aaron huffed and rubbed at his eyes. "None of that answers my question, though. Is there something wrong with me? To want a man to control me that way?"

"There's nothing wrong with you," Lauren said reassuringly. "What you do in bed with your boyfriend doesn't matter so long as it gives you satisfaction and pleasure. Aaron, being submissive, if that's what you're implying, isn't a bad thing or a good thing. It's just a way of being, just like me being asexual is just a way of being. It's not a big deal one way or another."

"You're asexual?"

"Yes. Maybe even aromantic. I'm not sure. I don't really crave being with another person, not like you do, or like my other friends. Or the way my mom seems to think I should." She rolled her eyes. "Maybe you've played out a certain innate, Dom/sub dynamic with your mom and that got toxic between you. But that was with your *mom*, Aaron. Not a man you were choosing to play with."

"Eww. Stop."

"No, listen." Lauren took hold of his chin, and he couldn't look away. "There was no choice with your mom. No consent. Just domination and control. It's an entirely different ballgame when you're consenting to that dynamic with a man you're in a relationship with. It's not the same as being stuck in a dynamic against your will with the woman you should have long ago grown *out* of dependency on."

"I didn't realize you knew so much about this stuff."

Lauren shrugged, her hair sliding off her shoulder. "I've got that counseling degree underpinning my education degree, remember?"

"Right. But you know a lot about sexuality. I thought you'd studied developmental psych and counseling for students."

"It took some trial and error for me to make peace with my asexuality." Lauren smiled at him, and she looked a little vulnerable now. "I don't mean that I physically tried out things and rejected them. But I did a lot of research and self-examination. I read a lot. I scoured the Internet. I might not want to have sex, but I enjoyed learning about it." Flinging away her introspection, she grinned. "Are you guys keeping it safe, sane, and consensual?"

Aaron rolled his eyes. "Of course."

"Then you're fine. But if you're seeing a connection between the way your mother treats you and the way that you *want* to be treated by a partner, then keep in mind that it's only abuse when it's not consensual, safe, or sane. And nothing with your mom has ever been consciously consensual. I mean, one could argue tacit consent since you never fought back until now, but you grew up in it. So…no."

"I'm really disturbed that you're applying BDSM principles to my relationship with my mom."

"It's a little twisted, I agree, but it doesn't mean there isn't a connection. You spotted it yourself."

"I know." Aaron stared off into the distance, seeing indoor Christmas trees shine through the windows of the lakeside houses. "What am I going to do?"

"I can't tell you what you should do, but I'll tell you what I would do."

"Tell me."

"I'd call her. Not with apologies, which is what she'll be expecting, but with a clear list of what boundaries she'll need to start respecting in order for the two of you to move on, not only as principal and teacher, but as mother and son."

Aaron let out a shocked laugh. "Holy shit, that's terrifying."

"I know. I couldn't even do it with my mom and the *Days of Our Lives* updates. But maybe that's because in the end, it's not a big deal, and I had a lot less to lose. You've got your freedom and future wrapped up in this."

"A few days ago, you were advocating that I drop RJ so that I didn't offend my mother."

"A few days ago I was wrong." Lauren took hold of his hand. "Your mom has always scared you, and I hated seeing you like that. Like a whipped dog. But this is different. You're different. You're *angry*, and I've never seen that fire in you before. If that's because of RJ Blitz, our weird emo goth student of yore, then I can only say good on him, and good for you." She squeezed his fingers. "And go for it. If you want him enough to have grown a spine to have him? Then who am I to stand in the way over a little bit of 'that's my former student ick'?"

Aaron snorted. "I don't know if this is because of him, or if I'm just finally done with her." He licked his lips, considering. "I guess, in a way, it *is* him. Because for the first time ever, I've had a glimpse of what I could have if I'd just allow myself to open up to it. I probably can't have it with RJ. Though he's starting to act like he wants to see where this might go too…" Aaron met his best friend's gaze, certainty in his gut. "But I could have it with someone. I deserve to have it with someone."

"You do deserve that, honey." She kissed his fingers. "I'm proud of you for figuring that out. Really damn proud." She glanced at her watch. "Now I need to get home. My mom's *Days of Our Lives* update will be coming in t-minus thirty-six minutes and counting."

"Ah, and they must have started with the Christmas episodes by now. Who knows what Sami is getting her new lover for Christmas?"

"Speaking of, what are you getting yours?"

Aaron choked. "Fuck me. I don't know."

Lauren laughed as they pulled away from the park and headed home.

Chapter Twenty-Six

"W"HAT'S GOING ON?" Carter asked defensively as Mom and Doug ushered him into the living room. The little kids were still over at the neighbor's house. "Why are you here?" he asked RJ with narrowed eyes.

Mom said, "RJ is here because he's part of this family and apparently part of the problem."

Carter's eyes went wide. "There isn't a problem. I don't have a problem."

"But you did on Monday," Doug said. "When you went to the principal to talk about RJ and your teacher?"

Carter sputtered and looked ready to run out of the room, but Doug put an arm around him and guided him to the sofa, sitting beside him. RJ sat with his mom in the lounge chairs.

Doug assured Carter, "No one's angry with you, buddy. We just want to know what's going on. If you'd rather talk to just me and Betsy, we can send RJ upstairs for a while. But we get the impression that maybe clearing the air with RJ would be good for you too."

Carter stared at RJ, eyes wide and a little terrified.

RJ had no idea why he seemed to spark so much fear in the kid. "Look, I'm not mad at you. And neither is Aaron, er, Mr. Danvers."

It felt weird using that name outside of the bedroom now, but he plowed on ahead. "Aaron is a good guy, and he understands that discovering we're...dating..." He winced, and his mom shot him a dagger-filled glance. "Yes, dating," he said again, more securely. "That had to be awkward for you. Maybe it worried you? About your grades? Or maybe the kids at school finding out? Teasing you?"

"I don't know," Carter whispered, still gaping at RJ.

Doug shot Betsy a confused look, and she leaned forward to ask, "What did you say to the principal, honey?"

"I told her that Mr. Danvers was seeing RJ," he whispered, his eyes sinking from RJ's face down to the carpet. His cheeks stained red. He looked so young in that moment that RJ's heart hurt for him. He was just a kid, even if he was broader than Aaron.

"That's all?" Doug prompted.

"I said it didn't seem right," he whispered.

"Because they're gay?" Mom asked, almost making it sound like it would be all right if he gave that as his answer.

Carter shook his head.

"Then why?" Doug asked, squeezing him securely.

"Because he's my teacher and RJ is..." Carter swallowed hard.

"RJ is?"

"He's..." Carter looked up at RJ with shiny eyes and licked his lips. RJ braced himself for something awful. "I don't know! What do you want me to say?" His voice cracked, and he looked so miserable that RJ went hot and cold all over.

"Hey, it's okay," RJ said quietly. "Look, I get it. You don't know me and yet here I am in your house. Maybe I make you feel awkward or—"

"Stop!" Carter yelled, and Doug looked like he was about to scold him for it, but then Carter went on to say, "It's embarrassing. I don't want to talk about it. Stop making me talk about it."

"Son, RJ doesn't have to be here for this conversation, but you need to be polite to him."

"He messes with my head," Carter whispered, shrinking in on himself. "He makes me feel...ugh!"

"Who? Aaron?" RJ asked.

"You!" Carter hissed, anxiety leaking out of him. "*You* make me feel…" He looked miserable.

Clarity hit like light on snow. Carter had some sort of attraction for him. That explained a lot actually.

Mom inhaled sharply, almost like a half-laugh. Doug squeezed Carter even tighter like he was trying to hold him together—or maybe hold him in place to keep him from running.

"Oh," RJ said dully. "I, uh, wow. Thank you? I mean, I didn't realize that…um, yeah, that's…"

Mom put a hand on RJ's forearm, shutting him up, thank God. "You're saying that you think your stepbrother is handsome?"

What a mild way to put the scary, squirmy feelings of youthful attraction.

Wincing, Carter's eyes filled with tears. "It's wrong! I know it's wrong! Because you two are married, and he's related to me now! Even though he's not!" He covered his face. "I'm sorry. It's weird. I don't like it either. I don't want to think about it. At least at school I didn't have to *think* about it." He huffed, a small little shaking sob. "But the other day, I saw Mr. Danvers with you here. Out my window. I saw you leaving the house together, and the way you touched by the car…" He shuddered. "I hated thinking about that. I *hated* it."

"I see," RJ said lamely, looking to Doug for help. "I'm sorry."

"You know that being attracted to guys isn't wrong, right, Carter?" Doug asked. "I'm attracted to guys myself." He glanced toward Mom, and a tender, adoring look flashed between them. It was clear that the hour they'd had in their room alone had cleared up whatever hard feelings existed about that withheld information.

RJ was relieved about that. He was starting to hope he was wrong to be so hopeless about long-term love. For a lot of reasons.

"I know," Carter said, tears slipping down his cheeks. "I just wish I didn't feel that way about…about…him."

"So you told the principal that you were uncomfortable with Aaron and RJ dating because you were jealous?" Mom clarified.

"Because I shouldn't have to sit in my English class and wonder what my teacher has done with my stepbrother!" he bit out. "And yes, I was jealous. It made it suck even worse."

"I'm sorry," RJ said, looking Carter in the eye. "I really am. But I'm not going to stop seeing Aaron." He shrugged. "And while you're a great kid, obviously you're a little young for me. Even if we weren't related by marriage."

"I know." Carter ducked his head.

"But I'll tell you what. How about I promise to try to stop being so hot, if that helps."

Carter huffed a funny, embarrassed laugh. "Screw you."

"Oh man," Mom said, jumping in. "Carter, this is a complicated thing, I know. But maybe if you get to know RJ a little better, you'll stop thinking so highly of him."

RJ snorted. "Gee, thanks, Mom."

Despite his misery, Carter seemed impressed by the accidental burn.

"I won't be around long," RJ said. "If that helps at all."

Carter rolled his eyes. "Whatever."

"I know you haven't been able to see Dr. Thorne since she went on sabbatical last month, but you know you can always talk to the other counselor in the practice. We'd be happy to—"

"I don't need Dr. Thorne. I just need RJ to go away."

"Hey," Doug said.

"No, it's okay," RJ said awkwardly. "It's fine. I'm going soon enough. That's fair. In fact, if you want me to leave now, I will. Get a hotel or something."

Carter shook his head miserably. "No. It's your family too. I don't know. I'm sorry. I never wanted to feel like this."

"I know, buddy." Doug gave him a hug, and Carter seemed to relax a little in his arms.

The awkward moments dragged for a few seconds after Doug released Carter, until he said, "Putting all of that aside, I think that you owe Mr. Danvers an apology. Complaining to the principal has put his job at risk."

"But she's his mom," Carter said in confusion. "I just wanted her to make it stop."

"Well, Mr. Danvers is an adult, and his mother can't tell him who he can and can't date," Mom said. "I suppose, if she thought Aaron was giving you special treatment because of his relationship with RJ, then she might have some cause for concern. But as it is, it's put Mr. Danvers in an awkward position, especially since he's closeted at school."

"Mr. Danvers isn't closeted," Carter said, bewilderment warring with embarrassment on his face. "Everyone knows he's gay."

"Well, he doesn't realize that."

"He doesn't? But he's so…" Carter shifted around uneasily. "Gay."

"What's that even mean?" Mom asked.

"I mean, he's gay," Carter said, rolling his eyes.

"He doesn't flit his hands around or have any particular way of speaking," Doug said. He met RJ's eyes then. "I mean, I know that doesn't mean anything and that's stereotyping, but—"

Could this family conversation get any more awkward? RJ didn't think so, but then he wasn't sure he'd want to bet on it, either.

"No," Carter cut him off, annoyed. "He just…" Carter waved his hands around and squirmed. "Makes me feel…" He groaned. "Can we just stop? This is embarrassing enough."

"Well, if you have a crush on Mr. Danvers too, I get *that*," RJ said with a grin. "I mean, I had a crush when he was my teacher."

"You did?" Carter asked, narrowing his eyes.

"Oh, great. We maybe didn't need to let that cat out of the bag," Mom said. "Surely you can bond over something else."

"His dimples when he smiles?" RJ said with a wink. "Am I right?"

Carter flushed deeply and nodded quickly, shooting his eyes to the side. "You're right. And his…his…" He motioned in a way that indicated his butt.

"Nope, nope, nope," Mom said. "This discussion of Aaron's attributes isn't appropriate. For any reason. Even gay male bonding reasons."

"But Mom, his dimples *are* adorable."

"They are," she agreed. "But goodness, this has all been ridiculously frank." She pushed her hair off her face and took a deep breath. "Fuck me, let's stop talking about it before we're all required to seek therapy. Not that there's anything wrong with therapy. In fact, I should make a few with the family counselor we were seeing awhile back. I think we could stand a few sessions. Just to brush up on our communication skills"—here she looked pointedly at Doug—"and to work on how to have healthy, appropriate conversations about these issues going forward."

"That's a good idea," Doug agreed.

Carter shrugged, ambivalent, but not against the idea.

RJ said, "Well, I'll be on the road, so…"

"You can FaceTime in," Doug said.

RJ nodded. "I can do that."

"Wait, you like guys?" Carter asked his dad suddenly, as though it had taken all this time for those words to sink in. Then he cast a skeptical look at Mom. "But she's not…"

Mom said, "I think your father likes men and women."

"So are you gonna get a boyfriend?" Carter asked his dad. "Like, on the side?"

"No!" Doug said, startled. "Why would I do that? I love Betsy."

"Because she's not a man?"

"I'm a monogamous person," Doug said seriously. "And I feel like we've had enough difficult discussions for one day. We can discuss polyamory and such another time. Like at counseling, like we were just discussing. Suffice it to say that Betsy makes me very happy. I have no need for more."

"If you say so," Carter said, still clearly skeptical.

RJ couldn't help but think it was the skepticism of a very gay boy who couldn't fathom a future without dick. "So, with this all out in the open, I hope we can be friends," RJ said to Carter earnestly. "I came home for the holidays because I wanted to get to know my family. And that includes you."

Carter flushed but nodded. "We could play *Overwatch* sometime if you want."

"Sure. I'll suck at it. But that's okay with me, if it's okay with you."

"Yeah." Carter stood up, pulling free of his dad's embrace. "I'm going upstairs now." He paused and turned back. "I'm sorry if I caused Mr. Danvers any problems. What should I do?"

"Just apologize when you see him," Mom said. "That should be more than enough."

Carter nodded and turned to go again. "He won't lose his job, will he?" he asked as he reached the foot of the stairs.

"I'm not sure, buddy," Doug said. "I hope not."

"There's a lot going on between Aaron and his mom that has nothing to do with you," RJ offered. "If Aaron doesn't stay on as a teacher, Carter, it won't be your fault. It will be hers, okay?"

Carter nodded and dashed up the stairs to his room. The door shut hard, the eager bam of a kid who was dying to get away from an awkward situation.

"Well, that sucked," RJ said. "Note to self: never have kids."

"Does Aaron want kids?" Mom asked.

"Hell if I know, but I'm not having any." Though the idea of a little Aaron in the world was pretty cute. But no. No way. He wasn't going to start down that mental path. One of the great things about being gay was that his relationships could crash and burn, and only he and the other guy went through the fallout. No kids left behind. Although he supposed some gay people did have kids.

"I feel like it's not quite over yet," Doug said. "But we at least have it all out in the open."

"And I'll try to stop being hot," RJ said, nodding to himself.

His mother slapped his arm. "You're an asshole."

RJ laughed. "Merry Christmas, Mom. It's the messed-up family you always wanted."

"It is, actually," she said, joining Doug on the sofa. "Though maybe Doug's having doubts."

"Never." He threw his arm around her, dragging her close for a kiss.

"And now it's my turn to go up to my room," RJ said. "I have some presents to wrap."

BACK IN HIS apartment, Aaron was on the sofa when he finished the last of his end-of-semester grading and set aside his laptop. He still hadn't heard from his mother, but his father had texted earlier in the day.

Dinner will be at 6 on Christmas Eve but come spend the whole day. Bring that boy. Don't let yourself down. Just bring him.

Aaron fiddled with his phone, reading the last message from his mother before their big blowup. *You can be in charge of the sweet potato casserole for our Christmas Day luncheon this year. I'm trusting you not to mess it up.* And then switching back to his dad's message. Such different people. No wonder they hadn't lasted.

Not sure what possessed him, he thumbed his father's name on his phone, and the call went through. Too late to hang up. His dad would see his name on the caller ID and just call him right back.

"Cracker! What's going on, son?"

"Just wanted to hear your voice."

"Oh, yeah? Why's that? Something wrong?"

"Mom and I fought."

A low hum of understanding slipped through the phone, and Aaron wanted to wrap himself up in it like a blanket. "Must've been a doozy. You wouldn't be calling me if it weren't."

"Yeah. We fought a few days ago. We haven't spoken since."

Dad sighed. "She's a hard one, your mother. But it's not like you to be so tough on her. What's it about? That boy of yours?"

Aaron wanted to deny it, but of course he couldn't. He slid his fingers through Constance's soft, black fur and was gratified by her soft purrs. "Yeah. She's always said if I want to work in her school, then I have to stay in the closet."

His father was silent, and Aaron's hair stood on end. Somehow, he sensed his father's rage.

Rushing on, Aaron clarified, "Not that I ever fought her on it. I agreed. I didn't want the complications of being out as a teacher. What if... What if parents didn't like it?"

"Then fuck 'em."

Aaron laughed. "Yeah. I'm coming to see it that way. But Mom... She's never going to be okay with me being gay, is she?"

"You'll have to ask her, son. I'd like to think she'll come around, but she never came around on me being a farmer, even though that's what I was when she found me." Dad sighed heavily. "But I wasn't her son. You are. After the divorce, you became her primary relationship in the world. It wasn't healthy on a lot of levels, but what was I supposed to do about it? I think once she accepts she can't run your life, she'll come around to some sort of relationship with you. She won't cut you out. Not like she did me."

"I don't know." Aaron smoothed Constance's fur. "I think she might."

"I'm here for you. The family's here for you. You won't be alone in this world. But I know everyone needs their mama. I needed mine until her dying day."

"I miss Grandma. She was wonderful."

"She put up with a lot of hooey from us kids, and from Dad." He chuckled. "Listen to me. Bring that boy out for Christmas Eve, and if you haven't made it up with your mother by Christmas Day, bring him over again to watch your cousins' kids open their presents."

"RJ has his own family, Dad."

"Well, come out alone. We're always happy to have you."

"I know. I love you, Dad."

"Love you, too, Cracker. Hang in there. It's the season of miracles."

"So I've heard."

After disconnecting the call, Aaron considered reading a book in bed until he grew sleepy enough to drift off. But once he was beneath the covers, everything felt all wrong. His ass was tender from the braided belt, and he'd had to apply cream to it twice over the course of the day. He felt unsettled, like he needed something more. A spanking. A fuck. A simple kiss.

Was he allowed to ask for what he needed? He'd never been allowed to before.

Picking up his phone again, he opened the text thread with RJ. They'd exchanged something simple earlier when RJ had reassured Aaron that things were going to be okay with Carter, and they'd agreed that a night apart would be for the best. *To allow your ass to heal, and to allow me some time to convince my stepbrother that I'm a troll.*

At the time, Aaron had agreed readily enough. He'd had grading to do and he was tired after several sleepless nights. Plus, he'd realized that having RJ around was a distraction from thinking about his mother, and he owed it to himself to figure out what he wanted to do about her. But now, reading over the texts again, he couldn't help but wonder...

Girding himself for humiliation, he typed in a question and sent it.

If I didn't want to fuck you anymore, would you still want to spend time with me?

The *Read* message appeared. There was a long delay and then bubbles, then no bubbles, and then bubbles again.

I'm calling you.

The phone started to ring as soon as the message came through and Aaron shivered as he picked it up. "Hey."

"Did I hurt you? Are you okay?"

"You hurt me, but I liked it, remember?"

"I know, but…" RJ let out a frustrated growl. "What did you mean by that message?"

"I don't know." God, he felt like an idiot now. An adolescent idiot, even though he was coming up on thirty and was older than RJ. "I just got worried."

"About what?"

"That you just like me for my ass."

RJ barked out a laugh. "Baby, I like you for so much more than your ass. Though I admit it was the first thing that got my attention way back when…" He cleared his throat and grew serious. "Is this because I suggested not getting together tonight?"

"Maybe."

"Mmm. How about I come over there and prove to you how much I don't need your ass to enjoy being with you?"

"I thought you needed to stay home with your family?"

"They've all gone to bed. Give me twenty minutes."

"You don't have to—"

"Be ready, Mr. Danvers. I'm going to show you just how good it can be to *not* get fucked."

Aaron shivered as the call was disconnected. He wondered if he should do something to prepare, like clean Constance's litter box, or shower, but in the end, he simply lay in bed staring at the ceiling with a half-hard cock and a lot of ideas of what RJ might do to him when he arrived.

Which he did, exactly twenty-four minutes later.

Aaron shuffled down the hall in his pajama bottoms to let him in. Constance, asleep in the kitchen sink, woke enough to yowl and storm into the bathroom to scratch at her scratching pad.

"Hey," RJ said, coming in from outside smelling of snow, which had started to drift down again. Aaron wondered if it would stick. "You look good, Mr. Danvers." He tweaked Aaron's nipples with cold fingers. "Let me get out of these clothes and then we'll get on with the not-fucking, all right?"

Aaron chuckled, helping RJ off with his coat and smiling as RJ kicked his shoes off by the rack at the door. Then he took RJ's hand and led him back toward the bedroom, with RJ losing his shirt, socks, and pants along the way. He wore no underwear at all, and his cock was half-hard too.

Aaron brought him to a halt by the bed, his heart hammering and his dick rising slowly up. RJ took it in hand and held it loosely. He bent low and kissed Aaron's neck. "Sorry, baby. But this isn't going to get you anywhere."

Confused, Aaron let RJ push him down on the bed. "Get under the covers. It's late. We need our sleep."

"What are you doing?" Aaron asked as RJ went around to the other side of the bed and got in.

"Not fucking you."

"But... There are other things we could do?"

"There are. And I love doing them. But not tonight," RJ said with a smile. "I wouldn't want you to think I'm into you only for your body. I mean, the orgasms are impressive—best I've ever had—but I wouldn't want you to feel used, Mr. Danvers."

"I don't feel used," Aaron gasped, sliding up next to RJ and pressing their naked bodies together. He reached down to touch RJ's cock and was relieved to find it hard.

"Uh-uh-uh," RJ tutted. "That's a no. No sex tonight."

"Did you come here to torture me?" Aaron asked, his cock throbbing now that he was being denied relief.

"I came here to love you," RJ whispered. "Come here." He opened his arms and drew Aaron close, pressing Aaron's head to his chest and wrapping their legs together. He gripped Aaron harder with his thigh when Aaron tried to hump against him. "My mother says that trust is love. What do you think of that?"

"I don't know," Aaron said breathlessly. "I hadn't ever thought about it before."

"I don't think you could love someone you didn't trust," RJ said thoughtfully, his fingers skimming up and down Aaron's back, making him shiver and ache. "But could you trust someone you didn't love?"

"I don't know. It seems likely that if you trusted someone, truly trusted them, then you'd feel some affection for them," Aaron said, thinking of his mother and how much he didn't trust her. Did that mean he didn't love her, either? "Please let me touch your cock."

"No," RJ said firmly. "Roll over and turn the lamp out. We should sleep."

"I don't want to sleep. I want you to help me feel better."

RJ rolled over on top of Aaron, pushing his hard cock against Aaron's stomach and shoving Aaron's hands into the mattress. "I'm in charge here, and you'll come when I tell you to come. That won't be tonight."

Aaron shuddered hard. He nearly came right then, submissive pleasure coiling tight in his balls and cock, but he didn't. It was close, but not quite enough to send him over.

"Oh, you like that," RJ said, laughing and nuzzling at Aaron's neck again. "Maybe I'll get you a chastity device. Make you wear it while I tour. Keep the key with me, until I get back from going around the world. Let you come only for me."

"Fuuuuuuck," Aaron hissed, and just like that he *did* come. A sweet, rolling, throbbing orgasm pumped through him, and jizz spurted out in hot pulses between their bellies.

RJ laughed. "Holy shit, Mr. Danvers. Look at you. Such a dirty, naughty boy." He laughed again, lifting up to see the sticky mess between them. "I'm afraid I'll have to punish you for that."

Aaron shivered and quaked, his nipples tingling as he came down from the shock of orgasm. "H-h-how?" he asked, a flare of greedy hope in his chest. Maybe he'd spank him again. Or otherwise give him a jolt of pain.

"You'll see."

Aaron panted and shivered as RJ rolled out of bed, found a wash-cloth in the bathroom, and cleaned Aaron up. RJ's cock was still hard, but he didn't put it in Aaron's mouth or let him touch it.

"What's my punishment?" Aaron asked as RJ slipped into bed again.

"Sleeping here beside me," RJ said, tugging him close and shoving his hard cock against Aaron's hip.

"Let me help you," Aaron whispered, reaching for RJ's dick.

"No," RJ said, pushing his hand away. "Only good boys get my come. You, Mr. Danvers, were a very bad boy who didn't obey me. When you can show me obedience again, I'll let you have my come—in your mouth or in your ass—but until then, you'll have to live with the knowledge that you're on my naughty list, Mr. Danvers." He kissed Aaron's cheek before stretching out on his back, his cock tenting the sheets a little.

"You aren't going to jerk off?"

"No."

"But I won't be able to sleep," Aaron said softly. "I'll feel guilty that I came and you're still hard."

"Oh, you'll sleep," RJ said, turning onto his side and touching Aaron's cheek. "For the record, I think maybe it's *you* who only likes *me* for my body. After all, I was able to resist the temptation, and you weren't."

"I don't know what all I like you for," Aaron admitted as he turned the lamps out as he'd been asked. "But I want to find out."

"Me too, baby. Me too." RJ cuddled Aaron close and kissed the top of his head. "Now sleep. Tomorrow we can find out more to like about each other."

"And I'll be off your naughty list?" Aaron asked as a tug of relaxation took hold. It did bother him to be on RJ's naughty list for having actually disobeyed, even if he hadn't been able to stop himself from coming.

"We'll see. I'm sure I can find a way to help you get off it."

"By helping you get off?" he asked hopefully.

"Shh." RJ kissed his hair again. "Sleep."

From outside, the sound of carolers reached them. Aaron recognized them as a group from one of the downtown churches that went door-to-door every year as well as wandering up and down the streets of the city.

As the tune of "God Rest Ye Merry Gentlemen" floated in through the walls, Aaron slipped into sleep with RJ's arms tight around him.

Chapter Twenty-Seven

T HE WEATHER FORECAST was calling for a snowpocalypse on Christmas Eve, but no one really believed it. It was Tennessee after all, not the Finland of RJ's stories, and the dire snow predictions the weather people hyped every winter almost never came to pass.

The past week, Aaron had slept late, read books, scrolled social media, and pretended to look for new jobs while snuggled up on the sofa with a hot guy. He also had a wonderful orgasm almost every day.

This was the greatest Christmas ever. Well, aside from the single text from his mom that Aaron hadn't replied to:

Christmas Day starts at 11am. Bring the casserole like we discussed and a well-considered apology.

With nary a snowflake in sight so far on the twenty-fourth, Aaron rode in the passenger seat of RJ's borrowed SUV out to Strawberry Plains with a green bean casserole balanced on his knees. RJ had made it himself, saying that his mama had taught him that he was never to go to anyone's house for a meal empty-handed.

On the back floorboard, there was a Jell-O salad that Aaron had made, a favorite from his childhood that he always brought, though he couldn't say now just why. The little cousins seemed to enjoy it still, but he didn't even bother putting any on his own plate anymore.

"How many people am I going to have to impress today?" RJ asked, putting his hand on Aaron's thigh and squeezing.

"Around thirty people will come and go throughout the day, but my cousins will be the ones most interested in you. But don't worry, they'll be so distracted by their hellcat kids that they won't have time to do more than *wish* they could interrogate you."

And *me*, he thought. Aaron was glad his father had prepared the family for the fact that he'd be arriving with a male lover, and God, he hoped his dad hadn't used that word. Though he still really liked it. Even if he no longer hoped it also meant fleeting.

"Anyone I need to be warned about? Aggressive huggers or shoulder clappers? Or homophobes?"

"I'm not sure about homophobes," Aaron admitted. "I think they'll keep it to themselves since we'll be in my dad's home. But my cousin Rory Lynn is a big hugger, and her husband Nails is really fond of those aggressive bro-dude taps that knock you over. You know the kind."

"Closeted?"

Aaron laughed. "Maybe? But I don't know. He's always had girl-friends."

RJ nodded and made the turn down the farm's driveway. There were half a dozen parked cars near the farmhouse, and one of the goats was out headbutting the wheels of his cousin Woody's big-ass truck.

"Looks like most of them are already here," Aaron said, taking a deep breath and letting it out slowly. "You have your epi pen? In case you get into accidental eggs?"

RJ grinned. "Yeah. But I'll be fine. Don't worry so much. I'm used to navigating my allergy."

Aaron bit into his lower lip in worry. "Promise?"

"Of course. You ready?"

"I guess."

RJ peered at the house. "We can take a minute before we go in."

"Two weeks ago, I never imagined that I'd be here with you." Aaron spoke slowly, trying to figure out how he felt about what he was about to say next. "Never imagined I'd be here with anyone. Ever."

"It's a big change."

"Yeah." He broke into a smile. "A good one."

RJ squeezed his thigh again. "Ready?"

"I am."

They managed to get inside without being headbutted by any goats. Inside, the house was warm, cozy, and already overrun with people. Aaron's little cousins Silas and Garner shot by "flying" old-model airplanes from his father's collection. The youngest cousin, Annaliese, was crying and arching back out of her mother's arms, screaming for a cookie, while her older sister, Ruby, stood on a chair nearby eating one and dancing to the Christmas carols playing from his dad's stereo.

"Cracker! Let me take that!" Aaron barely had time to thank his cousin Rory Lynn before she swept the Jell-O salad from his hands, and his other cousin LeeLee swooped in for the green bean casserole from RJ. They both looked like they wanted to greet him with hugs and beg for an introduction, but there was a sudden shout and crash from the kitchen and a child's wail rose up from the middle of it.

"That'll be Raisin," LeeLee groaned, and she and Rory Lynn took off with the food to see what was going on.

"Raisin?" RJ asked.

"Like I said. Nicknames. It's a thing. Sorry." Aaron grinned. "Hope you don't mind if you end up with one?"

RJ shrugged and winked. "I'm a fan of Santa, myself."

Aaron motioned for RJ to take off his coat and scarf, and they tried to hang them up in the overflowing coat closet. In the end, they sort of draped their coats over other coats and hoped for the best. Then Aaron rolled back his shoulders, put his chin up, and decided to get this over with.

"Come on, let me introduce you around."

RJ seemed to blend right in, which was a surprise and a half. In some ways he was a better fit in the family than Aaron, what with his rough-sounding voice, hyper-masc presentation, and guitar-slinging lifestyle. RJ might not be a farmer or mechanic, nor was he into Harleys the way most of his male cousins were, but he had stories about life on the road, and a way about him that said, "*Don't fuck with me.*" Aaron's cousins could respect that.

As for the female cousins, they were delighted, though in a completely different way. Rory Lynn and Candace cornered Aaron on the staircase.

"So, how'd you meet him?"

"At a club." He'd already decided to obscure the full truth, though maybe he should have told RJ the plan because…

"He said you were his teacher back in high school."

"He did?"

Candace waggled her brows. "Indeed he did." She looked like she'd been drinking already. Her cheeks and nose were red, and her eyes were alight with more than excitement over the holiday. "Is it true?"

"I hardly remember him from back then."

"Oooooh," Rory Lynn said. "That's a little dirty, isn't it?" She'd obviously been drinking too.

"Definitely not the rumor I want getting around. For all intents and purposes, we met at a club downtown earlier this month. He was playing a gig and I was in the audience. We struck up a conversation afterward." He shrugged. "Voila."

"Oh, voila!" Candace said, laughing. "You're such a pompous prick, Cracker. I mean, come on. You're sleeping with a former student. Don't act like you're all that."

"Admit it. He was a one-night stand that stayed longer than you expected," Rory Lynn said with a chuckle.

"Why do you care?" Aaron asked, feeling hot all over.

"Look at him. Blushing like a virgin bride," Rory Lynn said. "Oh, Cracker. You're too much fun to tease."

"This is why he hasn't brought anyone home before now," LeeLee said playfully, coming down the stairs from having put her toddler down for a nap. "Leave him alone or he won't bring anyone else again."

"My hairdresser is gay," Candace said. "And my dermatologist too."

Aaron stared at her.

"Are they single?" Rory Lynn asked. "Because Jake's cousin Brian is gay, and he's single."

"And I'm not," Aaron said, frowning in confusion. "So…"

"Hey," RJ's voice carried up from the bottom of the staircase. "I've been looking for you."

Rory Lynn, Candace, and LeeLee all hustled away, smiling at RJ and squeezing his arms as they passed like they wanted to test to see if he were real or not. The noises from the kitchen—pots, pans, laughter—echoed down the hallway.

"Everything okay?" RJ asked, coming up the stairs.

"The bathroom downstairs was occupied, so I was going to use the one up here but got waylaid by nosy cousins. They wanted me to know that there are other fish in the sea if you throw me back."

"Is that what they said?"

"Not really. But I think that's what they meant."

"Kinda sweet of them," RJ said with a grin. "Wanting to matchmake for you if things don't work out with us."

"They're probably mad I didn't tell them before. Years of potential setups down the drain."

RJ followed Aaron up the stairs to the second floor and into the bathroom. "We can share," he said, shutting the door behind them.

With the door blocking out the waves of family sounds from downstairs, Aaron closed his eyes and lifted the toilet seat to take a leak. He put his hand on the wall over the toilet and leaned against it, trying to relax enough for his bladder to release.

"Your dad's happy I'm here," RJ said. "That's pretty cool."

With a sigh of relief, Aaron felt his piss surge, and he groaned as it hit the water in the porcelain bowl. He hadn't realized how badly he needed to go. "I think he's genuinely glad, but also I'm pretty sure he thinks he needs to make up for how awful my mom is being. So he's being extra open-minded."

RJ scooted in beside Aaron, his cock out and already taking aim. There was barely enough room, but if they both held still and concentrated, they could piss together at once without making a mess.

"This is nice, right?" RJ said as they washed their hands in the sink together.

Aaron nodded. It was nice. No doubt about it. He was surprised to find that having RJ with him made him feel more real and less like a hanger-on of the family. This was his lover, his father's house, and his Christmas. He wasn't just an observer, around for a few days here and there while the rest of the Danvers clan were the real family. Not this year.

Of course, when they went back downstairs, it was only a matter of time before the cousins broke out the embarrassing childhood stories. LeeLee even went so far as to get out his father's photo album. There were some horrendous pictures of her in there too with terrible early-2000s hair and clothing, but no one seemed to care. RJ seemed to enjoy the old pictures, and Aaron was grateful LeeLee didn't get out the actual baby book.

The kids played and danced. Adults drank and laughed. And before long, it was time to exchange gifts.

RJ had brought in a sack of small dollar items he'd picked out with Perri and Beau as gifts for Aaron's little cousins. He passed out the carefully gift-wrapped trinkets to each of them and seemed gratified by the squeals of delight. "Amazing how happy a plastic kazoo can make a kid," he said, laughing.

"And how furious it can make their mother," Aaron replied, nodding to where Rory Lynn and LeeLee looked like they might destroy the small plastic toys before the night was through.

"Oops. Did I make enemies?"

"Nah. It's not that bad. One year, my dad gave my cousin Dem Buns a chainsaw. He was fourteen."

"Dem Buns?"

"Long story. Involves bread buns. I swear."

"Right. These nicknames, man. They're killing me."

Aaron laughed. "I know, I know. The kazoos will no doubt meet a grisly end, but we'll be long gone by then."

"This is for you," Aaron's dad said, pressing a package into RJ's hands. "And this one is for you, son." He pushed a soft, wrapped square into Aaron's. Probably a sweater.

"I…" RJ stared at the gift. "I don't have anything for you, sir. Just the casserole."

"And it was a damn good casserole," Dad said. "Don't worry about it. It's nothing." He waved his hand toward the present. "Open it."

RJ tore into it. No saving the paper for him. Aaron's mother would have winced at the waste, but Aaron liked the enthusiasm. Beneath the paper was a picture in a frame, and when Aaron leaned closer, he felt a rush of heat go up his chest, neck, and into his cheeks. "Dad!"

"I've got more copies. He can have that one."

"Dad!" Aaron repeated. He'd brought RJ to family Christmas, yes, and he was pretty sure he was in love, but they weren't to this stage yet. No one got to *this* stage until they were engaged.

RJ laughed and laughed, tears starting from the corners of his eyes, and he wiped at them with his knuckles. The cousins were curious about what had Aaron's guy losing it like that, so they crowded around. Hoots were followed by exclamations that his dad had gone too far.

"Uncle Rutty, that's not nice," LeeLee scolded.

"I think it's great," RJ said hoarsely, still laughing.

Aaron groaned and tried to scoot away on the sofa, but RJ wrapped an arm around his shoulders and dragged him back in against his side. The framed picture remained balanced on his knees, there in all its embarrassing glory.

"Uncle Rutty, he's naked in it!" Rory Lynn reprimanded, though she was laughing too.

"Naked on Santa's lap," Woody crowed. "And crying. What the hell,

Uncle Rutty, that's messed up."

Aaron wiped his hand over his face, hoping the photo would disappear, but of course it didn't.

"It's a great picture!" Dad said. "That was his first picture with Santa. And he was so mad about having to wait in line for it that he took all his clothes off in protest. Helen was *furious*, so she left me there with him. She said, 'He's yours. You deal with him.'" Rutty laughed too. "So I just led him on up to Santa, buck-naked, and the guy picked him up. Aaron screamed and screamed, and just when—"

"Dad!" Aaron said desperately.

"Just when Santa put him down, he walked over and peed in the potted plant. He was something else."

"Holy shit," RJ said, laughing so hard that he could barely breathe. "Oh my God. Oh, baby, look at you."

Aaron couldn't help but laugh too. "I had to go. I was trying to tell them."

"He couldn't talk much yet," Dad said. "Helen was so impatient with him. She tried to teach him sign language, but he refused to learn."

"But when he did finally talk, didn't he do it in full sentences?" Woody asked. "I remember he went from being a grunting, pointing baby to speaking in big long sentences."

"That's right," Dad said. "I think he was waiting until he could do it 'right.' You know how Aaron likes things to be right."

"Prissy," RJ murmured in Aaron's ear, too low for anyone else to hear.

"He just knows what he likes and is willing to wait for it," LeeLee said. "There's no shame in that." She winked, clearly indicating that RJ was further evidence of this.

Aaron took the photo from RJ's hands and put it aside, tearing into his own gift—yes, a sweater—to hide his still-red cheeks. He was embarrassed but somehow thrilled too. RJ's reaction was a gift that made the photo even better.

THE NIGHT WOUND down slowly. Cousins drifted off and out of the house one by one, taking their rowdy or sleeping kids with them. The snow started to come down around dinnertime, but they ignored it, assuming that it wouldn't stick. But by the time Aaron and RJ had helped Rutty with the dishes and put the house back to rights, the tire tracks from where the cousins had left were all covered up, and there was a good foot and a half of snow on the ground. RJ knew there was no way they were driving anywhere.

"Might as well wait until morning," Rutty said, clapping his hands on their shoulders. "The roads out this way don't get salted and it's dark. I'd feel better about you making it home safely in the morning light."

RJ didn't protest, catching Aaron's eye though to make sure he was comfortable with it.

"You two can share your old room," Rutty said. "I changed the sheets in case you wanted to stay over anyway."

RJ followed Aaron upstairs, and they both said an only slightly awkward good night to Rutty on the landing before going in separate directions. RJ pulled his phone out as he walked, sending a fast text to his mother to let her know that he'd gotten snowed in but that he'd be home for sure by noon the next day.

"The kids are going to be so mad at me," he said as he shut the door of Aaron's old room behind him and gazed around with curiosity in his eyes. "I promised I'd be home for Christmas morning."

"We can get up early."

"They'll be up before dawn," RJ said, walking over to a framed photo on the wall. It was of what looked to be a seven-year-old Aaron kissing the snout of a baby pig by the barn. "Mom was complaining about how she won't get to sleep in on Christmas Day for the next ten years."

"I'm sorry."

"It's not your fault. I wanted to come here tonight. I'm glad I did. Meeting your family was sweet. And that picture of you with Santa…" He laughed softly. "I can't believe your dad gave it to me."

"I don't think he understands the kind of relationship we're in."

RJ turned away from the pig picture. "I think he understands perfectly."

Aaron's eyebrow twitched up. "That's the kind of gift you give someone who will want it in ten years' time. Not someone who—"

"I'll want that picture in ten years' time," RJ whispered, coming closer to Aaron with his hands outstretched. He grabbed Aaron by the hips and dragged him close. "I'll want that picture for the rest of my life."

"But—"

"Shh." RJ nuzzled Aaron's neck and whispered, "We're supposed to be seeing where this goes. Stop trying to control or define it. Just let it be."

"Me?" Aaron shivered as RJ's lips traced his jaw. "I'm not the control freak here."

"Oh, baby, of course you are." RJ laughed, his breath hot on Aaron's earlobe. "That's why you love it when I take it away from you."

Tension hung between them. RJ held Aaron close. White snow piled up on the windowsill. Coldness seeped in from an unseen crack in the wall, and Aaron shivered.

"RJ?"

"Yeah?"

"I don't know how to do this."

"We'll figure it out together."

Aaron clung to RJ's broad shoulders, pressing so close he could feel RJ's heartbeat through his nice, button-up shirt. "I'm scared to hope."

"You're not alone in that."

Aaron released RJ and pulled out his phone to send a text of his own before undressing. The cold from the crack continued to seep in, and RJ watched as Aaron got down to just his underwear and jerked back the quilts and slipped beneath them.

"I have a present for you," RJ said as he stripped to his boxer briefs.

"You do?" Aaron asked with a yawn, his short, light brown hair rubbing over the white pillow as he turned to face RJ. "I thought we weren't going to exchange presents?"

"We weren't, but I have something." He climbed in beside Aaron, curled on his side to face him and said, "I'm going to give you something special. I just thought of it, actually. Just now."

Aaron blinked at him sleepily. "Okay?"

"I'm going to give you some clarity."

"Huh?"

RJ took hold of Aaron's chin. "I love you. I know we've said that before, but the fact remains that I do. I love you more and more every second. I don't know how long we'll last, but I think we should start acting like we're going to last a long time. Because if we don't, then we definitely won't."

"If we don't, then we won't?" Aaron repeated confusedly.

"Yeah." RJ stroked his thumb over Aaron's mouth. "I remember telling Becca once that if she wanted to be a drummer, she needed to go at it one hundred percent. Because if she wanted to be a drummer but decided to style hair as a backup plan, then I could guarantee that in five years' time she'd still be a hairstylist. And she is. A hairstylist."

"*And* a drummer?"

"Not really. She just drums for fun."

Aaron kissed RJ's thumb. "Right."

"So if we want to make it, even if we don't really believe it's possible to make it, we have to start acting like we can. Or we'll be over and done with before we ever start."

"I had too much eggnog, or maybe you did, because you've gone goofy on me."

"Let's commit."

"Um?"

"To monogamy. I mean, we've already basically agreed to that, but it should be explicit. And to being boyfriends."

"Lovers."

"Whatever. So long as it means we plan that next Christmas we'll still be together. We have to *plan* on it."

"RJ…"

"Don't overthink it."

"I think you're the one overthinking things."

"I'm not. I didn't become a touring guitarist entirely by chance. I did it by not giving myself the option to fail at it."

"RJ?"

"Yes."

"I really think I love you too."

"I know."

"And I want to believe, but…"

"No buts!"

Aaron huffed. "You're ridiculous."

"It's Christmas. Let's give ourselves this ridiculously expensive gift."

"Expensive?"

"If we're wrong and it all goes to shit, it'll cost us a lot more in heartbreak and lost time than some dumb material object we could have bought. But if we're right and it works out, then it's priceless."

Aaron's dimples broke through. "You're a secret romantic."

"I'm not. I actually think love is bullshit."

"Right. Okay. And yet—" Aaron put his hand over RJ's where it still cupped his cheek.

"I know. I know. I want this. I don't want to believe that this will be the only Christmas I'll ever spend here."

Aaron chuckled. "Were my cousins that fun?"

"No, but I just want to be with you. Next to you. I want your dad to give me more baby photos, and I want to hear more cousin stories, and I want to become a story of my own... 'Remember that Christmas when RJ showed up? We didn't even know Aaron was gay!'"

"They knew I was gay."

"Did they though?" RJ chuckled, and Aaron did too.

"They suspected."

"It doesn't matter. What matters is that I want a nickname too."

"Do you?"

RJ grinned. "We have to plan for that future, baby. We have to commit to it working. Unless you don't want it?"

Aaron leaned close, kissing RJ and whispering, "I do."

Chapter Twenty-Eight

THE SOUND OF a scream woke RJ from his sleep. He jerked up in bed, heart pounding with a rush of adrenaline. "What was that?"

Aaron, who'd been curled up next to him, snuggling in for warmth, chuckled and tugged on RJ's arm. "Rooster."

"Are you sure? It sounded like a scream to me."

"I'm sure."

The noise came again, and RJ thought it didn't sound a damn thing like the cockle-doodle-do of his childhood books. "That's terrifying."

Aaron murmured something incomprehensible and snuggled close again. RJ ran a hand through Aaron's soft hair and down the chill of his scratchy cheek before climbing out of bed. The house was snug, but still cold, and he shivered in the morning air. It was dark out the window, but he could make out that the snow had mostly melted in the night. The temperature must have lifted well above freezing.

So much for a white Christmas. The kids would be disappointed.

The kids!

RJ hustled over to the night table and grabbed his phone. Five-ten in the morning. Not even close to dawn. The rooster crowed again.

"The sun isn't up yet," RJ whispered. "Why's he screaming?"

"Internal clock. He always crows at five or shortly after." Aaron yawned and rolled over. "C'mere. It's cold without you."

RJ put the phone down and was just climbing under the covers when he heard a door open and shut from the hallway. Heavy footsteps started down the stairs. "Your Dad's already up?"

Aaron nuzzled RJ's shoulder, his nose all cold against his skin. "Farm life. Going out to the barn."

"Now I see why you didn't want it. Way too early." RJ cuddled up to Aaron, breathing in his sleepy morning scent and considering. As much as he loved holding his sweet Mr. Danvers, soft and pliant in his arms, he also had a promise to keep. Well, if he could.

"Aaron, wake up."

"Mmm?"

"I had a thought. If we leave now, I could still get home in time to see the kids come down for their gifts. Be there on Christmas. Like I promised." He winced. Unless the little ones really did wake hours before dawn like his mom said they might. "Maybe."

Aaron wiped at his sleepy eyes. "But the snow..."

"Gone."

Aaron held very still and quiet for a moment, but then he sighed and sat up. He stretched and made a few morning snuffling sounds before announcing, "Okay, yes. We should try."

"Thank you."

Aaron kissed his cheek and said nothing more.

They scrubbed up quickly in the hallway bathroom, using guest toothbrushes and razors that Rutty kept in there. Then they put on the same clothes they'd had on the day before. Heading downstairs, they were met in the front hall by Rutty, who was just coming in from the barn.

"I didn't disturb your sleep now, did I?" he asked, tugging a stocking hat off his head, exposing his reddened ears and cheeks. He sat on a bench in the entryway to pull off his boots and put them aside in a box that caught the dirt.

"Clucky woke RJ," Aaron said with another yawn and a wide stretch of his arms. He looked adorable and delicious with his soft smile and his dimples on display. "He's not used to the sounds of the countryside."

RJ snorted. "It sounded like someone screaming."

Rutty laughed. "Old Clucky has a unique crow, I'll give him that. Heading out so early?"

"Yeah," Aaron said, reaching out to help tug his dad up off the bench in an unnecessary but affectionate way.

RJ said, "I'm so sorry to leave this early, but I promised my little brother and sister that I'd be there on Christmas morning when they came down for presents. I'd hate to disappoint them."

"I can understand that. Good thing the snow melted. There'll probably be a few icy spots left. So be careful anyhow." Rutty nodded down the hall toward the kitchen. "Spare a minute and I'll brew you some coffee for the road."

They followed Rutty to the toasty-warm kitchen. The woodstove was burning already. The final dishes from the party yesterday were dried in the rack. The view out the back windows showed a long field that ended with the silver stripe of the Holston river, lit up with the still visible white light of the low-hanging moon. RJ wanted to be welcomed back to Rutty's home again and again. He hoped Aaron was still committed to their promise the night before to try. To *really* try.

"It was right nice having you here for Christmas Eve," Rutty said to RJ after brewing a fresh pot of coffee and handing him a steaming travel mug. "I hope you'll be back before too long?"

Aaron eagerly took his own travel mug and moaned at his first sip, clearly comforted by the heat and caffeine.

"I hope so, sir," RJ said, taking Rutty's hand in a firm shake. "I wish we could stay longer this morning. Spend some of Christmas Day with you."

"That'd be nice, but Aaron has always been with his mother on this day." He looked to Aaron now and cocked his head. "And this year, I assume it's the same? You're welcome to stay with me, son. I can carry you on home later."

"No, I plan to go to Mom's," Aaron said quietly, his contented, sweet expression completely dropping away and dimples disappearing. "I have some things I need to discuss with her."

"All right." Rutty looked worried but didn't argue. "If you change your mind, I can break away from the family to come pick you up again." He put his arm around Aaron's shoulders and gave him a squeeze.

RJ's heart ached to see Aaron snuggle in closer, taking his father's offered affection so easily, obviously needing the reassurance. When they broke away from each other, RJ shook Rutty's hand again and they were off.

On the way back to Knoxville, the empty roads sang with the slushy wetness beneath the wheels of the SUV. RJ put his hand on Aaron's knee and held it there, letting the pink glow of a raw, new Christmas morning open up behind them and do all the speaking. Some sunrises were like that. Full of meaning.

Eventually, he broke the silence. "Do you want to come to my house with me? Watch the kids do their thing?"

Aaron smiled and wiped at his still-tired eyes. "I think I'd love to see that some year, in that future we promised to try for. But I need to get ready to face my mom."

"All right." RJ didn't like the thought of Aaron dealing with his mother alone. "I could come with you to your Mom's place? Meet her. Maybe I could help put her mind at ease about us and you and Carter?"

Aaron shook his head. "No. This is something I have to do on my own."

"On Christmas Day?"

"New beginnings. Death of the old, birth of the new. All that jazz."

"I thought that was New Year's Eve."

Aaron snorted. "I suppose. It's something I have to do. For myself. Alone." He took RJ's hand from his knee and held it instead, their fingers knitting together comfortably. "No matter what happens with my mom, I'm glad we met again."

"None of that, Mr. Danvers," RJ said gruffly. "That sounds like a goodbye and we've agreed to pretend that love can last."

Aaron laughed a little giddily. "This is crazy. We've barely met."

"That's how it always starts, right? At some point, everyone's 'barely met,' but they choose to keep on meeting and it grows." RJ squeezed Aaron's fingers. "When a mother gives birth, she's barely met her baby, but no one would say she doesn't love it. What makes us different? Just because we're grown-ups? Didn't that Baby Jesus charge us with loving each other?"

Aaron squeezed his fingers back. "You're a strange one, RJ Blitz."

"You love it."

Aaron kissed RJ's knuckles and said solemnly, "I do."

STILL-WARM CASSEROLE HEATING his hands, Aaron was sweating when he pressed the doorbell with his elbow. His smile must have been gruesome given his mother's expression when she finally opened the door.

"Merry Christmas," he said, lifting the casserole dish. "I made the sweet potatoes like you asked."

His mother wore a Christmas sweater and jeans, and her hair was soft and loose around her shoulders. Her makeup was casual. Her smile, like Aaron's, was tight and horrible. She beckoned him inside. "Did you compose the apology I requested too?"

"No, Mom, I didn't." Aaron walked stiffly through the living room, ignoring the tinkling piano Christmas music playing from the speakers above the TV and the Christmas tree decorated with his own handmade ornaments from childhood.

He stepped into the long, galley kitchen, inhaling his mother's savory green bean casserole and a roasting turkey. Steeling himself, he said, "I don't intend to apologize. Because I didn't do anything wrong." He put the sweet potatoes on the counter and turned around.

His mother stood in the doorway, arms crossed over her flat chest, eyes narrowed ominously. "I can't believe you're going to ruin Christmas over this, Aaron."

He took a careful breath. "Let's go into the living room. I have a few things I need to say."

Rolling her eyes, she moved into his space, crowding him against the counter. "There's a lot still to do in the kitchen. I don't have time for this nonsense. Apologize and let's get on with it."

"No," Aaron said firmly, though his voice quivered with emotion. "I've met someone I care about, Mom."

She lifted a brow but said nothing.

"His name is RJ Blitz. And he was my student once. But he's a grown man now and I like him a lot. I might even love him."

She scoffed. "Love."

"Yes. Love. It's not without complications and it's not perfect, but when is it ever?"

"Aaron." She shook her head warningly. "You know and I know that you're talking about infatuation. Lust, not love."

"Mom, please. Just hear me out."

"Fine." She turned her back on him and stalked into the living room. Aaron followed her. She swept her hand toward the sofa, and Aaron took a seat. She stood over him.

"Sit down, Mom."

"How long will this take?"

"As long as it takes."

She glanced at her watch. "I have things to do in the kitchen. This can wait. We'll discuss it over lunch."

"No, I don't want to fight while I'm eating. Let's just get it done now so we can enjoy our meal."

She gritted her teeth, her thin jaw clenching, and sat in the lounge chair across from the sofa. "All I ever asked was that you not embarrass me, Aaron. And—"

"And I'm in love. I love him."

She threw her hands up.

Aaron bulldozed on. "It's too soon, but we're going to try to make it last. We're acting like it's going to grow into something, because otherwise is never will. We're *believing* it."

She pursed her lips. "Listen to yourself. What is this madness?"

"It's not mad for me to be gay, Mom."

Her jaw clenched. "I don't see why you need to flaunt it. Why date someone so much younger? A former student! People will talk. People already talk about you, Aaron."

"I don't care. Let them." Aaron put out his chin. "I ran from being talked about for so long. And recently it's occurred to me that I actually have very little to lose. I never got to explore what I really wanted from my life. Hell, I don't even know who I *am*, Mom."

"Evidently." She pressed her lips together again.

"I know one thing. I like who I am with RJ. And he never makes me feel like I'm less than perfect. Less than I should be."

"No one is perfect. Not you. Not even me." She lifted her chin like she was disabusing him of a long-held notion.

"Exactly. So I might as well give them something real to talk about."

"You already have one ethics code violation—"

"That was bullshit and you know it," he snapped. "Why did I get the stick for that while McAllister is still coaching like it never happened? I bet he still goes on Grindr trolling for hookups. If anything, he might be a little smarter about it, but you know he didn't turn into a saint who honors his marriage vows overnight." Aaron put up his hand when his mother started to speak. "Like I already told you, I didn't know he was married."

"Regardless, you have the mark against you. You could lose your job, Aaron. For what? For a late-twenties crisis? We all have them. For *love?*" She said the word like it was grotesque. "Please. What happens between you and these men isn't love. It's lust. Nothing more. Nothing lasting."

Aaron took another slow breath, trying to keep from crying or screaming or both. "It doesn't matter what you think is between me and RJ. All that matters is what I believe is between us." His throat ached. "I know now that you aren't ever going to be okay with me being gay. That 'don't embarrass me' was code for 'put my needs above your own,' and I'm done doing that. I'm your son, and I'd like to think you'll love me no matter what, but I guess you won't."

His mother glared at him. "You sound like your father. He was the same."

Aaron took a shaky breath. "The same? How?"

"He wanted me to love him even though he didn't deserve it."

Aaron lurched to his feet, checked his pockets for his keys and phone, and started toward the door. His chest ached, his mouth was dry, and he thought he might throw up.

But he didn't stop walking until his hand was on the doorknob.

"This again? Leaving as soon as I say something you don't like?" She followed at his heels.

"You've said things I don't like my whole life. And I still love you. But I deserve to be loved too, Mom. Because I'm a good man and a human being. I *deserve* it. Do you understand? And so did dad. He deserved love too."

She pressed her fingers between her eyebrows and shook her head. "Look what you've done. Christmas is ruined. All you had to do was say you were sorry. Is that so hard?"

Aaron released a bitter laugh. "All you had to do was love me! And I could ask the same."

She dashed her fingers through her hair. "Yes, Aaron! It's hard! You're making it very hard to love you!"

"How?"

"You're too old for this teenage rebellion," she said, taking a different tack instead of answering his question. She let out a long sigh. "I love you. Don't be silly. Come back and sit down. Don't spoil our lunch."

Aaron whispered, "You just said I made it hard to love me. I heard you."

"I was angry. I *am* angry." Her smile was brittle, and she reached out for him. "But it's Christmas. Let's have our meal and talk about this later when we've calmed down. I need to get back in the kitchen. The corn might boil over."

"I need to leave."

"Aaron—"

"No, Mom. I'm done with this conversation. I'm going." He jerked open the apartment door. "And I *will* be tendering my resignation. So you should probably spend the rest of your winter break starting a hunt for a new teacher. Because I'm not interested in remaining at Pineview."

"What?" She gawked at him like he'd grown another head. "That's absurd. How will you pay your bills? How will you live, Aaron?"

"Now you care?"

"I have always cared. I love you. I'm your mother."

"Don't give me that now. I don't owe you my plans."

"I'm your *mother.*"

Aaron thought of Betsy and her evident and easy love for RJ, how she'd effortlessly accepted the situation with Carter, and the way she'd embraced Aaron too. He thought of his own father's reaction to RJ when Aaron brought him to the farm the first time, and the holiday sweetness of the night before, spent in the loving embrace of his extended family. All of them so much more welcoming than his own mother.

"You're my mother? Act like it."

Aaron left then. He didn't look back.

When he reached the car his mother had texted him: *What about the casserole dish?*

Keep it.

Chapter Twenty-Nine

RJ DIDN'T KNOW what Helen Shock's problem was, but he wouldn't mind shaking the woman until she stopped being such a horrible person.

"Is she religious? Is that it?" he asked, holding Aaron as the little spoon, his chest pressed to Aaron's back, their bodies fitted together. Jeans against jeans, T-shirt to button-up cotton shirt. As close as they could be.

Aaron shook his head.

"What did your father see in her?" RJ was determined to solve the puzzle.

Aaron shrugged. "I think she must have been different once? He said she grew more ambitious after their marriage, less satisfied. But we don't usually talk about her. He moved on with his life without her."

"Maybe she'll come around," RJ said. "Not today, but someday."

Aaron shrugged. "I told her I was resigning."

RJ's heart skipped. "Good thing you've already been looking for jobs."

Aaron snuggled back against him and said a little timidly, "I think I'm going to travel first. I have some savings. Nothing much, but enough that I could go to a few places. See a few things. You know, before I have to commit to some sort of career again."

The implication hung in the air between them. RJ wasn't misreading it, was he? He decided he had nothing to lose by checking to see.

"Have you ever thought about going to Finland in winter?" RJ whispered against Aaron's hair. "The northern lights are stunning."

Aaron turned around in RJ's arms so they were facing each other. His eyes still gleamed, but the active crying had stopped. "Is that where you're heading?"

"I don't know actually. I haven't given my agent the okay to book me on a new tour." RJ touched the places Aaron's dimples should be. "Would you like that? Would you want to come with me?"

"Could I?" Aaron whispered it, like he wasn't sure he was allowed.

RJ's heart soared. He'd never imagined, never thought... "Yeah, of course. We don't always stay in nice places," he babbled. "Hotels, I mean. It can be a little rough."

"I can do rough."

RJ chuckled. "Hell yeah, you can, Mr. Danvers."

Aaron gazed at him, studying him closely. "Seriously, you'd want me to go along? I wouldn't be intruding?"

"No. I mean, yes, and no you wouldn't be intruding."

"This is impulsive."

RJ grinned and nuzzled Aaron's nose. "Yup. It is."

Aaron's face flushed, but this time with fervor instead of grief. "Yeah. It really is. It's crazy." But he didn't sound like he was backing away from the idea. He sounded thrilled by the wildness. "And what about..." Suddenly he deflated and looked away. "But will you still want me if I quit teaching? You know, if I'm not Mr. Danvers anymore?"

RJ tenderly took hold of Aaron's chin. "You'll always be my Mr. Danvers. You don't have to teach a class of pubescent balls of hormones to be that. But would you be happy? You're a great teacher. The best. Carter loves you, and the other kids must as well. Would you want to stop teaching?"

"Right now? I want to burn it all down and start over." He shuddered. "I just want to breathe." Aaron frowned, the dimples that had almost made a new appearance vanishing entirely again. "Do you know why I became a teacher? Because my mom wanted me to, and I knew I'd be good at it."

"That's fair."

"Yes. I suppose. I don't hate it, but I don't feel about teaching the way you do about music. I've seen you in Chip's studio. The way your eyes light up, the way you come alive with the music. On the stage too. You radiate. I wanted to fuck you the moment I saw you up there." He paused before going on, "I still do. Every time."

"I know what that's like," RJ growled in his ear. "That ass of yours. Shaking. While you wrote on that damn smart board."

Aaron's dimples blinked on. "I don't know what I'm doing. I don't think it's smart, or prudent, or well-considered, or any other mature thing. But I think it's what I want to do. If you want it too. And if you don't? I can travel on my own. I'll hike through France, and kayak the Amazon—"

"Oh, don't do that. That seems a little extreme." RJ laughed. "Besides, I want you with me. But what about Constance? She can't travel with us."

Aaron frowned again. "I don't know. Impulsivity has its complications."

"You don't have to decide now." RJ kissed Aaron's nose. "We have some time."

A small knock came at the door. RJ stood up to answer it, glancing over his shoulder to see Aaron wiping at his red cheeks and trying to compose himself. Opening the door, RJ found his mom with a plate of cookies and two mugs of cocoa on a tray, and big, worried eyes. "I thought these might help?"

His heart was so full of love for her that he almost cried too. Maybe things hadn't been ideal between them for some time. But she'd never been the kind of mom Aaron had grown up with. RJ, even at his most neglected, had known she loved him.

RJ took them from her and gave her a kiss on the cheek. "Thanks, Mom."

"Tell him he's welcome to stay. As long as he needs. We have another guest room we can make up for him. He'd need to sleep there, though. For Carter's sake. You know I don't care."

"I know, but I think I'll go home with him in a bit." There it was again. Thinking of Aaron's apartment as "home." "After dinner, maybe. If that's okay?"

"The kids will make a fuss."

"I know, but he needs me."

She tugged him down close. "And you love him?"

"Yes."

She looked over RJ's shoulder to where Aaron was still wiping at his eyes on the bed. She whispered, "He needs that."

"He does. And, Mom?"

"Yes?"

"Thank you. For always loving me. I'm sorry I've been an asshole."

She shrugged but her eyes filled with tears. "You had good reasons to be resentful. I could have done a better job. I should have." She cleared her throat and waved it off. "But—look, Aaron needs you now. I should shower and put on actual clothes." She motioned toward her snowman pajamas. "We'll talk more later. Doug wants to speak with you at some point today too? Before you leave, if that's okay."

RJ's stomach went sour at the thought, but he supposed it wasn't too much to ask. He should completely clear the air with the man. Figure out what was holding him back from trusting Doug. Or, well, loving him, his mother would say.

If Aaron could talk to his mother, then RJ could talk to his nice, supportive stepdad and work his shit out. Montmartre sunrise promises and all that.

ABOUT THIRTY MINUTES before dinner was supposed to be served, RJ was sent out back to the grill and Doug with a plate of veggies. They fired up the gas and stood awkwardly beside each other for a few minutes before Doug said, "So. I've been meaning to tell you." He cleared his throat. "I'm glad you came home for Christmas."

"Oh?" RJ had been half expecting Doug to give him grief about how little time he'd actually spent with his mom and siblings after he rediscovered Aaron.

"Yes, it's meant a lot to your mother. And your brother and sister. And even to Carter." He used tongs to put the veggies on the grill and concentrated on them as he finished up his declaration. "It meant a lot to *me*."

RJ shrugged, unsure what to say. "Oh, um. You're welcome."

Doug put the plate aside, lowering the gas so the flames died back a little. "I'm serious, RJ. I never got the chance to know you. I came along after you were gone, and you never came around. I thought you were…" He coughed. "I thought you were like your dad. But I was wrong."

RJ crossed his arms over his chest, trying not to feel defensive. But how could he deny it? He'd done to his mom what his father had done, hadn't he? He'd abandoned her. Hadn't looked back. Left her to fend for herself. Doug was the one who'd saved her.

"I owe you a debt," RJ said gruffly. "I let Mom down, but you—"

"Your mother is proud of you. You didn't let her down. Don't worry about that."

"I left her behind."

"You're the son, RJ. You're supposed to leave. That's what we raise our kids to do. If your dream had been accounting, then sure, you could have gotten work in Knoxville. But your dream was music. Your mother was only ever proud of you for following that with your whole heart, and for making it work."

RJ scrubbed at his leather jacket sleeves, shivering despite the heat of the gas grill. "Thanks. Still, I should have—"

"No shoulds," Doug said. "We could all should ourselves to death.

I'm just grateful you came home, that we had this time, and that we know each other a little better now. I'm glad for all of it. Even the hard conversations that came up because of Carter's crush. I should have come out to Betsy ages ago. I was worried she'd—" He shrugged. "She loves me. It didn't matter."

"She does love you," RJ said. "And you love her. I…admit it's hard for me to believe that love can last. Even with Aaron…" He cleared his throat and tried to explain. "Even with him, when I feel so much for him already and can imagine our future so clearly, I'm afraid that if I believe in it, I'll be wrong. And that will hurt too much to survive." He said the last in a whisper.

"Your father was a jackass. I'm sorry, but he was."

"I'm not sorry. It's the truth."

"He left you not once, but twice. Now the fact that his leaving was for the best for—"

"He hit her," RJ said, darkness lapping at his heart. His fists clenched.

Doug nodded, his hand clenching the tongs tightly. The scent of veggies rose around them and Doug removed them from the grill, covering them with aluminum foil to keep them warm. He turned off the grill.

"You're right that there are no guarantees in life. Maybe it won't work out with Aaron, but maybe it will—"

"That's what I'm saying," RJ said. "That's what we've agreed. That we have to try. That we've got something special enough that we both know it already. So we should try."

"Exactly. That's all you can do." Doug clapped a hand on RJ's shoulder. "Thanks for coming home."

"Thanks for giving my mom a home."

Doug hugged RJ with a few manly slaps, and they took the veggies inside and sat down to Christmas dinner. Beau and Perri clamored to sit beside RJ, and Aaron agreed to give up his seat to sit across from him.

"The view's better from here," he said with a wink as he took the seat. His eyes weren't red anymore and his smile looked genuine.

"Is it?" Perri asked with a toss of her light hair. "I wanna see."

"You sit there," Mom said. "He just wants to look at RJ."

Carter sat down next to Aaron and said, "Eh, it's an okay view, I guess. I've seen better." But his voice was all wonky, and he looked at RJ with those same eager eyes that he hadn't been able to shake since he'd confessed to his crush.

And everyone laughed. Even Carter. Happy family. Handsome lover.

Merry Christmas.

As CHRISTMAS DAY waned, Aaron had enough fun with RJ's family that he was able to forget from time to time that he'd lost his mother's approval and love—assuming he'd ever really had it.

When it was time to say goodbye to the Ward family, Aaron was grateful when RJ announced he was coming back to the apartment with him. If he'd had to leave on his own and go home alone, he knew the weight of all that had happened with his mom would have crushed him. At least RJ would distract and comfort him.

RJ would make sure that he felt it was still Christmas.

On the ride home, as RJ drove Aaron's car, citing Aaron's three glasses of wine over dinner as reason for commandeering the vehicle, Aaron's phone dinged. He glanced down, for a heart-stopping moment hoping it was his mother, before remembering he'd blocked her calls.

Hope it went well with Helen. I love you. Merry Christmas.

"Lauren," he offered when RJ tilted his head curiously. "She hopes it went well with my mother."

Aaron started to laugh. Shocked, hysterical, almost sobbing laughter, until it shifted once more to tears and he was sobbing. Actual hard, heaving sobs that sounded like his heart was breaking, and he couldn't make them stop.

RJ made soothing sounds from the driver's side, but they were on the interstate now. There was no safe place to pull over, so Aaron knew comforting noises was the best RJ could do.

All of it—even the old stuff like the divorce and the constant displeasure he'd faced growing up, plus the new stuff like the hiding, the hurting, the hating himself—welled up and out of him like a forced purging, and when he finally stopped, they'd been parked in the lot behind his apartment for God only knew how long. The lights were on in the church, and the Christmas trees from all the downtown buildings and lofts sparkled in the darkness.

"Here," RJ said, stuffing a handful of napkins into Aaron's hand. "Found them in your glove box."

Aaron nodded and rubbed the scratchy paper over his nose and eyes. It was overly warm in the car between his feverish crying and the heater, so he rolled down the window. The night was quiet, aside from the usual bursts of noise from the city and the hymns from within the church. The organ and the muffled but sonorous sounds of voices lifting and falling in welcome of a new baby.

A new start.

"Okay," Aaron said at last, the cold night air rushing over him and stirring between them in the car. "That's enough of that."

"I didn't mind."

"I know."

They shared a smile, and Aaron wiped at his eyes with the papers again. "I don't think I've ever cried like that in my life. Not that I remember. I guess I needed it."

RJ smiled sadly. "I'm sorry about your mom, Aaron."

"Birth is hard," Aaron said. "Even if you're just birthing yourself."

"Ah, there's my English Comp teacher. Similes abound."

"Metaphor, actually."

"My bad."

Aaron smiled and the sound of the chorus within the old church rose with the entire congregation joining in. "I know you said that you wanted me to go with you on the next tour, whenever that is, but you don't have to stick to that, RJ. If it turns out that we don't work, or that you don't—"

"Mr. Danvers," RJ said, his dominant voice breaking over Aaron's hot skin like a rush of cold wind. "Stop. No doubts. No second-guessing. Just give in to this. Let it happen. You can't struggle your way out of the pain you're feeling or the confusing months ahead. You have to just give in and go with it. See how it turns out. We'll deal with everything as it happens. Stop trying to control it."

"I'm not."

"You are. Do you need me to smack your ass to remind you that you're not the one in control here?"

"Right. You are."

"Nope. Not even me." RJ smiled. "Though it's a fun game in the bedroom, and I'm honored that you trust—love—me enough to let me do whatever I want to your body." He flushed. "What we both want. But even I'm not actually in *control*, Aaron. I have no idea what tour I might get signed on to. I don't even know if it will be country music, or rock, or jazz, or what. I just go. Where they say. *When* they say. I surrender and roll with the punches, and sometimes it sucks, and it's tiring and hard, and sometimes it's glorious and fun. And there are those Montmartre sunsets to offset the hardship." He shrugged. "And other times, there are lovers overdosed on bathroom floors."

Aaron winced, reaching for RJ's hand.

"No one is in control. Not you. Not me. Not Santa Claus." He nodded toward the church. "Despite being a Christian, I'm not even willing to say that Baby Jesus has his hands on the reins. What I do know is you have to learn to ride the horse without fighting the gallop. Loose body, loose knees, take those jumps and roll with the beast. Sure, sometimes the horse just walks along the stream and you get a break, right? That's nice when that happens. But that's not life. That's a metaphor. Look at me, Mr. Danvers. I learned that from you."

Aaron stared at him, the light from the city Christmas lights spackling the car window behind him. "RJ, I don't know if I can live that way, but I want to try. I've always been, like you said, prissy. I've always had things 'just so,' but I want to see what happens if I let go."

"I know you can handle it, Mr. Danvers," RJ said roughly. "Have you ever seen yourself take a spanking? Because if you had, you'd know you can handle anything that comes to you."

They kissed, the windows fogging up with their breath. "I'm so glad you're my Christmas lover," RJ murmured.

"Not just for Christmas."

"No. My lover-lover."

They kissed more, their mouths growing sensitive and tender. The winter night blew cool outside, but it grew even hotter in the car.

RJ whispered, "Let's go inside. There's something I want to show you."

Twenty minutes later, Aaron was ass-up over his dining table.

He wasn't sure about this idea. Everything he'd ever taught his kids said that letting yourself be filmed naked, cock hard and a small plug in your hole, was a terrible idea. The video could be uploaded, forwarded, sent anywhere. Lauren would lose her mind if she knew what he was letting RJ do.

But he trusted RJ.

And RJ said he wanted Aaron to see.

"Ready, lover," RJ asked in his ear, smoothing his hands over Aaron's back and shoulders. "Keep your head this direction. I want the camera to pick up every expression. I don't want you to miss your surrender."

Aaron's breath came in harsh, wretched pants, and he nodded. After all he'd been through with his mother today, he felt close to lifting out of his skin as it was. He hoped RJ was right that this was a spanking he could handle.

"Relax."

"I can't."

RJ massaged his arms and his back, his big, strong, warm hands rubbing up and down, then parting his ass cheeks to slip fingers up and down his crack. "There," RJ murmured when Aaron finally unclenched his hands and loosened up on the table. "Perfect."

Aaron stared at the iPhone set up to record this encounter. He *should* say Hermey. He should call this off and erase the file. He shouldn't let this happen. His mother would be horrified if the video got out. What if someone hacked RJ's phone, what if he left it behind somewhere, what if...

"You're thinking too much," RJ said, dropping a kiss to Aaron's shoulder blade. "I'm going to help that go away now. All of it. The worry. The fear. The anxiety. Fly away."

Aaron shivered and kept his eyes trained on the iPhone camera lens. "What are you waiting for?" he gritted out.

"Oh, Mr. Danvers, you're so naughty. What a thing to ask."

And then it began.

RJ used a long, thin black belt he'd taken from Aaron's closet, and the snap of it over Aaron's ass was instantly shocking and scary. When it hit the base of the plug, the jolt to his prostate was ecstasy. He shifted, but RJ put his hands on the other side of the table again and told him to hold still.

"Eyes on the camera," RJ said again. "Don't look away."

Aaron tried to obey, but the fire burning into his haunches, sinking deep beneath his skin and into his bones, was so strong that he had to clench his teeth and squeeze his eyes closed to keep from screaming. RJ backed off and rubbed a hand over the blazing pain of his ass cheeks and hips.

"Beautiful. But you need to let it out, Aaron."

"I'm tired of crying."

"Let it out," RJ said again, the dominance as firm as his hand on Aaron's ass.

Aaron guessed that RJ had decided not to give him any choice. Because the next layer of slaps the belt laid down were harder, and Aaron crumbled under them. He shook and squirmed and finally shouted, his body convulsing in pain as harsh, broken sobs burst forth, and the tears ran free again.

He hadn't thought he had more in him, but as RJ continued to lay on the stripes, the shame, guilt, horror, and sadness of what he'd lost—of what he'd never had—forced its way out of his mouth and leaked from his eyes and snotted from his nose.

It wasn't pretty. He didn't feel pretty. He felt raw, completely stripped down, and honest.

"That's so good," RJ said, easing off the spanking. "I think you've needed all this for a long time now."

Aaron sobbed as RJ lifted him from the table, kissed his lips, and held him close. His cock throbbed urgently, and he wished he could come and obliterate this intense, broken-hearted sorrow inside. But he felt too far away from himself, too outside his body to reach orgasm, and almost certain that he couldn't even if RJ tried to make him.

"Let's go back to your room now," RJ whispered. "I think tomorrow, when you see what we did, you'll understand. You're already free, baby."

Aaron couldn't fully comprehend what RJ meant. His body was a livewire of pain, but he hobbled back to the bedroom with RJ's arms around him. Under RJ's tender care, he flashed back in his mind to the last time he'd let a trucker fuck him. Hot, grimy, against the side of a wall near the end of an alley.

He thought of being bent over Coach McAllister's desk taking his veiny cock. He thought of the men he'd let spank him, just a swat or two, and then fuck his mouth. And he started to cry again. Not in shame, but in sheer sadness. He could have had *this*. He could have had RJ. Or something like it.

He could have been loved all along.

IN THE MORNING, bleary-eyed and snuggling, RJ asked Aaron if he wanted to watch the video.

Aaron tensed, for only for a few heartbeats. He exhaled and said, "Later."

RJ wasn't sure if Aaron would really need to see it—maybe the act of filming it was enough. It was Aaron's call. RJ kissed him deeply as the sun rose, gleaming off the church spire through the window.

Nuzzling RJ's neck, Aaron whispered, "Next Christmas, can we play Santa and elf again?"

RJ's heart lifted, his joy at hearing the question asked so easily, the assumption of their togetherness in a year so clear. "Yeah, but we can play that game any time you want, baby. You're always on my naughty list." RJ kissed him, and the wonder of holding the man of his dreams in his arms hit him all over again. "You're my Christmas dream-come-true, Aaron."

Aaron's dimples were on display, a fever in his eyes. "Thank you for asking me if I'd been stood up."

"Thank you for staying to talk."

"Thank you for fucking me."

"Thank—" RJ laughed as Aaron grinned. "Thank you for making me believe that love is worth trying to make last. For making me believe that it will last. With you."

Aaron pulled RJ down on top of him again, spread his legs, and whispered, "Fuck me, Santa. Fuck your bad elf and show him how you do it."

RJ laughed. "Damn, Mr. Danvers. Santa Claus is at your service."

Epilogue

Two years later

SCRUFFY CITY HALL was all done up for Christmas again. Silver and gold stars hung alongside tinsel garlands, draping from the ceiling, and colored lights wound around the banister of the upper level and all around the stage. A decorated tree or two brightened the stage and the corner by the bathrooms. The band played a tight Christmas set that inspired drunken sing-alongs, raucous dancing, and vigorous shaking of the plastic tambourines that had been tossed out into the audience. There was no doubt that the show was another success.

Leaning against a wall where he could easily see the stage, Aaron nursed his whiskey, training his gaze on the delicious man playing lead guitar. Reindeer antlers and tinsel garland bracelets be damned, RJ was as hot as ever.

Aaron's nipples tingled and his dick rushed with blood. It never got old seeing his lover onstage. As they'd traveled together, he'd watched RJ play to massive crowds in London and L.A., and he'd watched him play to small theaters in Nashville and Berlin. But every single time he ended up hard and horny, aching for RJ's touch and hungry for RJ's cock.

It was nearly Pavlovian.

Luckily, RJ felt the same way most nights, leaving the stage flushed and racing with adrenaline. Aaron was an eager recipient of all of that energy. He could never get enough.

As the rollicking version of "Marshmallow World" wound down, RJ cleared his throat and wiped the back of his hand over his sweaty forehead. He peered through the lights, out into the crowd, and finding Aaron easily, he smiled. Then he cleared his throat.

"Y'all having fun tonight?"

The crowd banged tables and stomped their feet, whooping with delight.

"Good. That's good." He fiddled with the tuning of his guitar before bending down to get a capo before clamping it over the fretboard. He glanced over his shoulder at Joel and Becca, and then over at Madison on piano. "It's good to have the old gang back together again. I've been away for a long time, but there's nothing like being home for the holidays."

Cheers went up and Aaron sipped his whiskey again, enjoying the way RJ worked the room.

"Don't get me wrong. It's been a fun two years. Really fun. I made some music, put it up on Spotify, and some of you listened to it."

More shouts and shimmers of tambourines.

"Yeah. That was cool." He noodled a little on his guitar. "And I went with some good bands on a few tours. That was neat. Traveled a lot, which can be tiring, but this time I was with someone I love. So that was cool, too."

The crowd cheered, though Aaron had to laugh. Cool was a bit of an understatement. He and RJ had traveled the world. First as part of a tour with a rock group, and then with a female-led country band. The latter had taken their young families on tour with them, and Aaron had been hired to be the kids' teacher. In fact, the band was going out again in the spring to support a new album, and Aaron and RJ would be going with them.

Constance was able to go with them on the US legs of the tours. It turned out she traveled well, and Aaron preferred to keep her close. When they went abroad, though, Constance stayed with his cousin Dem Buns in Aaron's apartment. Dem Buns—well, Frank, as he preferred to be called for obvious reasons—was getting his Bachelor's Degree from

U.T., so taking care of Aaron's apartment and cat was a good way for him to keep costs down.

Aaron and RJ had been home only five times since they'd first left, and only for a few days at a time. Aaron hadn't talked to his mother since his final text with her (she had kept the casserole dish), and he'd spent his first holidays without her quite happily, going between his dad's place and RJ's folks' house. Doug and Betsy were as in love as ever, and possibly trying for another kid, if the hints dropped during FaceTime calls were any indication. Carter had thankfully moved on from his crush on RJ and now had a boyfriend his own age. A sweet little guy with glasses and a mop of curls. Aaron thought they were adorable together.

Still, this trip was their first visit back to Knoxville that had lasted long enough to catch their breath and make some plans. RJ had made the most of it, rehearsing and playing more Christmas shows, and making another batch of songs to upload to Spotify. Aaron had sorted out the details of their next tour and put his grandmother's Sapphire Regal up along with a host of Christmas decorations. He'd really nested in cozily and enjoyed the downtime, making everything in the apartment "just so" for both of them. Yes, Aaron loved the time off, but he also adored their whirlwind life together.

He'd never imagined he could be so free.

"But this next year…" RJ gave a smirky grin, nailing Aaron with his gaze. He put his guitar on the stand and wiped his palms on his jeans. "I was thinking about a way it could be even more fun."

Aaron blinked. Whatever RJ was talking about was news to him. More fun? Had he already booked another tour for the second half of the year?

"Aaron?"

Aaron straightened up and stared at RJ, sweat slipping down the back of his neck. When would he stop wearing sports jackets to these shows? He always got too hot.

"Come up here."

Aaron blinked at him, but when the crowd started shifting restlessly, looking his way, he did as he was ordered, his heart pounding and his head awhirl. Was this...? Could RJ...? No. That was...he wouldn't. Would he?

When he reached the stage, RJ tugged him up next to him. "This is Aaron. He's my lover," he announced to the crowd to a mix of very vocal reactions, though it was mostly positive. A few girls looked disappointed. "We started out as a Christmas fling, but you know how those tend to end, right? It's either true love or tears. No other way out of a Christmas fling."

The crowd yelled and laughed. Aaron laughed, too, but his heart was beating so fast that he sounded giddy.

RJ squeezed Aaron closer, sweat glistening on his exposed collarbones above the wide neck of his T-shirt. "I told Aaron once that if we wanted to last as lovers, then we had to act like we'd last forever. Remember?"

Aaron nodded, his throat going tight. Oh, wow. Was this...?

"Because love is trust," RJ said to the audience, with a sly smile cast toward his mother who now stood with Doug in the front row. Where had they come from? *Oh, wow.* There was his dad, too. Oh, God, this was really happening. "So we did. We acted like we'd last, and now it's been two years"—more cheers from the audience—"and I love him more than ever."

The room echoed with screams at that proclamation.

"He loves me, too," RJ said, looking down at Aaron, and his eyes were soft with affection. "I know because he gives me everything he has, all the time, every time. I'm lucky. You should all be as lucky as me."

Aaron eyes burned with tears, and he opened his mouth to speak, but RJ shook his head and put his finger on Aaron's lips.

"I'm not done yet," he growled gently, but he punctuated it with a smile. "Two years ago tonight a couple of assholes stood this guy up—

yeah two in the space of a few hours. Ouch, right?" Aaron winced, but RJ grinned. "And I'm grateful to both of them for passing up this man every single day of my life. Also, they weren't just assholes, they were idiots, because they missed out on the best person in the world. But I didn't. I was smart." His grin turned wicked. "I took him home and—"

Laughter and cheers roared.

RJ winked at Aaron. "And I fell in love with him. Christmas miracles and all that stuff. Being his lover has been the best thing to ever happen to me. But I'm hoping that after tonight, we won't call ourselves just lovers anymore." He released his hold on Aaron quickly, and Aaron's legs went weak when RJ dropped to one knee. A shiny ring materialized from the depths of RJ's jeans pocket. He held it up and the Christmas lights played on the gold. The room exploded with joy and the sound of shaking tambourines. "Baby, will you make my dreams come true again tonight?"

Aaron's heart filled with so much joy it overflowed, and he didn't bother wiping at his streaming eyes as he put his palms on RJ's shoulders to steady himself. He nodded vigorously, already mouthing yes, as RJ went on, "Aaron Danvers, will you marry me?"

"Yes, yes, yes! I will!"

RJ rose up and tugged Aaron to his chest as the sound of tambourines and shouts of congratulations filled the air, along with a rousing clatter of piano keys as Madison added to the cacophony.

RJ kissed him so long and deep that Aaron was panting by the time their lips broke apart. They clung together as the band started to play, and they swayed to the music. Suddenly, Aaron recognized it as Dolly Parton's "Here You Come Again," and he started to laugh, remembering that it had played from the Market Square skating rink that first night just after RJ had kicked out the patio chair and told him to take a seat.

"What do you say, Mr. Danvers," RJ said into his ear, careful that the mic didn't pick up his words. "Now that you're my fiancé, do you still want to pretend you're on my naughty list tonight?"

Aaron nuzzled RJ's throat, pressing a kiss to the place where he felt the beat of his pulse. "I do, yes. Yes, I do."

"I do," RJ repeated back, eyes warm with love. "Yeah, I like the sound of that."

THE END

Letter from Leta

Dear Reader,

Thank you so much for reading *Mr Naughty List*! I had so much fun writing this steamy story of a teacher and his former student, and I hope you enjoyed reading it as much as I enjoyed crafting it. Extras and deleted scenes for the *Mr. Christmas* series, as well as other book universes, can be found at my Patreon.

Be sure to follow me on BookBub or Goodreads to be notified of new releases. And look for me on Facebook for snippets of the day-to-day writing life, or join my Facebook Group for announcements and special giveaways. To see some sources of my inspiration, you can follow my Pinterest boards or Instagram.

If you enjoyed the book, please take a moment to leave a review! Reviews not only help readers determine if a book is for them, but also help a book show up in site searches.

Also, for the audiobook connoisseurs out there, *Mr Frosty Pants* (the first in the Mr. Christmas series) will be out in November 2019, narrated by the wonderful John Solo. Many of my other books are also in audio, narrated by Michael Ferraiuolo or John Solo. I hope to eventually add my entire backlist to my audiobook roster over the next few years.

Thank you for being a reader!
Leta

Book 3 in the Mr. Christmas series

MR. JINGLE BELLS
by Leta Blake

Opposites attract as frosty business partners become fake boyfriends in this Christmas gay romance!

After an emergency forces Ashton Sellers from his apartment, all he wants for Christmas is new lipgloss, zero contact from his abusive family, and a place to stay for the holidays. Cue his business partner begrudgingly taking him in.

Walker's a fuddy-duddy with no sense of fun, but he does have a safe, warm home with four adorable dogs and delicious food on the table.

If it turns out Walker's also a secret softy with a tender side and a hot body beneath his endless parade of golf shirts? Great, good, cool. And if Walker wants Ashton to pretend to be his boyfriend for his sister's Christmas-themed wedding? Awesome, amazing.

Could Walker be the safe haven Ashton missed out on as a child? Could they be falling in love for real?

But when Ashton uncovers a painful mistake in Walker's past, it hits too close to home. As the jingle bells quiet and the snow settles, will Ashton be able to forgive Walker, or will their relationship be over before it ever truly begins?

Mr. Jingle Bells is a gay Christmas story by Leta Blake featuring forced proximity, opposites attract, fake dating, office romance, steamy scenes, and a taffy-sweet happy ending. It's set in the *Mr. Christmas* universe, which began with *Mr. Frosty Pants*, but **can be read as a standalone.**

Content warnings for childhood abuse, past addiction issues, PTSD episodes, and gambling.

Book 1 in the Mr. Christmas series

MR. FROSTY PANTS
by Leta Blake

Frosty former friends get a steamy second chance in this Christmas gay romance!
Can true love warm his frozen heart?

When Casey Stevens went away to college four years ago, he ghosted on his straight best friend, Joel Vreeland. He hoped time and distance would lessen the unrequited affection he felt, but all it did was make him miss Joel more.

Home for the holidays, Casey hopes they might find a way to be friends again. But Joel's frosty reception reminds Casey of just how hard he had to fight to be Joel's friend in the first place. It's going to take a Christmas miracle to get past that cool façade again.

Joel isn't as straight as Casey believes, and his years of pining for Casey have left him hurting and alone, caring for his abusive father and struggling to get by. Unable to trust anyone except his rescue dog—and with no reason to believe Casey is interested in him for more than a holiday fling—Joel's icy heart might shatter before it can thaw.

Can Casey and Joel's love overcome mistrust, parental rejection, class differences, and four long years apart? *Mr. Frosty Pants* is a stand-alone, Christmas gay romance by Leta Blake featuring a virgin hero, childhood friends-to-lovers, second chance romance, and steamy mm first times.

Standalone novel featuring winter holidays

SMOKY MOUNTAIN DREAMS
by Leta Blake

Sometimes holding on means letting go.

After giving up on his career as a country singer in Nashville, Christopher Ryder is happy enough performing at the Smoky Mountain Dreams theme park in Tennessee. But while his beloved Gran loves him exactly the way he is, Christopher feels painfully invisible to everyone else. Even when he's center stage he aches for someone to see the real him.

Bisexual Jesse Birch is a single dad with no room in his life for dating. Raising two kids and fighting with family after a tragic accident took his children's mother, he doesn't want more than an occasional hookup. He sure as hell doesn't want to fall hard for his favorite local singer, but when Christopher walks into his jewelry studio, Jesse hears a new song in his heart.

Smoky Mountain Dreams is a heartfelt gay romance with a single dad, winter holiday highlights, found family, and steamy scenes to warm even the coldest heart!

Full-length novel featuring winter holiday scenes

TRAINING SEASON
by Leta Blake

Can a cowboy's firm hand help discipline this feisty figure skater—on and off the ice?

Matty Marcus fears he doesn't have what it takes to achieve his Olympic dream. His self-esteem is at an all-time low after figure skating coaches and skating judges have told him he's not skinny enough, good enough, or masculine enough to win.

Matty wishes he could afford the kind of coach he needs, a top-notch one who specializes in keeping their skaters focused. But those coaches are ridiculously expensive, and Matty is financially strapped.

Until a lucrative house-sitting gig brings him to rural Montana.

And to Rob.

No one has ever looked at Matty the way rural cowboy Rob Lovely looks at him. No one has ever touched him, loved him, and healed him from the inside out. No one has ever made him feel so valuable and adored. Worthy. Strong.

No one has ever taught Matty how to fly. Or how to lose.

Rob might be a cowboy and a single dad who knows nothing about figure skating, but after only a few months, he's trained a new kind of bravery into Matty's soul.

But to achieve his Olympic dream, Matty will have to face the ultimate test. Has he truly learned what it means to win—on and off the ice—during his training season?

Training Season is a MM romance with a feisty, flamboyant figure skater and an easy-going dominant cowboy, opposites attract, hurt-comfort, single dad, winter holiday highlights, love beyond reason, multiple steamy scenes, and a well-earned happy ending. *This book contains some BDSM elements.*

Standalone

ANY GIVEN LIFETIME

He'll love him in any lifetime.

Neil isn't a ghost, but he feels like one. Reincarnated with all his memories from his prior life, he spent twenty years trapped in a child's body, wanting nothing more than to grow up and reclaim the love of his life.

As an adult, Neil finds there's more than lost time separating them. Joshua has built a beautiful life since Neil's death, and how exactly is Neil supposed to introduce himself? As Joshua's long-dead lover in a new body? Heartbroken and hopeless, Neil takes refuge in his work, developing microscopic robots called nanites that can produce medical miracles.

When Joshua meets a young scientist working on a medical project, his soul senses something his rational mind can't believe. Has Neil truly come back to him after twenty years? And if the impossible is real, can they be together at long last?

Any Given Lifetime is a stand-alone, slow burn, second chance gay romance by Leta Blake featuring reincarnation and true love. This story includes some angst, some steam, an age gap, and, of course, a happy ending.

Gay Romance Newsletter

Leta's newsletter will keep you up to date on her latest releases and news from the world of M/M romance. Join the mailing list today.

Leta Blake on Patreon

Become part of Leta Blake's Patreon community in order to access exclusive content, deleted scenes, extras, bonus stories, rewards, prizes, interviews, and more.

www.patreon.com/letablake

Other Books by Leta Blake

Any Given Lifetime
The River Leith
Smoky Mountain Dreams
Angel Undone
The Difference Between
Omega Mine: Search for a Soulmate
Raise Up Heart
Heat for Sale
Bring on Forever

The Mr. Christmas Series
Mr. Frosty Pants
Mr. Naughty List
Mr. Jingle Bells

The Training Season Series
Training Season
Training Complex

Heat of Love Series
Slow Heat
Alpha Heat
Slow Birth
Bitter Heat

Stay Lucky Series
Stay Lucky
Stay Sexy

'90s Coming of Age Series
Pictures of You
You Are Not Me

Co-Authored with Indra Vaughn
Vespertine
Cowboy Seeks Husband

Co-Authored with Alice Griffiths
The Wake Up Married serial
Will & Patrick's Endless Honeymoon

Gay Fairy Tales
Co-Authored with Keira Andrews
Flight
Levity
Rise

Audiobooks
Leta Blake at Audible

Free Read
Stalking Dreams

Discover more about the author online
Leta Blake
letablake.com

About the Author

Author of the bestselling book Smoky Mountain Dreams and the fan favorite Training Season, Leta Blake's educational and professional background is in psychology and finance, respectively. However, her passion has always been for writing. She enjoys crafting romance stories and exploring the psyches of made up people. At home in the Southern U.S., Leta works hard at achieving balance between her day job, her writing, and her family.

www.ingramcontent.com/pod-product-compliance
Lightning Source LLC
Chambersburg PA
CBHW050519110726
47899CB00005B/1515